PSYCHO

BY THE

SEA

LYNNE TRUSS

PSYCHO
BY THE
SEA

R A V E N B O O K S
LONDON · OXFORD · NEW YORK · NEW DELHI · SYDNEY

RAVEN BOOKS
Bloomsbury Publishing Plc
50 Bedford Square, London, WC1B 3DP, UK
29 Earlsfort Terrace, Dublin 2, Ireland

BLOOMSBURY, RAVEN BOOKS and the Raven Books logo are trademarks of Bloomsbury
Publishing Plc

First published in Great Britain 2021

A catalogue record for this book is available from the British Library

Library of Congress Cataloguing-in-Publication data has been applied for

ISBN: HB: 978-1-5266-0987-8; EBOOK: 978-1-5266-0985-4

2 4 6 8 10 9 7 5 3 1

Typeset by Integra Software Services Pvt. Ltd.
Printed and bound in Great Britain by CPI Group (UK) Ltd, Croydon CR0 4YY

To find out more about our authors and books visit www.bloomsbury.com
and sign up for our newsletters

For Hoagy,
captain of my heart

'Every detective must be a psychologist, whether he knows it or not.'
Anthony Berkeley, *Roger Sheringham and the Vane Mystery*, 1927

'The cosmetics manufacturers are not selling lanolin, they are selling hope. We no longer buy oranges, we buy vitality.'
Vance Packard, *The Hidden Persuaders*, 1957

Just what is it that makes today's homes so different, so appealing?
Title of Richard Hamilton's Pop Art collage, 1956

'Adelaide Vine's hair was technically chestnut, while her eyes were almond-shaped, and hazel-coloured. As her mother used to say, Adelaide had been born with all the nuts.'
Lynne Truss, *The Man That Got Away*, 2019

Author's Note

Psycho by the Sea is the fourth Constable Twitten story, set more than a month after the events recounted in *Murder by Milk Bottle*. Although it can be read as a stand-alone book, actions occurring since June 1957 – when Twitten first arrived in Brighton – will continue to have dramatic consequences for the four main characters: Constable Twitten, Sergeant Brunswick, Inspector Steine, and Mrs Groynes (station charlady and secret criminal mastermind). For the convenience of new readers, here are some brief (helpful) notes.

On 5 August, Summer Bank Holiday, Inspector Steine shot dead London gangland boss Terence Chambers at a seafront milk bar.

Barrow-Boy Cecil, ostensibly a simple cockney street trader with a tray of clockwork bunnies, is in fact employed by Mrs Groynes. In *Murder by Milk Bottle*, he sold a handgun to a minor, which was morally questionable.

Mrs Thorpe, a glamorous widow, owns a gracious Regency house on Clifton Terrace, where Constable Twitten is now a paying guest.

Miss Sibert is a heavily accented Viennese émigrée and known associate of Terence Chambers.

Adelaide Vine is a stunningly attractive young criminal who was reared by a group of four ruthless con artists, one of whom was her mother.

Pandora Holden is a precocious and beautiful young woman of nineteen with misplaced romantic hopes concerning Twitten.

Blakeney is a dog who enjoys travel.

The action of this book takes place over
one week in mid-September 1957.

One

If the disappearance of Barrow-Boy Cecil aroused no suspicions at first, it was for one very good reason: since the beginning of the month, Brighton had been subject to constant, drenching rain.

The September seafront was grey and deserted; striped shop-awnings sagged and flapped; street drains backed up; overexcited schoolboys wrote rude words, backwards, on the steamed-up windows of the trolley-buses. No wonder that the town's dodgy street characters, one and all, turned up their jacket collars, pulled their sodden headgear tighter to their heads, and raced indoors (through puddles) to sit it out.

Any visiting academic engaged in studying the Petty Criminal of the South Coast of England could have had a field day in the cheaper cafes and milk bars of Brighton during this unlooked-for monsoon season. Even the respectable Lyons tea room towards the top of North Street was full of minor hoodlums. In every establishment it was the same: damp, disgruntled men and boys (some with livid facial scars) sat around formica-topped tables in loose, taciturn groups, waiting with charmless impatience for the pubs to open at half-past eleven while their clothes steamed unpleasantly.

Conversation was scant. Each man nursed a cup of strong tea, smoked roll-ups down to the stub, miserably totted up halfpennies dug from deep trouser pockets, or idly polished a flick-knife blade with a handkerchief – or at least until the proprietor yelled 'Oi!' from behind the counter.

It would have been madness for Barrow-Boy Cecil to be out. 'See the bunny run, madam?' was his perpetual patter, as he wound up the plastic mechanical toys on his felt-lined pedlar's tray and waved a showman's hand, as if the world offered nothing more splendid than their stiff, arthritic hopping. 'See the bunny jump, sir! Only half a crown! See the bunny jump!' Well, what sort of idiot holiday-maker would be in the market for a cheap, foreign-made clockwork toy in weather like this?

But there was another good reason. Cecil's regular pitch was at the Clock Tower – a location that tended to bear the brunt of inclement conditions, what with its being a major crossroads, exposed to winds whipping straight up West Street from the sea. In some ways it was an excellent spot, providing a 360-degree vantage point for a trusted lieutenant in a well-organised criminal gang headed by a woman cunningly posing as a charlady at the police station. It made him the visible hub of the organisation; almost its talisman. 'What's the lay, Cecil?' Mrs Groynes would traditionally ask, smiling, as she stood in front of him at least twice a week, pretending to purchase a bunny for a favourite niece. Alternatively, if she needed him to act as an urgent bush telegraph, she would get hold of young Shorty (trusted juvenile messenger) and hiss, 'Get this to Cecil. He'll tell the others.' So there was no gainsaying the topographical advantage of Cecil's position, but there was also no denying that it was dismal when the wind blew hard from the south and the rain came down like bullets.

So, that's why no one missed him initially. There were four perfectly good reasons for Barrow-Boy Cecil to be absent from the streets. In the first place, there was zero passing trade; second, standing in his usual place, it would be like having buckets of water chucked in your face; third, he secretly received a regular substantial stipend from Mrs Groynes anyway, so the revenue from the bunnies concerned him little.

But the fourth factor was probably the clincher: in conditions like these, the bunnies not only blew about on the flimsy tray suspended from Cecil's neck; their mechanisms seized up, and they toppled over onto their backs, making a heart-breaking noise (*Fzzzzz, fzzzzz, fzzzzzzz* ...), with their little legs kicking feebly at the air.

———

Sergeant Brunswick was the first to ask where Cecil was. For several years the sergeant had, deludedly, been passing money to the bunny-man every couple of weeks in return for information about criminal activity in the town. Sometimes this outlay was later reclaimed from petty cash; more often, it came from the sergeant's own pocket (he wasn't very clever about money). It was only ten shillings, but you could buy quite a lot for that: two tins of salmon; sixty cigarettes; several quick haircuts from Rodolfo the Barber on Western Road. However, if the sergeant wished to throw his money away on Cecil, it was up to him, and it made him feel he was doing his job properly.

For his own part, Cecil quite relished the comic role of underworld 'grass'. Sometimes, alone in the evening, he practised in a mirror tilting his hat forward, tapping his nose, and speaking shiftily out of the side of his mouth. At one point he toyed with having a toothpick clamped between his jaws, but it turned out to be almost impossible to say 'See the bunny run' with your jaws clenched. Also, for proper authenticity, you had to manoeuvre the stick from one side of your mouth to the other, and the first time he tried this he nearly swallowed it.

But Cecil didn't assume the role of double-agent for his own entertainment. It was entirely for the benefit of the gang. For Mrs Groynes's purposes, this 'informer' arrangement was a reliable means of sending the police (in the person of Sergeant Brunswick) on well-timed wild goose chases when she had important criminal business to conduct.

'Word is you should keep an eye on that new Buy Rite supermarket, Sergeant,' Cecil would murmur, conspiratorially (head down, lips exaggeratedly lopsided, like Popeye), as he picked up a toy, wound it up, and placed it on the tray. Then, loudly, with the usual flourish of the arm, 'See the bunny run, sir? Lovely, innit? Lovely bunny, sir! Only half a crown! See the bunny jump, look!'

'Good man, Cecil,' Brunswick would murmur in reply, and then announce for the benefit of anyone passing, 'I'll take that pink one, mate.'

'Pink one? Good choice, sir. Look here, sir, on the bottom. Made in Hong Kong, only the best!'

Then the sergeant would hand over a folded ten-bob note, put the toy in his pocket, and walk off without any change, glowing with achievement, while Cecil called 'See the bunny run, madam?' at a fresh member of the public.

And usually the information paid off – but only because it was a fair bet in this town that if you set out to uncover criminal activity in any location, you would succeed.

Acting on Cecil's insider dope, Brunswick (taking several men with him) would lie in wait at the new supermarket and, sure enough, apprehend a couple of unwashed kids smuggling tins of peaches up their moth-holed jumpers. What Brunswick had so far failed to notice was that, invariably, just as he triumphantly grabbed a scarpering juvenile delinquent by the ear and said 'You're nicked, sonny!' (to gratifying cheers from female shoppers), a high-end jeweller's shop in another part of town was successfully raided by masked villains.

Meanwhile Brunswick's desk drawer was filling with wind-up bunnies, as testament to his acumen and perseverance as a police detective. When she was alone in the office, Mrs Groynes sometimes turned from her special locked cupboard – filled with gelignite, armed-robbery equipment, hot jewellery, and gold bullion – and opened the sergeant's drawer, just to see the bunnies. They always made her smile. Much as she liked Sergeant Brunswick personally, there was no escaping the tragic fact that he was, basically, *such easy meat.*

Still, it was Brunswick who was the first to notice that the bunny-man was missing. 'Barrow-Boy Cecil hasn't been around much lately,' he observed on this dismally wet Tuesday morning in September, hanging up his soaked hat and mackintosh to drip on the lino, and gazing in despair at his sodden, half-ruined shoes. 'I hope he's all right.'

The overhead lights were on in the office, and heavy rain drummed at the window. Mrs Groynes, a lit cigarette in one hand, was waving a feather duster along the tops of picture frames (mostly for effect), while young Constable Twitten was absorbed in a book. It was quite cosy. The air smelled of cocoa-flavoured biscuits, fresh from the packet.

But before Brunswick could properly relax, he nodded at the inspector's empty room.

'The inspector … ?' he said carefully. 'Still *elsewhere*?'

'Thank Christ, yes, dear.'

'You're sure?'

Twitten chipped in, without looking up from his book. 'The inspector is still in London, sir.'

Brunswick narrowed his eyes. Something was different. 'It's very quiet.'

This was true. No phones were ringing.

'Oh, I got them to deal with all his calls at the switchboard,' said Mrs Groynes.

'Blimey, you've got some nerve, Mrs G!' said Brunswick, impressed. The fierce female telephonists at the station were notoriously unaccommodating to requests of this sort. They also had surprisingly well-developed arm muscles from all the reaching across each other to connect the jacks to the board. Once, without properly thinking it through, he had asked out a petite redhead from the switchboard and over their first drink in the saloon bar of the Cricketers pub she had challenged him to arm-wrestling, with embarrassing results.

'Oh, they don't scare me, dear. I said if they put one more call through to this office, I'd rip the wire out of the bleeding wall. I said the bags of post piling up are bad enough.' As if to prove the point, she kicked an unopened sack of fan letters that stood against the wall with a dozen others. 'All this interest is on account of that shocking Chambers business last month, of course,' she sighed, shaking her head as if this vague 'Chambers business' was a regrettable train of events with which she'd had nothing to do (when she had in fact engineered the whole thing). 'Cup of tea, then? Come on,

Sergeant, there ain't nobody here but us chickens. Take the weight off those massive plates of yours.'

Brunswick exhaled with relief and sat down. Naturally, everyone was very pleased that the psychopathic London villain Terence Chambers had been shot dead in Brighton last month, making the world a better place; and yes, they were proud that Inspector Steine was the man who pulled the trigger. But had the shooting marked the end of anything? No, it had been more like the flaming beginning. Because afterwards came ... the *accolades*.

It started just a day or two after that momentous Bank Holiday Monday, when the inspector came bursting out of his office with the news.

'Men! Men! Listen!'

'Yes, sir?'

'I'm receiving the Silver Truncheon award from the Commissioner of the Metropolitan Police!'

'Ooh, well done, sir. Well deserved, sir.'

'Bleeding well done, dear.'

'Thank you. I'm very excited. It's the highest honour bestowed—'

'We know, sir.'

'I know too, dear. Good for you.'

'I am absolutely overwhel—'

'Cup of tea to celebrate?'

'—med. Oh. Well, yes. Yes, please.'

But it didn't stop there. It escalated.

'Men! Men! You won't believe it!'

'Gosh, sir. What is it now, sir?'

'They want me to be a guest on *Desert Island Discs*! Roy Plomley just telephoned personally! I nearly fell off my chair!'

'That's flaming marvellous, sir. Well done.'

7

'I know. It's a huge honour.'

'Yes, sir. Bally well done.'

'Men! Men! You won't believe it! I've been invited to the Palace!'

'Men! Men! They want me to appear on something called *The Sooty Show*!'

'Men! Men! If I am willing to lend my name to Brylcreem, which is apparently a hair preparation of some description, they'll pay me a fee of five hundred pounds!'

Much as Brunswick and Twitten tried to say 'Congratulations, sir!' with consistent gusto, it soon grew hard to do so. Inwardly they groaned with each fresh salute to Inspector Steine's greatness. One evening, when Brunswick and his auntie sat cosily at home watching *Panorama*, a handsome young man with a guitar started singing a witty topical calypso about Inspector Steine, 'Cleaning the Streets of Bright-on', and Brunswick was so upset he burst into tears.

But there was more to it than having to offer constant congratulations. For those who knew Inspector Steine well, to observe him on the receiving end of so much hero-worship was seriously alarming. The big question was: *could he cope?* After all, it takes strength of character to treat fame with the contempt it deserves, what with the natural temptation to measure one's own self-worth by it. Many great men have fallen victim to hubris. What hope could there be, then, for Inspector Steine – a man of small achievements, feeble intellect, and no self-knowledge whatsoever?

So this was why Brunswick was relieved to find the inspector out of the office, and was free to remark (again) that Barrow-Boy Cecil hadn't been seen lately, causing Twitten to stop reading for a moment and look up at Mrs Groynes. Knowing full well that the bunny-seller was, secretly, one of this ersatz charlady's most trusted gang members, he was keen to observe her response.

She didn't let him down. 'Barrow-Boy *who*, dear?' said Mrs Groynes, still flicking the feather duster with one hand and dropping fag-ash on the floor with the other.

'Cecil,' said Brunswick. 'You know, Mrs G. *See the bunny run*? By the Clock Tower.'

Mrs Groynes frowned, as if trying to place the name. 'Oh, yes. Tall cove with a tray. Ain't he out and about, then?'

'Not that I can see.'

Twitten closed his book. 'I can't imagine how a chap like him actually makes a living, can you, Mrs G?' he asked, in a conversational tone. 'Even if he sells the bunnies at two shillings and sixpence each. I wonder sometimes whether such colourful Brighton street characters in fact obtain the bulk of their income from other, more nefarious sources.'

Mrs Groynes reached over to pat him on the shoulder. 'You're asking the wrong bleeding person, dear. Now, how about that cup of tea, Sergeant?'

'Ooh, yes, please,' said Brunswick, idly picking up the *Police Gazette*. 'The thing is, it's been at least a week since anyone clapped eyes on him. I hope he hasn't got that flaming Asian Flu everyone's talking about. The doorman outside the Essoldo said he saw Cecil talking with a glamorous young woman—'

But at this point, unfortunately, all talk of Cecil abruptly ceased. With a cup of tea in the offing, more important matters had come up.

'Kettle, sir!' interrupted Twitten urgently, jumping to his feet. 'Sir? Sir? The electric kettle!'

Kettle? What was going on? Why was Twitten so excited by tea-making all of a sudden? But then Brunswick remembered. 'Right, son. Yes!'

'Give me strength,' said Mrs Groynes. Year after year she had made the tea for this lot and no single bugger had taken the remotest interest. But now? Good grief. Rolling her eyes, she withdrew her hand from the kettle's switch.

'Go on, then, Constable. Do the honours.'

Twitten blushed. 'May I?' he breathed. 'May I *again?*'

And so the electric kettle was switched on by the good graces of the constabular digit, and all three of them stood in silence to watch it in action.

The cause of all this unusual excitement was that Mrs Groynes had lately acquired an up-to-the-minute electric kettle that *turned itself off once it had boiled.* Formerly, she had made tea using water from an enormous hot-water urn that she trundled, clanking, along the corridor from the lift on a rickety steel trolley. This urn was distinctly old-fashioned: the fact that it provided the requisite hot water for tea-making was utterly dull and unremarkable. Whereas who could fail to be thrilled and transported by the sheer novelty of this shiny, futuristic kettle, with its little switch that sprang out – with a wondrous 'tock' noise – once the boiling process was complete? Truly, making an everyday hot beverage was now like living in the twenty-third century!

All conversation was suspended while the appliance noisily heated to a boil on its special new tin tray. Both Twitten and Brunswick were tense. Would the switch duly pop out when the time came? They listened to the sound of the water starting to rumble and bubble, and looked at each other. Would it? Would it ever? The kettle was by now boiling fiercely. Hot steam was issuing from the spout. *Would it? Shouldn't it have done it by now?* But then, just when they started to think that the mechanism must have failed (and that it was time to call the fire brigade), 'Tock!' it went, and the boiling subsided, along with their groundless fears.

'Gosh,' sighed Twitten, sinking back onto his chair.

'Blimey,' exclaimed Brunswick, with a chuckle.

'And about bleeding time, dears,' muttered Mrs G, as she poured the water into the prepared teapot, and gave the contents a stir.

———

At Gosling's Department Store, on the London Road, the weeks of rain had been highly beneficial. Sales of swimwear and sunglasses might have dropped abysmally, but the sales of umbrellas had soared, along with stewing steak, tapioca, warm vests, jigsaw puzzles and the new (huge) fifteen-inch television sets.

Gosling's was one of several department stores in the town, the most prestigious and central being the mighty Hannington's in North Street. Like its competitors, Gosling's took what you might call a 'gamut-running' approach to retail lines (or 'indiscriminate' if you were being unkind), and dealt in everything from Dutch lard to fur coats, bedroom furniture to dog meat, surgical appliances to coach trips. Promotional signs were displayed everywhere: KEPEKOOL REFRIGERATORS! CHILPRUFE THERMAL UNDERWEAR! EASICLENE OVENS! (In the exciting consumer boom of the mid-fifties, brand names adopted an ostentatiously *faux-naïf* approach to spelling.)

It was a bustling, lively sort of shop, arranged over four floors. Many Brightonians preferred Gosling's to the more sedate Hannington's, because in the London Road store there was always something entertaining to gawp at. The original Mr Gosling (known to staff as Mister Edward) had founded the shop in 1912, and laid a foundation of good service; his forty-three-year-old son (known as Mister Harold) was more of an extrovert, and although he was a cheapskate by nature, his retail instincts were excellent.

Since Mister Harold took the helm, Gosling's had become *the* place to go on a rainy day. Every morning in the kitchen-ware department, a high-heeled woman with a tiny waist and pencilled-on eyebrows (and an unfortunate pained expression suggestive of a headache) demonstrated how to make such fashionable dinner-party staples as crabmeat puffs and chocolate chiffon. In the record department, customers could listen to LPs of their choice in little booths lined with soundproof pegboard, thanks to the modern-day miracle of speaker-wire. And in the dairy section of the food hall, little cubes of exotic cheese (such as Edam) were offered on sticks by a blonde teenaged girl from Patcham dressed up in a rough approximation of Dutch national costume. For people who had recently endured a drab decade of post-war rationing, the invitation from Gosling's to sample a morsel of seafood canapé, then listen to the latest Pat Boone and scoff free cheese from the Netherlands, was almost unbearably exciting.

It was in Gosling's that Mrs Groynes had purchased the electric kettle. For reasons that will become apparent, she received a discount there. But it was Inspector Steine who had paid. In a rare access of munificence (on the day he discovered he was to receive the Silver Truncheon, which came with a cheque for a hundred pounds), he had searched his mind for ways to share his good fortune with his immediate staff. But what did they like? What were their interests? He considered each of his men in turn, trying to picture them in their leisure hours – and, interestingly, came up with nothing. In the end, he decided to consult the charlady, calling her into his office for a private conversation.

'Well, dear,' she said, when he had put his proposal to her, 'I wish I could say this needs a lot of thinking about, but I'd be lying. If you ask me, the sergeant would like nothing better than a trip to one of them poncey film studios up London way.'

Sitting back in her chair, she produced cigarettes and an expensive-looking lighter from the deep pocket of her flowery (but deeply ugly) pinny, and lit up a Capstan Full Strength. Tilting her head back, she took a satisfying drag.

Steine was mystified. 'What poncey film studios?'

'Oh, come on, dear. You know. Pinewood, Shepperton, Merton Park; one of those. And as for Constable Clever Clogs, I can promise you he'd love you for ever, dear, if you got him a year's membership of that bleeding London Library he's always banging on about.'

'Really? Are you sure?' Steine pulled a face. Film studios and a library? Personally, he hated the sound of both of those things.

'See this?' From the pocket of her pinny Mrs Groynes produced a page torn from a film magazine. It featured a competition, with the words 'WIN A TRIP TO FABULOUS PINEWOOD' across the top in red lettering. 'The sergeant goes in for this every bleeding month, dear.'

'No!'

'Yes, and it's not free. You have to send a postal order. It's a proper scam, of course, but he can't see it, bless him. If you look in his desk, you'll find he's got several postal orders ready, *and* a stack of ready-addressed envelopes, so he can post off his entry the minute the competition opens.' She shook her head knowingly. 'As if that would make a blind bit of difference.'

'Good heavens.'

Steine took the page and perused it, frowning. Evidently, entrants to this competition were required to study a series of studio photographs of somebody called Patricia Neal and list them in order of 'loveliness'. He sighed. Here was proof enough that it was a bad idea to dig beneath the surface of the people you worked with. 'And what on earth's the London Library?'

'Ah,' shrugged Mrs G, 'search me, dear. But I'm guessing on the available evidence that it's a library up London. Constable Clever Clogs is always after some obscure book or other, and I've heard him on the dog-and-bone nagging his poor old mum to make him a member of it.'

'I see.' Steine considered what he had heard, wrinkled his nose, and came to a decision. 'Well, thank you for those imaginative suggestions, Mrs Groynes, but I can't think of anything I want to encourage less than Sergeant Brunswick mooning over more actresses, or Twitten with his head in more books.'

'That's a shame, dear. You could have made them very happy.'

'Even so. My first instinct was new silver-plated whistles.'

She let out a laugh of surprise. 'Oh, my good gawd. *Whistles?*'

'Yes.' He refused to be mocked by the charwoman. 'Whistles coated in silver, and *engraved*. So they will be very special.'

'They'd still be bleeding whistles, dear.'

'Yes. But look, Twitten and Brunswick are both policemen, Mrs Groynes. The whistles will be engraved with the date of my shooting Terence Chambers. In their old age, Brunswick and Twitten will explain to their grandchildren that they were fortunate enough to be in Brighton at the time of the momentous event, even if they didn't actually play a part in it, and weren't in fact present when I heroically pulled the trigger.'

'Right, dear. Well, you know best.'

'Thank you.'

'But in that case, can I put in a request for one of them new electric kettles that switch theirselves off?'

'A new what?'

'Kettle, dear. That turns itself off. It would benefit everyone, but it would also save me wrestling with that bleeding tea-urn for the rest of my life, risking life and limb.'

Steine brightened. This was more like it. 'It turns itself off? How?'

'Well, I'm no thermo-bleeding-physicist, dear, am I?'

'Well, no.'

'But as I understand it, it's got a bi-metallic strip in the rear of the kettle—'

'Bi-metallic?'

'Made of two metals.'

'Ah.'

'And this strip is cunningly exposed to the steam rising from the water, and due to the steam this metal expands to a point where it knocks the switch out, thus turning off the element, stopping the boiling process, and saving everyone in the area from a gruesome fiery death.'

Steine looked impressed, but also a bit thoughtful. 'Mrs Groynes, how do you—?' he began.

'But don't listen to me, dear,' she interrupted, laughing. 'What do I know about technological advancements in domestic appliances and whatnot? Hovercrafts, dear?

Araldite? The many-worlds interpretation of quantum mechanics? Ha, I mean to say!'

And so she had trotted along to Gosling's to buy the recently launched Russell Hobbs K1 model, with the revolutionary automatic shut-off. As she sailed through one of the pairs of swing doors on London Road, greeting the uniformed doorman holding it open, and tucking the customary ten-shilling note into his hand, she reflected that Brunswick and Twitten would sadly never know how close they had come to gaining their hearts' desires. If Constable Twitten ever so much as entered the stately catalogue hall of the London Library in St James's Square (where she had herself been a member since 1945), he would set up home there for the rest of his life. If Brunswick once saw inside a film studio, it would be much the same story, but with busty actresses being the attraction, instead of dusty tomes. However, neither of them knew that she had made such wonderful suggestions on their behalf, and it was better that they didn't. If there was ever a woman who whole-heartedly maintained that *what you don't know can't hurt you*, it was, obviously, Mrs Palmeira Groynes.

On her way through Gosling's to buy the kettle, she had said a discreet hello to various gang members who'd been in place in the store for months, posing as everything from migraine-victim cookery demonstrator to carpenter-cum-handyman. She had come up with the plan the previous Christmas, and had been patiently slotting the pieces into place all year. In all her days in the business of crime, the upcoming Gosling's Christmas Job was the one that had excited her most. It was masterly. It would go down in history as the cleverest and cleanest (and most lucrative) commercial robbery ever carried out in Great Britain.

As she handed over a five-pound note to the sales assistant in Domestic Appliances, she watched with particular pleasure as he took a canister from a basket behind him, unscrewed its lid, and placed inside it the handwritten note of sale and the money. He then posted it into the shop's vacuum-activated tube system, where it was immediately sucked away. He smiled at Mrs Groynes, and she smiled back pleasantly. He then wrapped the purchase for her in paper and string, while they waited for the cashiers in the far-off basement 'tube room' to send the canister back.

It was quite a good idea for stores such as Gosling's to keep no cash on the shop-floors. Less tempting for opportunistic criminals; also, of course, less tempting for light-fingered staff. Some of the shops in town used an overhead pulley-system for transporting cash that involved a very entertaining pull-down catapult mechanism and a network of overhead wires. But Gosling's had lately taken down the untidy and obtrusive wires and opted for the more discreet vacuum tubes that ran next to (and sometimes through) the walls. It was a quieter system, and much neater. The local engineers who had installed it (on the cheap) promised it would go wrong only if a) someone accidentally posted a French baguette into it, or b) it sucked a cashier's arm off up to the shoulder.

Most customers had no idea where the canisters went. To them, it was a delightful mystery. But Mrs Groynes knew all about the tube room, where a row of seated girls and women dealt with every sale in the store – opening the canisters, entering the purchases in ledgers, calculating the change, and sending the canisters back, with the notes of sale stamped 'PAID'.

The thing was, one of these tube-room girls was Denise Perks, aged nineteen, orphaned older sister of Shorty the messenger boy, trainee gang member, and well on her way to becoming Mrs Groynes's deputy. (We will be hearing much more of Denise.)

'I see a lot of myself in you, dear,' Mrs Groynes told the girl once, when she was only fifteen and working as part of a whizz mob at the railway station (picking pockets). 'Just don't fall in love with someone pretending to be a bleeding war hero, and nothing can stop you getting to the top.'

It was good advice, and the cool-headed Denise had resisted falling in love with anyone. She was far too focused on her job. Having worked at Gosling's for only three months, she was already in charge of a team of twelve, and earning an extra seven and six a week. Right now, she was efficiently placing Mrs Groynes's change (one shilling and fourpence) in the canister and posting it back through the appropriate tube, thankfully without getting her arm sucked off, not even up to the elbow.

———

Back at the office, with the kettle duly boiled, Twitten returned to his book. It was very absorbing. These had been excellent weeks for him: Inspector Steine's absence and an unusual drop in violent criminal activity (due, as he was fully aware, to the understandable exhaustion of Mrs Groynes after all the shenanigans over the Bank Holiday weekend) meant that for several weeks Twitten had not been obliged to stand over a single bullet-riddled corpse.

But how best to take advantage of this little holiday? By reading, of course. True, under orders from the inspector, he had reluctantly started reporting for driving lessons on weekdays from a brisk police instructor, which were going far from well ('*Left foot, Constable! I said left, that's the accelerator! Eyes on the road! Mind that pram! What the blazes is wrong with you?*'), but mainly he'd embarked on a great reading spree at his desk, often with a sharpened pencil in his hand and a zealous gleam in his eye.

Lately, he had been reading a newly published book called *The Hidden Persuaders*, and he had rarely read anything that excited him more. It was so bally relevant to the modern world! It explained so much! He couldn't wait to describe it to everyone, and persuade them to look at the world in a new way – which was presumably why Mrs Groynes had taken the sergeant aside and warned him, 'Whatever you do, dear, don't ask the constable about that book of his. He's bleeding bursting with it.'

Brunswick, meanwhile, had also enjoyed the period of calm, by daring to turn his attentions elsewhere for a change. Very tentatively, and without much conviction, he was courting Twitten's attractive forty-one-year-old landlady, Mrs Thorpe.

'Please, Jim. Call me Eliza,' she had urged him warmly, on their first date, but somehow he couldn't do it. Any younger woman he could call by her first name automatically, but not Mrs Thorpe. She was older than him, for a start, and her late husband had been a general. She spoke beautifully, and was firmly middle class, with a nice house in one of the most desirable terraces in Brighton. Admittedly, her house had recently been the location of an upsetting and grisly murder (a playwright horribly slain with the general's regimental sword), but it had also for years played host to eminent stars of stage and screen. By striking contrast, Brunswick had received his education at the London Road Academy for Orphans, Waifs and Foundlings, and had joined the army at thirteen. He owned two decent suits, had never held a bank account, and he lived with his auntie in a flat above a bicycle shop.

So he couldn't call this woman Eliza, but he did enjoy her company, and he was intrigued (or, more honestly, pleasantly disturbed) by her undisguised interest in him physically. In all Brunswick's dealings with women up to now, the attraction had flowed emphatically in the other direction, with gum-chewing girls rejecting each romantic advance with 'No, Jim. Not interested!' Or 'Mind my nylons! These cost two and eleven!' He had experienced, in his miserable love life, a great deal of being pushed in the chest (and he had also shelled out for a lot of replacement hosiery). So he was naturally confused by Mrs Thorpe's strange erotic attraction to him. She throbbed with it. He once took her hand to help her out of a taxi and she was so thrilled by his manly touch, she started to hyperventilate.

But things had not progressed easily. They had seen a few films together; drunk a few frothy coffees. It was only when they went to see a new stage production of a comedy called *The Reluctant Debutante* at the Palace Pier Theatre that things moved on slightly. They would both always remember that particular evening. As they walked back uphill from the Clock Tower towards Mrs Thorpe's fine house on Clifton Terrace, they discussed the merits of the cast.

'I preferred Wilfrid Hyde-White in the original production, I'm afraid,' said Mrs Thorpe.

Now, Brunswick might have been hurt by this. After all, he'd paid for the tickets. Women weren't supposed to be critical of something a man had spent good money on. At certain levels of society, such an ungrateful remark would earn a woman a smack on the kisser. But Brunswick was deeply pleased by what Mrs Thorne had said, because he agreed with it. The chap in this production hadn't been a patch on Wilfrid Hyde-White.

'You saw it last year, then?' he said. 'At the Theatre Royal?'

'Yes. But why do you—?'

'I was there, too!'

'Oh, I see.'

'You're the first person I've ever told. I mean, I can hardly talk much at the station about light-hearted stage comedies about rich people. When the inspector's about, I have to read my monthly *Plays and Players* on the sly, tucked inside the *Police Gazette*.'

'Well, wasn't he good? Freddie, I mean.'

'Good? He was flaming brilliant!'

'Apparently they've cast Rex Harrison for the film,' she said matter-of-factly. 'But I can't quite imagine that, can you?'

Brunswick stopped walking, and looked at her. What an amazing woman this was. She knew about Rex Harrison being cast in *The Reluctant Debutante* in the part that belonged by right to Wilfrid Hyde-White? Who else would care about this but him? Who else would have an informed opinion? Who else would refer to Wilfrid Hyde-White as *Freddie*?

'James?' she said, puzzled.

And then, on a romantic impulse, he took her in his arms. As he pulled her close, she received the full force of his pungent after-shave – Cossack ('for Men') – but being well versed in acceptable feminine behaviour, she cleverly masked the gag reflex.

'James?' she said again, raising her face to his, and not breathing.

'Mrs Thorpe!' he exclaimed, and kissed her.

If we have started with a pause, it is deliberate. Because, back at the police station, the days of peace are about to end. Later on, all those present will remember how agreeable things were on this seemingly humdrum rainy Tuesday in the middle of September. Mrs Groynes is having a sit-down, while Brunswick whistles softly to himself, scanning the latest *Picturegoer*, and Twitten makes another scholarly note with a pencil. All is well in their world. The kettle makes comforting contracting noises as it cools. A clock ticks. Everyone has forgotten about the minor mystery of Barrow-Boy Cecil's disappearance – everyone apart from Mrs Groynes, who is reliably quick at putting two and two together.

—————

But beyond the police station, key events are taking place – events that will require someone to put two and two together, plus two, and two, and two, and two, and two. At the tiny Polyfoto shop in Western Road, for example, the manager returns from his lunch hour and finds the door hanging open and the place ransacked. Cameras have been stolen from the portrait studio at the back; furniture has been knocked over; storage boxes tipped out on the floor.

'Len?' he says, a quiver in his voice. He can't work this out. Has Len the Photographer done this? Has he gone berserk after ten years of taking pictures in here?

And then the manager turns round and sees Len lying unmoving on the marbled lino with blood puddling around his head. The sight makes him yelp and stagger. Then he picks up the telephone and asks the operator for the police.

—————

At about the same time, Ben Oliver of the *Brighton Evening Argus* receives a phone call from a woman with a strong Germanic accent who refuses to give her name. She is evidently in distress, but wants to tell him something important. She says she is a psychiatrist who's been working for several months at an unnamed hospital for the criminally insane in the county of Berkshire (clearly she means Broadmoor), attempting to treat an inmate with a history of extreme violence.

'They von't tell me any-zing,' she gasps, 'but I know some-zing hass happen. I sink he hass escape!'

Oliver raises an eyebrow. This news is interesting, but he doesn't see what the *Argus* has to do with it. 'Can you give me his name, please?'

'Of course,' she says, trying to calm herself. 'His name iss Chow-tza. Geoffrey Chow-tza. C-H-A-U-C-E-R.'

Oliver, who has just switched the phone receiver to his left ear in preparation for making notes, pauses, and briefly considers just hanging up at once. *Geoffrey Chaucer*? 'But that's the name of … well, that's the name of Geoffrey Chaucer, madam. English poet.'

'I know! Ve talk of ziss coincidence many time, belief me.'

Bemused, Oliver picks up a pen. He has to admit it's all been a bit slow recently in the crime-correspondent world, since the killing of Chambers by local hero Inspector Steine in August. Oliver has been so stuck for decent stories that he's been working towards a somewhat lame feature about an American academic who's been in town studying 'crowd behaviour' (whatever that is). He might as well establish the facts about this escaped Chaucer character, such as they are.

So he makes a note. 'Broadmoor?' he writes. 'Escape. Geoffrey Chaucer – REALLY?' Then he draws a circle around 'REALLY?'

'And why are you telling me this, exactly, madam?' he asks.

'Because he iss obsess wizz killing polizemen, and in particular he has grudge – "grudge"? Iss this correct?'

Oliver considers. 'You mean, a grudge against someone?'

'Precisely. It iss a grudge against a policeman in your own town of Brighton!'

Oliver finally sits up straight. 'Please tell me your name, madam.'

'*Nein, nein*, not important. But you must alert ze police! Geoffrey kills policemen, and not only zat! He cut off head and boil in bucket!'

'Ugh,' says Oliver, who is now making proper notes in shorthand. 'Why don't you alert the police yourself?'

'Why? You zink I not try? Zey never answer ze telephone!'

'And this policeman? I assume we're talking about Inspector Steine?'

'*Jah! Natürlich!*' says the woman. 'His name is Steine.'

'Oh, my goodness.'

'Yes! And if I were zis Inspector Steine, I would run at once for ze hill!'

In the tube room at Gosling's Department Store, it has been a very busy day, and Denise Perks is at full stretch, dealing with umpteen canisters a minute. If anyone had only heard of repetitive strain injury in the 1950s, she'd have been able to take this shop to the cleaners. The dozen girls working alongside her today are fast, too, but it speeds things up if Denise, as supervisor, takes each canister out of the basket as it arrives, unscrews it, and passes the contents to one of the others for processing.

It is just after lunch when she takes one such canister, and tips out something unexpected: a severed human finger with a ring on it, plus a small heap of crushed plastic, and a note that reads:

DON'T TELL MRS GROYNES ABOUT THIS
OR SHORTY WILL BE NEXT

This is an unpleasant surprise, to say the least.

'Oh, my God!' Denise exclaims, unable to moderate her reaction. In her defence, you don't see a human body part fall out of a canister every day.

'Something wrong, Miss Perks?' says one of the other girls, looking up.

'No, no!' she says quickly. 'Keep working.'

But Denise recognises the ring. It belongs to fellow gang member Barrow-Boy Cecil! What is happening? Has someone kidnapped him? Are they truly threatening Shorty? As her mind races, she recognises the significance of the shards of brightly coloured plastic mixed with springs and a little key. They are parts of a clockwork bunny.

———

Unaware of all this activity elsewhere, Twitten continues to read, and is so absorbed that he hardly notices the arrival of Mr Lloyd, the station's permanently miserable post-delivery man who daily, with a lot of wheezing and grumbling, dumps one of the large sacks of letters for Inspector Steine just inside the door. Today, Mr Lloyd pointedly pauses at the doorway, hand on handle, clearly waiting for the others to pay him attention.

It has been observed by many employees of Brighton Police Station that the notably dandruffy Mr Lloyd can never just shuffle in, make a delivery, struggle for breath a bit, collect the outgoing post from its designated pigeonhole, and shuffle out again: he always has to start a conversation. This is not because he is sociable by nature. Being the long-standing shop steward of a major union, he is a professional troublemaker who tirelessly angles for any affront or infringement (or misspoken word) worthy of protest, rebuke or even industrial action. As a consequence, people are very careful around him and speak little. He once attempted to call the whole branch out on strike because a boy in the pay office called him 'Mr Death Rattle' (in a whisper) when he was twenty yards away.

'Now I've got here something for young Constable Twitten,' he says, locating a large envelope in the top tray of his trolley but not passing it over. He wheezes a few times, while he gets his breath. 'But I have to tell you (*wheeze*) this is highly irregular, and I am in two minds (*wheeze*) what to do about it. Deliver it or not? In fact, should I even be touching it?'

He holds the envelope and stares at it, as if deciding.

'You see, a *very* pleasant and polite young lady handed it in at the front desk as I was setting out on my rounds and said it was urgent. So ... (*multiple wheezes, for dramatic effect*). So, seeing as it was not received into the building via the agreed union-approved channels ... well.'

Brunswick and Mrs Groynes look at each other, but say nothing. They know better than to interrupt this display of union muscle. Twitten opens his mouth to speak, but Mrs Groynes says 'Shh, dear', so he closes it again.

They all look at each other. Twitten looks (quite hard) at Mr Lloyd; Mr Lloyd looks challengingly at Mrs Groynes; Mrs Groynes looks steadily at Brunswick; Brunswick looks at Twitten. It's like a stand-off without the guns, and then – in a flash – it's all over. Because the telephone in the inspector's office loudly rings ('Oh, my good gawd,' yelps Mrs G, clutching her chest), and an unknown woman of grave proportions, in a mauve tweed suit and small bottle-green felt hat, appears in the open doorway, blocking it entirely. Mr Lloyd slings the envelope at Twitten, and smartly turns to go.

'Steine's office?' demands the dragoness, entering.

Confusion reigns. This woman is very intimidating. 'Um, yes,' says Twitten, standing up. 'May I help you?'

'I'm the inspector's new SECRETARY. Miss LENNON. And I have brought whistles as a gift.'

Stopping only to slam two silver-plated whistles in front of the startled Brunswick and Twitten, she strides into Steine's office and answers his phone.

'The office of Inspector STEINE,' she booms. 'Miss LENNON speaking. How may I HELP you?'

While the postman quickly wheels his trolley out, Brunswick and Mrs Groynes exchange anxious glances while Twitten, absent-mindedly, opens the envelope, unaware that the contents will threaten to alter the course of his life.

'What just happened?' hisses Brunswick. 'Who's Miss flaming Lennon? Why is the phone ringing again?'

'I don't know, sir,' says Twitten, bewildered.

He draws out the contents of the envelope and is bewildered further. It seems to be a photograph of Terence Chambers outside the Metropole Hotel in the company of Mrs Groynes. Twitten gapes. He says, 'Oh, crikey.' He looks up at Mrs G and then back at the picture. This is enormous. He has in his hand incontrovertible evidence of Mrs Groynes's true criminal nature! He can use this to expose her, at last! *Oh, crikey,* he thinks. *Oh-crikey-crikey-flip!*

'What have you got there, dear?' says Mrs Groynes, moving closer.

'Nothing,' he says. 'Nothing.' Quickly sliding the photograph back into the envelope, he pathetically picks up the whistle, saying, 'Gosh, look, Mrs G.'

'At what? It's a bleeding whistle, dear. You said "crikey".'

'Yes, but … oh, look, it's engraved in tiny letters. Is yours the same, Sergeant Brunswick, sir?'

Miss Lennon emerges from Steine's office and stands looking at them all, big hands on ample hips. They all shrink back; they can't help it.

'I'd like a cup of tea with TWO SUGARS, please, Mrs Char. But you must get rid of that kettle, it's against regulations and a serious FIRE HAZARD.'

No one says anything. They are too shocked. *Did this woman just call Mrs Groynes 'Mrs Char'?*

She pulls on the locked door of Mrs Groynes's stash-cupboard.

'And I'd like the key to this AT ONCE, or I'll get the station carpenter to come up tomorrow and open it BY FORCE.'

Two

In some ways the attack on Len the Photographer was a godsend. Not to Len himself, perhaps (he nursed the headache for weeks). But the call to investigate the Polyfoto shop break-in gave Brunswick and Twitten a perfect pretext for fleeing the awkwardness of the police station: awkwardness that had arrived in the shape – the emphatically tall and well-upholstered shape – of Miss Roberta Lennon, MCAPS (Member of the Chartered Association of Police Secretaries).

'I can't quite believe what just happened, sir,' said Twitten, as the two men trotted with relief down the stairs to the entrance hall.

'Nor can I, son. Did you notice how she made the room look smaller? She's like flaming King Kong.'

'In fairness, I suppose the inspector was very much in need of clerical assistance, but still ... ' Twitten frowned. He really didn't know what to make of this development. A fifth person landing on them without warning was hard to process, although he had to admit that the look on Mrs Groynes's face – of sheer, slack-jawed discombobulation – had been delightful to observe. In his three months on the job, he had never seen her even slightly wrong-footed before, let alone discombobulated.

But talking of things that were too hard to take in, what about this incendiary picture?

'You're not bringing that with us, Twitten?' Brunswick indicated the envelope Twitten was holding to his chest.

'Ah.' He looked down at it. 'No, sir. I suppose not.'

'What is it, anyway? Who's it from?'

'Oh, it's just from, um … ' Panic rose in his chest. There was no way he could explain the importance of this photograph to the sergeant. 'It's from … I think it's from bally Miss Holden, sir,' he said. 'I think. I mean, yes, of course it is, what am I saying? Ha-ha, I mean it is *definitely* from Miss Holden because it's … um … ' He held up the envelope as if in proof. 'Because it's … definitely … from her.'

'The Milk Girl?'

'You remember her, sir! Well, that's excellent.'

'It was only a few weeks ago, son.'

'Ha! You're right. So, yes, I mean the lovely, lovely ex-Milk Girl who promoted milk consumption by appearing at beauty contests and opening milk bars, and is a bit self-involved, and is going up to Oxford to study classics, and calls me Peregrine all the time when I wish she bally wouldn't, and lives in Norfolk.'

Brunswick made a face and nudged him. 'I told you she fancied you, didn't I?' he said.

'Yes, sir. You did tell me that – several times, in fact, despite my heartfelt protests. But I have to admit, to judge by the contents of this, I think she jolly well does.'

'Red-hot love letter, then, is it?'

Twitten reddened. Why not? He was already in so deep. 'It bally is, sir, yes. Scorchingly so. Miss Holden is a very, very passionate young lady.'

'Well, good for you.'

Relations between Twitten and Brunswick had recovered somewhat since the dramatic happenings in August. On Mrs Groynes's firm advice, Twitten had stopped openly psycho-analysing the sergeant (helpfully pointing out his deep-seated problem with 'self-esteem' and so on), and this development alone had improved their relationship no end.

Twitten assumed a brave expression. 'But given how very red-hot this letter is, sir, I think I'll just pop it in my locker, if you don't mind waiting.' And with that, he took the stairs to the basement.

But once safely in the locker room, with his little silver key already in the lock, he paused. Was this sensible? It was true that Mrs Groynes had not seen the contents of this envelope, but she had obviously sensed something significant – not least from the way he'd unguardedly gasped 'Oh, crikey', and looked from the picture up to her, and then back again. Leaving it locked in a flimsy metal box downstairs on the premises would hardly serve to foil a genius master criminal, especially one with zero conscience, everything to lose, and easy access to explosives.

He sneaked another look at the picture, and felt a thrill. Golly, it was *so* incriminating! It must have been taken just before last Bank Holiday Monday. He imagined it being presented in court at the Old Bailey, and Mrs Groynes fainting in the dock. He imagined it emblazoned on a dozen national newspaper front pages, under the headline 'EVIL POLICE STATION CHARWOMAN BROUGHT TO JUSTICE'. Obviously, he briefly wondered who had sent it to him, but there wasn't time to think about that. Right now, the only important issue was how to keep the evidence beyond the reach of Mrs Groynes. He left the locker room and stood outside it, breathing hard.

And then he heard her voice.

Flipping hedgehogs! Mrs G was already coming for him! And he was cornered! There was no exit down here in the basement except through the post room, which was, firmly, Postal Workers Only. From the top of the stairs, he heard her ask, 'Down here, Sergeant, dear? Popped to the latrines, has he?'

Twitten chewed his lip and whimpered. Should he tuck the envelope into his tunic, perhaps? Or put it in his helmet? But then, what if Mrs Groynes simply killed him? She might murder him in cold blood, just to get her hands on the photograph! If only he hadn't said 'crikey'!

'You all right there, son?' called Brunswick, down the stairs. 'We ought to talk to this Len bloke before he gets carted off to hospital. And Mrs G wants a word; she's coming down.'

'Right, sir,' he called back, his voice unsteady. 'Thank you, sir. Nearly done!'

And then Twitten spotted Mr Lloyd's trolley. It was standing just outside the nearby WCs. A few yards further on was the entrance to the post room with the forbiddingly unpunctuated notice 'POST ROOM PERSONNEL ONLY THIS MEANS YOU KEEP OUT' roughly glued to the door. A light trail of dandruff led towards it on the shiny tiled floor, indicating (in case there was any doubt) that this was Mr Lloyd's regular route. Taking a pen from his tunic pocket, Twitten quickly readdressed the envelope to the first person who came to mind: *Pandora Holden, The Old Rectory, Waffham, North Norfolk*, and slid it in with the outgoing post.

'Here, have you been tampering with my trolley?' demanded Mr Lloyd, emerging from the Gents and finding Twitten jumping back – as if stung by a bee – from a piece of rickety old equipment stringently reserved for approved forms of postal actuation by officially authorised union members only.

'Gosh, I would never do that, Mr Lloyd,' Twitten assured him, thinking quickly. 'Oh, and here's Mrs Groynes, how lovely.' With an effort, he turned his back on Mr Lloyd, and assumed an expression of innocent surprise.

'Did I forget something upstairs, Mrs G?'

Behind him, Mr Lloyd bent to examine the trolley as if it might reveal the secret of what had just occurred. Then, shrugging, he started slowly pushing it towards the sanctuary of the post room. It clanked as it crossed the tiles, each interstitial bump causing Mr Lloyd to mutter. Twitten had to fight every instinct to turn and watch him go – or indeed to shout at Mr Lloyd for flip's sake to speed up.

'Forget something?' Mrs Groynes repeated. 'No, dear, nothing like that.' She smiled at him, but with her eyes narrowed, like a cat's. It was quite clear what she was thinking. *What the bleeding hell has he done with it?* 'I just wanted to check you was all right, dear. We've all had a bit of a shock, and then you and the sergeant were out the door like greased lightning, leaving me on my tod with Lady Foghorn.'

'Yes, I'm sorry about that, but duty called. And I'm so sorry about your cupboard, Mrs G –'

She winced.

'– but all things must pass, I suppose. Perhaps Miss Lennon is very pleasant once you get to know her.'

Again, he resisted the urge to look round and see what progress Mr Lloyd had made.

'Been utilising our precious locker, have we?' She tilted her head towards the locker room.

'What? Oh, yes. Gosh. That's right. I had a letter. A letter from, er, from Miss Holden—'

'Oh, yes?' she said, standing uncomfortably close. He knew she didn't believe him.

'But I really must go, Mrs G.'

And with that, he led her back upstairs, all the while listening to Mr Lloyd making his slow, shuffling, wheezing progress along the corridor, until … *slam!* The door to the post room had banged shut and Pandora's envelope was safe.

Len the Photographer couldn't remember much about the break-in. He had been hit from behind, while setting up the studio in the back room for an afternoon portrait shoot. It would have been quite dark in the shop at the front, he supposed, what with its being like blooming Judgment Day outside and all the lights switched off. The street door had been locked because it was the manager's lunch hour. Len wouldn't normally be there himself at dinner-time, but today the volume of precipitation had given him pause. His shoes were new and he didn't fancy ruining them just for the sake of a half-pint of Bass and a stale ham sandwich in the pub.

'Ow, my head,' he groaned. 'Someone must have broken in. Ow! Ow, my head.'

It was silly to keep him here. The ambulance men were waiting in the rain; Brunswick decided to let him go.

'You'll be fighting fit in a couple of days, mate,' the sergeant called to him in the back of the ambulance. But Len pulled a face. He wasn't in the mood for comforting words. 'The bastards took my Hasselblad,' he said. And then (muffled by doors slammed shut), 'Ow! Ow! *My head.*'

'I wonder what else they were looking for, sir,' said Twitten, when the vehicle had gone. 'All this disorder wasn't necessary if they just wanted to steal cameras.' It was a fair point. Box files had been pulled off shelves and chucked about, cabinets had been rifled. Short shiny strips of negatives were scattered across the floor. 'It's as if they were looking for something specific.'

'You might be right, Twitten,' said Brunswick. 'Or you might not. It could be they were looking for something, but it might just be opportunism. Kids, you know. Or of course someone who just fancied making a flaming mess.' Brunswick called to the manager, Mr Peters, who was standing in the doorway, smoking, his hands unsteady. He was evidently very upset.

'Tell us what you do here, exactly, Mr Peters.'

Mr Peters turned, sniffed, and tried his best to seem normal. 'We process people's films, Sergeant. You brought us a roll yourself, if you recall, a few weeks ago. I don't know what else you want me to say. We process films and make prints. I mean, Len does.' He took a handkerchief from his pocket. 'Oh, poor Len! When I saw him lying there, I thought for a moment he was dead!'

'Take your time, Mr Peters. What about the studio in the back room?'

Mr Peters steadied himself. 'Len takes the portraits – you know, for passports and so on. Family groups; engaged couples. We've been here *ten years*, and nothing like this has ever ... '

'No. Of course.'

'It feels so personal.'

'But it probably looks worse than it is. Make a list of everything missing, and we'll circulate it. You might get some of it back.'

Mr Peters took a deep breath. 'He'll be all right, won't he? Len?'

'Absolutely,' said Brunswick. 'And you can follow him to the hospital, if you want, once we're finished here. We won't be long, will we, Constable?'

'What, sir? Oh, no. But there's just one thing, Mr Peters, sir.' Twitten had conspicuously taken no role in this interview: despite all his training in interview procedures, he could never see the point of asking questions when he knew the answers already. But now a significant matter had arisen.

'You mentioned that roll of film we brought in, Mr Peters,' he said. 'On the Saturday before the Bank Holiday.'

'Yes. What of it?'

'Well, I'm just wondering what happened to the photographs.'

Brunswick frowned. He'd forgotten all about that roll of film. He and Twitten had found it in the home of an AA man whose favourite pastime was snapping pictures of known villains, including Terence Chambers. Brunswick remembered Twitten's cheerful exclamation, 'It's a wonder he didn't get himself killed!' – a wildly insensitive thing to say to the man's grieving sister, given that the AA man had just been found murdered.

'I never saw the developed pictures, did you, Sergeant?' Twitten persisted. 'In all the excitement around the shootings, that roll of film must have slipped my mind.'

'Are you accusing us of not delivering them, young man?' Mr Peters sounded defensive. 'I can't believe you'd do that. Not at a time like this!'

'No, sir,' Brunswick answered hastily. 'Of course he's not accusing you of anything. But if you could check your records, perhaps?'

'I certainly can!' Mr Peters drew a large ledger out from under the shop counter and flicked back a few pages to the Saturday before the Bank Holiday.

'Here we are, look.'

He indicated an entry, in triumph.

'Thank you, sir,' said Brunswick. 'And what does it say?'

'That you brought in the film at precisely half-past twelve. Len did the prints as a priority, and our boy Nigel delivered them into the hands of your desk sergeant just before two o'clock. A Sergeant Baines.'

This was good enough for Brunswick. 'So, they'll still be somewhere at the station,' he said to Twitten, with an air of having settled the matter. He reached out a hand to Mr Peters. 'We'll go now, sir.'

But Twitten was peering at the ledger. 'What does this mark mean, please, sir? It says *D-U-P* in a little circle.'

'Does it?' Mr Peters followed the direction of Twitten's pointing finger, and his face softened. 'Well, you see, that just tells you all you need to know about Len, doesn't it? That's the sort of professional he is. He must have made an extra set of prints, you see, on account of this being a police matter.'

Twitten and Brunswick followed Mr Peters into the back-room studio. 'He'd have put them in here, in his special tall green box file … '

'This is very good of you, Mr Peters,' said Brunswick, looking round. 'Can we help?'

But Mr Peters wasn't listening. 'Green, green, green, green,' he muttered to himself, as he scanned the room.

'I can't see a green one,' said Twitten.

'Nor can I,' echoed Brunswick.

Mr Peters pulled a face. 'Well, what do you know?' he said, at last. 'It's gone.'

Unsurprisingly, young Ben Oliver of the *Argus* was keen to locate Constable Twitten at once and alert him to the worrying news about a violent escaped lunatic with murderous designs against Inspector Steine. Though Oliver entertained no illusions about the inspector (the happy phrase 'unrelenting idiocy' always came to mind when Steine's name was mentioned), he would be disappointed in himself if he failed to prevent an episode of wanton head-boiling.

On top of this, Oliver felt a duty towards Constable Twitten, even though their relationship was hard to define. He and the constable were not friends as such: they had never spent an evening in the pub; they hadn't roller-skated at the Ritz in West Street, flirting with gum-chewing girls in tight sweaters. But to be fair, both of them were too single-minded about their jobs to waste their leisure time on such inane activities. All Oliver knew was that over the past three months, his acquaintance with Twitten had been largely beneficial to his career, and because of that, there was a bond between them. They had sometimes shared useful information, and Twitten had generously steered him away from a few false leads.

There were just a couple of stumbling blocks to their having full trust in each other. From Twitten's point of view, he couldn't trust Oliver for the obvious reason that he was an ambitious journalist who would race to publish anything he was told. Oliver pursued truth, of course; but not as passionately as he pursued headlines. In the near future, Oliver would surely leave Brighton for Fleet Street, and he wouldn't look back. Twitten quite understood the reporter's rapaciousness, but it made him uneasy. It was just too clear that Oliver regarded other people largely as professional stepping-stones.

From Oliver's point of view, there was a more unusual obstacle to full trust: the fact that the poor constable harboured a delusion of tragic proportions – a delusion that would surely be his ruin. He genuinely believed (or claimed to) that the person running all the organised crime in the town was the cockney charlady at the police station. Of course, having a fatal flaw was not uncommon in members of the police force, but the usual ones were dishonesty, corruptibility, alcoholism, and a taste for disproportionate violence. Alongside such commonplace police foibles, Twitten's idiosyncratic charlady/ master criminal delusion (which had been planted in his mind by a stage hypnotist in front of a thousand witnesses, including Oliver himself) stood out quite starkly. Oliver would never forget the tragic moment at the Hippodrome when Professor Mesmer suggested to Twitten that the charlady was a criminal, and Twitten replied, with vehemence, 'But she is! She was behind the Aldersgate Stick-up, and she also shot Mr Crystal!'

But right now, Oliver had urgent news to deliver to the constable, and wasn't entirely sure where to start. For example, was it worth trying to telephone the police station? As his thickly accented Broadmoor informant had brutally pointed out, zay neffer answered ze telephone. In Oliver's experience, you could leave messages with the switchboard until you were blue in the face, but it made no difference (mainly because, unbeknownst to all, Mrs G intercepted the handwritten memos and tossed them out of the window).

So it was quite a surprise when the station switchboard put him straight though, and a woman efficiently answered, 'Inspector STEINE's office, Miss LENNON speaking, how may I HELP you?' and then dealt quickly with his enquiry, informing him of Twitten's precise whereabouts.

'Thank you, Miss Lennon,' he said. And before ringing off, 'I assume Inspector Steine is in London at the moment?'

'Yes, he IS. But he will RETURN in a DAY or so, and we shall REJOICE.'

'Well, thank you. You've been unusually helpful. Are you new?'

'YES,' she said grandly. 'I am VERY NEW. And there will be CHANGES here, I promise you. Inspector Steine is an IMPORTANT MAN and a HERO who deserves FAR, FAR BETTER. There are not only COBWEBS in this office, but this is the WORST CUP OF TEA I HAVE EVER TASTED.'

In his haste to meet Twitten, Oliver unfortunately neglected to consult his desk-diary, in which was clearly written: 'Prof. Milhouse, 2 p.m. Gosling's'. This oversight would have unfortunate consequences. The appointment at the London Road store was to have been his last with the visiting American sociologist, who was in the process of wrapping up his Brighton field studies.

Luckily, Professor Milhouse had no idea what sort of sarcastic, mocking and anti-intellectual piece Ben Oliver was planning to write. The young reporter had seemed genuinely interested in observing crowd behaviour alongside an expert in this burgeoning academic discipline. Over the past two weeks they had made notes together in many locations around the town, and photographs had been taken of the good professor, with his distinctively American buzz-cut hair and wire-rimmed spectacles, sheltering on the lea-side of the squally West Pier, holding out an arm to indicate the seafront beyond. The constant rain had not quelled Milhouse's academic ardour one jot. He was determinedly upbeat. 'Many interesting properties of crowd behaviour are merely intensified by inclement meteorological conditions,' he had said. 'Especially those at the anti-social end of the Goffman Scale. I refer you to the work of Riesman, Glazer and Denney. See *The Lonely Crowd*, page 165.'

Oliver had reported such snippets to his editor, Mr Ackerley. 'It's hilarious, sir,' he said. 'It's like he's swallowed a book! He keeps talking about how there are some people who are guided by "inner gyroscopes", while other people consult their "inner radar", and—'

'God's clogs, does he really?' chuckled Ackerley. The editor was from Yorkshire originally, and maintained an abrasive manner with most of his namby-pamby southern staff, but had a soft spot for Oliver.

The young man consulted his notebook. 'People are either *inner-directed* or *other-directed*, and society as a whole is becoming more *other-directed*.'

'Is it, by gum? What's the difference?'

'Ah, well, I wasn't planning to go into that too deeply, sir.'

'Ha! You mean you don't know?'

'I mean it's all patent nonsense, sir! I thought it better to take the line that even when you're just out and about in Brighton, minding your own business and choosing washing powder, *you are being watched*.'

'I see. Go on. That's not bad.'

'Earnest flat-headed Americans are lurking in the aisles of the supermarket. And the *Argus* asks: *Is it for this that we won the war?*

'That's good.' Ackerley gave Oliver an appreciative nod. 'You can never go wrong asking people if this is why they won the war.'

41

'We've got one more outing together, to Gosling's. He wants to show me how people's "blink rate" slows down when they're confronted with a choice of products.'

'What? Why?'

'Apparently they go into a kind of trance, sir.'

'Do they?' Ackerley pulled a face. 'I have to say, I find that quite interesting. But let's get this straight. The angle will be: *Remember to blink when you're shopping! Some nosy Yank is lurking nearby with a notebook?*'

'That's right, sir.'

Ackerley sat back in his chair. 'Well, lad,' he said. 'I'm seeing a spread.'

'Really? Thank you, sir.'

'Fifteen hundred words. With a byline. We could offer ten bob to the first person who spots him, how's that?'

'Well, he's leaving very soon, sir.'

'Is he? Good. Then make it five quid!'

So this was all set to be another career-enhancing assignment. But then a murderous lunatic with a hard-to-credit name escaped from a famous high-security psychiatric hospital and Oliver forgot all about blink rate and even about his fifteen hundred words. Thus it was that the mild-mannered thirty-five-year-old Professor Henry Milhouse II of the University of Nebraska – author of two authoritative books inspired by cutting-edge sociological theory – waited genially under an umbrella outside the swing doors of Gosling's for a quarter of an hour on that fateful afternoon, and finally went inside alone, leaving a message with the doorman in the hope that Ben Oliver of the *Argus* would eventually show up.

Meanwhile, up in London, how was Inspector Steine faring? Was it marvellous, being feted as the heroic killer of Terence Chambers, and receiving crate-loads of free Brylcreem at his hotel?

Well, contrary to all outward perceptions, the answer was actually no. Sudden celebrity was not entirely marvellous for the person experiencing it. For one thing, Brylcreem turned out to be disgusting, but mainly the inspector was lonely, homesick and fed up. What he particularly resented was the baffling social whirlpool he'd been sucked into: being introduced, tediously, day after day to crass famous people he'd never heard of, and being constantly reminded what a privilege this was.

'There's Douglas Fairbanks Junior, Inspector! Isn't that exciting?'

'May I introduce Donald Campbell ... Norman Wisdom ... Bela Lugosi ... Antony Armstrong-Jones?'

'You've been invited for drinks by Jimmy Edwards, and to be in the audience for an episode of the popular TV programme *Whack-O!*'

It was no good protesting, 'Well, I've never heard of him.' It was no good saying, 'I have no interest whatever in this thing called *Whack-O!* Which by the way sounds as if it irresponsibly condones sadistic violence towards children.' For years he had effectively put an end to any putative office chit-chat about famous people (usually initiated by Brunswick) by dropping the never-heard-of-him conversational bomb. But now he had been transported to a world where such a response was simply impermissible. Being a celebrity himself meant that he was expected not only to recognise but also to admire all other celebrities – and how many of them there turned out to be! They hailed from sport, from public life, from entertainment, from the arts, from the church. His face ached from continually feigning mute delight as he shook hands with people whose names and accomplishments meant nothing to him whatsoever.

He pined for his quiet life at home in Brighton, where his evenings were largely spent listening to orchestral concerts on the wireless while reading Somerset Maugham, with Johann Sebastian (the cat) curled up on his lap. Here in London, there had been grand dinners in his honour; invitations to glamorous galas in Shaftesbury Avenue; honorary membership of a Pall Mall club where he sat for three solid hours one evening pretending to be humbled and awed (but actually bored to tears) by a roomful of dinner-jacketed and cigar-smoking Tory grandees. To his credit, he managed not to ask Lord Astor where he lived or what he did for a living, but only because he had learned the dangers of such seemingly innocuous questions on a previous occasion when the chap turned out to be the Archbishop of Canterbury.

But Inspector Steine had an additional reason for wanting to go home. It wasn't just that he was fed up with shaking hands with these puffed-up individuals. There was one particular London journalist who was making a nuisance of himself, and it was getting serious. This wasp of a man had attended every press conference and from the start he had probed Steine in awkward and embarrassing ways.

'Clive Hoskisson, *Daily Mirror*,' he'd said, standing up at the first, hugely well-attended press conference at Scotland Yard, a few days after the events of the Bank Holiday Monday. He wore a distinctive white raincoat and a brown trilby. Steine, expecting further anodyne questions of the 'How does it feel to be a national hero?' variety, benignly nodded at him to proceed.

44

'My readers would like me to ask you a few questions, just to clarify the order of events on that extraordinary day, Inspector.'

'Of course. I'd be happy to explain again.' Steine leaned forward, folding his hands. 'Over the weekend, Mr Chambers had shot and killed ten well-known regional organised crime leaders at the Metropole Hotel, leaving their bodies in a room on the sixth floor. You may have seen the list. On the Monday afternoon, Mr Chambers left the hotel and proceeded to the House of Hanover Milk Bar on the seafront where his luck ran out. Mr Chambers was a well-known villain, and since he had just slain ten people and was still armed, I shot him.'

'Thank you, sir.'

There was a spontaneous round of applause.

'You're welcome.' Steine smiled then looked around. 'Next question?'

'But, Inspector—?' Unconventionally, Hoskisson had remained standing. He also still had his hat on, which showed a regrettable lack of breeding.

'Yes?'

'What my readers are wondering is why you happened to have that gun with you, sir, when you were ostensibly expecting only to announce the winner of a local ice-cream sundae competition.'

'Why I had the gun?' Steine laughed. 'Well, it was a good job I *did* have the gun. Think about this logically, for goodness' sake. If I hadn't had the gun, I couldn't have shot him!'

The press corps laughed along with Steine, and there were calls for Hoskisson to make way for others. But he didn't.

'My readers are confused, sir,' persisted the reporter. 'Are you saying you knew what Chambers was up to, killing all those men at the Metropole Hotel? Because the way my readers see it, if you *were* aware of his plans, wouldn't it have been your duty as a policeman to stop him? But if you *weren't* aware of those plans, they ask again – and it's a very simple question, sir – why were you armed?'

Steine shook his head and sighed. 'What's your name again?'

'Clive Hoskisson. *Daily Mirror.*'

A small jeer was heard, and some tutting. Someone said, 'Take your hat off!' Hoskisson was unpopular with some of his counterparts, it seemed.

'Well, Mr Hoskisson,' said Steine sternly, 'I think you and your so-called readers are deliberately missing the point. By common consent, the shooting dead of Terence Chambers was a very, very good thing. Your own newspaper called it a "Boon to Britain". The man was a known psychopath and kingpin of organised crime in London, who was evidently planning to expand his empire by removing all his rivals.'

'I know, but—'

'There are no buts. I accept no buts.'

'But—'

'I repeat, no buts.'

'But—'

'Everyone is glad he's dead, and so should you be.'

'Yes, but all I'm asking is: did you *know* what Chambers had just been—'

Steine was starting to lose patience. 'I don't see how this is any of your business. The question is irrelevant and you are making a fool of yourself.'

'But why did you have a *gun*?'

Steine shook his head, exasperated. One minute you're expected to know that the primate of all England lives in *Lambeth*, of all places; the next you have to account for your heroic actions to a worm like this? He pointed a finger at the reporter and looked around for help. 'Can this man in the hat be removed, please?' he said.

At which, to the general approval of all the other assembled journalists, Hoskisson was bundled from the room by two constables, and his notebook illegally confiscated.

But the wasp-reporter didn't give up. In the ensuing weeks, Steine received daily requests from Hoskisson for an interview (which he ignored), and he spotted the objectionable white raincoat and brown trilby virtually every time he left his Mayfair hotel. On entering Broadcasting House to share his *Desert Island Discs* with Roy Plomley, he saw Hoskisson lurking outside. And when he came out, the man was still there.

'What records did you choose, Inspector?' called the reporter. 'Did you ask for Betty Hutton singing "You Can't Get a Man with a Gun"?'

Steine had had enough. It was on this day that he decided to share his annoyance with the Commissioner of the Metropolitan Police, and it was the commissioner who, imaginatively, sanctioned the immediate secondment of the legendary Miss Roberta Lennon to Brighton, as Steine's special personal secretary (i.e. effective human shield). If there was one thing the commissioner really enjoyed, it was using his powers to quash legitimate concerns raised by a pesky press.

'Miss Lennon will protect you, old boy,' he said, patting Inspector Steine's shoulder. 'Trust me, she's a force of nature. I've been meaning to suggest it since this whole thing kicked off. Send her ahead of you down to Brighton tomorrow, then you follow the next day; sneak out of your hotel the back way at the crack of dawn and I'll have a car waiting.'

The inspector was both grateful and impressed. 'Thank you, sir. It's a mite underhanded but necessary in the circumstances.'

'Which is my exact personal motto, Steine! Oh, yes. Trust me. Pragmatism, that's the key to success in this profession.'

'Is it?'

'Of course!'

Steine attempted to absorb this, but couldn't.

'By the way, before you go.' The commissioner lowered his voice. 'I hope my Soho chaps haven't been too hard on you over this Chambers business.'

'No, no!' laughed Steine. Then, confused, 'For what?'

'Well, for halving their income, in some cases!'

Steine had no idea what the commissioner was talking about.

'I mean, I shouldn't say it, but between you and me, my own lady wife is furious with you. Furious! Chambers flew us out to Torremolinos last year for a fortnight, and she said it was the best holiday she ever had. And then of course there were the cases of spirits at Christmas.'

He sat back and lit a cigarette. 'Oh, well. Win some, lose some. But I can't imagine that boy Nicky Garroway carrying on those honourable traditions, can you? Far too green. And not much up top either.'

Steine gave up trying to understand. Who was 'that boy Nicky Garroway'? Why would a notorious villain send alcohol to the highest-ranking officer in the police? Where was Torremolinos?

He changed the subject. 'I'm wondering, sir, should I be scared of this Lennon woman myself?'

The commissioner roared with laughter and clapped him again on the shoulder. 'Not at all, old boy! That's the joy of it! Miss Lennon is loyal to an almost insane degree. When it comes to protective instincts, there's no one like her. If that reporter comes near you, she will chew him up whole and spit out his bones.'

When the commissioner so glibly mentioned young Nicky Garroway in connection with future backhanders, he little knew how empty were his hopes for more Spanish holidays from that particular quarter. Because, at the time he spoke, Nicky was lying lifeless beside an abandoned Humber on a grass verge just a mile west of Brighton. He'd been struck on the head with a rock, dying instantly. Since the shooting of Terence Chambers, the great man's young acolyte had barely been seen around Soho, and he'd been notably absent from the ostentatious funeral, with its intimidating slow-march procession of scar-faced hoodlums through the sombre streets of Stepney. If Nicky had ever intended to take up the reins of the organisation, the funeral would have been the ideal moment to stake his claim.

But in fact he had never entertained such ambitions. With the death of Chambers, Nicky did not sense opportunity. He felt only youthful shame, anger, and an unquenchable lust for revenge.

But what designs had he formed? In what cause had he been killed? It was as yet unclear.

When his body was eventually reported to the police, the attending officers found evidence of another person in the vehicle – a person who had, presumably, delivered the killer-blow and then scarpered. A suit of prison clothes lay crumpled up on the back seat, together with a large-scale map of Berkshire, with a route drawn on it in ballpoint pen towards the tiny village of Crowthorne. Also in the car were a shovel and some stout wire-cutters, a tarpaulin and a thick wool blanket.

On inspection, the prison clothes revealed that they were the 'PROPERTY OF BROADMOOR', and also that the prisoner's number and name were '142, CHAUCER, GEOFFREY'.

'What, like the poet?' said the constable at the scene, in a disbelieving tone.

'See for yourself,' said his partner, holding up the collar of the jacket with the name-tag turned out.

'Unusual,' commented the PC, snapping his notebook shut.

***

Back at the police station, with Brunswick and Twitten still sensibly preferring to stay out of doors (despite the rain), Mrs Groynes wheeled a trolley with a newly filled tea-urn along the dimly lit corridor from the lift. She took her time. In ordinary circumstances she would be keen to get back to the office and implement the first stage of a cunning plot to annihilate her sizeable new enemy in the shortest possible time. Nobody quoted fire regulations at Palmeira Groynes and got away with it. But today her fury with the interloper Miss Lennon kept being displaced by worries of other sorts; there was just too much to think about.

The main thing was: what had been sent to Twitten in that envelope? Who had sent it, and where was it now? (She had opened his locker with ease and found nothing.) Secondly, where had Barrow-Boy Cecil got to, and why hadn't she noticed he'd gone? Thirdly (and most importantly), why was she overcome with a sense of foreboding? Was it just the abysmal wet and overcast weather, or something more?

Stopping to light a cigarette, she winced to remember the encounter with Twitten outside the locker room, when he had so obviously lied to her. There was no mistaking the expression on his face: he had looked afraid, but also triumphant. This was not a welcome development. For a very enjoyable three months the clever-clogs constable had been powerless to make a case against her, and a friendship of convenience had formed as a result. She had helped him, advised him, confided in him, and (when necessary) gently pulled the wool over his eyes. But today she had seen a different Twitten – a Twitten who believed he had the upper hand – and she didn't like the way it made her feel.

How far would she go to stop him? That was the question. How far would she go against Constable Twitten if she knew he was in a position to expose her?

'Mrs Groynes?'

She looked round. It was a boy's voice, whispering.

'Shorty?'

'I'm over here, Mrs G.'

A rolled-up copy of the *Beano* poked out from behind an open cupboard door, and she went to investigate. And there he was, this adorable boy in shorts who *every day* gave policemen on patrol a plausible (and slightly revolting) excuse as to why he wasn't at school. 'My mum's taking me to the nit clinic; she told me to meet her here; she says I'm *over-run*'; 'They had to shut the school because of the *rats*.' He was a very promising juvenile, Shorty; a sharp kid, quick to learn. As his employer, Mrs Groynes cared about his welfare. Nevertheless she was cross with him right now.

'I told you never to come in here, Shorty!'

'I know.'

'So what are you playing at?'

'Sorry, Mrs—'

'How did you even get in?'

'Ah.' He smiled at her, and proudly kicked a damp cardboard box on the floor. 'Said I was delivering that, didn't I?' he said triumphantly. 'I said it was a *cake*!'

'Well, that was clever.'

'People never say no to cake, see?'

'You're not wrong, Shorty.' She patted his head. 'You might say my whole career is based on that one principle. But that doesn't explain why you're here.'

'Look, I told Denise you wouldn't want me coming, but she told me I got to. You should-a seen her, Mrs G! She was right shook up. She told me to bring you this.'

From his pocket he retrieved something wrapped in a large handkerchief and handed it to her. 'I ain't looked at it,' he said. 'But she said to tell you it come down the tube!'

Mrs Groynes gently folded back the hankie to reveal – well, we know what it revealed: the ghastly severed finger; the upsetting shards of shattered bunny; the note saying that Shorty would be next in line if Mrs Groynes was informed. When she opened it up, part of the mechanism went (faintly) *Fzzzz-zzzz*.

She gasped, and staggered. It was as if she'd been struck. *Oh, Cecil! What have they done to you? And I hadn't even noticed you'd gone! I just thought it was too rainy for selling worthless toot on street corners!*

She swallowed. What should she do? 'You're sure you didn't read this note, Shorty?'

'No, Mrs G. I told ya. Denise told me not to.'

'Good. That's good. You're a good boy.'

'She was white as a sheet, Mrs G. I never seen her like it afore. She went the colour you've gone now!'

'Right. Well, I'm not surprised.' Mrs G felt faint. If someone knew to target both Cecil and Shorty, they knew far too much about her.

'But she said to ask, did she do the right thing telling you?'

'Oh, yes. Yes, of course.' Mrs Groynes crouched down and gave Shorty a quick hug. 'But don't you go running back to tell her that, not now.'

'No?'

'No. We'll see her later, together. I've got to think about what's best for everyone, dear.'

Standing up again, Mrs Groynes put her hands to her face. *Who was doing this? Who was behind it?*

'Tell you what, Shorty. Can you pretend to be my nephew? I'll take you back to the office and you can read your comic until it's time to go home.'

'All right. Can I push the trolley?'

'No, dear. There's a knack.'

Shorty pulled a face. He would have liked to push the trolley.

'Are we *at war*, Mrs G?' he asked conversationally, as they made their way along the corridor together. 'Denise said we might be, but when I said at war with who, then, she said, how the hell did she know, and gave me a clip round the ear!'

Three

In the annals of crime, it's surprising how few violent criminals have shared their names with those of the great English poets. Well-informed readers will of course point at once to the cases of Johnny 'Bloodbath' Keats and Elizabeth Barrett 'Bone-crusher' Browning – but those are famous anomalies.

So, in the early 1950s, when Geoff Chaucer from Billericay started his extraordinary campaign of boiling the heads of recently decapitated policemen, you'd have expected it to cause more of a stir in the public imagination. But, alas, in philistine post-war England, even the greatest of fourteenth-century poets were held in shockingly low regard (as were the police), and our Geoff had boiled up the bonces of three London constables before he was arrested, determined unfit for trial, and wisely committed to the top-security hospital we have recently identified as Broadmoor. Meanwhile, the case was kept as quiet as possible, for fear of causing both a sharp rise in public anxiety and a concomitant plummet in police recruitment.

What had made him commit these atrocities, though? He never explained, because, in truth, he didn't know. Chaucer was a man who suffered short episodes of extreme mania

sparked by a mystery stimulus – which was as far as his official diagnosis went until, in August 1957, a new psychologist
presented herself to Broadmoor's governor, formally asking
permission to conduct some interviews. It was an unusual
request. The governor was surprised, and a bit suspicious, but
the lady's credentials were excellent, and the more he thought
about it, the more inclined he was to welcome her to his
gloomy institution. What harm could she do? Besides, she
would be a new person to talk to, and he was catastrophically
lonely. It was two years now since his wife had left him, by
ignominiously running off to Cumberland with the gardener.

The new arrival's name was Miss Sibert. She had worked
with Sigmund Freud in Vienna before the war, and then
travelled with him to London. Her speciality was recovering
buried memories, and her plan (she said) was to write a case
study of Mr Chaucer, whose name she pronounced 'Chow-
tza'. She hoped to name a psychosis after him. Until recently,
she explained, she had been helping Mr A. S. Crystal, a
famous London theatre critic, retrieve details of a traumatic
experience, and the process had been progressing in a highly
satisfactory manner until he was unfortunately shot in the
head.

'Shot in the head?' repeated the governor, when she related
the story. They were seated in his dark, monumental office,
either side of his vast mahogany desk.

'*Jah*,' she said matter-of-factly. She mimed pulling a trigger
next to her ear. '*Beng-beng.*' And then, for clarification, she
mimed an explosion of brains and eyeballs.

'I see, yes.' The governor was taken aback but reminded
himself that he had hoped for relief from monotony, and here
it certainly was.

She shrugged. Her eyes twinkled. 'But to be fair, Mr Crystal deserve this.'

'Yes?'

'He was *ein Schweinhund.* There are many days I want to shoot him myself!' Was this woman joking? It was hard to tell. '*Und* zo smelly!' She waved a hand in front of her face at the memory of A. S. Crystal's toxic body odour. 'Ach, *mein Gott.*'

The governor observed Miss Sibert with interest. In her mid-forties, at a guess, she was refreshingly brisk, rather comical, and strangely attractive. Rosy face, flat lace-up shoes, battered leather briefcase, blonde hair braided and pinned up, a mauve silk square neatly pinned to her high-buttoned blouse. She brought impressive letters of introduction, and a dog-eared black-and-white photograph of herself as a dreamy young woman in a town garden, sitting beside a snowy-haired old man in a bath chair, whom she identified as 'dear, dear Sigmund!' There was little doubt in the governor's mind that she was precisely what she claimed to be. There was also little doubt in his mind that he had never met anyone remotely like her before.

By way of fair exchange, the governor showed her the grisly scene-of-crime photographs in Geoffrey Chaucer's file. In all three cases the 'scene of crime' was of course divided between the site of the assault and then the dingy scullery where he enacted the head-boiling. The governor's motives in showing her these pictures were twofold: first, he thought it important that Miss Sibert understand the kind of violence Chaucer was capable of; second, he had always derived pleasure from observing a woman's confusion when exposed to something disgusting. (He thought no one had guessed this secret perversion of his, but it was in fact the principal reason his wife had left him.)

Disappointingly, Miss Sibert scarcely batted an eye when confronted with images of violent bloodshed.

'Where is this picture taken, please?' She indicated the site of Assault One: a grand, high-ceilinged room full of tables and chairs in disarray with a magnificent floor of black-and-white chequerboard tiles, marred slightly by the ugly corpse of a headless police constable slumped on it.

'Show me,' said the governor. 'Oh, yes. That was a Lyons' Corner House in London. At Sloane Square. The policeman just happened to come in. He ordered cheese on toast and a cup of tea from one of the nippies, and Chaucer went berserk.'

'How did he … ?' Pulling a face, she mimed the act of concentrated sawing, and blood spurting.

'Oh. On that occasion, he happened to have a sharpened saw within reach.'

'I see.'

She flicked through the others, and was about to return them when she was evidently struck by a thought. Lightly resting her hand on the pictures, she eyed him suggestively. 'We play cards for these, Herr Governor?'

'Of course not!' Shocked, he snatched back the pictures and replaced them in the file. *Play cards for them*? His heart was beating fast. It was a long time since he had felt so alive.

'So … ' He coughed, and steadied himself. 'So you think you might be able to recover Chaucer's reasons for committing his terrible crimes, Miss Sibert?'

'I do. *Jah*. Easy like off log falling.'

'And what is the desired effect of this?'

'That his mind will be liberated, Herr Governor!'

'But his body will still be under lock and key?'

'Of course! But when he understand *why* he commit these crimes, he will be heppy.'

'And you, Miss Sibert, will have a case study that might make your name?'

'Ah.' She smiled. '*Natürlich.*'

'Aren't you afraid to spend time with such a man?'

'Me?' She laughed. '*Nein, nein!*' Dimples appeared in her cheeks when she was amused like this, and the governor liked it. Her eyes twinkled again. 'But perhaps this man should be little afraid of *me.*'

They had then drunk a small glass of sherry together, to seal the deal, but she couldn't stay long because a taxi was waiting. And after she'd gone the governor locked his door, sat back down at his enormous desk, put his head in his hands, and succumbed to such a tidal wave of loneliness that he seriously thought about taking his own life.

And so the daily Geoffrey Chaucer sessions began – always with an armed guard present, of course, because even if the governor was an emotional ticking bomb, he wasn't an idiot. Every weekday afternoon Miss Sibert arrived by taxi from the station at 2.18 p.m., rang the bell, submitted to a search, and was admitted to a large, cell-like room lit only by a skylight, with a table and chairs that were bolted to the floor. She was permitted a notebook and pencil (and the pencil was checked at the end of the session, for obvious reasons). For a couple of minutes, she sat alone, gathering her thoughts. It was always chilly in this room, and intimidatingly quiet. And then, at 2.30, a heavy door was unlocked, and Chaucer was brought in, manacled. Every day she tried not to shudder, but she could never help it. When he walked in, a gust of chill air came in with him, like a blast of reality.

Chaucer, at twenty-seven, was a slender man but tall and broad-shouldered. He had exactly the right physique, funnily enough, for a policeman. He even had a prominent jaw, ideal for a secure helmet strap. What struck everyone most on first meeting him, however, was the intensity of his unblinking gaze. He seemed to look right through you.

'What do you want?' he said, at the first meeting with the psychologist. His voice was low and gravelly, his manner challenging without being aggressive. Despite the manacles and the fact that he was a psychiatric hospital inmate unlikely ever to taste freedom again, he exuded such a sense of power that the term *Übermensch* came unbidden to Miss Sibert's mind – although, to be fair, it was more likely to occur to her than to most people, given that she was a lifelong German speaker.

'I come to talk,' she said. Instinctively, she reached up a hand to clutch at her silk scarf, but it wasn't there. The guards had removed it, for fear it should be used by Chaucer to strangle her. They had also taken the belt from her waist and the laces from her shoes, and extracted all thirty-seven pins from her hairdo. When the interviews were over each day, it took her a full fifteen minutes just to reassemble herself.

'You're scared,' he said, that first day.

'*Jah*,' she admitted. 'Also I am cold. But I am please to meet you, and I think I can help.'

'No, you can't.'

Bravely, she looked him in the eye. 'Mr Chow-tza, you kill three men. Three policemen. Yes?'

'That's what they say.'

'Yet you say you commit these murders in a kind of trance? And you have no knowledge of what pulls trigger in your mind?'

'That's right. I just went mad.'

'No one just *goes mad*, Mr Chow-tza!'

He shrugged. 'I did.'

'I help you. We bring it beck. You trust me. Whatever it was making you do this thing, together we *bring it beck.*'

It may be remembered that when Miss Sibert was working with the notably odoriferous critic A. S. Crystal earlier in the year, her motives were mixed. The unfortunate smelly man was keen to recollect details of a bank robbery during which he had been trussed up and hooded; ostensibly Miss Sibert was helping him write a memoir, and had used her Freudian insights to open his eyes to many additional aspects of his personal history – for example, pointing out that when his dear old mother served him consoling oxtail soup in his convalescence, it was symbolic of castration.

But she was playing a double game. Twitten's investigations led him to the shocking discovery that, all along, Miss Sibert had been in the secret employ of the dastardly Terence Chambers. When Twitten found out the truth, he was quite upset.

'Good heavens,' he exclaimed to Mrs Groynes. 'So Miss Sibert was *a plant?*'

So, to be clear, we should assume that Miss Sibert's current interest in the multiple-murderer Geoffrey Chaucer is not purely academic. For all her bona-fide connections to the father of psychoanalysis, and her genuine devotion to her therapeutic calling, she probably has an ulterior motive for attempting to locate this homicidal maniac's secret trigger.

He is, after all, a walking human powder-keg.

In the right hands, with the right target, such a man could be very, very useful.

What Miss Sibert soon discovered, to her confusion, was that Chaucer's traumatic memories were not in fact buried. He just possessed no sense of proportion about them. To an unusual degree, he was dissociated from normal feelings; he had no mechanism for sorting life events in order of magnitude or significance. In an early session he described to Miss Sibert how his own father – a successful accountant employed by criminals during the war – was shot dead by police when he foolishly resisted arrest. But when Miss Sibert claimed this as a breakthrough ('You have classic reason to hate policeman!'), he shook his head and disagreed.

'Father shouldn't have drawn a gun,' he said flatly. 'There was blood everywhere and Mother wouldn't stop screaming, so they hit her and knocked her out. It was all his fault. What's the weather like today?'

It was an unusual problem. He had no happy memories; no unhappy memories. It was all the same to him. Just once, when Miss Sibert was exhausted, and was asking him routine questions about his early life, had he briefly shown a flutter of agitation.

'Did you play cards with your parents?'

'Yes.'

Miss Sibert made a weary note. 'Was this enjoyable?'

'I suppose so.'

'Did you play Snep?'

He frowned. 'Oh, you mean *Snap*. Yes, we played Snap.'

'Heppy Families?'

'Yes.'

'Chess?'

There was silence. Miss Sibert looked up, queryingly. 'Did you play chess, Mr Chow-tza?' she asked again.

'Yes.' But Chaucer's face had clouded. Miss Sibert continued with her questions, but made a note later about his interesting reaction to the word 'chess'. It stood out in contrast to the way he had reacted (with a simple, flat 'yes') to questions about whether he thought killing was a bad thing, and whether, in childhood, he had entertained incestuous fantasies about his mother.

But it would be fair to say that progress was slow until the day of Miss Sibert's fifth session, when she was ushered into the governor's office by a grim-faced medical assistant.

'But why?' she asked. 'What is happening? Is it Mr Chowtza? Is he unwell? Please *Gott* he is not dead.'

'Ah, Miss Sibert,' said the governor gravely. 'Do sit down.'

The office smelled so strongly of male cologne that it made her eyes water. A vase of garish flowers stood on the desk. Whatever was going on, Herr Governor had evidently been looking forward to seeing her.

'I'm afraid there has been an incident,' he said, when they were both seated. 'Chaucer attacked a guard this morning.'

Miss Sibert's eyes widened. 'He attacks guard?'

'Yes. I'm sorry to say, he did. So I've decided—'

He stopped, confused. A highly inappropriate smile had appeared on Miss Sibert's face, as she closed her eyes and nodded.

'*Gut,*' she said. '*Gut, gut, gut, gut.*'

'Did you just say *good* in German, Miss Sibert?'

'*Jah.* Why not? It is breakthrough.'

'He hurt a guard! The poor fellow's in the infirmary.'

She waved it away, as a trivial concern. 'Herr Governor, the important thing is—'

But he didn't want to hear about the important thing. He stood up. He paced up and down. He had made a decision. 'I'm afraid I must suspend your visits to Chaucer forthwith.'

'What? But why? Herr Governor—'

'For one thing, I feel that it isn't safe for you to spend time with him.'

'Nonsense.'

'It's a security issue.'

'No, it isn't.'

'And for another thing—'

'Yes?'

'It's all your fault!'

'What? What did I do?'

'You've stirred things up! I should have known you would! You've stirred him up, and you've stirred up … ' He tried not to say what was in his heart. 'In fact, look, you've stirred things up generally! I mean, for me! You've stirred me up! Unpinning your hair! Letting it dangle like that! For God's sake, I'm only human! You've got to stop coming here!'

Miss Sibert cast a pitying look at the man. He was very distraught. 'Herr Governor,' she began gently.

'Leave me alone.'

'Please.'

'I blame you for this.'

'I don't understand, Herr Governor.'

'Oh, for pity's sake, Miss Sibert,' he wailed, sitting back down at his desk. 'For pity's sake, *call me Gerald*!'

The cry hung in the air for a while, and then she reached across his desk and gently touched his hand. He didn't move it. 'Herr Gerald, then.'

'Thank you,' he said quietly. 'I'm sorry. My wife … ' His chin wobbled, in anguish.

'I know.' She smiled at him encouragingly, and then realised this was the wrong expression, so changed it to one of extreme sympathy. 'I know,' she said sadly.

'She's gone!'

'Yes. This I hear.'

'She ran off with the gardener!'

'I know. Everyone talk of it. They laugh, ha-ha. But I tell them it is not funny.'

'I just can't describe how it makes me feel.'

'No?' She seemed faintly amused. Could he really not put it into words? 'Well, perhaps I help, Herr Governor,' she said kindly. 'After all, it is standard in such a case. You feel emasculated, *jah*?' Her tone was sympathetic, but the terminology was so blunt that he could only gape at her.

'What? No!' *Emasculated*? 'That's not it, no, no, good grief, no.'

'But yes, yes. This is normal. You feel as if your penis, he is gone?'

'My—? Oh, my God, no!'

'But you are right to feel this, Herr Gerald. Don't deny. This gardener fellow, he reach into your trousers. He reach down, and he snep off penis – *snep!*'

She waited a few seconds for him to absorb this.

'But, Herr Gerald, we must set aside such feelings. They are standard reflex only and not of interest. But this attack by Mr Chow-tza! This is positive sign. It is breakthrough and we must pounce.'

'What do you mean, pounce?' If the governor couldn't quite concentrate, it was understandable. The image of George the Gardener walking up to him, thrusting a manly arm down the front of his trousers and, with an expert upward twist, pulling up a carrot, was one that would surely recur in night-mares for the miserable remainder of his life.

'Pounce! Take advantage! Learn! For example, at what time of day is this attack?'

The governor took a deep breath. 'At – er, at exactly seven o'clock in the morning. The guard remembered hearing the clock chime.'

'And what is guard doing? Does he provoke Mr Chow-tza in some way?'

'Hardly! He was doing a crossword!'

'Really?'

'He was stuck on a clue, so he asked Chaucer to have a look at it. Poor old Timkins just showed him the grid in the newspaper, and Chaucer looked at it for about thirty seconds without saying anything, and then one of the female cleaners came up to ask a question—'

'You have females here?' she queried. 'Is this wise, Herr Gerald?'

'Well, to be honest, I thought I'd try it because they're so much better at cleaning! And usually there's no interaction with the patients. But I'm regretting it now, because Timkins offended this woman in some way and the next thing he was on the ground with Chaucer getting ready to kick him in the head! Luckily another guard intervened, but Chaucer didn't calm down for an hour or more. He flipped, Miss Sibert. They all saw it. He flipped because of a damned crossword.'

'*Mein Gott.*' Miss Sibert held her head at an angle as she considered what she'd just heard.

The governor rose to his feet. He looked serious. 'What's your first name, Miss Sibert? I know it begins with a C. Is it Charlotte? Christine? Clara? Cherry? Clementine? Please tell me.'

She ignored the question. Her mind was racing. 'You show me crime pictures again, Herr Gerald. I must see them. Quickly!'

He opened his desk drawer. 'Here.'

Together they pored over the photographs, ignoring the headless corpses, looking for something else. It was Miss Sibert who found it.

'It is the pattern,' she breathed excitedly. 'Do you see? The floor! *Schachbrett* – black and white! Like crossword puzzle! Like chessboard! Yes!'

She selected another picture. '*Und* here!' She showed him an Art Deco room, with black-and-white striped wallpaper. In a third was a man dressed as a monochrome harlequin. She flung herself back in her seat, flushed with success. She had cracked it!

The governor wrinkled his nose. 'You're saying the man just has to see a black-and-white pattern to go mad? But that can't be it, Miss Sibert. We see those patterns every day. Those floors are everywhere. If that's all it takes, he would have killed hundreds of people. Oh, please.' He leaned close to her. 'You look magnificent at this moment, with your porcelain cheeks flushed like a Dresden shepherdess! Please let me kiss you.'

She waved him away and sat up properly. It wasn't unusual for men to throw themselves at her, and of course she completely understood the attraction (because it was Freudian). But she wasn't going to let this man's pathetic advances obstruct an important train of thought. She was getting close to cracking the mystery of Chaucer's manic episodes.

'Perhaps it is black-and-white pattern *und* the presence of a policeman!' she said. 'But perhaps one other element also. Perhaps a word, yes? So to sum up, there are three triggers.

One: pattern. Two: policeman. Three: a word. *Ein, zwei, drei* – and he *sneps!*'

'Please don't say snap again.'

Ignoring him, she chewed her lip thoughtfully; and slowly a smile of triumph lit up her face. 'It is *perfect*, but I must discover third trigger.'

While she turned over the implications in her mind, she barely noticed that the governor had dropped down to his knees and was beginning to untie the laces of her shoes.

'Herr Gerald? What you do?'

'Please let me. Please. Your feet are so small. And your shoes are so – they're so *practical*.'

'Very well. But I must see Mr Chow-tza today, Herr Gerald. And since you ask me, my first name is Carlotta.'

'Carlotta?'

'That's right.'

'Carlotta, I must tell you something. I love you.'

'I know.' She laughed. 'You fall in love with me the first time I walk in room! It is not first time this happen to me. But no more talk of terminating visits. No more talk of Dresden shepherdess also! We are on brink. *On brink*. You understand?'

'I think so.'

'Like—' She tried to think of an analogy, and smiled. 'Like when penis is about to ejaculate, *jah*?'

He choked. 'Oh, my God.'

'What?'

'Please don't keep referring to my penis, Carlotta.'

'But you love it, Gerald. Admit this. We are building and climbing, building and climbing, *jah*? Until we get to point and go … *Beng!*'

For the next few days, Miss Sibert avoided the governor, and focused on the events surrounding Chaucer's father's death. As usual, Chaucer was entirely – and flatly – matter-of-fact about them, and wasn't particularly agitated when talking about the black-and-white Art Deco surroundings of the hotel room where it happened. He agreed that there had been an unusual amount of black-and-white stuff at the scene. His mother was wearing a black-and-white dress; Chaucer and his father had been playing chess; the floor was tiled in the inevitable pattern; there was even an enormous chiming black-and-white clock. And, of course, when the police broke in, they had black-and-white check trimmings on the cuffs of their uniforms. All these patterns had been splashed or smeared with his father's bright red blood during the shoot-out that ensued. But Chaucer could describe it all without emotion, as if it had happened to someone he barely knew, or in a film he hadn't particularly been engaged by.

One morning in the third week of interviews, Miss Sibert rose early at her flat in Bloomsbury and quickly reread all the reports of the murders, hoping for inspiration. The trouble with such reports, of course, was that they were written by stolid policemen who had no interest in (or flair for) scene-setting or dialogue. For the J. Lyons murder, for example, the report said that the victim, Constable Fry, had spoken to a waitress named Doris Fuller (aged seventeen, of Chiswick), ordering cheese on toast and a pot of tea, and that this had made Chaucer – sitting within earshot at a nearby table – grab a heavy mallet, and then a handsaw, and run mad.

Exasperated, Miss Sibert telephoned the Sloane Square branch of Lyons and asked if Doris Fuller still worked there. The manageress, who was a bit flustered, and not accustomed to talking on the phone, said in an affected posh accent that

Doris had left the hemploy of J. Lyons five years ago following a hunfortunate hincident, but had left a home address in case anyone needed to contact her hurgently. Was this henquiry hurgent? Miss Sibert replied that it certainly was. Thinking quickly, she said she was calling from a solicitor's office about a possible inheritance.

'Oh, good for Dolly,' said the manageress warmly (and lapsing back into her normal voice). 'She deserves a bit of blooming good luck after all that murder malarkey!'

Address in hand, Miss Sibert set out at once to find Doris. 'Single-minded' would be the kind way of describing Miss Sibert – she was single-minded to the point of monomania, and it was not an appealing quality. It made her peremptory and impatient, especially when she was on any sort of mission. 'Hogarth Street! *Where?*' she barked at the dithery natives on Chiswick High Road, once outside Turnham Green tube station, and then charged off without stopping to say thank you. 'Number twenty-nine! *Where?*' she demanded of a scruffy boy in a home-made go-cart in Hogarth Street. 'Doris Fuller, *now!*' she said at the front door when Doris's mother, wearing a bright nylon housecoat, opened it and said politely – somewhat taken aback by the sight of this small, pent-up European woman on the doorstep – 'Hello, can I help you?'

Luckily Doris was at home. She was a sweet young woman, who had been proud of her job as a nippy at Lyons. The day of the incident had seemed unremarkable, she said, up to that moment when the young man went berserk at the policeman. It was five years ago, but she had never gone back to work with the public again. These days, she worked evenings as a telephonist at the local exchange, which was a better job anyway, if you didn't mind saying 'Number, please' all the time. She had loved the training for the job, learning all the names of the exchanges and the abbreviations: RIC for Richmond, POP for Pope's Grove in Twickenham, FRE for Fremantle at Earls Court. A friend of hers worked at the EMBerbrook exchange at Thames Ditton, and she thought the name Emberbrook was the prettiest she'd ever heard.

Unsurprisingly, Miss Sibert was impatient with all this. She just wanted to know the exact words spoken at the time of the attack, and when Doris demurred, saying that she'd rather not think about it, thank you, she had to resist an impulse to grab the girl and shake her.

'Why do you care so much?' Doris asked. It was a good question, which Miss Sibert was unwilling to answer. How could she explain what was *in it for her* if she got to the bottom of Geoffrey Chaucer's mania?

Doris's mum brought the tea things on a tray into the little front room that was reserved for the visits of strangers. She set it down on a dark-wood Utility table. 'What's going on?' she said.

'I was just saying, Mum, I don't understand why anyone would care about that awful man. He's a ruddy murderer and he's behind bars. I hope he rots.'

'I understand. But is hard to explain,' said Miss Sibert. She opened her handbag and took out three one-pound notes. 'I must know what happen, that's all. I must know what happen *before* he kills the policeman.'

She laid the notes on the table, and pushed them towards Doris.

'She can't remember everything; she's blocked a lot of it out,' warned Doris's mum, unable to take her eyes off the money.

'Let me try.' Gently, Miss Sibert took Doris's hand. 'Let me take you beck, Doris. Let us be calm now, and I take you beck.'

'You're not going to *hypnotise* me?' said the young woman, frowning.

Miss Sibert's eyes twinkled. 'You allow this?' she said. She added another pound note.

Doris and her mum exchanged glances. They looked at each other, and down at the money on the table, and then at the teapot (awkwardly) and then at each other again.

'Make it guineas,' said Doris's mum. 'And it's a deal.'

———

So this is what happened. It is a warm and sunny day in September 1952, and J. Lyons in Sloane Square is half-full. At a quarter to two, people are eating hot lunches and drinking cups of tea; others are tucking into fancy cakes. There are small family groups in the restaurant – mostly stout aunts taking small schoolboys in blazers out for a treat – but also a number of people sitting alone: Territorial Army soldiers from the nearby barracks; neatly dressed women with library books; respectable working men on their dinner break.

One of the latter is young Geoffrey Chaucer, qualified carpenter, who is employed across the road at the Peter Jones department store. His boss hired him because he seemed so gentle and well-spoken; he could interact well with customers if required. By a stroke of bad luck, Chaucer has with him a set of carpentry tools, fresh from being cleaned and sharpened. They are on the spare seat opposite him as he methodically cuts and eats his steak-and-kidney pie and winks occasionally at Doris, who seems like a nice girl. The jazzy black-and-white floor has no effect on him whatsoever.

Just before two o'clock, a policeman later identified as Constable Fry enters and sits at a table near to Chaucer's. He orders a pot of tea and cheese on toast. And that's it.

Really? Does he say nothing else? Doris, Doris, can you remember? What else does this constable say? He does say something, doesn't he?

'Yes, he does.' Doris looks surprised. How could she have forgotten this? 'He says to me, *Well, you're a nice little piece of goods.*'

'Men!' exclaims Doris's mum – but Miss Sibert shoots her a glance, and she says 'Sorry' very quietly.

'A *nice little piece of goods*, that's it. And then he pats me on the bottom, and I say, *Here, you. Take your hands off me.*'

'He assault you, this policeman?'

'No, no. It's just a pat. It happens all the time.'

'And does this Chow-tza man take notice of this?'

Yes, he does. Doris has never remembered this before: that it all started when she told the policeman to stop touching her. A cloud passes across Chaucer's face and he drops his knife and fork. 'You heard the lady,' he says, standing up. 'Take your hands off her, you lousy rozzer!' People look round. There is an air of impending violence.

But it still might not happen. There's something else before he goes nuts; there's *something else*.

'What? A sound? A car outside go beng, perhaps? Does the policeman say something to him?'

'No.' Doris slows her breath. She has never wanted to revisit this moment, but now that she's there, it's so clear!

'The clock chimes,' she says, at last. 'There's a really fancy clock in the Corner House and it strikes the hours and the quarters, you know?'

'Yes.'

'And it drives you mad hearing it all bloody day, I can tell you. But that's what happened. It started to chime like Big Ben, you know – *bing, bong, bing, bong*?'

'Yes? Yes?'

'And then when it strikes the first *bong* for the hour – that's when the man grabs this mallet from out of his bag and swings it at the policeman. And then the policeman hits the ground, and everyone starts screaming, and I'm shrieking, and he turns around to me and – no, no.' Doris stops. She looks puzzled, disturbed.

'He says something?'

'Yes, but— Sorry, but it can't be right, it don't make sense. Can we stop now, please?'

But Miss Sibert is not going to stop now. 'What does he say, Doris?'

The girl starts to cry. She looks pleadingly at her mum, but her mum can't help.

'He turns to me; he definitely says it to me, but it don't make sense. He says, *Run, Mummy. Run.*'

Four

True to her fearsome reputation (and nature), Miss Lennon wasted no time reorganising Inspector Steine's department. By the time Mrs Groynes threw open the door to the office next morning at half-past seven – having grudgingly manoeuvred her unwieldy urn-trolley along the corridor from the lift – the outer room was unrecognisable.

'Oh, for crying out loud,' she huffed.

Both desks (Twitten's and Brunswick's) had been pushed back from their usual positions, and Miss Lennon now sat in the dead centre of the room at a large shiny table with Twitten's favourite typewriter set upon it. Also on her table-top were a posy vase, a telephone, and a small ornate silver picture frame containing a sepia-coloured studio photograph of two children, presumably relatives. In the far corner of the room, where Mrs Groynes usually made the tea and dished out the biscuits, was a tall wooden filing cabinet. Ominously, the tea-making equipment was nowhere to be seen. Rain pelted against the window (the weather still hadn't let up), and the lights were on.

'Ah, Mrs GROYNES,' Miss Lennon said, glancing up. She was quickly sorting copies of the *Police Gazette* into date order, and had nearly finished. All the mail-sacks were empty, and the opened post was neatly piled. 'There. We. ARE,' she said, pleased. She stood up and gave her attention to the bewildered charwoman. 'Mrs Groynes, the inspector returns this morning, so everything must to be PERFECT for his arrival. And what an IMPROVEMENT!'

She didn't pause for a response. She seemed impervious to the shock on Mrs G's face. 'So I'd like a cup of tea, please, with two spoons of sugar. I've found a new place for you to make beverages and store your cleaning materials. I'll show you; it's not far. When I arrived yesterday the office felt more like a cafeteria than a place of work, and the reason was obvious: a charlady seemed to have taken up residence! You'll understand why it was CRUCIAL to change that?

'Now, I haven't had a chance yet to establish your exact TERMS OF EMPLOYMENT but in my extensive experience of police stations, it is normal for charwomen to work for a maximum of four hours, not ALL DAY.' She made a disapproving 'tut-tut' noise. 'It is also normal for charwomen to service a whole floor of a station, not just the officers in ONE ROOM. Mrs Groynes, I have to inform you that being at this station ALL DAY, and devoting yourself to just ONE SMALL DEPARTMENT, is HIGHLY IRREGULAR, which is why I feel duty-bound to curtail it henceforth.' She held out a crumpled paper bag. 'By the way, I found these SLIPPERS and this FRILLY SATIN EYE MASK in the corner. Am I right to assume they are YOURS? I wouldn't like to think they are SERGEANT BRUNSWICK'S!'

The phone rang on Miss Lennon's desk. 'Ah, excuse me,' she said, handing the bag to Mrs Groynes and picking up the receiver. 'Inspector Steine's office, Miss Lennon speaking, how may I help you? ... May I ask who's calling? Could you spell that, please? ... G-O-S-L-I-N-G? Like a young goose? You DO realise it's only seven-thirty-five a.m.?'

While Miss Lennon dealt with the call, Mrs Groynes lit a Capstan and took a thoughtful drag, but otherwise didn't move. She still had her coat and hat on. Both were still wet from her journey to work. Her handbag was over her arm. The only question was: should she walk out now, or walk out later? On the whole, walking out now was preferable: better to do it before anyone else arrived.

Having made up her mind, she took a deep breath. So this was it. She had always understood that this cosy police charlady performance couldn't run for ever, but if she had pictured the ending at all, it was very differently, with herself dramatically unmasked as a ruthlessly clever criminal, to assorted gratifying cries of 'Good heavens! You must be very clever!' (Inspector Steine) and 'Well, I knew all along, of course, but no one believed me' (Twitten) and *No-o-o-o-o-o-o!* (Brunswick). Instead of which, here she stood, being ticked off as a lazy charwoman who had craftily extended her working hours.

It was hard to take in. Since yesterday, many of the certainties of her existence had been overturned. She had learned that Shorty was in peril, and that Barrow-Boy Cecil had been snatched; meanwhile the long-gestated top-secret Gosling's Job was looking dicey, to say the least, what with Cecil's sawn-off digit being posted down the tubes for her attention.

And what about her stable relationship with young Twitten? It was interesting how upset she was by the change in the constable. Why did she care so much? They weren't *friends*. She had known him only three months; they were on opposite sides of the law; he was an annoying clever-clogs who had – when a whole universe of cake was open to him – panicked and chosen Dundee as his official favourite. How could she respect someone who did that? Dundee cake made everyone choke, himself included! And yet she hated the new way he had looked at her yesterday after receiving that mystery envelope of his. He'd regarded her as if he were a lost dog and she were a Wall's pork sausage.

But when things are over, they are over.

'Sod this for a game of soldiers,' she said quietly, snapping shut her handbag. Her glorious police-station tea-making days were at an end. Miss Lennon was still on the phone, taking notes, and didn't look up.

Searching for a positive, Mrs Groynes glanced at the frilly eye mask in the paper bag. It was nice to have it back. At home she had searched for it high and low.

'I certainly owe the cat an apology,' she thought, as she opened the door and marched out, leaving the urn-trolley behind her.

———

It is 'Mister Harold' who finds the body of our American professor. Ever since he took over the running of the family store four years ago, the forty-three-year-old has lived on the top floor, in a large, sunny penthouse, decorated to the latest style and fitted with all the latest mod cons. It is a stunning flat, like something from the latest *Daily Mail* Ideal Home Exhibition, but with the additional benefit of spectacular views across Brighton's rooftops, all the way to the Pavilion and the sea. Mister Harold's beautiful new assistant, Adelaide Vine, often stands at the windows up here, looking down at all of Brighton spread before her, and is visibly moved by the sight.

'Look at all *this*,' she sighs.

The sunlight glints on her beautiful chestnut hair, and is reflected in her hazel-coloured eyes, which are shaped like almonds. Looking at her lovely face as she smiles up at him, Mister Harold often finds himself pondering, for no fathomable reason, the nuts department. Traditionally it has been open only in the run-up to Christmas, but should it perhaps become an all-year-round affair?

Because the thing is, Harold's thoughts are always skewed towards retail opportunity: that's just the way he is. Show him a gorgeous young woman with nut-like attributes and he thinks of brazils in heaps, and filberts and cashews, and outsized market scales, and stout brown paper bags expertly gripped in the corners, then (flick of the wrists) neatly flipped to keep them closed.

He was born into retail: it is his life's blood. He blesses his luck that he has taken over the shop during a consumer boom, when there are massive profits to be made and the market for everything is changing fast. He loves the new spirit in advertising ('The Best Kipper is a MacRae Kipper'; 'Washday White without Washday Red') and the raft of saleable British brand names: from Lion's Head sherry to Wheatsheaf shoes; from Belgrave bedroom furniture to Burgo washing machines; Snugdown blankets to Evenglo light bulbs. His favourite brand of cigarette is Puffins, and he favours them not only because the name is clever: he is drawn to the picture on the packet of cliffs, waves and seabirds. Against all logic, the image makes him connect cigarettes with cool and bracing fresh air.

He is not married. While his wealth and bachelor status make him a perpetual target for gold-diggers, his single-minded devotion to retail successfully protects him from them. Determined women can snag him easily enough, but they can't retain his interest. 'What are you thinking about, darling?' they might ask breathily, wiggling their eyebrows and snuggling closer. And he replies brightly, 'Well, since you ask, why the new Murphy Swing-screen TV doesn't outsell the Pye Continental! It's really got me stumped!'

Sometimes these would-be girlfriends fall at a different hurdle, when they thoughtlessly break Mister Harold's cardinal rule, even though it is absurdly simple to remember: *Never mention Hannington's in his presence.* His feelings about the rival store are intemperate, and he has been known to venture out under cover of darkness and daub red paint over posters proclaiming 'Hannington's – Brighton's First Choice!' Other stores he can tolerate: Vokin's, the Co-operative, Peter Lord in East Street. But not the mighty Hannington's. When people speak the name to him, he feels they have spat in his face.

So he is a driven man, this Mister Harold, and an insomniac, and part of his morning routine is to visit – and give fresh consideration to – every inch of the shop-floor before even the cleaners arrive at half-past six. This time spent communing alone with his shop has inspired many a brainwave in the past: not least, to remove all the overhead wires from the old cash-canister system and install the more modern pneumatic tubes. Some of the staff were understandably scared of them to begin with. Such powerful suction! But thus far the only accident was quite a comical one, when the girl in the Dutch costume (with the cubes of cheese on sticks) bent her head too close to a carelessly uncapped portal and her wig – complete with plaits – flew off like a blonde flying squirrel and was sucked away down the hole.

This morning he is just about to leave the music department on the second floor when something catches his eye in one of the soundproofed booths. Mister Harold is proud of this little corner of the shop, and often lingers here because the smell of vinyl is so intoxicating. His decision to sell records (and compete with specialist music shops) entailed a substantial investment in fittings: not only the sturdy browsing racks for the heavy long-players, but the system of hidden wires and speakers and soundproofing for those essential little listening booths. Mister Harold had insisted on having two types of booth: four 'duck-ins' for teenagers who were happy to stand and dance – heads together – to their rock-'n'-roll records; two larger, more sedate booths for classical music lovers, with bench seats and closable half-glazed doors. He took the idea for the cubicles straight from the film *Strangers on a Train*, which one of the would-be girlfriends had made him take her to see. (The design of the cubicles in the music store was, of course, the only thing he took away from the evening. Disappointingly, the rest of the film didn't concern retail at all.)

But what's this? There is something red smeared on the internal glass of Booth F. He opens the door and is surprised to find a man lying there – a large man in wire-rimmed glasses. At first he is simply confused. *Are people sleeping in Gosling's now? Why didn't the nightwatchman find this man and throw him out?* But then – and, well, this is what separates a retail genius like Mister Harold from ordinary people – a Big Idea flickers to life, and he puts a thoughtful hand to his chin. Would customers *pay* to sleep in Gosling's? Would they see it as a privilege to spend the night here? Should the shop hold a competition? It could be used to relaunch the bedroom furniture section, which is in need of a new lease of life!

But the brainwave is short-lived. As he looks more carefully, he can't help noticing that the man has a small gun in his hand, and the back of his head is missing. The red on the glass is blood. Mister Harold gasps and backs away. A suicide? A man has shot himself in *Gosling's*?

As he pushes Booth F's door shut again, his first thought is, *I must telephone the police, of course. I will ask for Inspector Steine.* His second is, *But don't forget the sleeping-the-night idea, because Belgrave Furniture might be persuaded to sponsor the whole thing.* And his third thought – with a grin of triumph – is the supremely comforting, *Ha! So Hannington's wasn't someone's first choice, then, was it?*

By the time Inspector Steine had arrived back at his desk, there was rather a lot for his officers to tell him. He wasn't pleased. Since he had just been driven from London in the pouring rain, and had been obliged to rise extremely early, he would have appreciated a couple of hours sitting quietly in his office, perhaps having constructive thoughts for his memoirs. But this was not to be. He would also have enjoyed holding court with his men, relating his many triumphs in the capital (he had brought home a clanking holdall full of trophies, gifts and medals). But apparently he could wave goodbye to those fond hopes as well.

Here was the perpetual downside of being a policeman, in his opinion: the fact that random and unpleasant criminal activity *always* dictated the order of business. The inspector deeply resented the reactive imperative of the policeman's lot, especially when it interfered with a grand triumphal return. A perfect day might be in prospect, but if some tiresome idiot of a criminal took it into his head to rob or kill, you had no choice in the matter. You had to shelve your own plans while all your colleagues focused their attention on *him*.

'So you're telling me, Brunswick,' he sighed, 'that a man has just been found shot dead in Gosling's Department Store?'

'Yes, sir. An hour ago. In the record department. In a listening booth.'

'It *might* be suicide,' chipped in Twitten excitedly, 'but we suspect not. From what I can gather, sir, the man had everything to live for. He was on the cutting edge of important sociological research.'

'Well, I wouldn't know about that, sir,' said Brunswick, 'but the constable and I will set off for Gosling's the minute we've finished here. Your new secretary Miss Lennon allowed us to talk to you first because of the gravity of the situation.'

The inspector nodded. Miss Lennon had greeted him with more enthusiasm – and volume – than he was accustomed to ('Thanks HEAVENS! Our HERO returns!'), and he had scurried past her, confused.

'I'm told she's very efficient,' he said. 'The commissioner in London said she was the soul of loyalty and would be able to protect me.'

'Well, she can certainly be jolly fierce, sir,' said Twitten.

'Can she?'

'I should say so, sir,' said Brunswick. 'Sergeant Baines on the front desk has already started ducking out of sight when he sees her coming. And she only started yesterday.'

'But on the other hand,' said Twitten, 'she *does* seem refreshingly efficient. For example, she answers the phone and takes messages instead of kneeling down like Mrs G and threatening to cut off the cord at the skirting board with a penknife. I'm not suggesting that one approach is inherently better than the other, but it's certainly a very different sort of energy.'

Steine huffed. 'Well, I can't pretend I'm not disappointed to be welcomed back with this unpleasant news about this dead fellow. And it's your loss, too, I'm afraid. I'm sure you are both burning with curiosity about my time away.' He indicated the holdall on his desk.

Brunswick and Twitten looked at each other.

'Not really, sir,' said Twitten. 'Personally speaking, I'd much rather investigate a potential murder.'

'I see. And what about you, Brunswick?'

'Well … ' This was tricky for the sergeant. He had long dreamed of being awarded the Silver Truncheon himself, and was pretty keen to hold one.

'Well?' repeated Steine.

'I'm sorry, sir, but I mean, flaming hell, this man is *dead*—'

'Yes, well, in that case, let's not labour the point.' With a long-suffering air, the inspector dragged the heavy bag off his desk and placed it on the floor. 'Off you both go, then. What are you waiting for?'

Brunswick gaped in surprise. 'There's a bit more to tell you first, sir.'

'*More?*'

'Well, yes.' Brunswick produced his notebook, and took a deep breath. 'You've been gone for weeks, sir. I didn't want to leave anything out, so I prepared a list. Paint the big picture, as it were. So, *one*, yesterday at approximately one p.m. at the Polyfoto shop in Western Road, an aggravated robbery was perpetrated by a person or persons—'

'You love all this, don't you, Brunswick?'

'Pardon, sir?'

'I'm just saying. You love it.'

Brunswick shot a look of panic at Twitten: *What's going on?*

'I don't understand, sir.'

'Crime. Murders. *Aggravated robberies.*'

'Are you all right, sir?'

'The thing about criminals, Brunswick – and I believe I've mentioned this to you before – is that they are scum. They are the scum of the earth, and yet look!'

'Look at what, sir?'

'Look how they succeed in setting the agenda!'

Brunswick and Twitten exchanged glances. Twitten shook his head. All they knew was that this was an awkward situation. They waited.

Steine gave up. 'All right,' he sighed, 'how many items are on that precious list of yours?'

Brunswick glanced at it. 'Five, sir.'

'*Five?*'

Twitten cleared his throat. 'I think the sergeant really should be allowed to paint the whole picture, sir. I don't want to spoil it for you, but in terms of you personally, sir, it's a very big picture; in fact, it's bally *titanic.*'

'Oh, very well. Go on, Brunswick.'

And so, the inspector folded his arms, pursed his lips, and grudgingly listened to Brunswick's report.

'Thank you, sir. Constable Twitten can help me if I've forgotten anything, but as I see it, these are the five matters worthy of bringing to your attention.' He held up his list. '*One,* as I've already mentioned, an aggravated burglary at a photographer's studio, apparently with the aim of securing pictures taken by the AA man who you may remember was murdered in August; *two,* a notable missing person, going by the street name Barrow-Boy Cecil, long-standing police informant and popular trader, who's not been seen now for several days; *three,* an escaped violent lunatic who kills policemen and reportedly has murderous designs on you specifically, sir—'

'You specifically, sir!' echoed Twitten, unable to contain himself.

'*Four*, a murdered henchman of Terence Chambers's who evidently helped the lunatic escape from Broadmoor, name of Nicky Garroway; and last but not least, I'm afraid to say, *five*, Mrs Groynes has left us this morning, sir, and I just can't flaming believe it!'

'*What?* Mrs *Groynes?*' The inspector put his hands to his mouth. 'Why didn't you start with that? I just bought her a new kettle!'

'It's true, sir! She's gone!' chipped in Twitten. 'And as far as we can discover, the miraculous kettle has gone, too!'

'Good heavens.' Steine frowned. 'Mrs Groynes? Are you *sure?*' He had a vague feeling that perhaps one other item on Brunswick's list ought to have snagged his attention more, but for the moment he couldn't quite call it to mind.

'I am, sir,' said Brunswick, his voice a little unsteady. 'Apparently Miss Lennon spoke to her early this morning, about moving her tea things out of the office, and she turned on her heel and left. Without a word of goodbye! She'd been here with us for *years!*'

'She didn't explain at all?'

'All Miss Lennon overheard her say, sir,' said Twitten, 'was "Sod this for a game of soldiers." Which was one of her lovable cockney expressions, of course, but not very helpful in divining the precise cause of her departure.'

Brunswick sat down (without being invited to). He was trying not to give way to his feelings, but he was visibly moved. 'I just don't know what to think, sir. Mrs G was like a flaming mother to me.'

'That's quite true, sir,' said Twitten. 'She did seem to have a particular maternal fondness for the sergeant.'

'She made blancmange specially, just to cheer me up! She brought in Battenberg just because I like it.'

'I bally hate marzipan, sir,' chipped in Twitten.

'As do I, Constable,' agreed the inspector, with feeling. 'It's utterly vile. Well, this is very serious, both of you. I am saddened by this news. Partly on account of the kettle, of course. Did it work?'

'It bally well did, sir.'

'It turned itself off?'

'Beautifully, sir. Every time.'

'Well, I have to say, I leave you for a few short weeks and come back to – to what? Five items of very bad news – was it really only five?'

'Yes, sir.'

'I repeat, five items of bad news. And on top of that, no prospect of a decent cup of tea!'

———

At Luigi's venerable ice-cream parlour on the seafront, a grim-faced Palmeira Groynes sat with Diamond Tony, her back to the rain-spattered window. Wind rattled the steamed-up glass, and whistled through the door whenever it was opened to admit the dribs and drabs of desperate (and desperately unlucky) off-season holiday-makers, who shook the rain off their hats and umbrellas before ordering hot frothy coffees or large mugs of Ovaltine.

Mrs Groynes looked round every time the door opened. She was definitely jumpy, and not just because she had purloined the office kettle as a parting gesture of defiance. It now sat beside her on the bench seat with her coat over it.

'Thanks for coming, dear,' she said, patting Tony's hand. Mrs Groynes had a lot of time for Diamond Tony, her favourite psychopath-cum-loyal-assassin. He lived in style in one of the penthouses of the Metropole Hotel, and with his crisp suits and pomaded hair he was a right Flash Harry, but he was a good man in a crisis: straightforward to the point of bluntness, and brilliantly professional, taking proper pride in his stealthy work. In criminal circles Diamond Tony was something of a legend. No one garrotted with more finesse; no one slipped a stiletto between the ribs with more elegance and discretion. His victims neither saw him coming nor heard him. On his fingers he wore the rings of the last few people he had dispatched. At the moment they numbered five on each hand.

But if Mrs Groynes had good cause to rate him highly, he felt the same way about her. She had worked wonders in this town, keeping dozens of men on a generous payroll. As for him personally, he owed her everything. It was she who first awarded him the life-changing epithet 'Diamond' when he was just a fresh-faced dreamer starting out as a killer-for-hire. 'You're a diamond, that's what you are, Anthony,' she'd said. And thus Diamond Tony was born.

'So who do you think is doing this to me?' she said.

'Who's doing this to you?' he repeated, stirring his coffee with a nine-inch blade (out of habit, merely; a teaspoon would have been far more efficient). He pulled a face. 'What if it's nobody, Palmeira? What if it's just a run of bad luck?'

'It's not, Tony. It bleeding isn't.'

'Well, stop a bit. This new secretary you talked about. She was sent by someone at bloody Scotland Yard! I'd call *that* bad luck.'

'All right. I grant you, this Lennon woman, she's just my reward for making Inspector Steine the big hero, isn't she?

That's bleeding irony, that is. I work my backbone to a string of conkers making him the Big I Am, and in return for my kindness, I get to spend four hours last night clearing my stash out of the cupboard at the station!'

'What? The jelly and everything?'

'I had to. That woman was threatening to have the doors off.'

Tony grimaced. 'Where did you put it all?'

'Hove. Vince's lock-up.'

'Well, I'm not denying that's bad luck, Palmeira. I'm not. But like I said, it's not a conspiracy.'

'Yes, but everything else? Come off it. How did this person let me know about Cecil getting nabbed? By using my girl Denise in the tube room at Gosling's! Denise is in deep cover! No, they're telling me they know about the big shop job. Then there's poor Cecil, and now the threat against Shorty.' She shook her head. '*Shorty*, Tony. I mean, how low can you get, threatening a kid?'

They drank their coffees, and Tony took a spoonful of banana split. They did a phenomenal banana split in Luigi's.

'Well, my first guess would have been that Nicky Garroway bloke: you know, Chambers's little sidekick. He's got every reason to come after you. But they're saying he's dead.'

'I did think of Nicky. But as far as he was concerned, his boss was shot by Inspector Steine, do you see? As far as he knew, I had nothing to do with it.'

'Yes, but—'

'Most of the people who've got good reason to hate me *don't know it*, Tony! It wasn't me behind the Middle Street Massacre. It wasn't me who got Terry killed. I mean, I'm not bleeding daft. I cover my tracks.'

'I still think this is to do with Chambers.'

'Tony!'

'You're telling me that no one outside the gang knows it was you behind all those mobsters heaped up in the Metropole last month? No one *at all*?'

'*No one*,' she said, emphatically. But a cloud passed across her face. Because, oh, my good gawd, someone *did* know. What about clever-clogs Twitten?

'You've thought of something,' said Tony.

'No, no.'

'Tell me.'

'No, it's nothing. Eat your sweet, dear, your scoops are melting.'

Quickly she asked herself: *How much have I told that boy?* And the answer was: *A ridiculous, foolish, shaming amount.* Over the past three months she had told the constable virtually everything about her operations; she had shown off in the certain knowledge that he was powerless to stop her. But now she couldn't help (internally) screaming at herself: *Certain knowledge? Why did you ever think of it as* certain *knowledge?*

Tony must never know this, however. If he did, he wouldn't hesitate to seek out Twitten and slit his throat.

'No, no one at all,' she assured him. 'I'm positive.'

'Well, all right. But if you're right about this not being revenge for Chambers, it means someone just wants to take over the show down here.'

'I know.'

'Someone's moving in.'

She chewed her lip. 'Yes.'

'What about Fat Victor?' Fat Victor's gang had been wiped out in the Middle Street Massacre in 1951. On his subsequent dawn-raid arrest at a Littlehampton love nest, he had famously vowed to return.

'No, he's washed up. He won't come back here when he gets out. Heart condition. But keep thinking; this is useful. I tend to forget the people I've rubbed up the wrong way.' (By 'rubbed up the wrong way', she meant ruthlessly annihilated with maximum bloodshed.) 'I'd forgotten all about Fat Victor.'

'Did Chambers have a brother, maybe?'

Mrs Groynes made a face as she tried to remember whether she'd ever known. 'He might have, yes. I think he had an older brother called Bobby, but he wasn't in the business as far as I'm aware.'

'What about those Bensons who used to run the night club? They were scared to death of Chambers, so they kept their noses clean. But now he's out of the way, they might see their way clear to come back. I can picture them making a move against you.'

'Right. I'll tell the boys to keep an eye out for the Bensons.'

'And the more I think about it, this feels sort of personal.'

'Like someone hates me?'

'Yeah. They want to hit you where it hurts. I mean, it was clever to target Cecil and Shorty, on account of how much we all rely on them for getting the word out. But at the same time – and don't take this the wrong way, Pal – you've got an obvious soft spot for both of them, haven't you?'

She snorted. 'Soft spot?'

'Yeah.'

'*Me?*'

'Oh, come off it. You've got a soft spot for those useless coppers, too.'

'No, I bleeding haven't!'

'Of course you have. I mean, why else are they even still alive? If it was down to anyone else down here, Sergeant bloody-useless-undercover Brunswick would have been fitted for concrete boots five years ago.'

———

'The weird thing, sir,' said Twitten thoughtfully, 'is that everything was perfectly quiet until yesterday.'

Inspector Steine's debriefing was still going on.

'I was reading my book about the evil underhandedness of advertising – which is jolly fascinating, incidentally, but Mrs Groynes wouldn't allow me to talk about it, not a *single word* is what she said, or she would "duff me up good and proper"; she would "bleeding crease" me, she said, whatever that means – so, as I say, I was reading it quietly without a care in the world. Then we all stood together in silence and watched the kettle boil, and it was just so jolly nice.'

'I don't wish to hear any more about the kettle, Twitten.'

'It was quite something, sir,' said Brunswick apologetically.

'Yes, I'm sure it was.'

'And then suddenly Miss Lennon arrived, and it was as if someone had fired a bally starting-pistol. But if you don't mind my saying, sir, I think that although there are many things competing for our attention right now, especially our very bleak future in which there are no lovely cups of tea, and also of course the as-yet incalculable effect of Mrs Groynes's desertion on Sergeant Brunswick's already well-established abandonment complex, the main thing we should focus on is the lunatic.'

'The *lunatic*, that's right!' said the inspector, pleased. 'Well done, Twitten. I knew there was something else in Brunswick's list I needed to ask about. Remind me, would you? I noticed it, certainly, but I didn't quite flag it down.'

'Well, sir,' said Twitten, 'he escaped from Broadmoor a few days ago—'

'Broadmoor the hospital?'

'Yes, sir.'

'Quite a famous place, I think?'

'Yes, sir,' said Twitten. 'And very secure. My father took me once on one of his professional visits.'

'How did this man get out?'

'We don't know yet,' said Brunswick. 'We only know that he seems to have killed Nicky Garroway, the person who drove him to Brighton – a man who had very good reason to hate you, as it happens, because he worked directly for Terence Chambers.'

'He hated *me*, this Nicky person?' The inspector frowned. Hadn't the commissioner in London mentioned such a name? Yes, he was almost sure of it. A feeling of unease was beginning to creep over him.

'Yes, sir,' said Twitten. 'Because you killed Mr Chambers. This is all about you, sir. I'm so sorry if you didn't realise. Nicky, *who had very good reason to hate you because he worked for Terence Chambers*, helped the lunatic escape.'

'Oh. Oh, I see.'

'We think it's a plot, sir,' said Brunswick. 'A plot to kill you. Based on people hating you.'

'Oh,' said the inspector again. 'But you could be wrong about that, surely?'

'I don't think so, sir,' said Twitten. 'The escaped man does sound bally dangerous. He has killed three policemen, and according to his psychiatrist he is obsessed with you, sir. It's a fair assumption that this Nicky man helped him get out so that he could come and kill you.'

Steine put his hands to his face. The news seemed finally to have sunk in.

'I did explain earlier, sir,' said Brunswick quietly. He indicated his notebook. 'I definitely said, " ... *three, an escaped violent lunatic who kills policemen and reportedly has murderous designs on you specifically*". Look, sir. The exact words.'

'Yes, but then you told me about Mrs Groynes!'

'The point is, sir,' said Twitten patiently, 'the matter is under control. Until the maniac is safely caught, you will receive constant police protection.'

'Is anyone out looking for him?'

'Oh, *sir*!' Twitten had never heard such a stupid question before, even from Inspector Steine. 'The entire bally force is looking for him!'

'Oh, good.'

'You may have noticed that you were escorted from your car into the safety of the station this morning by a protective phalanx of twelve constables?'

'Oh.' Steine *had* noticed the constables swarming around him, but things had all been so peculiar since he became famous and popular that he hadn't really questioned it.

'I see. Well.' Things were beginning to sink in. 'Very well.' He took a deep breath. 'I see. Thank you. So people hate me. I see.'

They waited. Steine blinked.

'He's definitely mad, this man?'

'Oh, yes, sir,' said Brunswick. 'He's as nutty as a flaming fruit cake.'

'No doubt at all?'

'No, sir.'

'Good. Good. And we don't know what he personally has against me?'

'No, sir.'

'What's his name?'

'Chaucer, sir. Geoffrey Chaucer.'

Inexplicably, Twitten giggled. 'But not the one you're thinking of, obviously.'

Steine made a face. He had never heard of anyone by that name.

'You said … he murders policemen?'

'And decapitates them –'

'Oh, my God.'

'– which means he cuts their heads off.'

'Thank you, Twitten, I do know what decapitate means! But what I want to know is, why does he want to decapitate *me*?'

Inside the old wax museum in Russell Place, Chaucer lay on a narrow cot-bed and stared at the ceiling. Yesterday's escape was still a blur. He clearly remembered Miss Sibert unlocking the door to his cell in the early hours of the morning and whispering that she was helping him, but everything after that was strangely vague.

Perhaps she had drugged him. He wasn't even sure how she had negotiated all the locked doors, but weirdly he felt that the governor himself was involved. Could that be right? Chaucer seemed to remember a male cry of anguish as he was bundled into a car waiting outside: 'Carlotta! You used me!' And then, as soon as the car drove off, he must have fallen unconscious.

How many people were in the vehicle to start with? Was it four? But he was never introduced to the two in the front, and they didn't speak. And then he was woken and told by Miss Sibert to climb into the back of another vehicle – it looked like a shop van – and when he next saw daylight he was at the grey seaside, on a stormy morning, where he was bundled inside this building through a side entrance.

Why had he been rescued? And where was Miss Sibert now? Over the past few weeks he had come to rely on her. She had been kind and patient, and after a while had stopped asking him awkward questions about the murders he'd committed: it was almost as if she'd satisfied herself of something. Recently she'd just been borrowing the hospital projector and showing him films! When he closed his eyes, images from these films flashed in his head, even ones he'd seen for only a fraction of a second.

***

'Here,' said Tony, brightening. 'What about those two blokes you shot dead at Brighton Station?'

Back at Luigi's, Mrs Groynes was getting a bit depressed by all these potential enemies Tony could think of. Who knew that a lifetime of ruthlessly wiping people out could have so many negative ramifications? She was beginning to wish they could change the subject.

'You can't have forgotten,' Tony carried on. He was clearly enjoying the memory challenge she had set him. 'Those con artists? In July?'

'Oh, yes. Fancy a bit of gateau, dear?'

'You didn't bother covering your tracks much that time, did you?'

Reluctantly, and with a deep sigh, she cast her mind back just a couple of months to Wall-Eye Joe and his gang, who had operated partly from that terrible old wax museum.

'The girl got away, Palmeira. We got four of the five, but not the girl. What was her name? Adelaide something?'

'Adelaide Vine.'

'Well, couldn't it be her doing all this?'

'No.' Mrs Groynes shook her head. 'I could go for something with cherries on, personally.'

'If you're looking for someone with a motive, she's got four. You snuffed out everyone she knew! Come to think of it, you got me to garotte her *mum*.'

Mrs Groynes looked pained. 'Look, Tony … '

'What?'

'I appreciate all the effort you're putting in, but—'

'I don't understand.'

'This is all a bit of a smack in the face for me, dear.'

'How do you mean?'

'All these enemies you keep raking up.'

'You asked me to!'

'Yes, but I didn't think you'd come up with bleeding cartloads of them, did I?'

He shrugged. 'What about that psychologist woman who worked for Chambers?'

'Oh, that's enough, now!'

'But—'

'And anyway, as I've already said, *no one knows it was me who got Terry killed*.'

'Yeah, but come off it, Palmeira. How long does it take for people to work out Inspector Woodentop didn't do it without help? There are coppers in London that are proper hacked off. When he was alive, Chambers saw them all right, didn't he? He kept them sweet. And now he's dead. Those coppers can see for themselves how stupid Inspector Idiot is. They're going to work it out that someone with a bit of brain was actually behind it.'

'They *don't know*, Terry. No one does.'

'Well, I hope you're right.' He grinned. 'Change the subject?'

'Yes, please, dear, for gawd's sake.'

'All right.'

'Thank you.'

'I'm sorry.'

'That's all right. But don't call him Inspector Idiot, Tony. Not like that's his name. Everyone's saying Sergeant Stupid and Inspector Idiot and Constable Crikey these days. I'm beginning to wish I'd never started it.'

Back at the station, the full force of the maniac-with-a-grudge news had finally captured the inspector's full attention.

'So look,' he said flatly. 'Was this maniac something to do with Terence Chambers as well? Why does he want to kill me?'

'We really don't know, sir,' said Brunswick. 'I telephoned the governor at Broadmoor to get more information, but unfortunately he couldn't talk. His secretary said that he seemed to be packing a bag.'

Twitten huffed. 'We should have driven there directly, sir. I did suggest it to Sergeant Brunswick. I kept suggesting it, in fact.'

'Well, we *didn't* drive there, son, so stop flaming going on about it,' said Brunswick irritably. 'But Twitten is right, sir: we probably should have gone to interview the governor as soon as possible. When I called again this morning, I was told he had left the premises, leaving a bunch of keys on his desk and no forwarding address. Meanwhile the foreign lady who telephoned the news to the *Argus* unfortunately preferred to be anonymous, and Nicky Garroway is dead. At present there is no one to help us understand what this Geoffrey Chaucer's got against you.'

'So, the absence of cups of tea is the least of my problems?' said Steine, with a feeble attempt at a joke. 'When a man wants to kill me for no known reason and then cut my head off and leave it … rolling in the dust.' He turned his face to the window and stared into the middle distance.

Brunswick and Twitten exchanged glances. The phrase 'rolling in the dust' reminded them both of a small but vivid detail of the inspector's fate they had not as yet disclosed.

'Talking of your head rolling about like that, sir,' said Brunswick, 'I think Constable Twitten has something he wants to tell you.'

'Oh, I really don't, sir.'

'Good,' said Steine, not looking round. 'Because I don't want to hear it.'

He continued to gaze out of the window. From experience, they both recognised this as a cue to leave him alone with his thoughts.

'Perhaps we should take ourselves off to Gosling's, now, sir?' said Twitten.

'Yes, yes.'

'Miss Lennon allowed us to have this debriefing, but she's very keen to bring you up to date on other matters. She has sorted the post already, sir! Weeks of it. She's a bally miracle, sir.'

'Of course. Yes, yes. Miss Lennon.'

'Ooh,' added Twitten. (He'd had a helpful thought.) 'If you do find that the name Geoffrey Chaucer rings a bell eventually, sir, it will probably be because of *The Canterbury Tales*, so you can put it out of your mind.'

Steine seemed not to have heard.

Brunswick turned when he reached the door. 'We're … ' He stopped, hesitant. 'We're both very sorry about all this, sir.'

'Thank you, Brunswick.'

'And I don't think we said it properly at the beginning … '

'Said what?'

'Well, sir,' said Twitten, with an encouraging smile. 'Bally well welcome back.'

Five

'Sergeant Brunswick, is that really you?'

As they reached the top of the stairs, a surprise was awaiting our two fine police officers on the second floor of Gosling's Department Store, and it wasn't just the bewildering range of disparate retail lines haphazardly shoehorned into the available space. Wringing her hands in lovely anguish was a slender and beautiful young woman they had expected never to see again.

'Flaming heck,' said Brunswick, skidding to a halt.

She wore a dress and jacket in canary yellow; her rich chestnut hair was swept up in a dramatic chignon, from which an artful wisp hung elegantly (or was it carelessly?) over an almond-shaped eye.

'Crikey,' said Twitten. 'Miss Vine?'

'Miss Vine?' echoed Brunswick. 'It can't be.'

'But it is!' The vision of loveliness put her hands to her face. 'It's me!' Her shoulders heaved, and her face contorted, and her eyes brimmed with tears. 'And, oh, thank heavens, Sergeant Brunswick! It's you!'

The two men looked at each other in understandable consternation. The last time they had seen Adelaide Vine, she had been an outlaw escaping into the blank whiteness of a summer fog, having waved a gun at the inspector. She had said, in a steely voice, 'I don't want to shoot you, Inspector. But, believe me, I won't hesitate for a second if anyone tries to stop me leaving.' Her gun, when it was knocked from her hand, had actually shot Sergeant Brunswick in the leg. So why was she saying 'Thank heavens' and greeting them as friends?

Many such questions raised themselves (to both of their minds) along with 'What is Adelaide Vine doing in this shop?' and 'Don't we have historic grounds to arrest her?' And also (just Twitten), 'What is the theme of this floor? I see Tri-ang scooters but I also see rat poison. How does it bally add up?' But on the other hand, look at how helpless Miss Vine appeared to be! Her crystal tears would surely melt the heart of any man – or perhaps any man save for the sensibly wary Constable Peregrine Wilberforce Twitten.

'Oh, Sergeant!' she said again, rather pointedly.

'Miss Vine!' said Brunswick, with feeling. Watching all this from the sidelines, Twitten was fascinated. Written plainly on the sergeant's stricken face was the age-old male struggle between sense and sensuality, in which prudence born of experience ('I shouldn't trust this woman') competes with a more primitive response ('But she's beautiful and seems pleased to see me!'). The effort of refereeing this unequal fight was already producing colour in Sergeant Brunswick's cheeks and small beads of sweat on his forehead.

'Oh, forgive me, dear Sergeant,' Adelaide wailed. 'I said to Mr Gosling, if they send Sergeant James Brunswick we will be in safe, strong hands!'

'Really? Did you hear that, Twitten?' Quickly dabbing his brow with a handkerchief, Brunswick indicated his constable. 'You, er – you remember Constable Twitten, of course?'

She ignored the prompt. Twitten shrugged. He had forgotten what a seductive voice she had: sweet and feminine but *husky* – curiously, yet another word that you might associate with nuts.

'And I wanted so much to see you again, Sergeant,' she was saying now, 'to tell you how sorry I am for hurting you, however inadvertently. I heard you received a bullet in the leg. Do tell me you've forgiven me. I explained everything but you never replied to my letters.'

Letters? 'Hold on a moment … ' said Brunswick, flustered, scratching his head.

'I've been so worried!'

'I didn't receive any letters from you, Miss Vine.'

'You *didn't?*' she wailed.

At this point, a man approached. 'Harold Gosling,' he said, holding out a hand to shake.

'I see you've met my assistant. She's very upset about my finding the body in the listening booth, but if you leave her to get over it, she'll probably recover more efficiently. The poor dead man is over here, and the shop is due to open in fifteen minutes. Time is money, you know! All the staff have arrived. Constable, perhaps you could … ?'

'Yes, sir,' said Twitten. He tugged at Brunswick's sleeve. 'We really should go and inspect the body now, sir. Look, the others are already here.' He indicated the police pathologist and his photographer, who had spotted their arrival and were impatiently gesturing.

'They've been here nearly an hour,' said Mister Harold.

'Yes, and I'm very sorry, Mr Gosling,' said Twitten. 'The sergeant and I had to brief Inspector Steine before setting out this morning. He's been away, and there was … well, there was a lot to tell him.' He lowered his voice. 'How long has Miss Vine worked here, by the way, sir?'

'Three or four weeks. Why?'

Twitten lowered his voice even more. 'I don't suppose you've discovered during that time that she is closely related to you?'

Mister Harold frowned, and looked across to Adelaide. 'Why on earth do you say that?' he whispered.

'You are a wealthy man, I assume, sir?'

'Well, it's mostly tied up in the shop.'

'But she hasn't told you yet that she's your long-lost sister?'

'I'm sorry. I don't understand.'

'Good.' Twitten pulled a face. 'It was just a thought, sir. But please be aware: *Miss Vine can sometimes have a hidden agenda.* Although I have to say,' he added, mostly to himself, 'it's not particularly well hidden at the moment.'

'What did these letters say, Miss Vine?' Brunswick was asking, his knees bending as if he were about to genuflect at her feet, while Adelaide was – rather cleverly – just too over-come by emotion to give a coherent answer.

What a curse it was to see the weaknesses of others so clearly! One look at the sergeant's slavish expression confirmed to Twitten that any internal struggle was over. In the matter of Adelaide Vine, Brunswick's inner prudence had been no match at all for those primitive urges of his. It was as if a kitten had tried to wrestle with a wolf.

Twitten tugged again at Brunswick's coat-sleeve. 'Sir? The body, sir?'

'Of course. Yes. I'm coming.'

Brunswick reached out a hand towards Adelaide.

'Ooh, please don't do that, sir,' said Twitten quickly.

But Brunswick did it anyway. He touched Miss Vine lightly on the shoulder and leaned close. Impressively, all this had taken less than three minutes.

'Are you going to be all right, Miss Vine?' he said quietly.

'Of course,' she said, smiling bravely. 'You're here as a policeman, after all, not as a man with feelings.'

Twitten rolled his eyes.

'Please don't distress yourself any further, Miss Vine,' said Brunswick.

'Thank you,' she breathed.

'Well,' said Twitten flatly, 'at least she's stopped crying, sir. Can we press on now, please?'

Having already quizzed his staff as they arrived for work, Mister Harold could provide useful information about Professor Milhouse's movements the day before.

At two o'clock, the professor had come in. At half-past four, a reporter from the *Argus* had shown up late to meet him – but at that point, curiously, he couldn't be found. The professor had been conducting research in the store for the past three weeks, and was very well known to the staff. His original letter requesting permission from Mr Gosling – and outlining his project – gave his temporary address as the Windsor Hotel in Russell Place, near the old wax museum (now closed and awaiting demolition). Mister Harold produced the letter and Twitten made a note.

'That's very helpful, sir,' he said. Mr Gosling was the sort of sensible, clear-thinking witness that Sergeant Brunswick liked best, so it was a shame he was missing this. The sergeant – aware of Twitten shooting him judgmental looks – had chosen to examine the body instead, and was currently squashed into Listening Booth F with both the body and the pathologist (although glancing from time to time through the glass to check on the emotional state of Adelaide Vine).

'I like these listening booths, sir,' remarked Twitten, looking round the department. 'They're very modern. In fact, the whole store reminds me of Richard Hamilton's recent collage *Just what is it that makes today's homes so different, so appealing?* Do you know that image, sir? It's about modern consumerism and it's insanely crowded with brand names and domestic appliances with a sort of Mister Universe in the middle and a naked woman to the side wearing a lampshade on her head.'

'I don't think I've seen it, no. What's it called again?'

'Just what is it that makes today's homes so different, so appealing?'

'That's a terrible title for a work of art.'

Twitten assumed an expression of weary intellectual despair, indicative (to those who knew him well) of, *You are so bally wrong that it would be a waste of my time to argue with you.* 'I suppose it depends how you look at it, sir,' he said politely. 'Now, about Professor Milhouse. Did he conduct interviews in the record department much?'

'Not particularly, no. Would you like to sit down, Constable?'

In Booth E, they settled themselves on the hard leatherette-covered bench, which was, presumably by design, just a bit too narrow to be comfortable.

'So,' said Twitten. 'Professor Milhouse. What was his research exactly?'

'I didn't understand what he was getting at, to be honest,' said Mister Harold. 'He would put words to the customers and write down what they said in response. It seemed more like a game. But it was popular. It actually brought people in, and kept them in the store longer, so of course I welcomed it. I just wished he'd got the *Argus* involved earlier. It would have been even better for business.'

Twitten looked at his notes.

'So the professor was conducting *word-association experiments* with people out shopping?'

'Yes. I suppose that's what you'd call them.'

'Well, I have to say, Mr Gosling, I find that jolly interesting.'

'You do? Why?'

Twitten was a little unsure how to take Mister Harold. The man had happily declared himself a total philistine in regard to new movements in modern art, yet now he was apparently inviting Twitten to expound on a fascinating new branch of sociology.

'Well, sir, I've been reading recently about the new, up-to-the-minute science of "motivation research". In books and journals and so on. About how American advertisers are increasingly taking advantage of psychological findings. Sociologists are following it all very closely, too. It seems that when consumers choose to purchase certain products over others, you see, their motivations are quite deep-seated. The professor's word-association experiments would be an effort to add to the understanding of their buying choices.'

Twitten paused, embarrassed. He was rarely permitted to 'harp on'. By this point, in the office, he would have been shouted down or at least pooh-poohed. 'But I apologise, sir,' he added hurriedly. 'I don't suppose you want to hear about this: no one else bally does!'

'Really?'

'Oh, gosh, no. I have been pooh-poohed mercilessly at the station whenever I've tried even to bring it up. Between you and me, sir, I am pooh-poohed automatically by my colleagues just for uttering the bally word "interesting"! But I think we should return instead to the events of yesterday. I wonder if the professor had an umbrella with him when he came in? There doesn't seem to be one with the body, and significantly there's no hat.'

But Mister Harold didn't care about umbrellas. 'Tell me more about this motivation ... this, what did you call it?'

'Motivation research, sir. Those who are "in the know" call it MR for short. Look, are you *really* interested, sir? You're not just being polite?'

'I run a large department store, Constable.'

'So you're not intending to pooh-pooh me?'

'Constable, I don't mind admitting it, I don't even know what pooh-poohing *is*.'

'Oh. Well, in that case ... gosh, this seat isn't very comfortable, is it, sir? But basically, as I understand it, MR *is* bally interesting. Today's unscrupulous advertisers have realised that when customers choose what to buy, their true impulses come from *beneath their level of awareness*.'

Twitten paused to check that Mister Harold was truly not bored. But far from it. There was a positive gleam in his eye.

'Do you think other major retailers would know about this?' he asked. 'Would ... ?' He paused as if it were difficult to think of an example of another major retailer in the area. 'Would, um, *Hannington's*, for example?'

'I shouldn't bally think so, sir!' snorted Twitten. 'No, this research is fresh from Madison Avenue! And it's quite shocking. I can lend you the latest study if you like: it's called *The Hidden Persuaders*. You see, the newer advertising no longer bothers to aim its sales pitch at the parts of our brains that make rational decisions. Because what they've found is that while people might claim they care only about value for money, or aren't influenced by fashions – and they might even believe these claims themselves – they actually buy items whose purchase boosts their self-esteem, or that they think will make them fit in better with others.'

Twitten sat back. He felt he had summarised the contents of *The Hidden Persuaders* pretty well, while also keeping the grammar on track.

'And why is that shocking?'

'Oh, because this knowledge is used cynically to persuade people to buy things they don't need or can't afford, sir! Or things that aren't worth having in the first place. Take cigarettes. All cigarettes are fundamentally the same, and although the so-called "cancer scare" of a few years ago has apparently passed, they are obviously not good for you. So smokers are encouraged to identify, at some deep level, with a certain brand, and it keeps them hooked. It's like legal brainwashing. The advertisers can exploit all our unspoken insecurities or unacknowledged desires, and all in the cynical pursuit of profit!'

Mister Harold frowned. He still couldn't see the problem. He raised an eyebrow as if to say 'Go on.'

So Twitten did. He knew he ought to exercise restraint, but he couldn't. This was too glorious. He saw his past as a track littered with the bodies of exploded pooh-poohs, scorched and shrivelled.

'So while the psychologists are experimenting with "subliminal advertising", which is jolly controversial and entails flashing persuasive images at people too quickly for them to see them consciously, what the *sociologists* are explaining is that, increasingly, people are guided less by their inner values, more by appearance. It's this that I find more interesting, to be honest. The book mentions a Professor Riesman in Chicago who has suggested that we are actually on the cusp between two types of people in society: people of the industrial age with more traditional values who consult – as he puts it – their *inner gyroscope*, and people of the new consumer society who consult their *inner radar*. And it's such an elegant idea, sir, that I just can't stop bally well thinking about it!'

'What's the difference? They sound the same.'

'Oh, the difference is enormous, sir. They are opposites, in fact. The gyroscope revolves within, you see, to maintain a steady core of personality, whereas the radar sweeps round all the time, checking for external blips, and the personality adapts accordingly. One sort of person looks *in* for, say, moral guidance, and the other looks *out*. For example, I would say that I am a gyroscope sort of person, whereas Sergeant Brunswick is more of a radar. But, oh, look, they're taking the body away and I really should stop talking about this, even though you must admit you positively encouraged me so it's arguably all your fault.'

Twitten stood up hastily. He felt ashamed – even a bit dirty. But if he judged himself harshly, he did it alone. Mister Harold had long since forgotten about the corpse, the inquiry, and everything else. He produced the packet of Puffin cigarettes from his pocket and showed it to Twitten, as he stood up.

'So this was what Professor Milhouse was doing? Explaining why I choose to buy these?'

'It sounds like he was trying to, sir.'

'Or why people buy the Pye Continental instead of the new Murphy Swing-screen?'

'Um, yes. I expect so.'

'I wish I'd realised. So why did he kill himself?'

'We don't know yet that he did, sir.'

'Oh, but—'

'I must get on now, I'm afraid. The sergeant and I ought to start interviewing the staff.'

Twitten closed his notebook and slipped it back into the breast pocket of his tunic.

'We'll need to preserve the actual crime scene for a few hours but the shop can be open otherwise. And I do apologise again for talking so much.'

'Constable, there's no need.'

'Really?' Still unsure, Twitten bit his lip.

'Yes! Really!' said Mister Harold, with feeling. 'And if you still don't believe me, I'm going straight out now to buy that fascinating book of yours.'

———

An hour later, Twitten and Brunswick convened in the bedroom furniture department on the third floor (between the coach excursion booking office and the fitting room for abdominal appliances) to share the results of their interviews.

The known facts were as follows. Professor Milhouse had spoken to Sid the Doorman at just after two o'clock, leaving a message for Ben Oliver of the *Argus*.

'Did the professor have an umbrella with him, sir?' Twitten asked the doorman, expecting him not to have noticed – but Sid said, yes, the professor always carried a very distinctive umbrella, with a silver buffalo head on the handle.

'What excellent observational skills you people have in this shop,' Twitten remarked, looking up from his note-book. 'Untrained civilians such as yourself usually fail to spot anything useful. At Hendon Police College they taught us a handy mnemonic: UCANAHAFAWSG, which stands for Untrained Civilians Are Nearly Always Hopeless As Far As Witness Statements Go.' He paused. 'It wasn't one of the best ones.'

The professor had then made a beeline for the household products section on the ground floor, where he had positioned himself next to a pyramid display of Fairy Snow, a popular boxed soap powder, which had recently, for no discernible reason, been outselling all the other brands with such appealing names as Omo ('Adds Brightness to Whiteness'), Daz ('It's New! It's Blue!'), and Rinso ('Extra Soapy'). He spent an hour chatting to customers, principally about the bizarre illustration of the baby on the Fairy Snow box, who was marching purposefully from left to right, arms swinging like a sergeant major.

'Have you ever seen a baby walk like that?' the professor had asked the regular sales assistant, Janice, and she had laughed.

'He made you notice things you see every day and don't think about,' Janice told Sergeant Brunswick. 'We all liked him down here in Household, although what he was doing was obviously an awful waste of time for a grown man. You should speak to the girls in Mantle, though—'

'Mantle?'

'Coats and dresses.'

'Oh.' *Mantle?*

'He really got in the way up there! He talked to them every day about popular colours – guessing which ones they had been especially asked for. It was a different colour every day, you see, but he always guessed right. It drove them crazy. They couldn't work out how he knew!'

Brunswick pulled a face. It irked him to think that this so-called professor from Nebraska probably made a very decent salary from guessing daft dress colours in a daft shop 5,000 miles from home – a better salary than an oft-wounded ex-paratrooper detective sergeant in the Brighton Police, anyway.

'One more thing,' Brunswick said to Janice. 'Did he have an umbrella with him? My constable thinks it might be important, so I promised I'd ask everyone who saw him. Did he leave it here?'

'No, I'm sure he took it with him. It had a buffalo head on the handle. I've never seen one like it.'

At around 3.15, the professor had purchased a cup of tea in the staff's subsidised cafeteria and made notes. He had stayed around fifteen minutes, and eaten his usual strawberry jam omelette, declaring it to be delicious. And then, still with his umbrella, he had vanished. No more sightings. When Ben Oliver arrived at half-past four, he was directed upstairs and down, from one end of the store to the other, but Professor Milhouse could not be found.

'I wonder what the story was with the dress colours, sir,' said Twitten. 'That's very interesting.'

Brunswick huffed and wordlessly shook his head. He never encouraged Twitten to enlarge upon the remark 'That's very interesting', for fear of hearing a blooming lecture.

So he changed the subject. 'He doesn't sound much like a man getting ready to shoot himself, that's for sure.'

Twitten, taken by surprise, snorted derisively.

'Twitten, could you *not* make that noise, please?'

'Sorry, sir.'

'You've been told about it enough times.'

'I have, sir.' In the past month, Mrs Groynes had cautioned the constable more than once about how this particular noise was guaranteed to 'put people's backs up' and could one day

Date Charged: 1/22/2022
2:16 PM

1. PSYCHO BY THE
   SEA
   Truss, Lynne
   Barcode:
   31024153262558
   Due: 2/5/2022

Mount Pleasant Public Library
350 Bedford Road, Pleasantville, NY
10570
Call To Renew: (914) 674-4169
(914) 769-0548 Pleasantville
(914) 741-0276 Valhalla

earn him 'a right old punch up the bracket' (which apparently meant a punch on the nose!).

'But the notion of him committing suicide, sir! Well, let's just say suicide was a problematic inference from the start. I mean, gosh, this man was surely murdered, sir – and presumably for noticing something going on in this store, which I am convinced is hiding all manner of secrets. It's like a bally Aladdin's Cave, isn't it, sir? An Aladdin's Cave of *clues*. I bally love it here.'

While Twitten had thoroughly enjoyed his month of quiet sociological study, this was more like it.

Brunswick shook his head. 'I don't understand. What do you love here, son? It's a shop.'

'But look, sir!' Twitten gestured expansively. 'It's so jolly stimulating! The bustle, the commerce, the lift going up and down, the senseless jumble of unrelated goods. A known criminal working as the manager's assistant, and staff who are conspicuously observant. And have you talked to anyone about the vacuum system they use to move the cash around the building? The lady doing the cookery demonstrations – the one with the pencilled eyebrows – told me how Mr Gosling got a cut-price local engineer to put it in, and consequently it's much too fierce. She allowed me to pop one of the canisters in the tube in the wall, and it nearly ripped my sleeve off!'

Brunswick laughed. Twitten's enthusiasm for solving crimes was the sole facet of his personality that wasn't irritating. 'Well, all right. But we should be going now, son. Milhouse's hotel next, I think.'

'Yes, sir. Of course, sir. It's right near the old wax museum, did you realise? Isn't that where you were last shot in the leg?'

Without discussing their options for descent, they headed for the stairs. The lift (to all floors) might be part of the jolly stimulating landscape of the store, but on the only occasion they had chosen to ride it, the elderly operator had refused to slide open the metal gates until he'd aligned the floor levels perfectly, and it had taken him six tries.

'Ooh, by the way,' said Twitten, as they trotted down to the second floor, 'I warned Mr Gosling to be wary of Miss Vine, sir.'

'You did *what?*'

'Look, I know she's jolly pretty when she's crying, sir, but that's no reason to forget what we already know about her dangerously devious nature.'

Brunswick stopped on the first-floor landing and glared at him. 'Twitten—' he began.

'No, really, sir. I've been thinking back to events earlier in the summer, and it occurs to me that you were never perhaps aware of the whole story.'

'Look, she said she sent letters explaining everything.'

'But that was obviously a lie, sir!'

'You can't say that. She cried her eyes out when she found out I never got them.'

They set off down the next flight of stairs, Brunswick taking the lead.

'Oh, sir,' begged Twitten, as he trotted behind. 'Please see reason. Miss Vine is a trained con artist with years of experience. I happen to know that as a child she helped in the callous deception and murder of at least half a dozen wealthy women.'

'Perhaps she didn't know what was going on. Like you said, she was a kid.'

'You shouldn't trust a single word from her, sir. Especially, if I may say so, when she's assuring you how bally wonderful you are.'

They had reached the ground floor, and Brunswick turned. 'Well, I notice she didn't say anything to you at all, Twitten. She didn't even look at you.'

'That's true, sir. And I won't pretend it wasn't hurtful.'

'Ha!'

'But perhaps she ignored me,' said Twitten, lowering his voice, 'because she knew that trying to trap me with her damsel-in-distress act would be *a waste of time*, sir.'

'How do you reckon that, then?'

'Well, sir, luckily for our investigations, I am proof against her; I am impervious to her charms.'

———

Back at the police station, Inspector Steine sat alone in his office with the door closed. It was deathly quiet. From time to time he heard the muffled ring of a telephone, and the muffled soft-soft-LOUD-soft-soft tones of Miss Lennon speaking on it. On each occasion a brief spark of hope would light within him (did someone want to speak to him?), but then be dolefully extinguished when the phone was hung up, and silence – punctuated with short Gatling-gun bursts of high-speed typing – resumed.

He was surprised by how much he missed Mrs Groynes. All these years he had mainly ignored her, especially when she was wittering, but the office was bleak and sunless with-out her. When she wasn't swabbing, she was dusting; when she wasn't whistling tunes from popular musicals, she was popping a nice cup of tea on the desk; when she wasn't avidly studying the *Police Gazette* and making careful notes (what a peculiar little woman she was!), she was laughing her throaty, cackling laugh. What was it she always said? 'Well, dear, all this standing around jawing won't buy the baby a quarter pound of peanut brittle, now, will it?' Or sometimes it was, 'All this standing around jawing won't get poor Rosalind Franklin the recognition she deserves for helping to discover Deoxyribonucleic Acid.' All these years he had meant to ask her what she meant by the word 'jawing', and now the opportunity had gone for ever.

Thankfully, there were pressing police matters to address. On his desk was a sheaf of papers, organised for him by his efficient new secretary, with a helpful note pinned to each. All of these might help, Miss Lennon had said in a kindly tone, to distract him from thoughts of the ESCAPED MANIAC who was apparently FIXATED on CUTTING HIS HEAD OFF.

'Pull yourself together, Geoffrey,' he said, and picked them up, determined to give them his full attention. First was a letter from a concerned citizen demanding urgent road safety action at an accident black spot on the London Road ('*I believe this could be a good publicity opportunity,*' said Miss Lennon's accompanying note); then, a less-than-glowing report from Twitten's police driving instructor ('*Our dear young constable is not a natural at the wheel, alas*'); an official police docket authorising the purchase of a new car for personal use, up to the value of £750 ('*Congratulations, Inspector! I will research the models available at this price, always remembering that purchase tax on such an item is a shocking 50%*'); three notes from Clive Hoskisson of the *Mirror*, demanding an interview ('*I'm very sorry. This ghastly man won't take no for an answer*');

and lastly, a letter – out of the blue – from Adelaide Vine, whose very name it pained him to see (*'This looks private, so I did not read'*).

Adelaide Vine? The beautiful young Brighton Belle who had wormed her way into his affections by pretending to be his niece only to be exposed as a con artist? He shuffled the papers' order. It didn't help. Despite the serious draw of the new car, he extracted her letter and began to read.

> *Dear Uncle Geoffrey,*
> *I expect you are surprised to hear from me after all the things that happened in the summer. You probably blame me for everything – but I assure you, you can't blame me more than I blame myself. I'm afraid I allowed myself to be influenced by some VERY bad people who knew about my true connection to you even before I knew of it myself.*
> *But they are gone now; I am free from them. And I am working at Gosling's, the department store, in quite a good position. As you know, being a Brighton Belle was only a seasonal—*

The inspector put down the letter, horrified. Was this artful young woman still claiming a family connection? Why else would she address him as 'Uncle Geoffrey'? Good heavens, this woman had quite recently threatened his life! And Twitten had made it very clear to him after Miss Vine's swift disappearance that she was *not* his niece, and had only pretended to be because she hoped to swindle him out of an inheritance.

He really must give no further thought to Miss Vine. But when he picked up the material about traffic accidents, the news that three shop employees had been knocked down at the same spot in the course of one weekend outside Gosling's did surprisingly little to take his mind off her. He picked up Adelaide's letter again and turned it over.

You will ask why I didn't leave Brighton. The thing is, I couldn't. It broke my heart to think how I had been persuaded by others to abuse your trust and our close family relationship. Would it be possible for us to meet, dear Uncle? Mother always said you had a forgiving nature. Even if you can't forgive me, I would love to return to you a brooch of hers with the Penrose family crest on it. She left it to me, but since meeting you and getting to know you, I feel it should be yours.

He didn't know what to think. The painful subject of the Penrose family fortune was one he had firmly put behind him. But when he closed his eyes, he could picture that old cameo brooch. His sister had indeed purloined it when she ran away, all those years ago. If Adelaide Vine really had it in her possession, didn't that mean … ?

He shuffled his papers again. How about this road safety thing? There was no scope for wistful thoughts of sham nieces to intrude on that. 'Concentrate, Geoffrey,' he told himself, taking a deep breath. Attached to the concerned-citizen letter was a file of cuttings on the effectiveness of zebra crossings, presumably supplied by Miss Lennon. He was glad to read the entire contents of the file, and for a while successfully banished all thought of pulchritudinous young female relatives from his mind. But then – oh, no! Visions of beautiful Adelaide getting knocked down by a car! Beautiful Adelaide shrieking: 'Uncle Geoffrey! You could have prevented this!' as a small child stands in the path of a speeding lorry! – and he thought, *No, no, stop this now*, and went out to consult with Miss Lennon, whom he found arranging his various trophies on the shelves of the large built-in cupboard. The surprise of this, given that the cupboard had been mysteriously locked for many years, did momentarily take his mind off everything else.

'Miss Lennon, it's open!' he said, delighted. 'I was always asking why this cupboard was locked, but no one could tell me.'

She smiled at him. 'I am so pleased you are GLAD, Inspector. I threatened to demand a CARPENTER, and the next morning the key was in the LOCK and the shelves were EMPTY. I wonder what was in here before?'

He had honestly never thought about it. When you couldn't see inside a thing, why would you speculate on its contents?

'I have no idea,' he said.

'But you MUST have been CURIOUS?'

'Well, I always assumed … ' He furrowed his brow. 'Helmets?'

'Helmets?' Her smile became somewhat glassy, as she tried to mask her reaction to this terrible guess.

He thought about it. 'Yes. Old helmets, if anything.'

Briskly changing the subject, she pointed to the file he was carrying. 'Ah, you saw the CUTTINGS I located.'

'Yes.'

'Now, you might think this IMPERTINENT of me, Inspector, but I have experience in this area. I was working in the police station in SLOUGH when the very first zebra crossing was inaugurated six years ago, outside BOOTS THE CHEMIST. Once people understood what it WAS, it was a LIFESAVER. I have been PASSIONATE about them ever since.'

'We do have zebra crossings in Brighton already, Miss Lennon. This isn't darkest Africa.'

'Well, of course—'

'And we found, at first, that they actually caused more accidents than they prevented. People dithered on the kerb, making cars run into one another, or they just marched out expecting cars to stop and got knocked down. I wrote one of my entertaining BBC talks on the subject. It was reprinted in *The Listener*, as I recall, with an amusing illustration. I received five pounds.'

'Yes, but people have become accustomed to the crossings by now, Inspector. And, you see, what I'm thinking is that if you opened it YOURSELF, in a well-publicised CEREMONY, it would show the public that you aren't intimidated by this HOMICIDAL MANIAC who is on the loose. I mean to say, you surely AREN'T intimidated, Inspector?'

He hesitated to respond to such a leading question, partly because the honest answer was, *Of course I am.*

'Come! You are too MODEST, Inspector!'

'Am I?'

'Of course you are not intimidated!'

'Aren't I?' He was wavering. When Miss Lennon stated the case with such conviction, for a moment he could almost believe it was true. On the other hand, while this Chaucer man was still indisputably at large, wasn't it prudent to keep out of sight?

'But allow me to suggest another reason, a FAR more important one,' she carried on, cutting off all negative thoughts of maniacs. 'Your appearance at such an opening would also help quash your current unfortunate image in Brighton as a MAN OF VIOLENCE!'

'What?'

'Yes,' she continued. 'Instead of being the hard-boiled policeman of popular MYTH, REVILED in the newspapers for indiscriminately shooting people at close quarters, you will be seen as the kind of CARING policeman who uses his powers to SAVE LIVES.'

Steine was stung. *Man of violence?* He had always supposed that the public regarded him as a kindly authority figure, thanks to his relaxed, informative talks about law on the Home Service. He was sure he'd been introduced on *Desert Island Discs* in precisely such endearing terms. 'Are you saying I'm known as a sort of authorised assassin, Miss Lennon?'

She gave him a sideways look. 'You didn't KNOW?'

'No.' This was terrible. He sat down at Brunswick's desk and put his head in his hands. 'I mean … *hard-boiled?*'

'Oh, dear INSPECTOR,' she laughed, 'I talk only of public PERCEPTION, not of your true character. People simply believe what they are told! And thanks to the enormous publicity surrounding the shooting of Mr Chambers – well, you can hardly be SURPRISED?'

But Inspector Steine *was* surprised. In fact, he was stunned. The injustice of it! But he saw the solution clearly. He *must* endorse this suggestion of Miss Lennon's!

'Look. Miss Lennon. How do we go about this zebra-crossing business? Do I talk to someone at the council?'

'Would you like me to set things UP, Inspector? It will be a simple matter for me. Given your ENTHUSIASM, I think we should act IMMEDIATELY.'

'Yes, do that, Miss Lennon. Right away.'

'Very good. Despite the lunatic still being at large?'

A moment's hesitation, then a decision. 'Yes. Yes, there are important matters at stake here. It's worth the risk. Just don't tell Twitten or Brunswick; they'll only argue with me about it.'

'Oh, good. Well DONE, sir. That's the SPIRIT!' She smiled conspiratorially. 'MUM's the WORD.'

The inspector felt quite excited now that the London Road zebra crossing was going to become a reality.

'Tell them I'd like – you know, those flashing beacon things.'

She picked up a notepad and pencil. 'Of course, sir.'

'Each end of the crossing, with stripy poles.'

'I think the Belishas are standard, Inspector.'

'Yes, but flashing?'

'Yes, sir.'

'All right, but do the tops have to be orange? Is that the law? Can we have pink? It seems more of a Brighton colour.'

She made a note. 'I'll check.'

'Excellent.' Steine felt better. He had enjoyed making decisions again. And Miss Lennon was so agreeable! 'I had no idea how marvellous it would be to have a secretary,' he said. 'But I have to say it, Miss Lennon: you are a pearl.'

She blushed. 'Thank you, sir.'

'Oh, and you can leave the trophies for now.'

'Very well.' She went back to her desk. She had been strangely softened by his words of praise. When she added, 'You've made a very good decision, sir,' she noticeably didn't bellow any of the words.

Sitting down, she remembered something. 'Oh, and by the way, Inspector—' She held up a small, sparkling gemstone. 'I found this valuable diamond at the back of that cupboard. So if it really *was* helmets being stored in there, they were of an unusually opulent variety.'

———

Their inquiries complete at the department store, Brunswick and Twitten were just setting off (in the rain) for Professor Milhouse's hotel when they spotted Mrs Groynes in the weekday shopping crowd. It would have been easy to miss her, especially through the thicket of umbrellas. She was coming towards them, dressed like a normal housewife, complete with unflattering concertina see-through rain-bonnet, with its tapes tied firmly in a bow beneath her chin. They knew her at once, however. Something about her lightness of tread; something about the intelligent angle of her head. Beside her – being carefully shepherded along – was a blond boy in shorts who was familiar to both of them as the child normally seen leaning against walls in the centre of town, absorbed in the *Beano*.

'Mrs G!' shouted Twitten, excitedly waving at her. 'Look, it's us!'

He expected her to be pleased to see them. But when she looked up and registered the situation, she shot Twitten a dark look of such fear and loathing that he stopped in his tracks. Then she turned her head and spoke quickly to the boy, who nodded.

Twitten was puzzled. 'Mrs G?' he called.

She did not respond. Instead, she grabbed the boy's hand and ran across the road, narrowly avoiding being hit by a Number 46 trolley-bus, while traffic tooted and brakes screeched.

'What the—?' exclaimed Brunswick. 'Why the flaming heck did she run off like that?'

'I honestly don't know, sir.'

'She could have got herself run over.'

'I know.'

'And the way she looked at you. Here, have you been accusing the poor woman of being a female Al Capone again? Was that why she upped and left us, because if I find out it was—'

'No, sir! I wouldn't dream of driving her out. To be honest, I can't come to terms with the idea that she's gone.'

Each man pictured the office waiting for them back at the station: an office devoid of Mrs Groynes and with Miss Lennon sitting at her big desk; the smell of smoking type-writer ribbon supplanting the familiar Mrs Groynes smells of brass cleaner and scouring powder mixed with freshly brewed Ty-Phoo.

'I'm glad we've got more calls to make, aren't you?' said Twitten. 'I don't want to go back ever again.'

'Nor me,' said Brunswick gloomily. 'It's the end of a blooming era, son. For starters, who's going to tell you off for making that horrible snorting noise if Mrs G isn't there to do it?'

Six

By the time Twitten got into bed at Mrs Thorpe's house at half-past nine that evening, he was too tired even to open the latest issue of *Motivation Research Quarterly* that his father had kindly sent him. He placed it on his bedside table, stroked its cover lovingly, and switched off the lamp. Rain pattered against his dormer window, but otherwise all was quiet. As he stretched out his toes, he sighed. Not much had been resolved in regard to any of the ongoing investigations, yet when he closed his eyes and posed the bedtime self-probing question (which he had asked himself nightly since he was twelve), *Were you clever enough today, Peregrine?*, the answer was, as usual, *Gosh, I bally hope so.*

Images from the day swam into his mind, not all of them pleasant. For example, here was Adelaide Vine in her yellow costume pointedly ignoring him, refusing to catch his eye. While it was true that he was by nature safe from her womanly wiles (because he could see through them so easily), it had still hurt to be treated in such a way, and he wasn't sure he deserved it.

On the more positive side was the surprising arrival at the police station – just as Twitten and Brunswick were returning from their Professor Milhouse inquiries – of a man claiming to be the erstwhile governor of Broadmoor, desperate to locate a female psychiatrist called Miss Sibert who had helped in the escape of Geoffrey Chaucer, the dangerous madman with designs on Inspector Steine. The man had seemed a bit deranged himself. 'Carlotta!' he groaned repeatedly. 'Oh, my Carlotta!'

'Not Miss Sibert!' Twitten had exclaimed with interest, on hearing the name. He remembered her very well from his first case in Brighton. She had supposedly been helping A. S. Crystal, the theatre critic, recollect details of a bank robbery. Twitten hadn't met her, but they had spoken on the telephone. *How on earth is she mixed up in this?* he thought now. *Didn't I discover she was actually working for arch villain Terence Chambers?* He didn't know what to make of her reappearance. He found himself thinking – with a pang – that this was exactly the sort of matter normally illuminated for him by a private conversation with Mrs Groynes.

After the exciting arrival of the governor there had been the daily driving lesson, of course, which was perhaps best forgotten – especially the instructor's scream of, 'Watch out! Watch out! Kerb! Lamp-post! Mother-to-be!' as the out-of-control car briefly mounted the pavement. But then a fine evening meal with Mrs Thorpe of *Poulet Véronique* (chicken in creamy sauce with tinned grapes) followed by pineapple upside-down cake and a very nice cup of tea as a *digestif.* As usual, Mrs Thorpe had wanted to know – once they were both replete – every detail about the dead man in the listening booth, but after listening politely for twenty-eight straight minutes to Twitten's eager explanation of 'motivation research' and how it related to Vance Packard's bally shocking book *The Hidden Persuaders,* she clapped her hand to her face and said, 'Oh, no!

I forgot! I've got a ticket to see Anton Walbrook and Moira Shearer in their play at the Theatre Royal! I must leave at once!'

'I thought you'd already seen it, Mrs Thorpe,' said Twitten, surprised. 'On Monday. You said it wasn't very good.'

'Did I?'

'Yes. I remember distinctly.'

'Well, I have a ticket tonight, whatever I said, and dear, dear Anton would never forgive me if I failed him! You must finish your fascinating account of devilish advertising practices another time!' And with that she had grabbed her coat and umbrella, and fled the house.

And that had been his day, up until he took his evening bath and climbed the steep stairs to his top-floor bedroom. Just as he was drifting into sleep, he heard a tiny noise from below, a soft *click* of the front door closing. *Mrs Thorpe is back early*, he thought. *She's left the play at the interval again. She did say it wasn't very good*. And, satisfied with this own brilliance in all matters, he sighed again and drifted into sleep.

'Don't be alarmed, dear,' said a familiar voice quietly, in the dark.

Twitten woke, his heart pounding. 'What? What? Who's there?' Deeply frightened, he wriggled to a sitting position, clutching at the covers. 'Oh, *crikey. Crikey!*'

'Shh, dear.'

'Please! Please don't hurt me.'

'Shhh, dear. Stop it.'

'Mrs G? What the—?'

'I'm not going to hurt you.'

'Oh, crikey! Crikey!'

'I just need a little talk. Look, don't make me gag you, dear.' She laughed. 'I mean to say, don't bleeding tempt me.'

He reached for the lamp switch, but she barked 'Don't!' so he withdrew his hand and instead pulled the bedclothes up to his chin. From what he could make out in the gloom – and from the startling proximity of her voice – she was standing right next to his bed.

'I was *asleep*, Mrs G,' he said, as if affronted.

'I know, dear. I waited until you switched your light off. Nice diggings, dear. Was that a pineapple upside-down cake you had with your supper? It looked lovely from out there in the rain. All that steam coming off it. And there I was outside, as wet as a haddock and as cold as workhouse cocoa.'

'What do you want, Mrs G? And why did you just walk out this morning? It's bally horrible in the office now, and it's all your fault.' The initial terror Twitten had felt had given way to other passionate feelings, such as righteous indignation and self-pity.

'Calm down, dear.'

'And why are you here?'

'Shhh.'

'*Why are you here?*' he said, with vehemence.

'Shhh! Look, I've got something to ask you.'

'In the middle of the night?'

'It's half-past nine.'

'Oh.'

'And it can't wait. It's very important.'

'How did you get in?'

'Oh, I copied your front-door key, dear. Ages ago. And not to alarm you, but this isn't the first time I've let myself in and stood here, either. Look, I need to know something, and

it's important. I need to know whether you've told anyone
– *anyone at all* – about my being behind the deaths at the
Metropole, and the shooting of Terence Chambers. And if
you lie to me, I'll know.'

'Did you just say you've let yourself into this house on
previous occasions?'

'Yes.'

'That's so shocking!'

'Well, then, best not dwell on it. But what I want to know
is whether you've told anyone about me—'

'Of course I haven't told anyone! No one would bally
believe me, you know that. Why would you think I had?'

'Because it's out there. Somehow it's out there. Someone
knows everything, and is using it against me. And you're the
only person I talked to about it.'

'Mrs Groynes, that's ridiculous. Your entire gang knew,
didn't they?'

'Yes, but—'

'You had dozens of accomplices, all of them untrustworthy
criminals.'

'So you didn't tell anyone?'

'No.'

'You swear?'

'Yes!'

'All right. So tell me something else. What was in that
bleeding envelope yesterday?'

'Ah.' He pictured the envelope being safely delivered this
morning to the Holden residence in North Norfolk, and
was struck by a thought. He really should have telephoned
Pandora to explain its contents: opening it, she would have
been completely baffled.

'Come on, dear. It's not a difficult question. Not for a brainbox like you.'

'You're right. But the thing is, where that envelope is concerned, I'd rather not say.'

'I'm sure you would.'

'Well, *good*,' he said, with an air of finality.

'But imagine you don't have a choice, dear.'

'What?'

'Imagine there's a gun pointed at you.'

'*Is* there a gun pointed at me?' he squeaked.

'What was in that envelope?'

'You brought a gun?'

'Just answer, dear.'

'I don't have it any more. It's somewhere you won't find it.'

'That's not what I asked, though, is it?' There was the unmistakable sound of a pistol being cocked.

'Please! Please don't shoot me.'

'Just tell me what I want to know. This isn't a joke, dear. I'm not arsing about. My bleeding life is on the line.'

'Oh, Mrs G, this is so *horrible*. I thought you liked me.'

'Yes, well, I thought you liked me too.'

'Look, when I saw the picture in the envelope, I'll admit I thought: *At last, some hard and fast evidence against Mrs Groynes.* But I don't mind admitting, I also felt *awful*.'

'So it's a picture, then. Of what?'

Twitten considered not answering. But then he asked himself how much the world needed him to be alive and deducing things cleverly in it, and the sobering answer was *a lot*.

'Oh, all right, you win,' he conceded. 'It's a photograph of you with Terence Chambers outside the Metropole.'

'Me with Terry?'

'You remember someone broke into the Polyfoto shop yesterday and coshed a man called Len? The robbers made a big mess to create confusion, but the significant thing they stole, I'm pretty sure, was a set of duplicates of Officer Andy's photographs of you and Mr Chambers. You remember how the AA patrol man's favourite pastime was taking pictures of major crime figures, which was bally reckless of him, considering how dangerous they are, but interestingly this wasn't the reason he was killed?'

In the dark, Mrs Groynes closed her eyes, but managed to say patiently, 'Go on, dear.'

'Anyway, the first thing these robbers did, it seems, was send one of the pictures to me.'

'I see.'

'They must want me to expose you. They must know that I've had my hands tied all this time. Which means, you're right, they must know quite a lot.'

Mrs Groynes sat down on the bed, thinking. Twitten bit his lip. It was worryingly unclear whether the gun was still pointing at him.

'Does the sergeant know about this picture?'

'Of course not! He adores you! His bally head would explode!'

'So it's just you, then? Like it's just you who knows everything else? You see the position that puts you in? You see the position that puts *me* in?'

'Please don't shoot me, Mrs Groynes. Please. I never asked to be your confidant, did I? And I know it's a cliché, but I'll say it anyway. Mrs G, I'm too bally young to die!'

———

Sergeant Brunswick gazed at the empty pint mug in front of him and dolefully considered whether to have another. It was only half-past nine, but it was cheerless and quiet in the saloon bar of the Princess Alice this evening. Perhaps all the regulars were at home watching those flaming swing-screen fifteen-inch televisions of theirs, or gazing with pride at their flaming refrigerators.

He hadn't realised until today how much he disliked being alive during a so-called 'consumer boom'; how much he resented it for showing him up. The visit to Gosling's had opened his eyes. At his age, he should be marching into just such a big shop with a happy wife and children in his wake (possibly all skipping), and buying a fashionable radiogram on hire purchase for his family's shared delight. 'Daddy! Thank you!' would be the general cry, as he patted their heads in turn (wife included), while smiling broadly and puffing on his pipe.

He should be going home every night to bright curtains and matching crockery and up-to-the-minute paraffin heaters in every room. Instead of which, he was nursing pints in a dingy boozer and mooning over a sensational, unattainable girl with shiny chestnut hair (seventeen years his junior), while at the same time feeling squeamish about a well-meaning older woman whose only fault was that (apparently) she was struggling to keep her hands off him.

He was so deep in such unworthy self-pity that at first he didn't notice the figure standing in front of him.

'Sergeant Brunswick?'

'Yes?' He looked up. The man's coat was wet: he must have just come in.

'Gerald Winslow,' the man said. 'From this afternoon. From—' He lowered his voice. 'From *Broadmoor*. They told me at the station I might find you here.'

'Oh. Yes. Of course. Well, I'm not on duty right now, Mr Winslow.'

'That's all right. But perhaps I could join you?'

'Oh?'

'I'm feeling a bit sorry for myself.'

'Ah. On account of that foreign woman you were going on about?'

'Well … ' Winslow shrugged and took the seat next to Brunswick's. 'Well, partly on account of sacrificing my job by abetting the escape of a very dangerous inmate – but yes, mainly on account of Carlotta.' He let out a pitiful moan. 'I've never met anyone like her, Sergeant! There *is* no one like her, and for a while, you see, I believed she could be mine.'

'Nice name, Carlotta.'

'She … she used me!'

Brunswick pursed his lips, in man-of-the-world fashion. A small burp was the unintended result. (He was a little bit drunk.) 'You sound surprised, mate. Oops, pardon me.'

'Surprised? I am destroyed.'

'But that's what they do, mate. That's what they do.'

'Who?'

'Women.'

'Really? Sorry, I've lost track. Women do what?'

'They use you. All we want to do is look after them and pat their heads a bit. Buy them fancy radiograms on the never-never. But all they think is, *How much can I squeeze out of this daft bloke without giving anything in return?*'

'I didn't know that.'

'Well, it's true. You got to buy them a ticket to this, a ticket to that; glasses of vintage port and Tizer; dancing at the Aquarium … then it's all, "Ooh, get off me, Jim! I'm not that sort of girl!"'

Mr Winslow nodded sympathetically. 'That sounds awful.'

'It is.'

'All Carlotta wanted from me was that I unlock all the internal gates in a top-security mental institution. I suppose I got off lightly.'

'And I'll tell you what,' Brunswick carried on, apparently failing to note the frank confession the governor had just so casually made, 'sometimes what they're after is your *body* ... '

He paused and considered. He didn't know quite what point he was making here. Was he truly complaining that Mrs Thorpe – a handsome, solvent woman with an unapologetic sex drive – was keen to manoeuvre him into bed, with no strings attached? Was this a legitimate position to take? Was he really expecting sympathy because Mrs Thorpe fancied him?

'*Women*,' he said, with feeling.

'I was thinking of ordering a Bell's, Sergeant. Would you join me?'

Brunswick glanced at the clock on the wall, and the maudlin mood only intensified. It didn't matter what flaming time it was, did it? There was no wife waiting for him at home; no kiddies lay asleep in their modern space-saving bunk beds; no New World gas cooker kept his meat pie and chips warm on a brightly patterned plate for his return. No adoring faces would be upturned for a goodnight kiss.

'Why not, Mr Winslow? That's very kind. A Bell's would really hit the spot right now.'

Mrs Groynes had put the gun down. She wasn't sure how they had got onto the subject of motivation research quite so quickly, but it had certainly defused the situation, and the weapon had soon grown heavy in her hand. She had always suspected that boring people to tears was Twitten's unique special talent, but she hadn't known until tonight that his fondness for his own voice could deflect actual bullets.

'So, to sum up, Mrs G – hold on a tick, are you still listening?'

'What? Yes. No. Not really.'

'Perhaps I could put the light on now?'

'No.'

'It's just that in the dark it's jolly hard to tell whether I'm completely keeping your attention. I mean, for all I know, you might be comically miming hanging yourself, as you do in the office sometimes! You know, with your tongue hanging out and your head lolling sideways. Anyway, to sum up, Professor Milhouse was doing this very important research but he must have stumbled on something going on at Gosling's and that's why he's dead!'

'I see.'

'But I'm feeling you're not particularly intrigued by the mystery of Professor Milhouse's death, Mrs G.'

'Well. I've got a lot of things on my mind.'

'Of course. I'm being selfish. You've lost your job, and some-one knows you were behind the killing of Terence Chambers, which must be bally alarming.'

She laughed. 'A bit more than that, dear.'

There was a silence.

'*Please* may I put the light on now, Mrs G?'

'Not on your life.'

'Why?'

'Just no.'

'Look, do you want to talk about the things on your mind? I mean, I'm wide awake now. And, much as you seem to

unfairly resent my comprehensive knowledge of your criminal activities – knowledge which you have consistently
foisted upon me – perhaps I'm in a good position to help you
in your current undefined difficulties.'

'All right, I'll tell you.' She let out a long breath. 'Someone's
undermining me, dear.'

'Who?'

'I don't know!'

'Oh. Then how can you be sure—'

'It's a bleeding conspiracy. And it's serious. They've taken
Barrow-Boy Cecil and they've threatened Shorty.'

'What do you mean, they've *taken* Mr Cecil?'

'He's bleeding disappeared. You heard the sergeant say so.'

'Yes, but perhaps he's just at home with a cold. The weather's
been terrible.'

'Well, he isn't at home with a cold! They sent me a finger
and a note with a crushed-up bunny!'

'That's horrible.' Twitten wrinkled his nose. 'Gosh. And
who's Shorty?'

'The boy you saw me with earlier.'

Twitten snorted. 'You call him *Shorty*?'

'Oh, stop it. And now there's this murder at Gosling's and
that's no coincidence, you mark my words. Whoever this is,
they're drawing all this attention to the store, which is where
I've been planning a job for bleeding months, dear.'

'Have you? A job? You never mentioned it to me.'

'Well, it's massive. My crowning glory. I've got eleven of
my top people in there – on the door, in the hats, up to her
elbows in crabmeat, down in the so-called "tube room". All in
place for Christmas week.'

'Heavens.' Twitten thought back to this morning's interviews. 'Do you know, I *thought* everyone was a bit too sharp

for shop work. I said as much to Sergeant Brunswick, but he said I was just being snobbish. But if you've got people there, you must know that Adelaide Vine is working there, too.'

'Is she?'

'Yes.'

'Blimey. That's news to me.'

'And thinking about it, Mrs G,' he added excitedly, 'Adelaide Vine has jolly good reason to be angry with you!'

Mrs Groynes sighed. Not this again.

'I mean, gosh, Mrs Groynes, not two months ago you killed her entire gang, including her mother! I remember thinking at the time that she might return and seek bally vengeance.'

'Well, I admit, I didn't know she was back, but I've been through this once today already. Yes, the Vine girl has got a motive, but this plot against me isn't about her and her mum. I wouldn't believe it at first, but I've come round. This has *got* to be payback for me getting Terence Chambers shot.'

'Well, I don't think you should underestimate her. She positively enslaved Sergeant Brunswick this morning in a matter of minutes. It was revolting, but also *so interesting*. All she had to do was to start crying, and it was as if someone had removed his spine! The sergeant's attitudes to women are very contradictory, but at the same time, I suppose – and I have given quite a lot of thought to this, actually – his ambivalence is entirely consistent with being abandoned by his mother when he was small.'

'Look, I'm not saying Adelaide isn't in on it. She might well be. But look at her, she's a baby. And this is *big*.' Mrs Groynes's voice shook. 'I've got the finger here if you're interested.'

'Oh. No, thank you.'

He heard the sound of a handbag catch being opened.

'No, really,' he insisted.

'What did Barrow-Boy Cecil ever do to anyone?' she asked, with sadness. (It was unclear whether she had retrieved the finger.)

'Well, I know for a fact he sold a firearm to a child quite recently, Mrs G. So perhaps you're romanticising him just a little.'

It briefly occurred to Twitten that, when he had so innocently applied to join the police, he had never expected to be talking like this one day, in the dark, trapped in his bed, helping a cunning and armed female master criminal to rank her sworn enemies in order of importance. And yet, in such a short time, this was precisely how things had turned out.

'This isn't like you, Mrs G,' he said gently. 'You're usually a step ahead.'

He thought he heard her sniff when he said this, but he couldn't be sure. To find herself *not* one step ahead must, of course, be jolly difficult for a controlling personality like Mrs Groynes.

'I think you should come back to your job at the station,' he said, with more conviction than he felt. 'Swallow your pride. Look after Sergeant Brunswick. He's lost without you. You can guard him from the wicked Miss Vine, and keep an eye on things from there.'

'Are you kidding? Not while that woman's there.'

'Miss Lennon? Well, at least you can rest assured *she* can't be in on this … this whatever it is. I checked up on her and Miss Roberta Lennon has worked at Scotland Yard for decades. She's chairwoman for life of the Chartered Association of Police Secretaries. It's just bally bad luck she turned up in Brighton this week.'

'Well, if you ask me—' Mrs Groynes began, but stopped. 'Hold up, what's this now?'

There was a sound from downstairs: a key in the front door. Mrs Thorpe had come home. Twitten and Mrs Groynes both sat silent for a while, and listened to the homeowner bustling below in the kitchen, making herself a warm drink, and no doubt entertaining equally warm thoughts about the lovely Sergeant Brunswick who had two weeks ago kissed her fervently out of doors and set her whole nervous system aflame. She would never forget the way he had suddenly taken her in his manly arms. She gasped every time she remembered it (which was several times a day at set intervals). If she could only get him to kiss her like that *indoors* ...

'Were you really prepared to shoot me just now, Mrs G?' whispered Twitten reprovingly. 'Because poor Mrs Thorpe would have had to find my lifeless body in the morning. What with the murder downstairs in the summer, don't you think she's been through enough of that sort of thing already?'

———

At his home in the Queen's Park area of the town, Inspector Steine switched off the evening concert on the wireless, placed his book on a side table, and listened to the rain. He felt sorry for the poor officers (four of them) who'd been stationed outside, in their helmets and capes, to guard him. His house tended to catch a breeze up from the sea, and there was little in the way of shelter. He sighed. These men were paying the price for his own sheer dauntless integrity as a policeman! If he'd been a lesser mortal, who shrank from action, they would be at home with their families, or tucked up in the section house with a nice cup of bedtime Horlicks.

So he blamed himself for creating this situation, but only in such a way as (predictably) to reflect more glory on himself. To his credit, he certainly had not shot Chambers in the expectation of trophies, cash, fame, a new car and a thousand party invitations. Still less had he considered unpleasant reprisals. But what was the reason he'd had no such thoughts of repercussions when he performed the act? Well, whisper the shameful truth: *he hadn't known who Chambers was when he shot him.*

This inconvenient fact was now all-but-forgotten, of course. Occasionally, the inspector's conscience piped up with the question, *'Did you know, Geoffrey?'* but then his ego rebelled, and the incipient heresy was ruthlessly suppressed. On that day in the milk bar he had been a hero, and now he must face the negative consequences, just as he had accepted the acclaim. A screen version of events, called *High Noon at the Milk Bar,* was already in preparation, after all: a companion-piece to *The Middle Street Massacre.* He had heard today that ABC Television (whatever that was) was now talking about a spin-off 'Inspector Steine of Brighton' series to be aired on Saturday nights. It wouldn't be long before all the world would know his surname was pronounced 'Steen' and not 'Stine' – a small matter, but it would be a great relief after a lifetime of correcting people.

He wondered if he should check up on the man guarding the front of the house. Constable Jenkins, was it? But on the other hand, was it wise to open the door? Why hadn't anyone apprehended this Geoffrey Chaucer man yet? The station had circulated his photograph and a full description, and the *Argus* had printed both, advertised by a not-at-all-alarmist placard 'KILLER LOONY AT LARGE IN BRIGHTON' – so the public were also taking part in the manhunt.

Meanwhile, a helpful Broadmoor warder had sent a box of files relating to all the Chaucer interviews conducted in recent weeks by that dodgy female psychiatrist (this warder had always been suspicious of her). Inspector Steine had brought these Broadmoor files home with him, but had been too terrified to look at them. The box was still on his dining table, full of crime-scene photographs, spools of cine-film, and handwritten files with ridiculous labels such as 'Doris Fuller, Waitress, J. Lyons'.

He looked at it now in despair. *Doris Fuller?* How could knowing about some lowly waitress named Doris Fuller help a man in his position? A man under threat from a lunatic who not only killed policemen, but cut off their heads?

There was a knock on the front door. He jumped.

'Sir?' said a muffled voice.

The inspector, his head pounding, approached. 'What is it, Jenkins?' he called.

'Just checking you're all right, sir. The four of us will be relieved at eleven o'clock, sir. Then the final shift arrives at three.'

Why are you reminding me of this? he thought. *I know this.* 'Very good,' he said. 'Carry on.'

'Um, it's normal in these circumstances to offer the men on duty a cup of tea, sir. I hope you don't mind me saying, sir.'

'Not at all, Constable. Not at all. But explain to me how I could pass cups of tea to you without opening the door.'

'Ha! Good point, sir. Silly of me, sir.'

'And perhaps you could also explain, when you are drinking your cup of tea, where is your truncheon?'

'Ah.'

'Where?'

'It's hanging from my belt, sir.'

'Precisely. Not easy to fend off a madman while holding one of my best cups and saucers, I imagine.'

'No, sir.'

'Good night, then, Constable.'

'Yes, sir.'

'You'll enjoy the eventual cup of tea all the more for the wait.'

'Yes, sir. I expect you're right. And I meant to say—'

'Say what, Jenkins?'

'Don't worry about a thing, sir. No one's going to boil *your* head in a bucket without having Brighton's finest to answer to first, sir.'

'Thank you, Jenkins. That's very reassuring.'

The inspector was halfway up the stairs before the full import of these words of encouragement properly hit home.

'What makes you think she's here in Brighton, anyway? This Carlotta of yours?'

It was a reasonable question from the sergeant, but Mr Winslow, after three whiskies in quick succession, had serious trouble focusing on it.

'*Carlotta*,' he breathed.

'Mm,' agreed the sergeant. After three whiskies of his own he was in a similar state and had forgotten the question just as soon as he had asked it. 'Mine's called—' For a moment, he couldn't remember! But in his defence, he did usually address her as Mrs Thorpe.

'*Adelaide*,' he said softly. 'No! *Eliza*.' He laughed. 'Blimey. It's Eliza.'

'Adelaide Eliza? That's lovely.'

'No, just Eliza.'

'Oh. And you say she *wants* you?' Mr Winslow's face crumpled. He raised his empty glass and put it down again with a clunk. Then he leaned close to Brunswick. 'What does she want you to do?' he breathed.

'How do you mean?'

'What *act*?'

'Flaming heck, mate. I can't talk about that.'

'Why?'

'Because she's a lady, for a start!'

'Oh, go on. Have pity.'

'No!' Brunswick inhaled deeply and tried to stand up, but immediately sat back down again. He fought the mental fog that had settled over him. 'Look, we've got to find that Chaucer bloke. Can you give me anything on him? Anything?'

'I'm tired, Sergeant. So tired.'

'In the morning, then? Come in first thing. One of your blokes sent some material over, I think. Hang on.' He blinked a few times, and exhaled. 'Yes. I remember. Big box. So you'll come in, then? All right?'

'All right.'

Brunswick helped the man to his feet. 'Come along, Mr Winslow. Upsy-daisy.'

They shuffled, arm in arm, to the swing doors of the pub.

'Umbrella?' said Brunswick, before pushing the door open to the rainy night.

'Umbrella,' confirmed Winslow, producing one with a flourish from under his arm.

'Good. So when I say three— Oh!'

'What's wrong?'

Brunswick stared at Winslow's umbrella, frowning. 'Where the flaming hell did you get that?' he demanded.

Back at Mrs Thorpe's, all was quiet downstairs. The lady of the house was sleeping contentedly after reading a couple of steamy chapters of the sensational bestseller from America, *Peyton Place*.

Twitten had begged her not to purchase this famously lurid book when they visited Hatchards in Piccadilly together on a special day-trip to town. In fact, he had caused quite a scene in the bookshop, urging her instead to buy Agatha Christie's jolly good new mystery *Dead Man's Folly*. 'Miss Christie is at the peak of her considerable narrative powers, Mrs Thorpe!' he was heard to say. 'And reading her book won't arouse base animal passions that can only make you unhappy!' But in the end, Mrs Thorpe had prevailed, and had purchased *Peyton Place* for herself while treating Twitten to a copy of *The Hidden Persuaders* – a lapse of judgment now condemned by everyone who knew him. But on the plus side, together they had decided on *The Untouchables* (the story of legendary special agent Eliot Ness) as a surprise gift for Sergeant Brunswick, and he had absolutely loved it.

Mrs Thorpe had long been determined to read *Peyton Place* – especially after Sergeant Brunswick refused point-blank to accompany her to the controversial, adult-rated film. And each morning at breakfast for the past week, she had regaled Twitten with the repulsive and seemingly never-ending saga of small-town New England incest, child abuse, illegitimacy and teenage abortion, sometimes in so much anatomical detail as to put him right off his bacon and eggs.

Now that she was safely asleep in the room below, it would have been sensible for Twitten to urge Mrs Groynes's immediate departure. But, for better or worse, he didn't do this.

The thing was, in the intervening period, he had begun to organise his thoughts. He had started to apply himself to Mrs Groynes's problem, because that's the sort of irrepressibly clever young policeman he was.

'Thinking about this logically, Mrs G,' he said, 'we have to assume that the source of your enemy's inside information is in fact the captured Barrow-Boy Cecil. He has presumably told them all about your gang and its— What?' He had heard her take a breath, as if she objected to something he'd said. 'Is there something wrong?'

'No, no. It's just that you said "gang", dear. Took me by surprise. Carry on, I'm all agog.'

'You'd rather I didn't refer to your gang as a gang?'

'Well, yes. It's more of an organisation, you see.'

'But it's still a gang.'

She tutted. 'No, it's a bit harder to define. I'd say it's not as rigid as an autocracy, but on the other hand—' She paused to consider the best way of describing her gang without using the word 'gang'. 'Not as loose as a what-do-you-call-it?'

'An association?'

'I was thinking, *congeries*. I'd say organisation is good as a compromise.'

'Right. Well. Organisation it is, then. So, we must assume that Cecil – either willingly or unwillingly – has told them all about your so-called organisation and its plans. Cecil was a very close associate, I'm assuming?'

'That's right. I've always been very close to Cecil. Always told him everything. Call me daft, but I keep going back to the Clock Tower, dear. I come at it from different directions, hoping that this time ... ' She couldn't finish the sentence. 'I just can't believe he isn't there.'

'So when you jumped to the conclusion that it was *me* spilling the beans about the Chambers business, you weren't thinking very clearly, were you, Mrs G?'

'I suppose not, dear.'

'Right. So we assume Cecil is the source, and we agree that it is definitely *not me*. Now, who sent the finger? You say your associate Denise found it with the bits of crushed plastic bunny in a canister posted within the store. Was it possible to trace which department it was sent from?'

'Denise said the canisters usually have numbers on for posting them back up the right tube, but this one was cunningly unmarked.'

'Mm. What we don't know – and I believe it's crucial – is whether this conspiracy is aimed just at you personally, or at your whole gang. Sorry, not gang, I mean outfit. Can we agree on "outfit"', Mrs G? It's just that, to me, the word "organisation" suggests something totally above-board and respectable, like the United Nations or the English Folk Dance and Song Society.'

'All right.'

'Thank you. So my question is: will these enemies destroy your outfit and replace it with their own, or will they just assume control of it? Which is more normal when it comes to criminal turf wars?'

'To take it over, dear.'

'Right.'

'To squeeze me out, top me, hack me up, drop the bits in the sea.'

'Oh, God.'

'*Or* expose me, and get me hanged by the neck until dead. But I think the hacked-up bits in the sea would be first preference, as it wouldn't involve the legal system, which is notorious for arriving at the wrong result.'

'Right.' Twitten's voice was unsteady. 'I can't believe we're talking like this, Mrs G.'

'Well, as usual, I can't believe I've told you as much as I have, dear. I'm a bleeding fool to myself.'

'I just keep thinking: *What if I never see Mrs Groynes again?*' His voice quavered.

'Oh, cheer up. You know me; I'll think of something.'

'You're bally clever, Mrs G,' he said, with a sniff. 'And you're incredibly devious. Don't forget that. I mean, you're the cleverest and most devious person I personally have ever met.'

'Thank you, dear. I know you mean that as a compliment.'

'And you're not on your own. After all, perhaps I could—?' He stopped himself. Did he really want to say this? Did he really want to say he would help a clever, devious criminal outwit her enemies? He could almost feel his inner gyroscope spinning and tilting, trying to reassert control.

'No, no, dear,' said Mrs Groynes. 'Don't say something you don't mean.'

Twitten pulled himself together. 'I'll help you, Mrs G. I mean it.'

'No, it wouldn't be right, dear. You seem to forget that half an hour ago I was threatening to shoot you.'

'Yes. Well. Gosh.' Since there was no getting away from this discouraging fact, it would just have to be set aside. 'But you've helped me lots of times, haven't you? With cases? When I was stuck? And time and again you've proposed a quid pro quo and I've refused. We could consider this the quid pro quo, if you like? For example, I can tell you that a certain Miss Sibert from Vienna was involved in the escape of that madman.'

'Miss Sibert?' Mrs Groynes pulled a face. 'Who's Miss Sibert when she's at home?'

'Oh, that's disappointing, I was sure you would remember. I put two and two together at once! It's probably because my brain is younger and therefore less worn out than yours. She was the psychiatrist who was working with Mr Crystal, the theatre critic, to recover his memories.'

She brightened, interested. 'And didn't it turn out she worked for Terry?'

'It did! You see, I *can* help. Between us we can solve this.' He leaned back on his pillow. 'I just keep thinking of Mister Cecil's bunnies hopping about on that tray, though, don't you?'

'No.' She sounded confused. 'What are you talking about?'

'You know! *See the bunny run! See the bunny jump!*'

'What of it?'

'Oh, I suppose it's on my mind so much because of the book I've been reading. How easily manipulated we all are! People just have to wind us up and off we hop, buying the soap powder and cigarettes they want us to buy; helping pretty girls simply because they cry. You've got your own "hidden persuaders", Mrs G! They've wound you up and set you running! Otherwise why would you have come here, to my bedroom, with a bally gun?'

———

Unable to sleep, Inspector Steine padded downstairs in his slippers, switching on lights as he went. At the front door – which rattled in the wind – he paused and knocked.

'Yes, sir?' responded Jenkins miserably. His voice was that of a sodden man who'd been standing in one spot – soaked with rain and blasted by a gale – for several hours now.

'No cause for alarm, Constable!' called the inspector. 'I just wanted to inform you I've come downstairs.'

'Very good, sir.'

'I thought I'd make myself a nice hot cup of Ovaltine.'

'Good for you, sir.'

'I found that I couldn't sleep,' he called, as cheerfully as he could. 'It was nothing to do with what you said about this madman boiling heads and so on. I knew all about that already, of course! Your mention of grotesque head-boiling wasn't any sort of news to me, not at all!'

At the dining table, the inspector drew the box of files towards him, and bravely dug in. Boiling heads? Why hadn't this been mentioned to him before? Didn't he have a right to know? Must he do everything himself? But at the sight of the very first photograph – of the mutilated Constable Fry on the chequered floor of a Lyons' Corner House – all his courage dissolved, and he pushed the box away with such force that it slid right across the table and fell off the other side.

He shook his head, exasperated with himself for looking at such a horrible image. Knowing more about this psychopath wasn't going to help, was it? This was an argument he so often had at the office, of course, with young Twitten. 'Why do you always want to know how criminals *think*?' he would say. 'It merely sullies you, and conveys on them far more attention than they merit. You're always talking about inner this and inner that! How many more times must I say this? Our job is to catch criminals, not to understand them!'

With relief, he opened instead the file of suggestions compiled for him by Miss Lennon, concerning the opening of the zebra crossing, which was being mooted for Friday (i.e. the day after tomorrow). He was glad to have this road safety project to divert him. As Miss Lennon had assured him, there was little chance the madman would still be at large by then. But even if he were, why would a madman risk appearing at a ceremony where there would be hundreds of witnesses?

'Let's not think about that SILLY MAN, Inspector,' she had said. 'Put him completely out of YOUR MIND.'

'IDEAS' was the typed heading on the first page, and beneath it was a suggestion that really caught his imagination.

To celebrate the bold black-and-white nature of the zebra crossing, why not make the event a black-and-white bonanza, Inspector? Just off the top of my head, we could arrange:
Black-and-white chequered flags
Real zebras
Giant chessboards
Giant panda
Harlequins
Dalmatians
Packets of liquorice all-sorts, with the coloured ones removed
Men in French onion-seller costumes
Penguins
Nuns

'Oh, Miss Lennon,' breathed Inspector Steine gratefully, sitting back. He felt so much better after reading this. 'What an absolute lifesaver you are turning out to be.'

Seven

The plan for the robbery of Gosling's Department Store had been conceived during the previous year's pre-Christmas rush, when Mrs Groynes experienced a *Eureka* moment while shopping.

Genius is hard to pin down, but in Mrs Groynes's case, this particular *Eureka* demonstrates how the creative mind of a seriously gifted opportunistic criminal never truly nods. When it happened, she was dressed as a respectable house-wife in a blue swing-coat and a scarlet beret, and was toting home a string bag holding a humble half-pound of sprats wrapped in newspaper (for Raffles, the cat). As she barged her way through excited family groups on the second floor of Gosling's, she was thinking of nothing at all. And then, when she least expected it, a tiny incident snagged her attention.

She stopped barging with such abruptness that several people bumped into her.

'Sorry!' she said, clasping the string bag to her chest. 'Just remembered something. Honest, I'd forget my own head if it wasn't glued on with epoxy resin!' People laughed politely and passed on, and she retreated to stand beside a pillar, out of their way.

What had she noticed? It took her a while to be sure of this herself, but she knew it had involved the nearby fur-coat department, where – ah, yes! There it was! She darted a look towards the counter where a cheerful young assistant in a smart calf-length black dress with a little white collar was busily cramming big white five-pound notes into a canister. It was this unusual movement – elbow sharply up, pushing down with effort – that had caught Mrs Groynes's eye. 'I've never tried to get this much cash in one before!' exclaimed the girl. 'Let's hope it doesn't get stuck in the tube!' Then she turned, opened a little flap in the wall and said, 'All right, then. Off it goes!' and with a satisfying *Foop!* the canister was sucked away.

Why was this everyday proceeding of special interest to a super criminal always unconsciously on the look-out for new and attractive ways of committing grand larceny? Mrs Groynes wasn't yet sure. Rumours had reached her in the autumn of the younger Mr Gosling choosing to commission a second-rate cash-carrying system for the store (this was, apparently, typical of the man: to have big ideas and then baulk at the cost), but she had not previously seen any potential benefit in this for herself. But as she stood in the centre of the shop-floor watching busy Christmas-week sales assistants in every corner expertly posting those little canisters into those tubes – *Foop! Foop! Foop!* – it was as if she could hear criminal opportunity calling to her from within the very walls.

All that cash! Moreover, all that cash being sucked away ostensibly out of the reach of criminals! *Eureka*, indeed. Bag of sprats notwithstanding, she felt like dancing on the spot. Gosling's in the week before Christmas must turn over a fortune. True, at one end of the scale, they sold cheap packets of fresh fish to doting cat-owners, but at the other end, they sold fur coats at ninety quid a go! From fashion to bedroom suites, from jewellery to televisions, the high-ticket items abounded; and the good news was, transactions were nearly all conducted in lovely, untraceable cash, because the sort of person who shopped here (as opposed to the more spiffy Hannington's) *did not possess a bank account*. As all these interesting facts came together in her fevered mind, she was obliged to lean her face against the pillar to cool down.

'Are you in need of assistance, madam?' a man had said, holding out a hand for her to shake. It was Mister Harold, on his rounds of the shop-floor. 'Can we help you with anything? Are you perhaps looking for a gift? We have some lovely bath pearls in Christmas packaging.'

Mrs Groynes could only look at him. *Looking for a gift* was such an apt choice of words. A gift was what Mrs Groynes was always on the look-out for, it seemed. And thank you very much, Mister Harold, she felt she had found one right here.

The very next day, Mrs Groynes began to form her plan. Barrow-Boy Cecil typically played an essential role. The first thing was to find out who had installed the tubes and in this she was lucky: it was a local firm of wide-boy engineers, brazenly imitating the system patented by the Lamson company. The architectural plans would still be on file at their offices near the railway station. What she needed to know next was precisely how the tube room worked, the identity and personality of the chief cashier, where the money was stored, and precisely how it was transported to the bank.

Thirdly, she needed to establish a timescale for gradually introducing specialist gang members onto the staff.

And after all that, she needed a cup of tea and a brief lie-down.

Denise Perks was the first recruit to the Gosling's Job. Young, pretty and impressively numerate for someone who left school at fourteen, she was the perfect person to act as inside coordinator, especially after a couple of years of having Mrs G as her mentor.

'Do people tend to underestimate you, dear?' Mrs Groynes had said, kindly, at their first interview, back in 1954.

'Yes! All the bloody time!' the sixteen-year-old had angrily replied. She was rough-looking, and a bit dirty.

'Well, that's good enough for me,' Mrs Groynes had said. 'You're in.'

'What, just like that?'

'Yes, dear. Being underestimated is tough, I know. But in our particular line of business, I promise you, it's a gift.'

Denise made it plain that her little brother Shorty came as part of the package, and Mrs G had never regretted the deal. Both new recruits were priceless additions to the organisation. Orphaned when Shorty was five, they had survived on their wits; and it was much to young Denise Perks's credit that when the time came to apply for the job at Gosling's, she was fully capable of suppressing her natural delinquency, dressing herself appropriately (although she hated the ugly shoes), and buckling down to it, never once missing a day.

'I know you'll be tempted to lapse, dear,' Mrs Groynes said sympathetically, at the beginning. 'It's a long haul, this job. You'll ask yourself, "Who'd notice a bit of pinching? Might as well keep my hand in!" But if this job goes to plan, Denise, you and Shorty walk away with enough money to buy your own billet. Whereas if you get nabbed for nicking half a dollar, that's it. The main thing to remember is this: don't ever let them adjust the power of that vacuum, dear. Always insist that it's hunky bleeding dory.'

And so Denise suffered the tedium, learned not to cry when she looked at her pretty young feet encased in horrible lace-ups, and bided her time. 'Underestimate me at your peril' was her daily mental mantra, and it kept her on the straight and narrow. She noted everything from the start: in particular, the routines surrounding the chief cashier, Mr Frost, whose well-secured office adjoined the tube room. The other girls talked in their spare moments about boys, clothes, and going dancing at Sherry's. Denise tried to join in, but it would be fair to say that all her attention was fastened on Mr Frost, who all day long received and processed bag-loads of cash and sales records through a special grille.

And, of course, there were the canisters to watch, too. Thanks to the unadjusted vacuum pressure, they came rattling and whistling at high speed down the tubes, then shot out of the single 'IN' tube, flew across the room, and landed in an angled basket eight feet away – and woe betide anyone who got in the way.

'Shouldn't we ask someone to come back and adjust that, Miss Perks?' one of the girls might ask.

'No, I don't see why,' Denise would reply sweetly.

'My friend works at the tube room in the Co-op, and she says their Lamson canisters just flop out nicely, they don't shoot across the room, making everyone duck for cover. Have you seen the bruise on Ginnie's face?'

But the youthful Miss Perks was immovable on the subject of the system's pressure setting, and so the canisters continued to arrive in the entertaining ballistic manner described. The person most affected by the decision not to turn the power down was a sweet girl called Mabel (just fifteen years old, and fresh from school) whose job it was to dart along a long line of tubes labelled from 1 to 48, posting the canisters back to the various departments. She was proud of the technique she'd developed of offering the canisters up: a fraction-of-a-second open-palm method, like feeding sugar lumps to a bad-tempered horse.

Only once so far had Mabel lost concentration at a key moment, and she'd been genuinely touched by how quickly the other girls sprang to their feet and responded to her cry of: 'Help! Help! Stuck!'

'Blimey, it's like you was all sitting there expecting that to happen!' she exclaimed cheerfully, when they had dragged her to safety.

———

Most members of Mrs Groynes's gang (because it *was* a gang, whatever she claimed to the contrary) were at some point involved in the evolution of their leader's brilliant, epic plan to rob Gosling's. However, certain key players were bound to emerge, and from the beginning she focused on recruiting individuals with particular skills. As she explained to Denise and Cecil at one of their early commit-tee meetings, 'I'm going to need a dropper, a whizz man, some general grifters and a flop artist.' Luckily, everyone present understood what these underworld terms signified, because if they hadn't, it would have been a really pointless thing to say.

The first was easy. Stanley-Knife Stanley was the best dropper in the business. He had dropped through skylights since he was a teenager. Dispatched to the offices of Trend & Co. (cut-price engineers), he let himself in one night, and removed the all-important plans of the Gosling building without disturbing anything.

Historically, the profession of dropper had always been tinged with a certain hidden peril: to wit, it was all very well dropping down, but what if you couldn't climb back out again? Sad to say, many novice droppers failed to consider this eventuality until it was too late. But Stanley-Knife Stanley was an old hand; moreover, he had just received from Mrs Groynes a new-fangled telescopic ladder that could be folded up to the dimensions of a briefcase. A specialist criminal-enterprise supplier in Belgium had sent her one of these collapsible ladders as a free sample, and she had immediately ordered six more, despite the exorbitant cost.

As for the whizz man, the candidate was obvious: Jimmy the Gimp was the best pickpocket in town. Not a fan of the hurtful 'gimp' soubriquet, he had once or twice tried to adopt the brighter name Jimmy Lightning instead – on account of the speed of his fingers – but the result was only to confuse people (they started thinking there must be *two* pickpockets called Jimmy), so he gave it up. He demurred at the Gosling's Job at first, arguing that he wouldn't be free until after the summer bonanza of visitors, but this reservation was easily accommodated: they agreed he would begin his duties only once the weather had turned.

Jimmy's role in the job was very specific and not at all onerous: to lift a particular key from the pocket of the chief cashier, and also to stall the lift for about fifteen minutes. But even if a lesser whizz man could have accomplished such simple stuff, Mrs G wanted the best and she always got it.

For the general-duty grifters (to pose as humble sales assistants), Mrs G was a little stumped. Ideally, they should be presentable teenaged girls. It was Denise who came up with the solution: 'What about Joan and Dorothy from the Palace Pier?' she said.

New to the Brighton scene, Joan and Dorothy were attractive identical twin sisters of seventeen who had always dreamed of a career in show business while growing up in the sleepy nearby village of Hassocks. Over the summer, they had defied their worried mother by dropping out of secretarial training at Mr Box's Academy in Brighton (a very respectable school), and taking a job on the Palace Pier assisting an escape artist of legendary uselessness named Alfred the Great. They had enjoyed themselves immensely, and decided never to return to the classroom. Twice a day they were cheered by crowds just for levering open a sealed coffin at the last minute (or cutting a rope) and saving a tragically deluded man from imminent suffocation.

Crowds always flocked to Alfred the Great's shows, and not because of any sort of gimmick. This wasn't like the hilarious magician Tommy Cooper doing tricks badly on purpose. The forty-five-year-old Alfred Gubbins really didn't know how to escape: he had never acquired the requisite skills. Yet he was always introducing new levels of peril into the act, such as big tanks of water and ferrets down the trousers, making the audience squeal and laugh in nervous anticipation. Denise and Shorty had been in the audience on several occasions over the summer, and Denise had been impressed by the clever way Joan and Dorothy coped with it all: untrained as they were, they somehow succeeded in making Alfred's desperate flailings and strainings (and even his screamings) seem like part of the act.

'Hear Alfred the Great start to shriek like a baby!' Dorothy would say, with a broad, distracting smile, parading in a frilly-edged short skirt in front of George's desperately writhing body, while Joan discreetly knelt down behind and unlocked a padlock or two. As a start in show business for two talented girls, it wasn't great, but they were young and pretty and not cut out to be secretaries, and after Alfred rolled off the pier in chains one August afternoon and sank like a stone, the world was basically their oyster.

So, on Denise's recommendation, they were in, and by the beginning of September they were working in hats (Dorothy) and fancy lingerie (Joan). Or perhaps it was the other way round.

Meanwhile other gang members were turning up at the store in finely calculated dribs and drabs. Ronnie the Nerk got a job as general handyman. Stanley-Knife Stanley, oddly, volunteered for window dressing, and against all expectations turned out to have quite an artistic flair, especially with unpromising display items, such as mousetraps and aluminium saucepans.

'This is all very well,' objected Barrow-Boy Cecil, quite early on. 'But what about Sergeant Stupid? If he was to walk into that shop, he'd recognise everyone and smell a rat in a second. How are you going to keep him away?'

'Don't call him Sergeant Stupid, dear,' Mrs Groynes had said reprovingly. (This was at one of the fortnightly meetings with Cecil and Denise.) 'I mean, it's true, Sergeant Brunswick *is* a bit stupid, but it's not nice to say so. And it's a fair point, I don't deny it, but it's just a risk we have to take. I mean, he *never* goes shopping, docs hc? And as long as there aren't any bleeding murders committed in the shop between now and Christmas, I reckon we'll be laughing!'

Last to join the job was Sid the Doorman, and it was Cecil who persuaded him. Sid was the flop artist – and a very good one he was. In the post-war years in London, once car owners could get hold of sufficient petrol, Sid had made quite a living on the streets of WC1, putting himself deliberately in the path of moving vehicles, being knocked down, and collecting on-the-spot compensation from horrified motorists.

Nowadays he performed the flop less often, but just as effectively. Drivers were mortified to find they'd knocked down an ex-soldier whose doorman's uniform was festooned with purchased campaign medals. 'My head!' he moaned, as he sat up woozily and pointed at his chest. 'And me a veteran of Monte Cassino!'

Up to this point, Sid had been working quietly at a hotel in Hove, but he had made no secret of being fed up with the hours. A shop job with a guaranteed gigantic Christmas bonus suited him perfectly. He fancied retiring as soon as practicable to the up-and-coming Balearic Islands. Just one thing bothered him.

'What happened to Benny?' he asked, frowning. He and Cecil were having this conversation in the newly opened House of Hanover Milk Bar near the West Pier, Cecil's tray of bunnies on the table next to their frothy coffees.

'Benny?' echoed Cecil.

'Benny, the usual doorman at Gosling's. He's been there since he was demobbed. He loves that job.'

'Oh, he's about to be knocked down by a car,' said Cecil, glancing up at the cafe's clock. 'Ironic, eh?'

'What? Did you say *about to be*?'

'That's right. Some time today. He'll be all right, just on crutches for a while. I've got the application form here for you, but obviously, don't submit it 'til he's safely nobbled.'

'Well, ta,' said Sid, taking it. 'You're a pal. I've really had it with the late nights. Poor Benny, though. Hit by a car, you say?'

Cecil laughed. 'Yeah, well. There's been quite a spate of them in the last few months. Accidents. Just there, outside the shop. And somehow always involving *staff from the shop*, if you get my drift, who then *have to be replaced.*'

He left this thought hanging – but he didn't have to leave it for long. Sid was no mug.

'God, she's devious,' he said.

'I don't know what you're talking about,' said Cecil, winking. 'So, are you in?'

In the old days before the Middle Street Massacre, of course, Mrs Groynes had not commanded a gang of such impressive capability and scope. When she first arrived in Brighton, in 1950, she brought down from the Smoke only Stanley-Knife Stanley and Diamond Tony: they arrived in a small brown van and settled into a set of dank furnished rooms in Little Preston Street above a jellied eel restaurant. And there they lay low for the next six months, until the hue-and-cry from the Aldersgate Stick-up had successfully blown over, and the smell from the restaurant downstairs became intolerable.

They were not a jolly group. Diamond Tony mostly grumbled and tended to his knife collection; Stanley went for runs; Mrs Groynes started to cook up the audacious notion of getting a job at the police station as a charlady. In one important regard, she had chosen her two confederates well. Stanley would happily carve up anyone who threatened her; Tony would garotte them and drop them off a pier. So they were terrific as bodyguards. But as sparkling company for the long evenings indoors, they were a little bit brainless (Stanley) and extraordinarily creepy (Tony). No wonder that, as soon as she felt it was safe, she started to recruit locally.

In those far-off days, the two rival organisations battling for control of Brighton's criminal activity barely noted her existence. As history proves, however, when the opportunity arose to ascend to dominance, she was more than ready to make her move. The 1951 shoot-out in Middle Street saw forty-five villains from those two entrenched underworld outfits mown down and killed: these included the entire Giovedi family, who had ruled Brighton for twenty years.

Cecil was her first recruit after the massacre. Having acted for years as the Giovedis' look-out man, he fitted her requirements perfectly. In the first place, he demonstrably had quite a nerve, operating in plain sight with his preposterous tray of bunnies; a man like that would be able to handle the important new gang role of 'police informant'. Secondly, she had an affection for street traders in general. Her own late father had been a proud East London barrow-boy, selling stolen bric-à-brac (or 'pilfered toot', as he always called it) at the famous open-air market in London's Petticoat Lane.

So, the day after the Massacre, she invited Cecil to her house for Sunday lunch, to discuss his future.

'Can I just say something, Mrs Groynes?' he asked nervously. He was sitting awkwardly at the shiny antique dining table in her spacious home in Upper North Street, while she bustled between dining room and kitchen, carrying provisions on a tray. It was a tall terraced house, painted a dazzling white, and quite intimidating – a far cry from those old dismal rooms redolent of jellied eels. Most of the houses along here were divided up for multi-occupancy, but this unusual woman seemed to own the whole building.

'What's that, dear?' she called, disappearing down the corridor.

'I don't bear a grudge or anything. About my friends.'

'Sorry?' she said, returning.

'I was just saying, I don't bear a grudge. That you killed my whole gang.'

'Oh. Oh, good.' It hadn't occurred to her that anyone might be loyal to the Giovedis. Although tightly knit as a family, they were cavalier when it came to non-family-members. In a shoot-out at the Arrivederci Roma restaurant a few years ago, they had used one of their longest-serving henchmen as an effective (if initially quite reluctant) human shield.

'Well, I'm glad to hear I'm not in your bad books. So you might like to join my little organisation, then?'

'I might. And what I'm thinking is, I'm ready to go into something a bit more exciting.'

But Mrs Groynes wasn't ready to talk about details yet. There were more hostess duties to perform. Cecil looked around. Was there a *Mr* Groynes in the picture? Judging by the evidence in this room (photographs of cats in frames), the answer was surely no.

He looked up. 'What is it?' he said. Mrs Groynes was looking at him with interest from the doorway.

'Oh. Nothing,' she said, smiling. Without his hat and raincoat (and pedlar's tray), Cecil was a nice-looking man. He had thick dark hair and very attractive eyes. He wore a lovely garnet signet ring on his little finger. But he was here on business, she reminded herself, as she finally sat down and passed him a plate of chops and mashed potato. In these days of rationing, such a dinner was a rare treat.

'But you were saying,' she said. 'You're ready for something more exciting than what, dear?'

'Than selling bunnies from a tray!'

'Oh, I see.' She passed him salt, pepper and mustard. He used them all liberally, and looked about for brown sauce. She started sawing her own chop, and said nothing. She wanted him to expand, and he did.

'Those bunnies are only one step up from selling Swan Vestas and razor blades,' he explained, spearing a piece of meat with his fork. 'I know it's good cover when I'm on look-out duty, Mrs Groynes, but it's hard for a man like me to keep doing it. People look at me as if I'm an indigent! You can't understand what it does to a man's self-respect, saying *See the bunny run!* all flipping day, and having people buy shoddy little toys out of pity. I want to hold my head up, that's all I'm saying.'

He paused. She hadn't responded, but he was quite pleased with the case he'd made. 'So? What do you think?'

'Ha!' Mrs Groynes dropped her knife and fork on her plate and sat back in her chair. 'I do hope you're bleeding joking, dear.'

'No, I'm—'

'Oh, come on, Cecil. This is me you're talking to.'

'How do you mean?'

'It's me! Mrs Palmeira Groynes, who chooses to pose as a lowly charwoman! The self-bleeding-respect argument's hardly going to wash with me, is it?'

'Yes, but—'

'I swab floors, dear. I dust picture frames. I make gallons of tea. I smell permanently of Brasso.'

'Yes, but—'

'No, the bunnies stay, Cecil. The bunnies are *genius*. Sergeant Brunswick knows you're underworld already: that's the whole beauty of it. He'll look at you at the Clock Tower and think, *Hang on. Barrow-Boy Cecil's lost all his former criminal mates! Blimey, he might be willing at such a time to start acting as a grass for me!* And if he doesn't think all that of his

164

own accord, of course, I'll be more than happy to give him a nudge.'

'Yes, but—'

'On top of which, Cecil,' she interrupted firmly, 'I propose to bung you a score a week. Will that help you hold your head up?'

'Well.' He was taken aback. This was an astonishing offer. The Giovedis had paid him nothing like as much, and never on a regular basis. He finished his mashed potato (still slightly regretting the absence of sauce), and pushed his plate away. Self-respect truly did have its price. The dinner had been delicious. 'That's a very generous offer, Mrs G.'

So this was how the gang started to establish itself in the days after the Massacre in 1951. Once the way was clear for Mrs Groynes to expand her network, more members were brought in, many of them on stipends. But always there was a hierarchy, with her longest-serving associates at the top: Stanley, Tony, Vince (volatile Punch & Judy man), and Cecil. These were the four men she trusted, consulted, and listened to. After that first meeting, Cecil had gone home to his little house near the railway viaduct, and sat in silence for a while. He could hardly believe his luck. He had loathed and feared the Giovedis. This new woman was not only smart, she appeared to be fair; and it was possible she also fancied him. Twenty quid a week (plus all profits from the bunnies) was a very nice little income.

He shrugged at the irony of it, though. 'Oh, those *sodding bunnies*,' he sighed. But what could you do? Much as he hated them, on the day of the Massacre they had saved his life, with

Papa Giovedi insisting he stay at his post. And now look. The little plastic bastards were providing him with a comfortable livelihood for the rest of his life!

Early in September (two weeks before the murder of Professor Milhouse in the record department) Mrs Groynes had called a Sunday night meeting of her four top Gosling's Job operatives:

Denise – established in the tube room

Jimmy – soon to take up work in the lift

Ronnie the Nerk – handyman

Stanley – window-display artiste *extraordinaire*

It was exciting. She was ready to outline the plan, and expectations were high as they all arrived at Mrs Groynes's house and trooped downstairs to the cellar. Denise prayed that the job would be somehow pinned on Mr Frost, the aloof chief cashier, because she had become weirdly attracted to him, which made her angry with herself. Meanwhile Ronnie the Nerk was hoping it would involve drilling into a vault, or at least through a very thick ceiling. Ever since Mrs Groynes organised a private screening in this very cellar of *Rififi* (sensationally tense French heist movie), Ronnie had been drilling-mad.

'First things first,' she said, unveiling a blackboard with a flourish. 'We're not drilling.'

'Aww,' said Ronnie, who had no talent at all for disguising disappointment.

'The plan comes in three stages,' she said, pointing with a stick at three lists. 'On completion of each stage, our work will be undetectable. I intend for us to walk away with the money scot-free. Our twin aims are 1) to maximise the haul, and 2) to leave no trace of foul play. By the time the theft is discovered – which will be three days later, on December the twenty-seventh – the unsuspecting chief cashier will have disappeared, sent on a wild goose chase, ostensibly leaving a convincingly incriminating note, which of course will be written by me.'

'You're going to pin it all on Mr Frost, then?' gasped Denise, with mixed feelings.

'Just for a while. Don't worry, there won't be enough evidence to put him away, but he'll have a few awkward days in rural North Wales. During which time, we can all decide what we want to do. The money won't be divided at once: I don't want anyone taking off and drawing suspicion. And you can't all leave your employment in the shop at the same time, for obvious reasons. Everyone has to seem innocent. But be in no doubt: you'll all get your share by the end of January. And by March, I reckon, the coast will be clear.'

She turned to the board again, and began to outline the details of the ingenious heist, to the delight (and occasional applause) of her impressed confederates.

Later in life, they all remembered it glowingly as one of the great planning meetings of their lives.

'You're a genius, Mrs G!' they said in wonder – both individually and together – as the scheme became clear.

'Simple, but original!'

'What a plan, Mrs G!'

'No one else could have come up with this!'

And so on. By the end, Mrs Groynes had to beg them all to calm down, they were so energised by the brilliant, *brilliant* scheme, which – sadly – can never be fully revealed in print, for fear of inspiring copy-cat crimes. Suffice to say that split-second timing came into it, plus some expert whizzing and flopping, and some brilliant driving from Mrs Groynes herself. And then, in the end … ? Well, there is no harm, on reflection, in reporting the scheme's crowning moment, since there is no danger of a modern criminal adopting it for himself.

'So then … the loot all disappears!' she said triumphantly. 'Just temporarily, you understand. But when those precious sealed bank-boxes – containing only the sheets and pillow-cases Joan and Dorothy have just swapped in – are carted off in the armoured van, where's the loot?'

She looked at her enraptured audience. Gratifyingly, they seemed to have no suggestions.

'It's not in the cashier's room,' she carried on. 'It's not in the tube room either. There is *not a trace*. There's nothing to give away the fact that we've tampered with those boxes while Sid the Doorman was performing his spectacular flop outside. The cash, to all intents and purposes, has *vanished*.'

Four expectant faces looked up at her.

'So where do you think it's gone?' she said, enjoying it.

'Don't know, Mrs G,' confessed Denise. 'Please tell us, for gawd's sake. I'm bursting!'

She grinned at them. 'It's up the bleeding tubes!'

But that was two weeks ago. And now Mrs Groynes is looking at a far less rosy picture. Now she is rattled. Someone is trying to knock her off her perch, and it's clear that they know a disturbing amount about her plans.

Not only has Barrow-Boy Cecil been kidnapped and possibly killed: Denise and Shorty have been identified as gang members, and unwanted police attention has been drawn to Gosling's by the gratuitous murder of an American academic. And on top of all this, apparently, a bleeding zebra crossing is going to be set up imminently outside the store, to prevent any future pedestrian casualties – although, secretly, Mrs Groynes has to admit that she might have brought this particular reversal on herself by engineering so many road accidents involving shop staff.

The only good news is that when Sergeant Brunswick entered the building to investigate the murder, he spotted none of her men – although they certainly saw him. Working on a new 'Back to School' window display of children's footwear, Stanley-Knife Stanley had no sooner seen the sergeant walking past than he had dived behind a cardboard fixture.

'What was that?' asked Twitten, stopping.

'What was what?' said Brunswick.

'In the window. Something moved.'

Meanwhile, Ronnie the Nerk, blithely hammering a new shelf in the bedding department, dropped his tools and fled to the Gents. Jimmy the Gimp was luckily not due to start lift-duty for another couple of days, but was nevertheless present in the building, dipping for purses and discreetly observing the incumbent (hopeless) lift-operator at work. At Brunswick's approach, Jimmy scarpered to nearby Lingerie, where Joan (or was it Dorothy?) helped him hide inside a low cupboard with some brassieres and girdles.

As she applies herself to this unprecedented threat, Mrs Groynes looks occasionally at Cecil's severed finger and remembers the first meeting with him at her house: the one with the chops and mash. She remembers this ring. She remembers how she stood in the doorway thinking she liked the look of Cecil, and she wonders why she never did anything about it. But now, presumably, it is too late.

The world had been opening up to her, back then. Now it is closing in, like at the end of *Little Caesar* with Edward G. Robinson.

'*Mother of mercy*,' she whispers to herself, dramatically, '*is this the end of Rico?*'

And then she takes a deep breath and pulls herself together. 'No, it bleeding isn't, Palmeira,' she says firmly. 'Not by a long chalk.'

Eight

Twitten rose early the next morning (Thursday), feeling drained and peculiar. What time had Mrs Groynes left? He didn't know. He remembered a moment of waking and whispering 'Mrs G?' and realising with relief that she had gone.

As he quickly washed and dressed now, he found he had a lot to think about, not least the encouraging fact that it had finally stopped raining. The image of Mrs Groynes chopped up into bits and dropped in the sea was, understandably, claiming some of his attention; also the image of the condemned prisoner dropping through a trapdoor with a noose around her neck at the dead stroke of nine. But looming larger than both by far was the image conjured by her unsettling claim: *And not to alarm you, but this isn't the first time I've let myself in and stood here.*

However, as he began to creep downstairs, for fear of waking Mrs Thorpe, he attempted to take stock of the more salient facts. Mrs Groynes was in a bally pickle. Her position as leader of a 200-strong gang was under threat, and the man known as Barrow-Boy Cecil was missing. Her hidden enemy seemed to be *au fait* with her plans to rob Gosling's Department Store. And by a tragic coincidence, she had been forced out of her cosy charlady job by the appointment of a zealous police secretary.

Why was Mrs Groynes so convinced that avenging Terence Chambers was the motive behind all this? The way she had batted aside all other suggestions was puzzling. It was true that a known associate of Chambers had reappeared on the scene (Miss Sibert); also Chambers's right-hand man was involved (Nicky Garroway). But still, if you half-closed your eyes and surveyed the current landscape of Mrs Groynes's life for a figure who might have a stand-out motive for destroying her, the result would be a blurry, distant, and sizeable group of London hoods, local bank managers, and bitter relatives of Middle Street Massacre victims. But in the middle of them, in sharp focus and three times bigger than everyone else, would surely stand Adelaide Vine.

Was Twitten jumping to conclusions, though? He paused on the top landing and thought about it. If Mrs Groynes couldn't see the threat from this artful young woman, was he mistaken? Was he perhaps swayed by personal prejudice? After all, there were many things he disliked about Adelaide Vine's behaviour, which for convenience could be boiled down to two:

her blatant manipulation of the impressionable male by cynical employment of her God-given nut-like attributes;

the way she had pointedly ignored him yesterday while fawning on Sergeant Brunswick.

But weighing heavily against these strong personal feelings were the indisputable facts confirming her as a force to be reckoned with:

she recently cozened Inspector Steine and pointed a gun at him;

she lost all four significant people in her life, including her mother, at the hands of Mrs Groynes just two months ago, so was likely to be jolly peeved;

she grew up in the long-con game – playing a part in murder-ous plots against several innocent women. Ergo, wickedness and deceit came as naturally to her as breathing.

He began his descent – but not for long.

'Constable Twitten?'

He stopped on the stairs, hand to heart. Flipping hedge-hogs, it was Mrs Thorpe. However hard he tried to get out of this house without waking his landlady, it never seemed to work.

'Yes, Mrs Thorpe?' he said, as brightly as he could. 'Please don't get up. I was trying ever so hard to be quiet. Perhaps it's the boots.'

He braced himself for her appearing at the door in the usual diaphanous night attire and feathery slippers, but it seemed she was happy this morning to restrict herself to speaking through the door.

'I forgot to tell you last night over supper, Constable. Your girlfriend Pandora called yesterday about something you sent her in the post.'

'Oh, no. Gosh, I'm sorry. She's not my girlfriend, actually, but I was meaning to—'

'She seemed quite annoyed, and was threatening to tear it up and throw it away. What on earth had you sent her?'

'Ah.' Twitten really should have warned Pandora about the photograph. There were many things to like and admire about the former Milk Girl, but an empathetic ability to put herself in someone else's shoes wasn't one of them. She would not be asking, 'Why has he sent this?' or even, 'Is Peregrine in trouble if he sent this?' She would only be thinking, 'Why has he sent this *to me*?'

'If she calls again,' he said, 'do tell her I'd like her to keep it in safe keeping. Could you stress that please? I'll try to make time today to explain everything to her. But if you could emphasise *safe keeping*, I'd be jolly grateful. And I really should make strides now, I'm afraid.'

He turned to go, but had achieved just two steps when she called after him, 'Will you be seeing Sergeant Brunswick, do you think?'

'Er, yes. I expect so,' he called, freezing again mid-motion with one leg extended. 'As you know, Mrs Thorpe, I see the sergeant every day.'

'Well, pass on my regards.'

'I will.'

'Do you know if there are any desserts he particularly likes?'

Twitten tried hard not to harrumph. He really needed to get to the station. The cold-blooded murder of Professor Milhouse wasn't going to solve itself! Plus, a large box of material sent from Broadmoor needed to be studied as a matter of urgency, given that the Brighton-wide manhunt had so far yielded no sightings of the dangerous Geoffrey Chaucer. And here he still was on the bally stairs, being expected to play Cupid? Mrs Thorpe was a lovely woman and a terrific landlady but she didn't seem to care at all about the position she was putting him in. If her relationship with Sergeant Brunswick progressed further, there could come a morning (Twitten gripped the banister rail tightly at the thought) when he would be making his way down these stairs and the person calling to him as he passed Mrs Thorpe's bedroom would be the bally sergeant!

But could he ignore a request for information, when he was in possession of it? He could not. He knew full well which dessert the sergeant liked best.

'Between you and me, Mrs Thorpe,' he said, in a confidential tone, 'Sergeant Brunswick likes *blancmange*.'

'What did you say?' she called.

'I said the sergeant likes blancmange!' he called, adding volume.

There was a stunned silence from Mrs Thorpe. She had probably hoped for something sophisticated and French. (He had noticed a tattered copy of an Elizabeth David book on the little table beside her armchair last night. It had occurred to him that Brunswick should be warned.)

'Oh. I was thinking more of *Gâteau de Rochefort*. Do you think he would like that? It uses shredded almonds!'

'Well, you could try it, certainly. But pink blancmange with a thick skin on top is the key to his bally heart, Mrs Thorpe. I've seen Mrs Groynes's blancmange work its magic on the sergeant on any number of occasions.'

Despite all this diverting hokey-cokey on the stairs, Twitten was still the first to arrive at the office. He had requested that everything from Professor Milhouse's hotel room be delivered to the station, and he was just flicking through a notebook headed 'Motivation Research: Brighton Field Observations Part One' when Brunswick burst excitedly through the door, evidently brimming with news.

'You know that umbrella you wouldn't stop going on about yesterday, son?'

'Gosh,' said Twitten, frowning. He had been deep in thoughts of his own, and it took him a moment to catch up. 'Ooh. You mean the unusual one with the silver handle fashioned in the shape of a buffalo head that belonged to Professor—'

'Of course I mean that one!'

'Sorry, sir. I was—'

'I only flaming found it!'

Brunswick drew up a chair and sat facing Twitten across his desk. His eyes were alight with triumph. Here was the best facet of the sergeant, in Twitten's view: his genuine zeal to detect. In all other respects, his life as a policeman seemed to make him so miserable that Twitten had often thought of urging a career change to something more inherently uplifting, such as lighthouse-keeper. But at times like this, Brunswick positively came alive.

'Gosh. Well done, sir.' Twitten put down Milhouse's notebook. 'Where was it?'

'Listen. Last night I was out having a pint or two at the Princess Alice and, well, I admit it – I was feeling a bit sorry for myself.'

'That doesn't sound like you, sir,' said Twitten supportively. (He had recently learned that lying through one's teeth for the sake of another person's feelings sometimes made conversations run more smoothly. Mrs Groynes had been the source of this excellent tip.)

'Anyway, who should come in but that Broadmoor cove.'

'Mr Winslow?'

'That's it. Winslow. And, blimey, I tried to be sympathetic to that story of his, but the way he let that Sibert woman twist him round her little finger … well, I was shocked, Twitten: flaming shocked! And he's not even embarrassed! He was putty in her hands, poor blighter.'

Twitten raised an eyebrow, but resisted making the obvious point about the sergeant's own credulity where attractive chestnut-haired females were concerned. 'What sort of thing did Miss Sibert get him to do for her, sir?'

'What *didn't* she get him to do for her! Listen, he only lets her interview Chaucer, *on her own*, for days on end.'

'No!'

'She gets permission to show him films!'

'Really? Did he say which?'

'It seems she's dying to get to the "trigger" that makes Chaucer kill, you see, and she starts to reckon it's – oh, I don't know, something to do with floor patterns or crosswords or chessboards or something. She's got an idea it's a combination of three things: "*Ein, zwei, drei,*" he keeps saying. Three things that will make Chaucer go *snep*!'

'*Snep?*'

'That's what he says. I assume she's got an accent. Anyway, that's by the by. He only takes all this nonsense seriously and gives her access to all the police files, including witness statements from the killings!'

'He shouldn't have done that, sir. Not without the express permission of the Home Secretary.'

'You're telling me. Then she even goes off and interviews some of the witnesses herself!'

'Good heavens. Didn't Mr Winslow receive *any* sort of vocational training for the job of governor, sir?'

'He's in love, son. He's crazy about her rosy cheeks and the way she pins her hair up in plaits. And don't get him started on her tiny feet! Anyway, all this time she's plotting to spring the loony the first chance she gets. And after all that, well—! Can you believe it, he isn't even angry with her? He's lost his job, and his home, and his reputation, and his blooming sanity, if you ask me. But he still thinks he flaming loves her!'

Brunswick threw up his hands, in comic despair. He had really enjoyed telling this story.

'Poor chap,' said Twitten. 'That's awful. But what's it got to do with the umbrella?'

'Oh, right. I forgot. Winslow had it with him.'

'No!'

'It's downstairs. I left it with the forensics boys. When I saw Winslow had it, I said, "Where the flaming hell did you get that?" And I was about to march him to the station, but he said he found it next to the front door at the boarding house he's staying in, and I believed him, so I let him go.'

'Gosh. I don't suppose you enquired who else is staying at that particular boarding house, sir?'

Brunswick gave him a steady look. Twitten bit his lip.

'Sorry, sir. Of course you did.'

'Thank you, Twitten. *Of course I did.* And, well, this is what I wanted to tell you. I mean, you'll never guess, you could have knocked me down with a—'

'Was it Adelaide Vine, sir?'

'Oh, flaming hell, Twitten!'

Brunswick harrumphed, sat back, and crossed his arms. Twitten really was the most annoying person in the world.

'But was it, sir?'

'Yes, it was flaming Adelaide Vine who left the umbrella by the front door of the flaming boarding house.'

'Ha! Excellent! I knew it!'

———

In the J. Lyons tea room towards the top of North Street, spaced along the cosy left-hand wall, three women sat at separate small tables, each with a hot drink and a fancy cake. No one would have paid particular attention to them – although the youngest of the three had hair of a striking chestnut colour that was hard to miss. They appeared not to know one another.

The woman at the first table was quite large and stolid-looking, with greying hair: she had an upright carriage, as if she had served in the forces. Let's call her Roberta Lennon of the Metropolitan Police. At the second table sat a rosy-faced foreign-looking woman with blonde plaits pinned up on top of her head, who for argument's sake we will call Carlotta Sibert, Viennese émigrée, expert in extreme psychoanalytic regression techniques. And there are no prizes for guessing the identity of the third solitary female customer, sitting the furthest from the door.

As was their daily habit, after half-past eight these women had entered the restaurant individually, bringing books to occupy them. Miss Lennon was reading *Peyton Place* with unfeigned rapt attention, while holding a loaded forkful of creamy *millefeuille*; Miss Sibert, with an academic air, jotted marginal notes in her copy of Carl Jung's *Gegenwart und Zukunft*, while occasionally picking up a macaroon and nibbling it in a squirrel-like manner (using both hands); meanwhile Adelaide Vine, ignoring the untouched second half of a delicious *tarte au citron*, seemed absorbed in *The Scapegoat* by Daphne du Maurier.

At a quarter to nine, Adelaide Vine stood up and brushed invisible crumbs from her turquoise raincoat. She reached into her lemon-yellow handbag and withdrew two envelopes. Passing Miss Lennon's table, she neatly deposited one of the envelopes on its surface, where *Peyton Place* was swiftly placed on top of it; passing Miss Sibert's, she deliberately dropped the second envelope on the floor, so that both women could bend down to pick it up.

'Butterfingers!' she laughed, as she crouched down.

'Ha-ha!' laughed Miss Sibert, in a friendly way.

'We're on for tomorrow!' whispered Adelaide into Miss Sibert's little pink shell of an ear.

'*Gut*!' said Miss Sibert. 'You remember ze clock? It won't work without—'

'All in the letter,' Adelaide assured her. Then, straightening herself and speaking at normal volume, she handed over the envelope, saying, with a broad beaming smile, 'I'm so sorry, madam, is this yours?'

Back at the station, the subject under discussion was still the umbrella found by Mr Winslow, and the way it seemed to incriminate Adelaide Vine.

'She was out at the time,' said Brunswick, 'but she's definitely staying there. The landlady actually remembered her bringing the umbrella in and putting it in the hall. I can't believe it. It means she might be involved in the murder.'

'Yes.'

'I just can't flaming believe it.'

'No, sir. You said.'

'She's so lovely!'

'Yes, she is. But the thing is … ' Twitten faltered. Mrs Groynes had told him off so many times for 'rubbing the sergeant's nose in it', as she called it. Perhaps this was the sort of occasion to practise a bit of diplomacy? 'The thing is, sir … ' He stopped. 'I really don't know what to say.'

Brunswick pulled a face. 'Yes, you do,' he said flatly.

'I mean, I know you felt very sorry for her yesterday when she was weeping and throwing herself at you and talking about your strong, safe hands and pretending she'd sent you letters … '

Brunswick winced. He had been distraught about those lost letters from Adelaide Vine. He'd had a row about it with his auntie Violet, because she'd insisted that no such items had ever been received.

'But as you were just now implying in regard to Mr Winslow's folly, sometimes you have to look at people clearly and judge them by their deeds rather than by their pink cheeks and attractive tiny feet. And if you remember, sir, Miss Vine did, on a previous occasion not so long ago, sort of shoot you in the leg.'

'I know. I know.'

'And she deceived the inspector wickedly.'

'Yes. All right. But why would she kill the professor?'

'Well, sir – you're sure you don't mind my saying?'

'No,' sighed Brunswick resignedly. 'You go ahead.'

'Well, I think I might have found the answer. I was just looking through these books of his observations, and it seems the professor was bally obsessed with her! Do you remember the women in the mantle department – you know, the coats and dresses – telling you that the professor could always guess what colour clothes the customers had been asking for on any particular day?'

Brunswick looked blank.

'It was a very striking comment, sir.'

'If you say so, son.'

'Or at least I thought so at the time. Well, if you look in these notebooks, from the beginning of his observations in the store Professor Milhouse starts to note every day what colour is being worn by one particular person; and the particular person is Adelaide Vine! Look, sir.'

Twitten held up the book to show the note in Professor Milhouse's handwriting: 'AV Chartreuse'. Then he flipped to another page, where it said 'AV Violet'.

'I'd only just noticed it when you came in. Isn't it fascinating?'

Brunswick frowned. 'Not to me, son, no. Why would that matter to Milhouse?'

'Because it influenced customers unconsciously, sir! Which is what the professor's research was all about! The thing is, Miss Vine looked so stunning in whatever outfit she had on, female customers unconsciously wanted to look like her, and shopped accordingly. I'd love to show you the relevant passage in *The Hidden Persuaders*, sir, but I shan't do that because, although I don't understand why everyone is so dead set against my reading matter in general even when it's directly relevant to our inquiries, I've learned from experience that even raising the subject is a bally red rag to a bull. But the professor's field was *motivation research* and I bet if you asked those customers what made them choose chartreuse or violet on those days, they wouldn't be able to tell you. They'd just say they really liked those colours. The effect Miss Vine had on them was perfect anecdotal proof of unconscious influence!'

'It doesn't mean she killed him, Twitten.'

'No, that's true.' Twitten's face fell, but then brightened again. 'But if the professor thought he was really on to something, he probably trailed about after her. And in the end – well, I don't know. Perhaps she got sick of it, or he saw something he shouldn't have. So she lured him to the listening booth and shot him.'

Brunswick gave it some thought. 'That's pretty thin, Twitten. Even for you.'

'I resent that, sir.'

'Possession of the murdered man's umbrella isn't much in the way of conclusive evidence, is it? And people buying frocks in funny shades won't get us very far, either.'

'No, sir. I suppose not. But you agree that we should at least regard her as a suspect?'

'Oh, definitely.'

'And I don't like to speak out of turn, sir … '

Brunswick narrowed his eyes. It was clear that Twitten was about to go all holier-than-thou. 'Yes, you do,' he muttered flatly, again.

'I think it behoves us, sir, as responsible policemen and trusted servants of the public, to resist Miss Vine's womanly wiles as far as we can on account of her being a suspect.'

'Womanly wiles!' scoffed the sergeant.

'Yes, sir,' said Twitten firmly. 'Womanly wiles. Miss Vine's womanly wiles are just as dangerous as the wicked Miss Sibert's, sir. More so, probably, as she doesn't have tiny feet and her hair pinned up in plaits, which for many men would *not* be effective as an aphrodisiac.'

'Right.'

Of course, what Twitten wanted to add was: *And I think she's out to chop up Mrs Groynes and drop the bits in the sea! I think she has already killed Barrow-Boy Cecil! She wants to take over the gang-cum-organisation-cum-outfit-cum-congeries that has been Mrs Groynes's for so long!* But of course he was obliged to keep this additional charge-sheet to himself.

So he changed the subject. 'Do we know if Miss Vine has been in touch with the inspector again, sir?'

'He hasn't mentioned it to me. But then he's hardly spoken to me at all since Constable Jenkins started guarding him day and night, and he's got this new secretary bustling round him and telling him how blooming marvellous he is.'

'Well, let's hope Miss Vine leaves him out of it this time. The poor man has enough to worry about with that madman after him. And as for that— Ooh!'

'What?'

'Ooh!' Twitten repeated, and pulled a face. It was a particularly annoying expression that Brunswick had noticed many times before. It usually came just before the annoying cleverclogs smugly picked him up on some detail that other people had overlooked.

'What was that you said about floor patterns triggering the madman's murders, sir? You mentioned crosswords and chessboards as well, I think? And Miss Sibert interviewing a witness? *Ein, zwei, drei*? May I follow that up?'

'Oh. Well, I suppose so. I mean, the manhunt hasn't flushed him out, has it? And thanks to your chum at the *Argus*, the whole town's out looking for him.'

'I *shall* follow that up, then, sir. If I can find the bally box of files. And— Ooh! There's something else.'

'Oh, what now?' Brunswick had been thinking he would go to the canteen across the road and get a cup of tea and a currant bun (maybe even two currant buns) to lift his spirits. It was funny how talking to Twitten always left him craving carbohydrates.

'Given the choice between *Gâteau de Rochefort* and pink blancmange, which would you plump for?'

'Well … ' Brunswick was taken aback. Why on earth were they talking about puddings? 'I'd have to say blancmange, son, not having heard of—'

'I knew it!' interrupted Twitten cheerfully. 'I'll tell Mrs Thorpe. Now, I wonder what happened to that box?'

———

An old, closed wax museum was in many ways the ideal place to house a recently absconded homicidal psychopath, and Adelaide Vine had chosen it quite easily. It was the place where her mother had been murdered; it was also the site of her own humiliation, when she had been disarmed with ludicrous ease by the clever Mrs Groynes.

But there were other, more practical, reasons for choosing it. For one thing, the building was empty and ignored; for another, she still had a key to the side door. This door opened into a tiny alley famously too narrow for anything other than furtive copulation. Given the well-established risk of getting wedged in (and requiring the assistance of the fire brigade), visitors to it nowadays were few and far between.

So, in some ways, how clever of Adelaide to think of the dark and defunct Maison du Wax, awaiting demolition. But from another point of view, was it wise to keep this same recently absconded homicidal psychopath in a murky museum full of gruesome effigies, some of them depicting scenes of execution? How might this affect his mood?

Chaucer himself knew none of the reasons for choosing this place. All he knew was that he hated it. His companion, Miss Sibert, kept promising him that this was a mere staging post, and that in a few days they would board a cross-Channel ferry. But he wasn't stupid. He knew she was lying. All those regression experiments back in Broadmoor had obviously been conducted for some nefarious purpose. He had gone along with it for one reason: because he could see she was planning to break him out. And escape was all he had dreamed of, day and night, ever since his arrest.

Thus, when Miss Sibert had come along, motivated by quite blatant self-interest, he had decided to turn the situation to his own advantage. If he played his cards right, *he* could use *her*. It didn't take him long to work out what was going on, either: she was digging to find the exact combination of factors that had been present on the three occasions he had gone berserk and deboncified a bobby. This was quite shocking, really; he found it offensive. Did she intend to set him on someone, like a dog? For a time he argued with himself that this supposition was too preposterous, but then she started showing him the films and he had to accept the truth. Because, quite crudely spliced into the celluloid, were fraction-of-a-second frames designed to convey the subliminal message, KILL INSPECTOR STEINE.

It had been a job for him not to laugh when that first message had flashed up in the middle of *The Titfield Thunderbolt*. Miss Sibert had sat with him in the semi-dark, pretending to be absorbed in the plot. Stanley Holloway was shovelling coal into the furnace of the steam engine, and the train was puffing along in virgin countryside and then, KILL INSPECTOR STEINE. He blinked with surprise, but otherwise betrayed no sign of having seen it. Later on, during a nice scene with the young John Gregson, another message flashed up, with Steine's photograph and the words HATE THIS MAN. The same messages turned up in *The Belles of St Trinian's* the following week. It was laughable. But if he wanted to get out of here, he knew he must play along. After each film, when the lights were switched back on, she had asked him, in a casual tone, if he had heard of someone called Inspector Steine, and he'd said, curling his fist and striking the tabletop, 'No, but I *hate* him!', which was apparently more than satisfactory.

So now here he was in Brighton: confined to the wax museum and biding his time. Miss Sibert went out each morning and returned smelling of coffee and macaroons and clutching a letter of instructions that she refused to show him. They slept in the old offices of the museum, upstairs.

They talked of what they would do when they got to France, and she seemed genuinely to believe she had nothing to fear from him. His madness was directed only at policemen, after all. And there had to be three triggers: *ein, zwei, drei.*

He was quite curious to see what would happen next. The thing was, he didn't mind if he killed another policeman. But if he once suspected that Miss Sibert's secret plan entailed getting him caught and imprisoned again, he would kill her, too. No trigger required. He would kill her brutally, and all her little friends as well.

———

Back at the station, Inspector Steine (HATE THIS MAN) was escorted upstairs to his office by three constables pressed so closely around him that he had to fight the urge to push them away. Much as he appreciated their loyal protection, he was getting fed up with it. Had it really been necessary to bring him to work in the back of a Black Maria? The blasted driver had instructed him, 'Lie on the floor, sir! That's right! Down, sir!' and the result was he'd rolled uncontrollably from side to side ('Help! Stop! Help!') as the speeding van careered round corners, and had emerged from it with his uniform caked in dust.

'Thank you, men. I can manage from here,' he said, with relief, when they reached the door. He made an unambiguous gesture with his arm as if to dismiss them, but they didn't respond to it, except to smirk. If anything, they shuffled nearer.

'Sorry, sir. Orders are to guard the door.' The speaker was Jenkins, the officer who had stood outside the house in the rain last night; the one who had dropped heavy hints about its being customary for bodyguards to be offered cups of tea.

Steine gave him a hard look. There was something about this man that was beginning to get on his nerves.

'Well, you can stand there if you like, Jenkins. I can't stop you.'

And with that, he entered the office and – intending it to sting – slammed the door so hard that his Silver Truncheon rattled on its mount and his framed Outstanding Policing Certificate jumped off its hook and slid down the wall.

Brunswick and Twitten pulled faces but made no remark.

'Morning, sir,' said Brunswick, as if nothing had happened.

'Brunswick,' he replied (minimally, through gritted teeth). 'Twitten.'

Years of experience had taught Brunswick that when the inspector was tetchy, you didn't ask questions or raise objections. Either you pretended to be deep in study, or you simply left the building to enjoy some delicious currant buns. Twitten, by unfortunate contrast, had not yet learned this.

'Ooh, that was a little uncalled, for, sir!' he piped up pleasantly. 'Poor Constable Jenkins! If you recall, sir, the threat to you from Mr Chaucer is very real.'

'Yes, yes.' Removing his peaked cap, Steine gave him a look. 'As it happens, I do recall that, thank you, Twitten. I believe the man boils the heads of his victims in a bucket, although no one chose to mention this to me, presumably because they thought I wouldn't be interested.'

'So it's about your safety, you see, sir.'

'Yes. Thank you.'

'He's an insane killer, sir.'

'Thank you. Yes. I think I've grasped it now.'

Brunswick shook his head discreetly at Twitten, but it didn't work.

'Oh, good. Because the thing is, sir, you seem quite angry for some reason.'

Brunswick groaned.

'Do I, Twitten?'

'Yes, sir. And I'm guessing it's because you're scared, sir. Anger is often a direct by-product of fear, you see.'

'Really? You surprise me. I must remember to write that down.'

'But I'm pleased you found out about the head-boiling, sir. Because the sergeant and I realised afterwards that we had neglected to tell you the full story of Geoffrey Chaucer's deviant modus operandi. Sergeant Brunswick, why are you signalling at me like that?'

Twitten bit his lip. Belatedly, he was beginning to suspect he had wandered out of his depth. He noticed that Sergeant Brunswick was keeping completely out of the conversation, and was studying the *Police Gazette* with far more assiduity than such a humdrum publication could possibly merit. He also noticed the inspector had gone quite red in the face.

'Would it help if I changed the subject, sir?' Twitten asked.

'I'd give it a try, son,' advised Brunswick quietly.

'Well. There was a reporter outside, sir, in a white rain-coat and a brown trilby hat. The desk sergeant said he's been determined to speak to you and has been lurking out there for hours, so I said I'd ask if you were available. Did I do the right thing?'

———

At that moment, three women – separately – arrive at their places of work. At the police station, it is Miss Lennon. This is a relief to everyone present.

'Lovely DAY, Inspector!' she booms, barging in and slamming her handbag down on her big shiny table. She pulls the cover off her typewriter, then picks up the framed certificate and rehangs it before adjusting the Silver Truncheon, which has slipped slightly from its proper position. At her desk, she lightly pats the little framed photograph, as if for good luck. 'It has stopped RAINING at LAST,' she announces, 'and I have MARVELLOUS NEWS, but for YOUR EARS ONLY, I'm afraid, Inspector!'

Grateful for the hint, Brunswick spots an opportunity to escape to the canteen. 'I think I'll go and get a cup of tea, sir,' he says, standing. 'That is, unless you want an update first on anything?'

'On what sort of thing?'

'The Gosling's murder, for instance, sir.'

Steine pulls a face. Gosling's murder? To be truthful, he has forgotten all about it. 'Oh, no. Not at all, Sergeant. You go ahead. A cup of tea's much more important.'

'Thank you, sir.'

'And here's a thought: take young Twitten with you. If you don't, I might forget myself and dismiss him from the force.'

'Ooh, but, sir?' says Twitten, getting up. 'I really wanted to look at that box of files from Broadmoor, sir. Do you know where they are?'

'They're on my dining-room floor. Why?'

'May I go and consult them, sir? I have a hunch.'

Steine considers. He sees a chink of light. 'How long will this hunch keep you out of my sight, do you think?'

'Quite a long time, I imagine. But if you want me back sooner, I could try—'

'No, don't try.'

'What I meant was, I could bring them back here and—'

'No, don't do that.'

'But—'

'No, really.' The inspector fishes a door key out of his trouser pocket. 'Take as long as you like.'

Miss Lennon writes the inspector's home address on a piece of paper. 'But don't forget your DRIVING LESSON, Constable,' she says, as he is leaving. 'Today it is at half-past ELEVEN. Your instructor Sergeant Masefield says that your test is due NEXT WEEK and he is in positive DESPAIR.'

And then, when both Brunswick and Twitten have left, Miss Lennon gleefully prepares to discuss with the inspector their exciting hush-hush plans for the opening of the zebra crossing the following day at noon – the one with all the black-and-white patterns, in spectacular abundance, as far as the eye can see.

———

Adelaide Vine arrives at her own office on the top floor of Gosling's to find Mister Harold waiting for her in his pyjamas. This is most irregular, but there is nothing sinister in it. He does live up here, after all. He is excitedly waving a book called *The Hidden Persuaders*, and clearly hasn't slept.

'Good morning, Miss Vine, and what a lovely morning it is. Did you know that people are like sheep? I mean, as customers? They are! They really are! It's been scientifically tested! You can sit them down in a cinema and flash images at them saying "Buy Puffin Cigarettes", and they just do it! It is fantastic news!'

He realises she is staring at him. 'Oh, I'll go and get dressed. But take a look at this, Miss Vine.' He hands her the book. 'I had no idea this was what the professor was doing in the store. Such valuable work! I feel – I positively feel that previously I was blind, but now I can see!'

Adelaide smiles at him. 'I'm so pleased for you, Mister Harold.' Then, once he is out of the room, she sets the book to one side and opens her desk-diary, where the main topic for the day is (a.m.) *'CLOCK ARRIVING'* followed by (p.m.) *'CLOCK BEING FITTED'*.

The phone rings on her desk. She answers it so beautifully, you would swoon to see it. It is news from the loading bay at the back entrance to the store. A large crate has just been delivered. She thanks them and calls the clock-fitters, who confirm they will appear at two o'clock.

'Excellent,' she says to herself, smiling. The others had worried about how to manage this element of the plan, but it had in fact been an easy matter to persuade Mister Harold to purchase a clock for the outside of the building.

'There will be a large crowd for this new zebra crossing on Friday at noon already, you see, sir,' she explained. 'And they'll gather to see it, and then, what a thrill! At exactly twelve, our wonderful new clock will strike the hour for the very first time. They will all look up in delighted surprise, and there you will be, leaning out of the window and waving! I know it's a bit wicked to distract attention from what the police are doing, but I'm sure once they see the amazing effect our wonderful clock has on the proceedings, they won't be cross with us one bit!'

And finally, Miss Sibert returns to the wax museum, letting herself in by the door in the side alley. As she walked down Russell Place, she had a feeling she was being followed, but whenever she glanced back she saw nothing out of the ordinary: just a few shoppers, a stationary car and a messenger boy carrying a box marked 'CAKE'.

'Hello?' she calls into the darkness as she shuts the door, her eyes not yet adapted. It is always the same, stepping in here: she has to wait, blinking, until the looming black shapes (waxworks under sheets) become more detailed silhouettes in the gloom.

If she were to ask herself the question directly, she would be forced to admit she is quite afraid of being cooped up with a known maniac in such a macabre setting, which is why she never does ask herself that question. Instead she keeps cheerful by remembering that tomorrow at noon, a policeman will stand on a new zebra crossing in front of hundreds of onlookers. Then Miss Lennon will suddenly exclaim, in a horrified manner, 'Take your hands off me, Inspector!' and at that precise moment a clock will chime, and Geoffrey Chaucer will emerge unstoppably from the crowd, to screams and panic, and the man who killed Terence Chambers will be struck down in cold blood just as her *liebling* Terry was.

'*Terry*,' she sighs, lost in the happy thought. '*Liebling.*'

'Boo!' says Chaucer. He has crept up on her, dressed in a musty, moth-eaten robe that for untold decades adorned the effigy of Cardinal Wolsey.

She barely flinches. He has done something similar every day. 'I think I see Inspector Steine while I am out,' she says offhandedly. 'You are acquainted with him, perhips, Mr Chow-tza?'

Chaucer gives her a look of total, blank sincerity. 'No, but I hate him,' he says. 'I can't explain it, but if I ever saw this Inspector Steine, I think I'd want to kill him.'

Nine

For the third time that morning, Sergeant Baines left his desk in the entrance hall of the police station. He'd had enough of this. He flipped open the hinged flap of the counter and let it fall with a bang. And he didn't care who heard it. Since *seven o'clock* a wasp of a reporter had been conspicuously waiting outside the door, lounging against a pillar. Dressed in a distinctive white raincoat and a brown trilby hat, this man was, of course, Clive Hoskisson of the *Daily Mirror.*

'You!' said Sergeant Baines from the doorway, wagging an admonitory finger.

'Sergeant Baines,' said Hoskisson politely, but without standing straight. If anything, he leaned more heavily.

Baines harrumphed. 'Look, you,' he said, irritated. 'I've told you before. Hop it.'

'Oh, that again,' said Hoskisson.

'Yes, *that again.* Have I not asked you *not* to lean against that pillar? I believe I have.'

'You have indeed.'

'I have said, in plain terms, do not lean against that pillar. I have also politely asked you to sling your hook. Now, for the last time, sonny, buzz off.'

'And I have replied, Sergeant, that I have every right to lean here if I choose,' said the reporter. 'I refer you to the Highways Act of 1950, which clearly states in Paragraph Sixteen ... ' But the desk sergeant had turned on his heel and returned indoors, so there was no need for Hoskisson to quote the exact wording of the Act in question, which was just as well, since it had no bearing at all on the current situation (it covered, in exhaustive detail, the laws concerning cattle grids).

It was typical of Hoskisson to stand his ground robustly. For one thing, he had every right, as a member of the press, to loiter outside the station, in hopes of confronting Inspector Steine. For another, refusal to budge was his defining characteristic: in fact, he was known in certain Fleet Street circles as the Human Limpet. 'Oh, give it up, Hoskisson!' was the regular cry of his colleagues and counterparts alike. 'Let it go!' But he was proud of his adhesive qualities, especially where stories were concerned. As for popularity, he didn't care what people thought of him at all.

This was just as well, since he was universally disliked. Even his editor at the *Mirror* had serious reservations. For preference, such a high-circulation paper would employ a crime correspondent of some personal flamboyance who would not only mix with criminals but boast in print of his connections; who would run up a vast expense account entertaining the bigwigs at Scotland Yard; who would appear on television drunkenly waving a cigarette, giving outrageous, headline-grabbing opinions of Old Bailey verdicts. For such a self-publicist, the editor would bump up the salary and gladly print a regular picture byline. But Hoskisson had no desire to play the fame game, and the *Mirror* just had to make do with a conscientious and incorruptible crime reporter whose main talent was stickability and whose current unbending goal was to expose a genuinely shocking story of police incompetence shored up by a bent establishment.

'It's a very big story, sir,' Hoskisson would explain. 'Inspector Steine is a complete fraud and also a coward, and I am working on collecting the evidence that he killed Terence Chambers in cold blood.' Hoskisson kept his cards close to his chest, for fear the newsroom boys would jump the gun and print too soon. But he had tracked down two witnesses willing to state that at the time of the celebrated milk-bar incident, Steine had shot Chambers *before the news of the bodies at the Metropole had been delivered.*

In the pocket of his raincoat Hoskisson had a list of all the people present when the shooting occurred – a list that included the name Pandora Holden, better known to the dairy-aware British public as the Milk Girl. She had appeared on a thousand billboards sucking milk through a straw; she had opened fêtes and jamborees; she was a human embodiment of health, vitamins and (above all) an opaque fatty bovine mammary secretion available quite cheaply for daily delivery to your doorstep. He quite understood why the *Mirror* would love her to go on record. Imagine the picture on the front page. Imagine 'STEINE IS LIAR, SAYS MILK GIRL'. But according to the Milk Marketing office in London, Miss Holden had recently quit the post and they refused to help him locate her. Their paths, alas, were very unlikely to cross by chance.

Sergeant Baines appeared at the door of the police station again.

'Off! Pillar! You!' he barked.

'Tell Inspector Steine I want to see him,' Hoskisson called to the desk sergeant's retreating back. 'He can't avoid me for ever.'

And then, as he leaned his shoulder more heavily into the pillar, it happened. The miracle.

'Did you say Inspector Steine?' said a female voice behind him. 'So this *is* the police station? Thank goodness!'

He turned around, and was about to snappily point out the telltale blue lamp suspended above the doorway (with the word 'POLICE' written on it) when he saw that the speaker was a charismatic young woman with cropped dark hair, clutching an envelope. A small golden dog sat at her feet, with a tatty piece of string attached to its collar. The dog looked up at him with an expectant expression and wagged its tail.

'Sorry about the dog,' said the girl, blushing. 'It's a long story, but he insisted on coming.'

'That's all right,' said Hoskisson. 'I like dogs. Don't I know you from somewhere?'

At long last, the reporter relinquished his leaning position and stood upright. He held out his hand to introduce himself.

'Hallelujah!' came (faintly) the voice of Sergeant Baines.

It was the answer to Hoskisson's prayers: it was the Milk Girl.

———

At Inspector Steine's house in the Queen's Park area, Twitten let himself in with the door key, feeling like a burglar. He was never comfortable in such situations: being alone in someone else's house. At his lodgings in Clifton Terrace Mrs Thorpe was always urging him, 'Use the wireless when I'm not here, Constable. Watch the television! Boil an egg! You are a paying guest!' But he wouldn't dream of doing any of that.

Softly shutting the inspector's front door behind him, he surveyed the rather elegant hallway with surprise. Although he had never tried to picture Inspector Steine's dwelling arrangements, this house was still somehow far more tasteful than he'd expected.

'Gosh,' he said aloud. In his days as a dedicated reader of educational *I-Spy* books, he had very much enjoyed *I-Spy Antique Furniture*, and the knowledge gained from this excellent booklet had stood him in good stead. It took him no time at all to recognise the inspector's pristine walnut console table as genuine Hepplewhite, and his cherry-wood grandfather clock as late Georgian, and he was just standing back to admire both of these splendid pieces when he was startled to hear a faint 'Thump!' followed by a 'Shhh!'

He froze. Oh, flipping hedgehogs, was Geoffrey Chaucer in the house? The man who beheaded policemen? The muffled thump noise had sounded like a cat jumping down onto a rug. But the 'Shhh!' could only have been human in origin. Was the rich patina on this beautiful grandfather clock about to be spattered with his own arterial blood as he was hacked down in this well-appointed vestibule? Was this attractive Hepplewhite console table the last thing he would see in this life? Would his head be later discovered in a large pan on the range in the scullery?

'Hello?' he called, in a low tone. 'Hello, kitty? Hello, puss, puss, puss?'

Stealthily, he opened the door to the front room. Light from a tall bay window illuminated a charmingly decorated parlour containing a piano and an expensive radiogram, but no cat. Shutting the door again quietly, he moved to the door to the dining room, and it was just as he began to turn the polished doorknob that he heard a further human noise, this one a bit like a gasp.

There was nothing for it. For the first time in his career as a policeman, he drew his truncheon. The resulting paperwork would be onerous, but he had no choice. If only he could remember the training for situations like this! But the form of words seemed to have vanished from his memory. 'Crikey,' he whispered to himself. 'Good luck, Peregrine.' Then he turned the handle and thrust open the door with such force that it banged against some rather desirable oak panelling within.

'Police!' he yelled. 'Police with bally truncheons!'

'Stay back!' yelled a woman's voice. 'It's only us!'

'Police!' he cried again, excitedly looking around and perceiving only one figure in the room, near the fireplace: a figure that was holding a cat in its arms and was self-evidently not the madman Geoffrey Chaucer because it was the beautiful Adelaide Vine.

'Drop the cat!' he commanded wildly.

'Constable Twitten?' she said, with a little sigh of relief. 'Oh, thank goodness. You really scared me.'

'I said, drop the cat!' he said. 'You didn't drop the cat, Miss Vine, and I told you to.' Twitten was trying – without success – to assume authority over the scene.

She tilted her head, as if in thought. She was extremely calm. 'Why would you want me to drop Johann Sebastian?'

'I don't know! I don't bally know!'

'*Miaow?*' said the cat musically, looking up at Adelaide.

'Shhh!' said Adelaide, again, and placed him gently on the floor. 'There you are,' she said. Then she smiled at Twitten. 'You really did scare me just then, Constable. I thought the intruder had come back.'

He scanned the room. What had she been doing here? Why had this wily woman broken into Inspector Steine's house? Well, the answer to this question was all too apparent. On the dining table stood a half-empty box labelled 'PROPERTY OF BROADMOOR', alongside a bottle of lighter fluid and an ashtray containing a half-dozen blackened matches. In the fireplace behind her, telltale embers shrivelled and glowed.

'What intruder?' he said.

'Whoever was here when I arrived, Constable. I must have interrupted him burning these files.' She pointed at the ashes in the grate. 'Look. Still warm!'

The truncheon in Twitten's hand stayed raised. Flaming hedgehogs, this woman was such a brazen liar! He had caught her virtually in the act of destroying evidence and she had instantly invented a cock-and-bull story to cover it.

'Miss Vine, please tell me why you're here.'

'I was hoping to see my uncle, of course. He gave me a key a couple of months ago.'

'You've been burning the contents of that box.'

She seemed puzzled, but then she laughed. She really was a tip-top fibber. Having observed the masterly Mrs Groynes at close quarters for three months, Twitten could recognise true quality when he saw it.

'No, no,' Adelaide said, smiling. 'That wasn't me. I just explained. About the intruder. He might still come back, so it's wonderful that you're here with your terrifying truncheon to protect me.'

Looking him steadily in the eye, she drew out a dining chair and sat down. 'So,' she said sweetly. 'You've got it all wrong, I'm afraid.'

Twitten sat down opposite, instinctively snatching the box away from her as he did so. Glancing inside, he saw it was still about half-full, and on the top was a file labelled 'Doris Fuller' – a name that rang no bells.

Rather childishly, he dropped the box to the floor beside him – but with great maturity managed not to stick out his tongue or chant '*Nah-nah-na-nah-nah!*' as he did so.

Back at the station, Miss Lennon bustled into Inspector's Steine's office with a clipboard. She found him staring out of the window, feeling sorry for himself. He felt he had very good cause. Good grief, a man puts his life on the line to rid the country of a dangerous criminal and this is how he is treated? Thrown about in the back of a van, jostled by his own officers, and subjected to gross impertinence? Meanwhile, in the world beyond he is painted not as a heroic champion of justice but as a *man of violence*, and on top of everything a reporter in a white coat dogs his every step like a confounded nemesis.

'INSPECTOR?'

He turned to face Miss Lennon. Yesterday, he might have assumed a more cheerful expression for her benefit, but he felt they had now passed beyond the need for such pretence. (He had known her roughly twenty-four hours.)

'Not now, Miss Lennon,' he said sadly. 'Perhaps later. I'm not in the mood.'

'I'm afraid it can't WAIT, sir. I need to update you on the arrangements for TOMORROW. Perhaps they will CHEER YOU UP.'

She gave him an encouraging smile and patted her clipboard. 'I think, considering the unusually tight time constraints, we have much to CELEBRATE, Inspector, but I will begin with the BAD NEWS. I have drawn a BLANK with the NUNS.'

He folded his hands. If she was determined to talk about these arrangements, the sooner he paid attention, the sooner it would be over.

'Nuns,' he repeated. 'So we have no nuns, you say?'

'That's right.'

'Well, that's a shame. But to be honest, Miss Lennon, I wasn't convinced nuns were necessary, and it was the penguins I was most looking forward to.'

Pulling a face, she looked down at her clipboard. Apparently there was more bad news.

'I'm afraid, sir, that the PENGUINS TOO were impossible to procure at such short notice.'

'Ugh!' The inspector threw up his hands. 'I can't even have *penguins*?'

'I'm afraid not.'

'I ask you, Miss Lennon, why did I bother to shoot Terence Chambers? Why? Why did I bother, if this is the thanks I get?'

'I sympathise, sir. But the Zoological Gardens in Regent's Park were quite SHORT WITH ME when I put my request to them. I apologise for raising the prospect of penguins without checking beforehand, it's really all MY FAULT. But they did once supply an ELEPHANT for a party I organised in LONDON for the COMMISSIONER so I suppose I took too much for granted.'

'So you did explain to them the penguins were for *me*? For Inspector Steine, milk-bar hero?'

'I did.'

Tears of self-pity pricked the inspector's eyes. 'Well, in that case I give up,' he said sulkily. 'I really do.'

'However, in all other respects I have been SUCCESSFUL. The Belisha BEACONS are already in place and generating interest. ORANGE, I'm afraid,' she added hastily, before he could ask the inevitable question. 'They said orange was NON-NEGOTIABLE. The council will arrange for the ROAD-PAINTING to be done this evening, taking advantage of the break in the rain. The shop Gosling's is by coincidence installing today a new chiming CLOCK on its broad London Road elevation which will STRIKE THE HOUR for the first time tomorrow when you set foot on the new crossing. Additionally, I have secured the SERVICES of four heavily accented French ONION-SELLERS in traditional garb, and have also acquired a very large number of black-and-white chequered flags that can be distributed to the CHILDREN.' She lowered the clipboard. 'I promise it will be a day that Brighton will NEVER FORGET, Inspector.'

He pulled a face. 'I don't know,' he said. 'I'm beginning to think … '

'Think WHAT, Inspector?'

'Well, is it really worth the risk of appearing in public?'

Miss Lennon gasped, as if shocked to hear such lily-livered qualms from him of all people.

'I mean, no one's caught that Chaucer man yet. It would be a perfect opportunity for him to get to me.'

She sat down and took a deep breath. 'Inspector,' she said quietly. 'I completely understand your misgivings, of course I do.'

'Thank you.'

'But our madman is HARDLY going to make an appear-ance THERE, is he, sir?'

'Well, he might. And if he does … ?'

If the inspector was hoping for absolution, it didn't come. He could see from her fallen face how appalled she was by both his cowardice and his ingratitude.

'Of course,' she said briskly, 'if it's your genuine wish I will immediately CANCEL EVERYTHING. I can explain to everyone that you are, after all, afraid to SHOW YOUR FACE.'

'What? No!'

'It truly doesn't matter to me that I have worked SO HARD to put this together. My job is merely to SERVE.'

'Oh, Miss Lennon. I'm sorry.'

'But I was SO hoping you would do this for the sake of your PUBLIC IMAGE, Inspector. It infuriates me that the public sees you – you gentle, honourable, caring man – as a man of violence. I RESENT and DETEST it!'

'You really think that if I do this, they'll start seeing me as a man of sensible road safety enforcement instead?'

'They will. Trust me.' She took his hand and held it, looking him directly in the face. 'Sir, I promise the people of Brighton will link the name of Inspector Steine with the words "zebra crossing" FOR EVER.'

The inspector extricated his hand. He still looked glum. 'I'm not sure people's attitudes are so easily manipulated, Miss Lennon. They have minds of their own.'

'That is CHARITABLE of you, sir. But in fact, it is sadly true, people are SHEEP.'

'Well, if you say so,' he said. 'But I'm glad to say that *I'm* not easily led, and I never have been.'

Miss Lennon regarded him, speechless. Then, with a little cough, she turned and left the room, shutting the door behind her. She patted the framed picture on her desk. This was a moment to be treasured for the rest of her life: Inspector

Steine claiming he was *not a sheep* when tomorrow she would lead him, frisking and *baaa*-ing, straight to his own personal abattoir.

Pandora was very happy to have a cup of tea with the reporter she'd met outside the police station. She had caught an extremely early train down from Norfolk, and had not stopped for refreshment. She didn't normally drink tea with strangers, especially representatives of the press, but once she had enquired and it turned out that Twitten was not expected back until later, she found she had time on her hands.

'He's got one of his blooming driving lessons at half-past eleven,' said the bluff Sergeant Baines. 'And I hope he don't miss it, because I changed my shift specially. The look on Sergeant Masefield's face when young Twitten settles himself behind the steering wheel and says: "Remind me what these pedals do, sir." Ha! It's blooming priceless.'

And so Pandora had accepted Hoskisson's offer of tea – partly because of Twitten's inconvenient absence from the station, but also because of the reporter's interesting reaction when he first recognised her. Normally people said, 'You're the Milk Girl – wait 'til I tell Mavis!' But Hoskisson had said, 'You're the Milk Girl – you're at the top of my list!'

As they sat in the tea room now, it occurred to Hoskisson that he'd never met anyone like Pandora before. Normally, he divided interview subjects into two types: ones who didn't mind talking about themselves, and ones who hated it and required a lot of coaxing. Pandora, however, represented a whole new category: people who were incapable of talking about anything else, and positively enjoyed seeing someone making a note of every word she uttered. Within twenty minutes of sitting down, he knew all about Pandora's long-standing crush on Peregrine Twitten, her schoolgirl years at an exclusive Brighton clifftop school, her year as the Milk Girl, her place at Oxford to study classics, and the clever way that Blakeney (the local station-master's dog) had managed to sneak into her compartment on the Milk Train at five o'clock in the morning. Just fifteen minutes after meeting Pandora, his notebook was half-full, and they hadn't even touched on the day of the Milk Bar Riot.

'Shall we get another pot?' he said, waving to a waitress. All this time he had been expecting Pandora to ask him what story he was working on. He was braced to come clean about it, if necessary, but she simply wasn't curious. When he had explained that he worked for the *Mirror*, she had immediately launched into a description of a large picture of herself the *Mirror* had once printed, listing the errors in the caption. And then, when he artfully mentioned the shooting at the House of Hanover Milk Bar, she happily launched into yet another story. For her, this last narrative was of precisely the same significance as all the others, but for him it certainly wasn't. It was – potentially – journalistic dynamite.

Was this *it*? Was he about to secure the story 'STEINE IS LIAR, SAYS MILK GIRL'? He listened to Pandora Holden's critical first-hand account of the milk-bar incident with mounting agitation.

'You see, I was sheltering under a table,' she explained. 'It was all very frightening, Mr Hoskisson. And my dress was ruined.'

'Oh, dear,' he said, purposefully not looking up from his notes.

'Someone had thrown a rock through the window and there was glass everywhere. The police cordon outside was keeping back a rioting crowd – and the noise! The noise was really awful. And that poor cow—'

'Did you say "poor *cow*"?'

'Yes!' She rolled her eyes. 'There was always a cow; that's one of the reasons I gave up the job as Milk Girl. You can tell your lovely readers that I was plagued by cows, Mr Hoskisson. This particular cow was called Pansy. Anyway, you probably know all the details about what happened with Mr Chambers, there was so much in the papers! When I close my eyes, sometimes I still hear the shots!'

She paused, waiting for him to catch up. 'Am I going too fast?'

'No, no.'

'Did you get the cow's name?'

'Er, yes.' He scanned back a page or two. 'Pansy?'

'That's right. Good. Well, and nowadays Inspector Steine is everywhere on the television and on the wireless, isn't he? I expect that's why he won't agree to see you: he's become such a big celebrity, you see. After the shooting I decided enough was enough, and I resigned as the Milk Girl and you can tell your readers that I don't regret the loss of attention one bit and that I hope to be married soon to a lovely young police officer, while at the same time continuing my budding career as an artist.'

Hoskisson glanced up at her. He had to be careful how he put this, so as not to arouse suspicion.

'Going back a bit,' he said. 'You're saying that you witnessed the actual shooting? I can't imagine what that was like.'

'Can't you?'

It was the first time she had queried him, and for a moment he was worried. Was she suspicious?

But then she smiled and dispelled any anxiety. 'Well, the thing is,' she said, in a friendly and confidential tone, 'it wasn't *a bit* like everyone said afterwards.'

'No?' In a bravado show of nonchalance, Hoskisson reached for his cup and took a sip of tea, still with his eyes cast downwards. When he replaced the cup in the saucer, there was a telltale rattle of china (from his trembling hand).

'The papers all said the inspector knew about what Chambers had done when he shot him! Do you know, though, it's a funny thing—'

Hoskisson closed his eyes. *Here it comes,* he thought. *I can quote the Milk Girl that when Steine shot Chambers, he did not know what had occurred at the Metropole! He just shot him anyway! I've got him! I've got him!*

'—but in fact, he didn't even know who he was!'

'*What?*' Hoskisson's jaw dropped.

'It's true! I know it sounds too funny for words, but Inspector Steine didn't even know that the man *was* Terence Chambers, not until afterwards. Also, it all happened at about a quarter to two, and not at noon, but I suppose when they labelled it High Noon at the Milk Bar they were using poetic licence, which we learned about in English for the General Certificate.'

She stopped and sipped her tea, while Hoskisson tried hard to remain calm.

'Are you sure about this, Miss Holden?'

'Oh, yes. I remember looking at the clock. It was one-forty-seven.'

'No, I mean about the other details of the shooting.'

'Absolutely! And I'm so pleased you're interested, Mr Hoskisson. No one else has wanted to hear about it. But what happened was, this man came in and walked up to the inspector and announced he was *from the Metropole.*'

'Those exact words?'

'Yes. Like it was a code. *I'm from the Metropole.* It was a bit odd. I was very close, you see, so I heard him even above the noise from outside. The inspector studied him for a while, then reached into a briefcase and seemed to be studying something in there as well – as if he'd got written instructions or something! So it didn't happen straight away. Then eventually Inspector Steine pulled out the gun and shot Chambers twice in the chest. It was *awful.* And he didn't look pleased with himself – not at all. In fact, when he put down the gun, he said, "Now someone should arrest me."'

'Oh, my God.'

'I know. Isn't it peculiar? Are you all right?'

'He asked for someone to *arrest* him? This is fantastic, Miss Holden! I mean, how awful for you to have to see all this, a lovely young woman like yourself with such a promising future ahead of her.'

'Thank you. Yes, it was.'

'But let's get this clear. You are saying that at this point Inspector Steine not only didn't know what Chambers had done, he didn't know who he was?'

'Yes.'

'Oh, my God.'

'But he soon did, of course, because there was a nice young reporter there who jumped up and said: "That was Terence Chambers; you shot Terence Chambers!" And I was saying, "I've never heard of Terence Chambers; who's Terence Chambers?" because obviously I don't know much about such things, I live in Norfolk, did I mention that? And then Peregrine – that's Constable Twitten – came running in with news about all the dead bodies at the Metropole. And then I suppose it was quite comical in a way, because Inspector Steine kept saying, no, the man *wasn't* Terence Chambers—'

'You're sure?'

'Oh, yes. He was very emphatic about it, but Peregrine and the reporter kept saying, "Yes, it *is* Terence Chambers, and you've been a bally hero!" And the inspector was saying, "*No, it isn't*," and so – really, are you all right, Mr Hoskisson? You look a bit peculiar.'

'No, I'm very well, thank you. Please go on. You've had such a packed and interesting life for such a well-brought-up young lady, Miss Holden. I'm a bit overwhelmed.'

'Well, that was it, really. After a little time, the inspector seemed to accept he had done this heroic thing, and told everyone not to bother about arresting him, it wasn't necessary after all. And then he cheered up and the papers called it High Noon at the Milk Bar and that's how it will be remembered, when in fact, as I said, it all happened at quite a different time! It *is* quite funny, looking back, though – the way at first Inspector Steine didn't have a clue what he'd done!'

Back at Inspector Steine's house, Twitten and Adelaide Vine sat opposite each other. Her turquoise coat was a perfect complement to her chestnut hair and hazel eyes. It occurred to Twitten that there would be another unexplained rush to the Mantle department at Gosling's today – this time in search of beautiful blues and greens.

'I suppose I should go,' she said, standing up.

'No, please don't do that, Miss Vine,' said Twitten. 'Please sit down again. I haven't decided yet whether to arrest you.'

She obeyed, prettily, but demurred. 'Oh, surely that's out of the question, Constable. I've explained what happened. The intruder!'

Twitten realised he had never spoken to her one-to-one before. It was troubling, and he wondered if he was up to it. How was it possible that he and she were roughly the same age? The difference in their mental outlook, and in their breadth of personal experience, was phenomenal. He had divided much of his (quite recent) adolescence between a) enthusiastically compiling a scholarly directory of literary locked-room mysteries (with sophisticated cross-referencing), and b) trying to establish a formula for calculating a fair target cricket score for the team batting second in a limited overs match interrupted by weather or other circumstances; meanwhile, she had spent all of hers as an active member of a gang of real-life con artists who tricked innocent women out of their money, slaughtered them, and melted their bodies in acid.

'Miss Vine, I think you should understand one thing,' he said, at last.

'And what's that?'

'Your womanly wiles. They're useless against me. I am impervious to them.'

She laughed. 'Oh, I know *that*, Constable!'

'You do?'

'Of course. I know that Constable Twitten is much too clever to be taken in by – what did you call them – my *wiles*?'

This was very difficult. On the one hand, it was important to be blunt with this woman. But on the other, she was bally beautiful and she was laughing at him. Adding to his discomfort was the unexpected fact that she was not even bothering to deny that she was a devious person.

'Yes, I call them wiles,' he said steadily. His cheeks might be burning, but he knew he had to be clear. 'Miss Vine, I have seen their effect on both Inspector Steine and Sergeant Brunswick. And since we are being frank, I don't blame you for using your beauty – your extreme beauty, if I may say so – on men who are so pathetically susceptible to it. I mean, the inspector and the sergeant are quite pathetically weak-minded when buttered up by a pretty woman, aren't they?'

'Yes. I'm afraid they are.'

'You're enjoying this, aren't you?'

'Of course I am. And I promise I shan't use any wiles on you.'

'Good.'

'Although I feel obliged to point out something, *since we are being frank*.'

'What?'

'Well, if I *were* using my wiles right now, you wouldn't know it. That's how wiles work, you see.'

This was worrying because it was true. But he decided to ignore it for now.

'But tell me one thing,' she said.

'What?'

'If you aren't affected by my womanly wiles, why were you so upset yesterday when I ignored you?'

He stiffened. 'I wasn't. I hardly noticed.'

She raised an eyebrow.

'Oh, all right, I thought you were being bally rude.'

As he said it, he heard how unconvincing it sounded. He was also aware that somehow the tables had turned and instead of Adelaide Vine answering his questions, he seemed to be answering hers.

'Miss Vine, I need to ask you about a certain umbrella that was taken from the scene of a murder,' he said, producing his notebook.

'Well, I don't want to talk about umbrellas,' she said, briskly. 'So put that thing away. I need to ask you something much more important.'

'What?'

'Why are you so loyal to the despicable Mrs Groynes?'

At the police canteen, Brunswick finished his cup of tea, and the second of his currant buns. On his way out of the station he had collected three notes left for him with Sergeant Baines. One was from Mr Winslow apologising for his drunken state the night before. One was from Mrs Thorpe inviting him to dinner at seven o'clock. The last was from Adelaide Vine requesting help. Could he meet her this evening at the old wax museum at six o'clock? She couldn't explain right now (she said), but she felt she was in danger, and he was the only person she could turn to, being a kind man with a big heart, who wasn't quick to judge a friendless young woman such as herself.

Had Mrs Thorpe witnessed the way Brunswick prioritised these notes, she would have been crushed. Whichever way he shuffled them, Adelaide Vine's kept coming out on top. Even worse, Winslow's was usually the next one down.

Naturally, the sergeant recollected Twitten's words of warning in regard to Adelaide. But then, with ease, he set them aside. Was there the slightest proof of her involvement in

Professor Milhouse's death? No. And besides, the words 'kind man' and 'big heart' described him to a T! Had anyone ever accused Constable Brainbox of being kind or big-hearted? No, they flaming well had not.

―――――――

Twitten felt more uncomfortable than ever once the subject turned to Mrs Groynes. For three months he had railed (mentally) at his strange and undeserved predicament. 'No one knows what I know about our charlady's criminal empire! I can't tell them because they won't flipping believe me! Everyone believes I was hypnotised!' All this time, he had yearned for a sympathetic confidante. But now that he had the chance to discuss the wickedness of Mrs Groynes with Adelaide Vine, he found he was tongue-tied. Shouldn't he be demanding to know what had happened to Barrow-Boy Cecil? What if the poor mutilated bunny-man were still alive somewhere? But if he pressed this line of inquiry, wouldn't that prove that he *was* loyal to Mrs Groynes? It would certainly prove he was in her confidence.

'I'm not sure that loyal is the right word,' he said eventually, with care. 'I mean, I have grown to like Mrs Groynes, it's true. But if you know so much, then you'll know I've been completely unable to expose her true nature. She played a brilliant trick that made it seem to the entire world that I'd been hypnotised onstage at the Hippodrome into believing she was a criminal. In her own words, she stitched me up like a bally kipper!'

'Pah!' said Adelaide contemptuously.

Twitten was shocked. 'I resent that immensely, Miss Vine.'

'Well, if you thought about things properly, you wouldn't. A "*Pah*" is what such a pathetic answer deserves. I sent you a photograph on Tuesday – a photograph that could expose her – and I know for a fact you've done nothing with it.'

'So it was you! Well, I guessed as much.'

'And … ?'

'And I did do something, if you must know. I sent it away for safe keeping.'

Again, his own words sounded hollow to him. What was happening here? It was like being cross-examined in a court-room drama by a merciless barrister over whether or not you stole a postal order from a fellow naval cadet. 'Look, I haven't bally decided what to do with it yet. And you hurt a photographer in retrieving that photograph, you know. He had to go to hospital and he kept saying "Ow, my head!"'

'I repeat, Constable Twitten: have you done anything with the photograph? Yes or no!'

'No!'

'Thank you.' Adelaide sighed. 'I need to explain something important to you, Constable, and it might be hard to take, but I advise you to listen.' She sounded very serious. 'You believe that, in your cleverness, you discern the hidden causes behind what other people do.'

'Yes, I suppose so. That's correct. My father is a noted psychologist, and I like to think I have picked up a working knowledge of the human psyche from the many scholarly books and articles I've read.'

'Yes, I know. Mister Harold showed me the book you recommended to him and I could see how it would appeal to you. But there is a significant gap in your understanding, Constable: you don't apply it to your own behaviour. I spent a lot of time talking with Professor Milhouse before he died, and I now regret I had to shoot him because I think you would have benefitted very much from talking to him.'

'You admit that you shot him?'

'Of course.' She pulled a face. 'You knew I did. That's not what we're talking about.'

'Why did you shoot him?'

She waved the question away. 'We'll come back to that. You know about his field of interest: he was convinced that people behave according to their deepest desires, even while shopping for clothes pegs. In the con artist's world, of course, this is hardly a revelation, but still, it was interesting to hear it being given so-called scientific validity. Knowing precisely where people are vulnerable – where to target them – is the key to the con man's success. I used to meet the professor every evening in the listening booth to hear about his theories. He thought I was his disciple, whereas in fact I was light years ahead of him. I played the part because I knew what *he* wanted, deep down, you see.' She made a face. 'And I know what you want, too.'

Had something happened to Adelaide Vine's vocabulary? She was using words like 'discern' and 'significant', and phrases such as 'scientific validity'. But she had also just accused Twitten of not being as clever as he thought he was, which was jolly hurtful but at the same time (weirdly) made him inclined to trust her. And now she seemed to be waiting for him to respond.

'Well, I was interested in the professor's work, too!' He sounded petulant, and wished he didn't. 'I've been reading about motivation research for the past few weeks, in fact, and I've been trying to explain it to anyone who would listen!'

'That's all very commendable. Well done.' She sounded so patronising! 'So you will understand how I deduce that what you really want, dear Constable, is not to expose Mrs Groynes.'

'What? No! No, that's not right at all. Hold on—'

'You admit you have done nothing with the photograph. Prevaricate as much as you like, but that's the truth. Now, tell me what you've done about the madman on the loose, threatening the life of the inspector?'

'I've done a few things. I mean, I came here to look at the contents of this bally box!'

'Pathetic,' she said, waving her hand.

'I know that the psychologist who interviewed him used to work for Terence Chambers and that she helped the madman escape.'

'But what have you actually done?'

'Look, I really resent this. Everything has happened very quickly and I am pursuing inquiries—'

'I'm sorry, but you need to hear this. You can see what's happening here, and you have not acted to prevent it. Therefore, Constable, you *want* Inspector Steine to be killed.'

'No!'

'And why not? He annoys you; he is stupid; by sheer luck he always seems to emerge from the blackest situation completely untarnished – indeed, often with his reputation miraculously enhanced! You are cleverer than him by far. It is preposterous that you are a mere constable, working for such a dolt. And as for the sweet but silly Sergeant Brunswick—'

'Are you saying I'm ambitious, Miss Vine?' Twitten thundered, leaping to his feet. 'Because if so … '

But there his protest trailed off. Ambitious? She had not even said the word. She sat back, arms folded, saying nothing, while his mind reeled and he sat down again.

Flipping hedgehogs. Ambitious? Mentally, he staggered and flailed. It was as if a thick veil had been slashed, letting the light of truth come flooding through. Because he *was* ambitious! Why had he never admitted it to himself before? Why had he told himself all this time that he was content to compromise his true worth, deferring to people who not only underappreciated him but actually belittled him? Why had he endured all those ignorant and anti-intellectual pooh-poohs?

'Now, we come to Mrs Groynes,' said Adelaide. 'I can see you're on the back foot slightly, Constable, but you'll just have to keep up as best you can. The important matter is Mrs Groynes to whom you *do* feel loyalty, whether you admit it or not. It's my job to inform you that you shouldn't. How she manipulates you is by confiding in you and talking to you as an equal, which flatters your ego while costing her nothing. In fact, she gets pleasure from taunting you with such confidences.'

'You're wrong,' he said feebly. 'You know nothing about it.'

'But think about her actual behaviour, Constable Twitten, and ask yourself how loyal she is to you. She makes a fool of you every day, which is profoundly disrespectful. She commits heinous felonies with impunity, making a mockery of your vocation. You accept this situation because you respect her cleverness and because she represents some sort of quasi-maternal figure who doles out sugary bakery products. For these absurd and paltry reasons, you are letting her cynically ruin your potentially stellar career in the police force.'

Twitten sat back, blinking. His father had told him about breakthroughs in psychoanalysis, and he'd never quite understood until now. He felt as if there were no floor beneath his feet.

'Oh, my God, Miss Vine,' he gasped. 'You're right.'

'Thank you.'

'You have completely overturned my idea of myself vis-à-vis my responsibilities to my gifts as a clever policeman.'

'I know.' She looked at the clock on the mantelpiece. 'But I should get back to work now, and I believe you have a driving lesson.'

'Golly.' It was all he could do not to plead weakly, 'Don't go.' On top of everything else, Adelaide looked devastatingly attractive to him all of a sudden.

She gave him an encouraging look. 'I know,' she said quite kindly. 'This has all been a bit of a shock, hasn't it? Take your time, I'll let myself out.'

'Did you know I was going to be here this morning?'

'Of course. A little bird told me. It worked out perfectly.'

'What have you done with Barrow-Boy Cecil?'

'You don't want to know. But in any case, this isn't about Cecil, Constable. Or about the devious Mrs Groynes. It's about you.' She stood up. 'But in case you're still in doubt, it really wasn't me destroying those files earlier. Someone else must be protecting the madman; trying to prevent your finding him. Someone else must want him to kill Inspector Steine. But who? Can't you smell something in the air? I mean, apart from the lighter fuel and the charred paper? It's quite strong, actually.'

He sniffed. She waited. He sniffed again. Oh, surely not?

'It's *Brasso*,' she said. And then, as he whimpered 'Oh, no!' she let herself out, leaving all his certainties shattered.

As she opened the front door, she smiled to herself. In the history of 'womanly wiles', surely no one had ever deployed them more skilfully than that.

Ten

It is Friday morning, and Denise Perks makes her way briskly downhill, through the smaller residential streets east of the railway station, towards the wide and busy carriageway of the London Road, where noiselessly efficient trolley-buses whisk passengers into the centre of town, and where the mighty Gosling's will be open for business in a quarter of an hour's time. Autumn is in the air and after the short dry spell yesterday it is raining again, forming puddles and rivulets. Denise misses Shorty. Until recently they made this morning walk together. But she mustn't get maudlin. The boy is safe, and Mrs Groynes has assured her that normality will very soon be resumed, once Barrow-Boy Cecil is avenged.

'Could it be the Vine woman behind all this?' Denise asked Mrs Groynes last night, at the beginning of a specially convened meeting of the Gosling's Gang.

'No, dear,' Mrs G replied, with a touch of impatience. 'It's *not* bleeding Adelaide Vine. Pardon my language, but I'm a bit sick of hearing it.'

Denise shrugged. 'I'm just saying. Ronnie reminded me that you killed her mum.'

'My money's on that Adelaide skirt, too,' said Stanley-Knife Stanley, looking up from the September issue of *Window Dressing Monthly* (to which he had just subscribed).

'Stanley, put the book down, please, dear.'

'Oh.' He was taken aback. 'Right, boss. A-course.' He folded down the corner of the page he was reading and placed the magazine on the floor.

As Denise now trots downhill towards the London Road, Sid the Doorman emerges from his usual doorway and falls into step. He reaches for her umbrella ('Allow me, Miss Perks?') and holds it over both of them.

'How's Shorty?' he asks, out of the side of his mouth.

'All right, ta, Sid,' she says. 'Vince has got him stowed, but they won't tell me where.'

'Jimmy the Gimp's first day today. Working the blooming lift.'

'I know.'

As they reach the London Road, they spot identical twins Joan and Dorothy arriving at Gosling's from the other direction, trotting through puddles towards the staff side door. Nobody waves, but they are all reassured to see one another. Denise notes that Stanley-Knife Stanley is already at work in one of the windows, arranging dummies of children and toddlers in thermal underwear into an attractive and colourful tableau. A very different side to Stanley is manifesting itself, it must be said. You would expect his windows to be full of shock-faced mannequins staggering back while clutching their crimson-slashed throats. But Stanley has embraced a sunnier aesthetic, and when Mrs Groynes told him to put down his magazine last night, the reason he did so with such reluctance was that he was halfway through an article headlined 'Make a Seasonal Cascade of Autumn Leaves'.

'The site's ready,' remarks Denise, subtly indicating (with a tilt of her head) some official-looking hubbub twenty yards to their right. Sid the Doorman, less subtly, takes a good look, nods his head, and says, 'We're on, then.' The beacons are already flashing on their striped poles, but the crossing itself is out of sight, covered by a loose grey tarpaulin designed to protect its pristine black-and-white paintwork from mud. Council workmen ensure that the traffic drives slowly across the muddy groundsheet; meanwhile other workers are sheltering in doorways nearby, waiting to implement the noonday road closure.

Under a makeshift marquee on the pavement opposite the shop, rain-dampened boxes of little chequered flags have arrived and are being unpacked on a trestle table by unenthusiastic council employees. A similar but smaller marquee is being erected on the Gosling's side, for the 'entertainers'. And from a window on the second floor of Gosling's, directly above this second marquee, Adelaide Vine surveys the whole rainy industrious scene with a beam of satisfaction. For someone who is *not* a devious mastermind, she is giving a very good impression of one.

———

Twitten's own walk downhill to work this morning is of an unusual nature, not just because it's raining again, but because Pandora Holden is with him; also Blakeney the dog, who hampers progress considerably by constantly stopping to cock his leg. This is adorable the first time, but the gleam soon wears off. It's not the urination *per se* that's annoying: it's the stopping.

'Does he have to do that *quite* so often?' Twitten asks impatiently, as the whole party pauses for the fifth time in twenty yards on Dyke Road.

'I think he does, yes. If I try to pull him along, he sits down in protest, so we get on even more slowly.'

'Couldn't you remove the string from his collar? Other dogs aren't on leads.'

'Yes, but other dogs aren't Blakeney. The moment I let him go free, he'll run off and jump onto an excursion coach to Bognor.'

'I need to get to work, Miss Holden!' Under Twitten's arm is an old brown briefcase containing the 'Doris Fuller' file, which he has now read with alarm, and which he needs to discuss with colleagues at the earliest possible juncture. In particular, he must warn Inspector Steine (and he can already hear the chorus of pooh-poohs!) that until Geoffrey Chaucer is caught, he must watch out for, and strenuously avoid, anything with a conspicuous black-and-white pattern on it.

'Of course. I'm sorry.' Pandora isn't really sorry, though. She adjusts her umbrella, looks down at Blakeney and sighs. The more the dog's drawn-out micturition routine holds them up, the more time she can spend with the man she has chosen to marry.

'Look, I'm sorry I didn't call to explain to you about the photograph,' he says. 'I really didn't mean for you to bring it back.' He would like to add, *Why on earth would you think I wanted you to bring it back?* – but he dare not, because Pandora always reacts very badly to being told off.

'I wish you would tell me what's happening, Peregrine. You're so buttoned up!'

'No, I'm not.'

'What's in the briefcase?'

'I can't tell you.'

'You see? And you were very off-hand at dinner last night. Mrs Thorpe had gone to a lot of trouble with that horrible pink *parfait.*'

'Yes, well … ' With Sergeant Brunswick failing to make an appearance at Mrs Thorpe's house last night, the specially made blancmange was best forgotten about. 'Look, I don't even like puddings very much, and besides I wanted to be on my own to think about things, and instead it was like a bally dinner party!'

Pandora nods understandingly, but she is thinking, *This is like a tiff between married people!* It thrills her to think that one day she and Peregrine will have bitter arguments just like this in their own North Oxford detached villa, when she has persuaded him to become an academic, and she is a professional artist with a growing international reputation, and they have two adorably brainy and bespectacled children called Sappho and Caligula (the names are a work in progress.)

'Well, I can tell you're excited about what's in that file, Peregrine. Mrs Thorpe could sense it too at breakfast. But when she asked you, you were quite rude. I really like her, by the way. She manages to be both refined and blowsy at the same time, and she was very kind to take me in for the night, and my little room was lovely. I hope you give Sergeant Brunswick a telling-off today for not coming to dinner and upsetting her. He didn't even telephone to make an excuse! But I suppose some people are just like that. Hurtful to women. I mean, look at you and me. I came all this way for your sake; all the way from *Norfolk*, and you've hardly spoken to me.'

They make a few yards' headway, then stop again for Blakeney. Fed up with all this, Twitten bends down and picks up the dog. The manoeuvre entails passing the briefcase to Pandora for a moment, and as she hands it back, she pouts.

'All right,' he relents. 'I'm sorry. If you want to know, I'll tell you why the file in this case is so bally important, if you promise not to tell anyone. There is a madman on the loose – a madman who attacks policemen.'

'I know that. And I hate it. Why did you have to join the police at all, Peregrine? I begged you not to, and I still don't understand it. And now you might get your head cut off instead of being safe and sound in the Bodleian.'

Finally, they are able to walk downhill at a sensible pace, the little dog quite contentedly surveying the world from his unaccustomed (and bouncy) elevation. Pandora is happy to think of the attractive picture they make – almost like a family group.

Twitten refuses to be drawn into old arguments about why he joined the police in the first place.

'What this file makes clear, Miss Holden,' he continues, 'is that on every occasion Geoffrey Chaucer has killed, there have been three triggers, all coincidentally occurring at the same time; all reminding him of a specific traumatic event in his childhood when police broke in and shot his father.'

'Oh, that's awful. The poor man. The police are like animals sometimes, and I can't imagine why you would—'

Twitten cut her off. 'Well, interestingly, Miss Holden, I looked up the case and the context rather exonerates the police. It seems that the father was a desperate and unstable man, cornered at a London hotel where he was armed and holding his own wife and child as hostages. Several times he stated that he was prepared to kill them. So when the police stormed in they did so, effectively, to save little Geoffrey's life. But either no one has ever explained that to him, or he just doesn't want to hear it. Either way, he thinks of the police as murderers, and sometimes he goes berserk and kills a policeman – but only when three very specific triggers occur simultaneously.'

'What three triggers?'

'Well, this is what Miss Sibert worked out. First, obviously, there has to be a policeman present. But the three triggers are: a woman has to say to this policeman, "Stop touching me! Leave me alone!" Then a clock with Westminster chimes has to start striking the hour. And on top of those two things, the whole scene has to take place in an environment of black-and-white patterns – like a black-and-white floor, or black-and-white striped walls.'

Pandora tips back her head and laughs.

'What's funny?' he asks.

'It's so unlikely, Peregrine! It's so unlikely that all those things could happen at once by chance!'

'Well, they *did* happen all at once right in front of this poor young woman Doris,' he says, indicating the briefcase. 'And now I really *must* get to the office and warn the inspector, because it's my guess that wicked people have sprung Chaucer from prison precisely to set him up to kill again – and Inspector Steine is the target!'

At the Clock Tower, Twitten places Blakeney on the ground and realises, with a pang, that Mrs Groynes had a point: this place does seem sad and dismal without Barrow-Boy Cecil and his jumping bunnies. He can't help looking round, expecting to see the street pedlar after all.

But it is time for them to part – Pandora to return to the railway station; he to proceed downhill. The short walk has been hard for both of them: Pandora has been hoping the whole time that he will compliment her on her appearance (she's wearing a lovely periwinkle blue skirt). Now she hopes he will kiss her goodbye, which is absurd since he has never done that in his life. He shakes her hand firmly instead and wishes her a pleasant journey.

'I'm sure no one could be trying to put all those elements together, Peregrine,' she says, in parting. 'It's just too complicated! If anyone wanted the inspector dead, why wouldn't they just shoot him?'

But Twitten doesn't want to hear this, and darts off towards the police station, glad to see the back of her.

Why is he so cross with Pandora? Well, not just because she brought the photograph straight back to him without checking. There is also the way she blabbed to the man from the *Mirror*. Last night, over dinner, happening to notice Mrs Thorpe's depressed demeanour, Pandora decided to entertain everyone with the amusing tale of her meeting with Clive Hoskisson in the tea room – how she sat down with him and described what actually happened when Terence Chambers was shot.

'He was *so interested*, Mrs Thorpe,' she gushed. 'He said he would write a big article about it in his newspaper. He said mine was an outstandingly helpful first-hand account, and that they might put me on the front page. He seemed to love the detail about how the inspector didn't actually know it was Chambers he had shot. I think no one ever mentioned that before.'

As it turned out, Pandora had seriously overestimated how much her anecdote would amuse her fellow diners. While Twitten sat frozen in horror, the story made no impact at all on Mrs Thorpe, who continued to dwell on her humiliation at the hands of the sergeant. 'Are you *sure* Sergeant Brunswick didn't say anything to you?' she asked Twitten for at least the fifth time. 'And why are you gaping like that, Constable? Do close your mouth, at least.'

As Twitten now canters downhill towards the police station, his annoyance with his *ersatz* girlfriend gives way to profound apprehension. If there is a dastardly plot against Mrs Groynes, there is clearly another against Inspector Steine. If a madman doesn't cut the inspector's head off in the very near future, Pandora's revelations to the *Mirror* will destroy him anyway. This has been a bally terrible few days. First Mrs Groynes banished herself from the office and found her position as gang leader under attack; now Inspector Steine is in the firing line, both physically and in terms of reputation; and as for Sergeant Brunswick, where *was* he last night?

'And on top of all that, I don't even know how I really feel!' Twitten inwardly wails, as he turns off North Street to wend his way past the big central Post Office and towards the police station. Since yesterday's epiphanies courtesy of Adelaide Vine, he doubts the honesty of all his own reactions. His certainties are certain no more. He thinks: *I am shocked by this surreal physical threat to Inspector Steine, but on the other hand don't I secretly desire him to be out of my way? I am friends with Mrs Groynes and I bally well offered to help her, but is the so-called friendship of Mrs Groynes just a cynical device on her part for holding me back, and why was she burning these files yesterday at Inspector Steine's house? Did she mean for me not to find out this plot against the inspector? Clive Hoskisson is the enemy, but why should I continue to collude in the lie that Inspector Steine is a flipping hero?*

Thank goodness for the reliable sergeant, he thinks, as he enters the station. *At least he's predictable to the point of irritating dullness.* But then Baines the desk sergeant stops him before he can go upstairs. Looking serious, Baines indicates a distraught-looking woman in a damp silk headscarf decorated with a border of bluebells.

'Auntie Violet?' says Twitten, recognising her. 'I mean, sorry, aren't you the sergeant's aunt? I'm Constable Twitten, I visited your flat once. Why are you here?'

The woman grasps his arm, and for a moment he thinks, *Sergeant Brunswick is dead!* But it isn't as bad as that.

'It seems the sergeant didn't return home last night, Constable,' says Baines, with a grimace. 'From what I can gather, he left here just before six o'clock and he hasn't been heard of since.'

At Gosling's, Mister Harold is extremely pleased with the new clock.

'Well done, Miss Vine,' he says.

'To be honest, sir,' she replies, 'I didn't expect the camels and palm trees and pyramids to be quite so prominent. Are you sure you like it?'

He waves away her concerns. He loves everything about this new purchase. It is huge and gilded, was bought at a knock-down price and even (after an argument) installed for free! If people start referring to Gosling's as the Camel Shop in the years to come, that will be fine by Mister Harold. Does the hoity-toity Hannington's department store have an enormous golden camel-and-palm-tree-and-pyramid clock on its frontage, grandly chiming the hours and quarters for the benefit of all? No, he rather thinks it doesn't. Does Hannington's *want* such a clock? Well, they might not in theory, but they will be green with envy once they've clapped eyes on this one.

The clock's casing is fully five feet across; the whole thing weighs more than a hundredweight; the Egyptian-themed decorations either side of the twenty-four-inch face are artistically not bad. Mister Harold's clock now sits atop a lintel on the second-floor frontage, in a newly made aperture, where it will chime in glory for decades to come. The installers wanted to use expensive chains and concrete to fix it in position, but it would have taken three days for the housing to set firm, so Adelaide said no: the clock must be ready to start striking on Friday lunchtime, and besides, the cost would cancel out some of the pleasure of the bargain. Mister Harold agreed. He didn't want to wait three days to start telling people the story of the exotic clock: how it was originally ordered for a British bank in Cairo, but then swiftly decommissioned at the time of Suez on account of its giveaway Westminster chimes.

As the reader will have gathered, the opening of the zebra crossing at noon on Friday is destined to bring many strands of our narrative together. But one man, above all, must be there: Inspector Steine. And at the same moment that the troubled Twitten is reaching the police station and finding the office deserted, that the triumphant Adelaide Vine is looking down with satisfaction at the street below, and that Jimmy the Gimp is making his first (and much too violent) attempt at operating the Gosling's lift, Inspector Steine is still at home and refusing to leave his house. He makes this decision when he opens his front door and finds not only the stolid Constable Jenkins already outside in the rain, but a Black Maria with its back doors open and its engine idling.

'Jenkins,' he says flatly. And then, with tears in his eyes, 'I can't stand this.' And with that, he shuts the door, and leans against it.

'Sir?' calls Jenkins, knocking.

'Go away, Jenkins.'

'But, sir … ? I'm afraid I must insist.'

'Go away.'

Inside, Inspector Steine turns to Miss Lennon, who arrived unnoticed by the guards ten minutes ago, letting herself in quite easily by way of the back gate.

'Brought the MEAT WAGON again, did he?' she asks boomingly. 'Oh, poor INSPECTOR.'

He laughs, weakly. How lucky he is to have this capable woman working loyally in his interests, when everyone else is so annoying.

'Constable Jenkins is not an IMAGINATIVE man, Inspector,' she says, in an attempt to mollify him. 'I suppose he is merely FOLLOWING ORDERS.'

'Jenkins is as bad as that confounded reporter,' he complains. 'Every time I look round, he's there. I feel trapped in my own home!'

'Poor YOU,' she says supportively.

'And he genuinely believes I should make him tea!'

'I KNOW,' she agrees.

'Sir?' comes Jenkins's muffled (and puzzled) voice, with some more knocking. 'We're just trying to protect you, sir.'

Steine sighs and straightens his uniform. He supposes he will have to comply. He can't stand here all day. But he will refuse to lie on the floor of the van this time. Yesterday, with all the rolling about, he got a lump behind his ear the size of a goose's egg.

Before he can act, however, Miss Lennon speaks up.

'Inspector, I've had an IDEA,' she says.

'What?'

'Why don't we just GIVE JENKINS THE SLIP, sir?'

'What? How?'

'I came via the garden gate and NO ONE SAW ME. We could ESCAPE by the same route and then LIE LOW until we are due at the London Road!'

He looks at her with gratitude and admiration.

'Did you just think of that?'

She blushes. 'YES.'

'Well, it's brilliant. Shall we go now?'

'Why not?'

But then he has a rather clever thought. 'Hold on. I'll buy us some time.'

He goes to the front door and knocks. 'Jenkins?'

'Yes, sir?'

'I've changed my mind. How do you take your tea?'

'Ooh, three sugars, sir. Lots of milk. That's very kind of you. But after that we really must get you safely into the van, sir.'

Miss Lennon gestures towards the back door and starts to tiptoe away.

'All right, Jenkins,' Steine calls through the door, as he takes an overcoat from his hatstand. 'I'm just going to put the kettle on.'

———

Meanwhile, others are, of course, working towards the same fateful deadline.

At the wax museum, Miss Sibert tells Chaucer that they will soon be heading to France on the ferry from Newhaven, but must first collect their tickets from the travel agency in Gosling's Department Store. As a kind of inconsequential afterthought, she suggests bringing the executioner's axe from the old Mary, Queen of Scots exhibit.

'Why?' he asks, suspicious.

'No reason!' she replies.

But as she places it in a convenient cricket bag, Chaucer notices that its blade glints in the low light, as if it has recently been sharpened and oiled.

Up in London's Regent's Park Zoo, the keeper of penguins makes a last-minute executive decision and starts packing a basket of raw fish for the journey.

Outside the police station, Clive Hoskisson bumps into Ben Oliver from the local paper, and learns the useful news that Inspector Steine will be appearing in public later outside Gosling's Department Store.

Inside the police station, Constable Twitten discovers there is absolutely no one to talk to about *ein, zwei, drei*. No Miss Lennon, even. *Oh, flipping heck, is the inspector dead already?* he thinks, at first. But then Constable Jenkins arrives and informs him that Steine has given him the slip, and that a person answering the inspector's description was seen clambering over a garden gate in the Queen's Park area in the company of a large woman who sounds very much like Miss Lennon. *So he is alive*, thinks Twitten (who isn't called a clever-clogs for nothing). *And thankfully he has the formidable Miss Lennon to protect him.*

But then, at ten o'clock, the telephone rings and – since he is the only person present – he answers it. The operator tells him it's a call for Miss Lennon from someone in the accounts department of London Zoo.

'Are you sure?' he says.

'Shall I put her through?'

'Um … ' Twitten doesn't quite know what to do. Taking messages isn't really his forte (or his job). On the other hand, Miss Lennon is exemplary in this regard, so he supposes he can for once return the favour. As he stands at her desk waiting to be put through, his eye is caught by the picture in the little frame that Miss Lennon sometimes pats so affectionately: it shows a brother and sister dressed in the fashions of the 1930s and it is dedicated 'To Bobby, the best sister in the world'.

'Can I help you?' he asks the mysterious person from the Zoological Gardens in Regent's Park.

'It's about the penguins Miss Lennon ordered for today,' says a brisk voice. 'Should we make the charge out to her personally or to Mr Chambers as we did last time?'

'Pardon?'

'The thing is, we've heard that Mr Chambers is unfortunately deceased, so we weren't sure what to do.'

'Ooh, can you hold, please?' asks Twitten, his mind racing. Penguins? London Zoo? *Mr Chambers?*

He sits down. He stands up again.

'Hello? Hello?' says the person from London Zoo. 'It's just that Mr Chambers paid for the commissioner's elephant last year, so I thought … '

But Twitten isn't listening. He has just noticed that underneath the dedication to 'Bobby' on the photograph is a signature that looks like 'Terry'.

Finally, at the railway station, four burly men with hold-alls step off the London train together and head for the Gentlemen's lavatories, where they proceed to bar the door and change their clothes. From the bags they produce multiple strings of onions, black-and-white striped jumpers, stick-on dark moustaches and black berets. If you are think-ing these must be the genuine French onion-sellers hired by Miss Lennon, however, you are only half right.

'Remember,' says one, who appears to be the leader. (He has a cauliflower ear and a broken nose.) 'We're only backup.'

'Yes, boss,' says another, tucking a gun into his waistband.

'Bobby'll give us the signal if she needs us to step in.'

Each man shows his gun.

'We're going to get the bastard one way or the other, then? The bastard what shot Terry?'

'One way or the other, mate. Yes, we are.'

When, oh, when will Constable Twitten learn of the zebra crossing? As he sits at his desk, typing an urgent note to the inspector explaining his suspicions about Miss Lennon ('I fear she is Mr Chambers's *elder sister*, sir, and therefore not to be trusted'), he is not asking this question, of course, but he knows there is something going on that he's not privy to, if only because of the surreal fact of the London Zoo penguins. It is not until half-past eleven, when he resignedly reports to the front desk for his daily driving lesson, that he hears the news – but not from the usual Sergeant Masefield. It seems that Masefield has suffered enough and at the insistence of his superiors has checked into a clinic for nervous exhaus-tion, so the lesson today will be conducted by the redoubtable Sergeant Baines.

'All right, lad,' Baines says, opening the passenger door of the regular training vehicle. 'Show me what you can do. It will be a different route today, though, what with London

Road being blocked at midday for that blooming road safety event.'

'What road safety event would that be, sir?' says Twitten, politely, as he slides into the driver's seat and adjusts his rear-view mirror.

'Wipers,' says Baines.

'Pardon?' says Twitten.

'Turn on your ruddy windscreen wipers, son. It's raining.'

'Of course, sir.' Twitten switches them on. The windscreen is already fogging up inside, though. 'Would you talk me through the pedals, please, sir?'

'No. You should know the blooming pedals by now, son.'

'Yes, but—'

'You've got the test next week.'

'I know, sir. But Sergeant Masefield always talks me though them again and I find it very helpful. But never mind, I expect it will come back to me. You mentioned a road safety event?'

'Needn't concern us, lad. So, we will make our way to Elm Grove and practise hill starts. I'd like you to drive to the end of the road here and then indicate left.'

Twitten checks his mirror, starts the engine, depresses the clutch, selects first gear and slowly applies the accelerator. As he eases the clutch, the gear engages and the car judders without moving, so he depresses the clutch again.

'I think it's broken, sir,' says Twitten, helplessly looking down at the pedals, as if they will provide an explanation.

'Don't look at your feet, son.'

'Right, sir. No, sir.'

'Handbrake, Twitten!'

'Oh, gosh, yes. Sorry, sir.' With his foot on the accelerator, and the clutch eased up, he releases the handbrake and the car shoots forward, grazing a lamp-post, and then ricochets back onto the roadway, where it stalls.

'Oh, flipping hedgehogs,' says Twitten. 'Shall I get out and see if there's any damage?'

'No, don't.' Baines rubs his forehead where it has just struck the windscreen.

'Look,' says Twitten, 'I don't mind admitting that driving doesn't come perfectly naturally to me, sir.'

Baines isn't sure if this is a joke.

'So I really wouldn't mind if you wanted to abandon this as a bad job. I can wait for Sergeant Masefield to get better. And you still haven't told me what's happening on the London Road.'

'Well,' says Baines, 'it was all Steine's new secretary's idea, as far as I can discover. That big woman with the booming voice.'

'Miss Lennon? What was?' In Twitten's mind, the word 'penguins' starts to loom.

'Well, this Miss Lennon said a new pedestrian crossing would be just the ticket for Inspector Steine's reputation. They painted it last night outside Gosling's. I just sent Constable Jenkins off there, actually. They're doing the grand opening at noon on the dot. Jenkins was furious about the inspector giving him the slip, you should have seen him!'

Twitten's mind races. 'When you say *pedestrian* crossing, sir, do you mean *zebra* crossing?'

'Well, yes. Of course.'

Twitten feels like screaming. A black-and-white crossing? In black-and-white stripes? *With penguins?*

'Now,' says Baines, with a sigh. 'I'd like you to restart the car, checking it is in neutral, and – what's happening? Twitten? What are you doing?'

'What's the flipping time, sir?'

'About twenty to twelve.'

'I'm afraid we are not doing hill starts in Elm Grove today, sir,' says Twitten, as he drives off – painfully – in first gear, indicating right when he is intending to turn left. 'We've got to get to Gosling's.'

―――――――

The penguins prove to be a huge hit with the gathering crowd. They are birds who enjoy a bit of applause, and always act up to it. It is a tragedy of natural history, really, that their habitat in Antarctica is so entirely deficient in this regard.

'So good of you to change your mind, Mr Geneva,' Miss Lennon says to the penguin-keeper quietly.

'Well, I remembered how much you got Mr Chambers to pay for that elephant. Between you and me, it kept her in buns for a year.'

He tosses a silver fish to each of the two penguins, who waddle on the closed road, making little charges this way and that, and occasionally drop down and bodysurf across the wet tarmac on their tummies.

Inspector Steine watches the antics of the penguins with pleasure. He does still worry a little about appearing in public when there is a lunatic at large, but he also loves the fact that this crossing will (according to Miss Lennon) be associated with his name for ever.

'You can remove the tarpaulin now,' she says. Glancing behind her, she sees in the crowd Miss Sibert and Geoffrey Chaucer, who appear – like everyone else – to be half bemused by the proceedings and half impatient to cross the road. Glancing up at the mighty new Camel Clock on the front of Gosling's, she sees the faces of Adelaide Vine and Mister Harold at an adjacent window. Below them, sheltering under the smaller marquee, keeping their onions dry, are four of Terry's top men in French outfits, pretending not to know her.

The tarpaulin is pulled back, and as the spotless black-and-white stripes are revealed, there is an 'Oooh' of appreciation from the crowd – which is generous of them, as they have seen many zebra crossings before. An interesting faraway expression appears on Geoffrey Chaucer's face. Miss Sibert wordlessly hands him the cricket bag and – quite unconsciously – he reaches inside.

Inspector Steine steps forward, taking a few folded pages of a speech from his tunic pocket. 'What's the time? Five minutes to go? I'll start,' he says. 'Now, can everyone hear me?' he calls.

And then he sees, on the opposite side of the road, lurking half-behind the small marquee with the onion-sellers in it, a reporter in a white coat and a brown hat.

'My nemesis!' he gasps.

Glancing the other way, he sees Constable Jenkins, a look of fury on his face.

'Jenkins!' he whimpers.

Inside the shop, at four minutes to twelve, it is Dorothy who first raises the alarm.

'Mister Harold, sir! Mister Harold, sir! Money! Something's happened to the money!'

Money? thinks Mister Harold. *How can anything go wrong with money?* But then he turns to look, and sees a sight that fills him with total horror. Large white five-pound notes are shooting out of the pneumatic tubes embedded in the walls. And it's worse than that. As they flutter down, excited customers – *customers!* – are not only snatching them out of the air, they are calling to their friends to do it too.

'What's happening?' he says. 'Let go of that money! Yes, you, madam! That's mine!'

He has never felt such a sense of panic in his life. 'Miss Vine? Miss Vine, there's something wrong!'

He rushes to the carpet department to retrieve a note from the hands of an elderly man who refuses to let go, and in the struggle, the elderly man trips over a pile of Turkish rugs and knocks his head on the floor.

Adelaide's eyes widen. *This is a trick!* she thinks. *Who's doing this?* She wants to stay and guard the clock, but what choice does she have? The caps are off all the tubes, and more money is exploding out of them, causing an enormous diversion. 'Cap those tubes!' she calls out to the staff on the shop-floor, but the caps are nowhere to be found, and still the five-pound notes keep coming.

———

'You can't go the whole way in first gear, Twitten.'

'This isn't a driving lesson, sir. This is bally life or death!'

'I appreciate that, lad, because you keep saying it, but why does that stop you from changing up?'

'Well, to be frank, sir, I'm in too much of a state to remember how to do it.'

They have been three times round the area of town called The Level, with Twitten trying to work out a route onto the London Road avoiding the roadblocks. Much of this has involved illegally driving in the wrong lane, with two wheels on the pavement, or between stationary cars with barely sufficient clearance.

'May I make one observation, Twitten? And would you please listen?'

'All right, sir. But time is of the essence.'

'You have a tendency to steer towards whatever catches your eye, so please focus only on the carriageway ahead.'

'I don't understand, sir.'

'So, for example, don't look at that bollard.'

'What bollard?' The car swerves to the right immediately.

'You see, now we're heading straight for the bollard.'

'Gosh, I see what you mean, sir.' Baines grabs the wheel, to save the car from smacking into the bollard head-on. 'Sorry, sir! Gosh, that was close!'

There is pandemonium on the second floor of Gosling's. No one is looking out of the window any more: they are focusing all their attention on catching free money, and fighting off the staff who attempt to recover it. Mister Harold has forgotten his Camel Clock and is trying to block one of the tubes, using his own jacket. Meanwhile Adelaide makes a bad decision. She jumps into the lift and instructs Jimmy the Gimp, 'Take me to the basement at once!'

Jimmy tips his hat and repeats, 'Yes, miss. Basement, miss. I can do that, miss, I'm sure.' Then – very slowly – he shuts each of the two metal concertina doors with a 'clang'.

'Come on!' she says.

'Pardon, miss?'

'I said, *come on!*'

'Yes, miss.' He looks at the lift control as if he's never seen it before, muttering 'Basement, basement, basement', and then with a big shrug – as if to say 'You can only die once' – he shoves the control forward with such inappropriate force that the lift plummets down two storeys.

'What are you doing?' shrieks Adelaide, in terror, her feet lifting off the floor.

'Sorry, miss,' he says. He corrects his mistake by pulling the control back again, and the lift jerks to a standstill. They both land heavily.

'Why did you do that?' she pants, furious.

He shrugs. 'I don't know, miss. But looking at the evidence, I suppose I must have received inadequate training.'

'Let me out at once.'

'Well, I don't think I can, miss.' He indicates their position, stuck between two floors. When he tentatively pushes the control, nothing happens. And together they are both distracted anyway by a combination of noises – the clock starting to chime, then a bang, perhaps? A lot of screaming? A car's brakes? It is infuriatingly difficult to make out.

Just a few minutes ago, Adelaide had been in the perfect spot to watch a brilliant plan unfold, but now she is stuck in this lift with an idiot and the chance of a lifetime has gone.

The person who sees everything is Inspector Steine, but – true to form – he doesn't understand any of it. All he knows is that a few seconds before twelve o'clock Miss Lennon signals to the onion-sellers on the Gosling's side to ready themselves, then she smiles at Steine and joins him on the crossing. 'This is it,' she says to him. A penguin tries to waddle across, but Steine orders it to go back and, astonishingly, it obeys.

As the clock commences its *bing-bong* chimes in advance of striking the hour, everyone looks up and sees that, beyond the clock, inside the shop, people appear to be rioting, which is odd. Children holding little chequered flags continue to wave them, though. Everyone loves a flag.

'What's happening?' mutters Miss Lennon.

Miss Sibert is similarly unnerved. '*Scheisse*,' she mutters.

But Geoffrey Chaucer is on track. He slips the axe out of the cricket bag and looks with approval at the sharpened blade.

'Ladies and gentlemen,' Steine begins, 'it gives me great pleasure to open this zebra crossing. In the past few weeks a number of accidents have occurred here, but I promise you—'

He stops. On the blocked road there is a police car coming towards them, not at great speed thanks to being in (straining) first gear, but with every appearance of purpose.

Miss Lennon takes her cue. The clock is about to chime.

'Inspector Steine!' she gasps. 'Leave me alone, leave me alone!'

'What?' says Steine. 'I didn't touch you, Miss Lennon.'

'Help, help!' she calls.

Chaucer grips the axe-handle tighter and steps forward. In his mind are explosions of scarlet on a black-and-white background – on his mother's dress, on the Deco walls, on the tiled floor. He sees the black-and-white checks trimming the policemen's uniforms; he sees chess pieces scattered.

The clock reaches the end of its *bing-bong-bing-bong*s, and then – when everyone is happily looking up at it – it wobbles.

'Good God,' says Steine. 'That's an enormous clock. Surely it won't … ?'

But it does. It is quite front-heavy, given all those ornamental pyramids, palm trees and such. Given a well-judged shove from inside by Joan and Dorothy in unison, it topples from its position and in less than a second has landed with mighty force on the marquee beneath, crushing all four of the *faux* French onion-sellers.

'Was that supposed to happen, Miss Lennon?' says Steine, confused. 'Weren't those people guests in our country?'

But Miss Lennon isn't there to answer him. She has run away into the screaming crowd, despite all attempts by a rogue penguin to trip her up.

Chaucer looks down at the axe in his hand, and understands everything. 'You set me up!' he cries. He wants to strangle Miss Sibert with his bare hands, but clever Carlotta has likewise made herself scarce. Following suit, he darts into the dispersing and hysterical crowd.

In the approaching car, Twitten can see the scene unfolding, but can't make the car go any faster (his foot is weary from holding the pedal to the floor). So he decides he must take the risk. He depresses the clutch and – praying – wiggles the gearstick to locate second gear.

'Oh, thank God,' says Baines, as the car finally picks up speed.

From his position still in the middle of the crossing, Steine sees that, fighting his way against the fleeing crowd, is Constable Jenkins, flushed red with annoyance. And as if to make matters even worse ...

'Inspector Steine?'

He looks round. It is Clive Hoskisson.

'Oh, for heaven's sake,' he says. '*Now*? Can't you see I'm in the middle of something?'

'I know it all,' says Hoskisson. 'I know you shot Terence Chambers while not even knowing who he was. I've got you, Steine. You're going down.'

Steine throws up his hands. Is all this really happening? Dead Frenchmen, a man with an axe, and on top of everything else, a car appears to be driving straight towards him (inside which, unbeknown to him, Baines is saying 'You're doing it again!' and trying to grab the wheel).

As it happens, Twitten is so aghast to see Hoskisson on the crossing that he is steering the car directly at *him*. Tragically, he has chosen the wrong person to target, because Hoskisson – as we already know – is a man who prides himself on always standing his ground.

'Brake, lad!' calls Baines.

'Oh, yes,' says Twitten. 'Of course.' And he looks down at his feet to select the right pedal.

'Sir, I have to get you off this crossing,' says Jenkins, taking Steine by the arm. 'There are loose penguins and everything. And there seems to be a full-scale riot in that shop.' But Steine shakes his arm free; he is irritated by Hoskisson's behaviour. 'Why don't you get out of the way, you stupid man?' Steine yells. 'Can't you see the car? Oh, my God, it's skidding!'

And then the inspector does something entirely out of character. Admittedly, the car in question is not approaching at any great speed; and admittedly, the main thought in Steine's head is the petulant, *I will* not *be told what to do by Constable Jenkins!* But it is heroic nevertheless in a slow-motion kind of way. Because at the last second, the exasperated Steine throws himself bodily at Hoskisson and knocks him out of the path of Twitten's car, which screeches and slews to a halt a few yards further down the road, Baines having grabbed the wheel and turned it sharply.

Twitten runs back in the rain to where the two men are still in a muddled heap of limbs on the road.

'Sir ... are you all right, sir?' he pants. 'Oh, thank goodness. Thank flipping goodness.'

'Calm down, Twitten,' says Steine. 'Not much harm done. I mean, apart from ... ' He glances towards the flattened marquee with the clock on top, from which a poignant smell of crushed onions is wafting. 'Are you all right, Hoskisson?'

But the reporter can't bring himself to speak. His life has just been saved by the man he was preparing to denounce as an idiot and a coward.

'I got here as fast as I could, sir,' explained Twitten, 'when I realised Miss Lennon had plotted to kill you using the crossing and the clock and the maniac and the penguins and everything, but to be honest I can't really drive, although I did just manage to find second gear all by myself so possibly I'm improving!'

Eleven

At a quarter-past twelve, making her way grimly through the rainy streets, following a figure hurrying along in a turquoise coat and carrying a lemon-coloured handbag, Mrs Groynes fingered the gun in her pocket.

It was satisfying to see Miss So-Called Adelaide So-Called Vine fleeing the scene at Gosling's. All her plans had just ended in humiliating failure: Inspector Steine was still alive; her co-conspirators had fled; a tall man with an unused sharpened axe was at large in the town; and, last but not least, four top members of the Chambers gang had died a deeply embarrassing death, crushed by more than eight stone of orientalist metalwork.

Mrs Groynes had witnessed it all, of course. While events in the London Road unfolded, she had been sheltering in the main Gosling's doorway with gang member Sid the Doorman and enjoying the results of her handiwork. Their position was so close to the point of impact that when the clock hit the ground, they both jumped in the air, gasping, and then laughed reflexively, holding each other up.

'Blimey, boss,' panted Sid. 'Couldn't you just have stuffed rags in it or something? There are easier ways to stop a clock than pushing it off a ruddy ledge.'

To any disinterested onlooker, their behaviour was unusual: these two people chatting light-heartedly in a doorway, while a hysterical crowd streamed past them.

'Now, don't be too disappointed, Sid, but I expect this has kiboshed the Christmas Job. I mean, we can hardly use the tubes again and I've told Denise to scarper at once anyway – ooh!' At this point, Twitten's car captured her attention, as it skidded past where she was standing and narrowly missed Inspector Steine and the man in the white coat on the crossing. 'Ooh, good gawd, that was a near thing,' she said, clutching her chest. The noise of the crowd made it necessary to raise her voice. 'I was saying, we can hardly use the tubes again, can we?' she shouted. 'But don't you make a move just yet, Sid. Don't go back to your flopping, it's too dangerous. You hold fast, dear. We'll wait and see.'

'How long can Jimmy keep that woman in the lift?' yelled Sid.

'Pardon?'

'The woman in the lift!'

Mrs Groynes nodded to indicate she had heard. 'I told him to let her out at ten-past.'

'When?'

'What time is it now?'

He produced a pocket watch and wiped off the rain that fell on it. 'Ten-past!' he yelled.

'Right. Good timing. There she goes!'

And now here Mrs Groynes was, following Adelaide Vine towards the centre of Brighton. In a way she felt sympathy for the girl. The plan to kill Steine on the zebra crossing was, admittedly, overambitious, but still, it had very, very nearly come off. Mrs Groynes had put two and two together only yesterday morning, when she had let herself into Steine's house to read all the Broadmoor documents regarding Chaucer's case.

About fifty yards ahead, Adelaide was zigzagging west and north through the grid of minor roads in the North Laine quarter of the town. She walked very purposefully – never looking back; never checking to see if she was being followed. This was fortunate for her pursuer, but also a slight cause for concern. This young woman had just escaped a débâcle. Shouldn't she be exhibiting at least a smidgen of anxiety about what was happening behind her? But Adelaide forged up Gloucester Street and then turned left into Kensington Gardens without once glancing back. Which was why Mrs Groynes began, at last, to smell a rat.

'That's bleeding odd, not looking back like that,' she said to herself. And then it struck her. *Unless she knows who's behind.*

Halfway along Kensington Gardens, Mrs Groynes made a decision. She stopped and turned … and there he was, just a few yards back, flanked by two other men wearing equally serious expressions. If it had been a film, the soundtrack would have gone, 'Dum, dum, DUMMMM'. Deep down, she had suspected it all along, but it still broke her heart to find it was true.

'Cecil,' she said, with a sigh of resignation. Rain that had collected on her horrible plastic rain-bonnet poured down onto her back as she looked up at the attractive face of her long-time favourite henchperson – those dark eyes; that handsome square jaw. Conflicting emotions flooded her: relief, fear, physical attraction. Without the bunnies, in a long grey raincoat and leather gloves, he stood straight and tall, a strikingly virile figure.

'Hello, Palmeira,' he said.

One of the other men held out his hand for her gun. It was Constable Jenkins. 'I'll take that weapon, madam,' he said, and, meekly, she took it from her pocket and gave it to him. The other man, who had the decency to look embarrassed, was Stanley-Knife Stanley.

'Oh, *Stan!*' she remonstrated. 'What did I ever do to deserve this from *you?*'

Cecil took her by the arm, and they walked on, this small middle-aged woman in her ghastly concertina rain-hat flanked by one big man in a homburg (Cecil), another in a tweedy flat cap (Stanley) and one in a policeman's helmet (Constable Jenkins). Without the presence of a policeman, passers-by might have guessed she was in peril. But as it was, they didn't.

'This your gang, then, is it?' she said, attempting conversation. 'These your boys? Well, I knew the Vine girl couldn't have come up with all this on her own.'

'Oh, yeah?'

'Yes, Cecil. You set her up well, I admit that. Everyone said, *It's Adelaide Vine doing this out of revenge for her mum*, and I kept on saying, *It's not, though; this goes bleeding deep*. But I tell you what, Cecil. That was cruel to make me think someone had hurt you.'

They all looked into the distance at Adelaide Vine, who had now stopped walking and was looking back uncertainly, as if waiting for an instruction. Cecil waved her on. Adelaide, with obvious relief, began to run.

'I suppose I should congratulate you on saving Inspector Idiot,' said Cecil. 'But he was only the icing on the cake. It's Sergeant Stupid who's your Achilles' heel.'

'Don't call him that, Cecil. I've told you before.'

'I'll call him what I like,' he said sharply, tightening his grip. 'Either way, his days of doling out ten-bob notes to me is over. Condescending bastard.'

'Listen, Cecil. Don't you go hurting Jim Brunswick, I won't stand for it.'

He laughed. 'You should hear yourself.'

'I mean it, Cecil. Anything else we could come to terms on, but not that.'

'Ha!' he said to the others, smiling in triumph. 'I knew it! Didn't I tell you? For a woman with no soft spots, she's got so many soft spots! Tell Mrs G what we're planning for Sergeant Stupid if she don't concede to me at once, Stanley.'

Stanley leaned in and grimaced. 'We're gonna start by shaving some bits off,' he whispered, drawing the Stanley knife from his pocket for her to see.

She closed her eyes. 'No, you're not.'

'I've had enough of this,' said Cecil. 'Why don't we go back to your place, Palmeira? Then you can put your affairs in order just before you unfortunately fall downstairs and break your ruddy neck.'

Back at the police station, Inspector Steine sat at his desk while Twitten busied himself in a small room along the corridor, trying to make them both a nice restorative cup of tea.

This job turned out to be much more challenging than he had anticipated. For one thing, there were no printed instructions to be found *anywhere*. For another, only tepid water was available in the urn, and the teapot, confusingly, contained old wet tea-leaves. He paused to think. Had he ever seen anyone empty a teapot? Honestly, no. Was it possible that you weren't supposed to? Yes, it was possible. For a start, where would the old tea-leaves go?

So he added some lukewarm water to the cold, soggy leaves in the pot, and then (to be on the safe side) emptied a half-packet of fresh tea-leaves into it, stirring with effort as he did so. Then he picked up the pot – which was surprisingly heavy – and attempted the deft swirling action that Mrs Groynes always accompanied with the mantra 'Show it the pictures on the wall.' He felt sure this would do the trick.

Forgetting to use a strainer, he poured the resulting chunky tepid liquid into a cup, then added a measure of milk and four spoonfuls of sugar. Then he took a sip, gasped 'Golly!' in a choking fashion, looked round for somewhere to spit it out, failed, and swallowed it with disgust, and went back to the office a few minutes later to confess that the tea things had unfortunately all been cleared away by persons unknown, and perhaps they should go out for a cup instead?

'Where's Brunswick?' said the inspector flatly.

'Ooh, well. That's a very good question, sir, because I don't know the answer. He's mysteriously missing, sir.'

'I don't understand.'

'You don't understand missing, sir? Gosh, I'm not sure how to explain it. But he didn't go home last night. His auntie is distraught, and I'm a bit worried myself. I didn't tell his auntie this, because I didn't want to add to her anxiety, but last night the sergeant passed up the chance of *home-made pink blancmange*, so I think it's quite serious.'

'Good heavens. The sergeant is quite partial to blancmange, isn't he?'

'He bally well is, sir. He once said in my presence that he'd like to "flaming marry it", sir.'

'Do you think he's actually tied up somewhere?'

'Well, he's either that or dead. With your permission, I'd like to start making inquiries. The trouble is, sir, I wonder whether it's advisable to leave you alone right now.'

This was a good assessment of the situation. The inspector had just been through a very traumatic ordeal, most of which was still not fully clear to him.

'You might be right.' Steine shook his head. 'Look, just explain again, Twitten. It was *all* an elaborate trap, you're saying? Even the zebra crossing?'

'The zebra crossing was at the heart of the plan, sir.'

'So Miss Lennon was behind it?'

'Well, she might not have conceived the plan herself, but she made it happen, sir. Didn't it strike you as odd that the preparations for the crossing came together so incredibly quickly, sir?'

Steine had never questioned it. 'Those poor Frenchmen with the onions. Did she mean for them to die?'

'No, sir. That was where the plan went wrong. What Miss Lennon wanted was for the clock to chime the hour, at which point Mr Chaucer would come forward and—'

'Yes, yes.' Steine shuddered. 'Yes, that's enough. You did explain, although I still don't see why it had to be in German. But remind me why she wanted me dead; I thought she liked me.'

'I'm afraid the pretending to like you was all a ruse, sir.'

'Good God, is nothing what it seems?'

'She nearly got away with it, sir. It was only because the person called from London Zoo about charging the penguins to Mr Chambers that I began to put two and two together. I've been bally blind, sir.'

Twitten handed the inspector the framed picture. 'That's her as a child, sir, with her little brother Terry.'

'Bobby?' said the inspector, puzzled.

'Roberta, sir. I suppose she preferred the name Bobby. Like the older girl in *The Railway Children*, sir. It must have helped Mr Chambers enormously to have his sister working as such a senior secretary at Scotland Yard. She was well placed to feed Chambers confidential information, destroy evidence that incriminated him, and of course she never come under suspicion, you see, because people always underestimate women.'

'Do they?'

'Yes, sir.'

'I'm sure I don't.'

'Oh, but everyone does. It seems to be a sort of universal rule.'

The inspector looked at the picture: of the young Terence Chambers holding hands with his big, big sister, whose greatest quality was that she was 'insanely loyal'.

'But I recall Miss Lennon was sent here by the Commissioner of the Metropolitan Police,' Twitten continued. 'So a rather larger and, may I say, darker issue presents itself, doesn't it, sir?'

Steine frowned. 'Does it?'

'Sir, I believe your killing of Mr Chambers might have made you a marked man with many high-ranking members of the Metropolitan Police who were accustomed to receiving money from him. I am therefore wondering whether the commissioner sent her here not in ignorance but actually *knowing who she was?*'

'Good God,' the inspector said again. He returned the picture to Twitten and faced the window. 'It's very shocking, isn't it?'

'What, sir?'

'Corruption. In the police, I mean.'

'Oh, I agree. It's bally awful, sir. You happily forget all about the subject of bent coppers. In fact everyone prefers to. And then, crikey! Up it pops again.'

'Do you think there's any corruption here in Brighton?'

'Oh, golly, I don't think so, sir. Or not of the conventional kind. Here it's done more with fruit cake and sausage rolls and—'

But Inspector Steine wasn't listening. 'You don't think Brunswick would ever … ?'

'No, sir! Absolutely not.'

'Good.'

'He is totally honest, sir. Too honest, arguably. His problem is that he's too trusting, especially where attractive younger women are concerned. But since you're asking, I do have suspicions about Constable Jenkins. His behaviour at the zebra crossing was quite peculiar, sir. When the plan to murder you collapsed, I saw him punch a brick wall with his bare hands.'

'Really?'

'Yes, sir. He realised I'd seen it, and came running over to check you were all right. But his knuckles were bleeding. And I've been meaning to say: did anyone ever *ask* him to be your bodyguard, sir?'

The inspector frowned again. 'That's a very good question, Twitten. I have no idea. When he started protecting me, I assumed he'd been ordered to do it.'

'Well, I think he deliberately overdid it, so that you'd get cross with him and be driven to put all your trust in Miss Lennon, sir.'

'But why would he allow himself to be *bent*, as you put it?'

'Oh, I expect the usual reasons, sir. He's been here for years and he's still a constable, for a start.'

Steine's gaze swept back and forth across his desk a couple of times, as if a lovely consoling hot beverage made with leaves originating in India or China might materialise. It didn't. Perhaps the shock was beginning to come home to him. He realised his hands were shaking.

'You ought to go and find out what you can about Brunswick, Constable,' he said, his voice as steady as he could manage. He cleared his throat authoritatively. 'Yes. It's probably best if you leave me now. Get someone from downstairs to guard the office until Chaucer is picked up.'

'Very good, sir. I'm so sorry I failed with the tea.'

'No matter. I need to take it all in, I think.'

Twitten picked up his helmet and turned to go, but paused.

'Sir? If I may … ' He blushed. This was a difficult thing to say, but he felt compelled. A day like this had never occurred before.

'That was a very selfless thing you did earlier, sir,' he gushed. 'Hurling yourself in front of the car. I can't get it out of my mind. It was—' He stopped and blinked, slightly overcome. 'Well, it was bally marvellous.'

To Twitten's surprise and alarm, Steine's eyes welled with tears. 'No, no, Twitten,' he said, distraught. 'You mustn't say that.'

'But, sir—'

'Listen, Twitten. This is the truth.' The inspector took a deep, steadying breath. 'When I jumped in front of the car it wasn't marvellous. I saw the stupid man fixed to the spot and … ' He trailed off and gave it some thought. 'And it just seemed like the right thing to do.'

Sergeant Brunswick heard the distant sound of a door being opened. He moaned, but didn't try to move, because he had tried it before and achieved nothing. His head hurt, his body ached and his hands were numb. But mainly he was angry. How quickly things had gone wrong for him last night! No sooner had he walked through the door of the wax museum with Adelaide Vine than *whack!* – he'd been hit on the head.

In his police career he was accustomed to walking into dangerous situations, but generally he did so *understanding the flaming risk*. This meant that when (invariably) his ill-considered undercover operations were tragically blown at the last minute, he was able to face his fate with equanimity. He was even able to tell himself that being shot in the leg so many times was a mark of his dedication as a policeman.

But last night's reversal was very different. He had met Adelaide Vine out of kindness, agreed to enter the old Maison du Wax, explained politely, 'I can't stay long, miss, because I have a dinner appointment at seven' – and the next thing he knew he was waking up with a blinding headache, tied to a blooming chair! He kept thinking of Len the Photographer, when he was taken away in the ambulance the other day, moaning 'Ow, my head!' At the time, Brunswick had thought, *Blimey, mate, you don't have to* keep saying it. *We all know what happened to you.* But now, with every conscious second that passed, he wanted to say, 'Ow, my head! Ow, my head! Ow, my head!' just as Len had done.

Of course, if he thought more deeply about it, he had to admit that Twitten had warned him about Adelaide Vine at least once. *Miss Vine is a trained con artist with years of experience, sir,* the pipsqueak constable had said. Also: *You shouldn't trust a single word from her, especially when she's assuring you how bally wonderful you are.*

But looking at it another way, didn't Twitten judge people quite harshly? Wasn't he basically a brain on a stick, without a shred of human feeling? 'There is no need to torture yourself remembering what Twitten said,' he told himself. 'None of this is your fault, Jim. You responded to a woman in distress, because you're a kind person with a big heart.'

But more of Twitten's warnings crowded into his mind. *And if you remember, sir, Miss Vine did, on a previous occasion not so long ago, sort of shoot you in the leg.* Also: ... *it behoves us, sir, as responsible policemen and trusted servants of the public, to resist Miss Vine's womanly wiles.*

Brunswick groaned again at the memory of that word 'behoves', and then, remembering the recent fateful sound of the upstairs door opening, looked up to face his beautiful nemesis. This wasn't how he had pictured his end. He had fancied a dramatic showdown on a Soho rooftop, followed by a lavish police funeral (with plumed horses) and a posthumous medal for bravery. But now his poor body would doubtless be left down here, mouldering in the dark basement of a condemned seaside wax museum, only to be found when the wrecking ball was sent in.

There were footsteps on the stairs, and a torch beam lit up fragments of the dusty exhibits. He closed his eyes. They were female footsteps, all right: high-heeled shoes clacking on tiles. A waft of female fragrance reached his nose. He held his breath.

'James, it's me!' called a female voice. 'Where are you? Are you in here?'

'*Mrs Thorpe?*' he called, opening his eyes. 'Ow, my head!'

'There you are,' she said, shining her torch at him. Her tone was, oddly, not one of relief, more one of accusation. 'Oh, James, James, I am only flesh and blood. That you would go to such lengths to avoid my dinner table makes me extremely cross!'

'Mrs Thorpe, what are you talking about? I'm tied up. And my head – my flaming head hurts.'

She dropped a large bag to the floor. It made a metallic clattering noise, as if she had brought the contents of her kitchen drawer. 'I want you to know that your not coming to dinner last night was very bad manners,' she said. 'In fact, we all agreed it was extremely rude.'

Just one thought had given hope to Mrs Groynes as she was frogmarched back to her house in Upper North Street by Cecil and his goons. When she had turned to face them in the rain, she had noticed something very interesting. She had seen that, a few yards behind Cecil and his men, another person was following *them*.

It was quite easy to pick out the man in pursuit, because when she stopped and turned to face Cecil's party, he likewise jerked to a halt. How fascinating it was that, just like Adelaide – and just like herself – Cecil had not checked behind him. If she survived this day, she would cite this case on one of her quarterly training sessions, because all these people were adept at following, yet oblivious to being followed. But for the time being, as she was propelled by Cecil along the wet pavements of Brighton, crossing the streets and dodging through the traffic, it pleased her to know that, twenty yards behind was a very conspicuous tall young man with wild hair and blood-shot eyes, carrying a glinting instrument of decapitation.

Cecil wasn't in the mood for talking, but Mrs Groynes had other ideas. 'Why are you doing this?' she asked him. 'Oh, let me bleeding guess, dear. Didn't I treat you like dirt enough? Was I too bleeding good to you?'

Cecil's grip on her arm grew more painful, but he said nothing.

Stanley leaned in. 'He don't like to explain, boss. I asked him the same thing.'

'Don't call her "boss", Stanley!' said Cecil angrily.

'Yes, boss,' said Stanley, shrugging. Half his mind was on the unfinished Gosling's window display he'd been torn away from. The other half was on the stunning autumn-leaf cascading theme that presumably he would never now get to execute.

They had reached Upper North Street. Mrs Groynes needed to slow things down before they reached her house. So she stopped walking.

'Tell me this isn't about the bleeding bunnies, Cecil,' she said.

'Of course it's about the bunnies, Palmeira!' he burst out. 'I told you at the start. But you said, "The bunnies stay; the bunnies are genius." And so I'm stuck acting the beggar on a windy corner 'til I'm old and grey, with people buying sodding plastic toys out of pity for me?'

'But you were brilliant at your job, Cecil. My key man. The bunnies were never the point.'

'I've dreamed of this moment for years, Palmeira. Ruddy years. And then it all came to a head, didn't it? When you took out Chambers, I thought, well, she'll be moving into the big time now, and she'll take me with her. I'm one of her four musketeers, and I work harder than any of the others – I work every day! But nothing changed, did it? Day after day, it's still bunnies, bunnies, bunnies; still *see the bunny run, see the bunny jump!*'

She pulled her arm free and stood back, facing them all, partly for dramatic effect and partly to check who was following behind. Also, she was genuinely angry. Was this man really complaining about having to say 'See the bunny run' a few times?

'You could have changed the form of words, dear!' she snapped. 'Be bleeding reasonable, Cecil, and for gawd's sake stop feeling sorry for yourself. No one was making you say the same thing for ever and ever, were they?'

'Shut up, Palmeira. Shut up!'

'Don't tell me to shut up! You're acting like a kid.'

Passers-by had already started sensing something amiss in this little group arguing so passionately in the rain, but Jenkins waved them past. 'Move along now, please,' he said firmly. 'There's nothing to see. Perhaps we should take this discussion indoors, madam?'

But people were looking at them anyway. And behind Cecil and his associates, a tall man with an axe was not only lingering, but listening.

'This is *my* story, Palmeira,' said Cecil. 'This is about how I brought you down. I started thinking about all the people you'd pissed off by killing Chambers – and guess what? Once I told them it was you who set the whole thing up, I was spoiled for choice.

'I got that Lennon woman involved – here, you never sussed she was his sister, did you? And she put me onto the Austrian bint who was in love with Chambers, and the Austrian suggested roping in the loony cop-killer, and then Adelaide Vine came to me and there we were! What a team!' He laughed. 'It seemed right, you know, doing all this with a bunch of women. You think you're unique, Palmeira! Well, you're not. And I've got a brain too, you see. It's a shame you never knew what an asset you had standing at the Clock Tower like a lemon.'

Jenkins pulled a face, and held out an arm, as if to repeat 'May we take this indoors now, please?' But both Cecil and Mrs Groynes had passed the point of caution.

'I never underestimated you, Cecil,' she said, with passion.

'Yes, you did,' he said bitterly. 'And then what about your precious Gosling's Christmas Job I wasn't part of? Why did you just assume you could leave me out?'

'Because—'

'I'd have loved to play a part in that! But I had to stand there all day telling everyone else how much money they were going to get – even that chit of a Denise girl. Bloody hell, even this idiot *Stanley* was standing to make a fortune.'

She gasped and looked at Stanley. This was her moment to show defiance; to get the show started. 'Are you going to stand for that, Stan?' she said. 'Cecil just called you an idiot.' At which the enraged Cecil – to a shocked response from onlookers – struck her face and knocked her down.

'Boss!' said Stanley reflexively. 'Are you all right?'

'Don't call her boss!' said Cecil, angrily swinging round.

'Move along, please, there's absolutely nothing to— Oh, my God,' said Jenkins feebly, as he caught sight of Chaucer advancing swiftly with his axe.

'Help!' shouted Mrs Groynes from her position on the wet pavement, holding her face. 'Somebody help! He hit me!'

'Oh, shut up, Palmeira,' commanded Cecil, with his fist raised. But then he felt a tap on his shoulder.

'What *now*?' said Cecil. And then he absorbed the sight of a man with an axe raised.

'Get down, Stan! Now!' shouted Mrs Groynes, as – with an impressive lateral swing – Geoffrey Chaucer landed a massive death-blow on Barrow-Boy Cecil's neck.

Mrs Thorpe turned out to be almost as bad at untying ropes as she was at absorbing new information in a crisis.

'That ghastly blancmange was entirely for you, James. No one else even liked it!'

'If you would start with the hands, Mrs T, then I can help with the rest.'

She positioned the torch so that it shone on his tied-up hands, and attempted to pull on the knots.

'And that sweet Pandora was there, and I felt her pitying me all evening. It was intolerable. Intolerable, James. I am very, *very* annoyed.'

'I said I was sorry, Mrs Thorpe,' he said grumpily. 'Ow, my head.'

'No, you didn't. You said, *I'm tied up*. It's not the same.'

Brunswick puzzled over this, and came up with nothing. He had a vague memory of a previous conversation with a woman that had gone just like this one, but he hadn't learned from it, so it didn't help. 'I don't see the difference,' he insisted.

'You didn't apologise!'

'I think I did. I said it wasn't my fault that I wasn't there. Which it patently wasn't! Ow, my head!'

'Aagh!' she screamed. 'For goodness' sake, James, just say you are sorry!'

'All right. I'm sorry, Mrs Thorpe, for being attacked and tied up! It was very, very rude of me to be in fear of my life when I should have been at your house eating a pudding!'

'Thank you!'

She went back to tackling the knots. His head had hurt quite a lot before the argument, but now it was exploding with pain.

'How did you find me, anyway?'

'A child came to the house this morning and told me that you came in here last night with a beautiful young woman! He said I should come here at once, but I didn't because – well, if you must know, I had to clear up a lot of shattered glass and pink blancmange from the scullery floor. He said he was intending to locate Constable Twitten and tell him the same thing, and I gave him sixpence for his trouble. He was carrying a box with a cake in it.'

'Well, if you want, I can explain about the beautiful young woman.'

She stiffened. 'Oh, please don't on my account.'

'I said I can explain, Mrs Thorpe. Her name is Adelaide—'

'So it's *true!*' she wailed, sitting back on her heels.

'Look, Mrs Thorpe. I promise we can talk about this later. But right now I am very worried a woman called Adelaide Vine will arrive here with a gun and kill us both. So, please, please, keep trying with the knots.'

She started fiddling again, but angrily. 'Oh, this is hopeless,' she said, standing up. She marched to the bag she'd brought with her and opened it. 'I'll have to use this,' she said, producing her late husband's regimental sword.

'Argh!' screamed Brunswick, at the sight of its sharp edge flashing in the light from the torch. 'No, don't use that.'

'Don't worry,' she said. 'I grew up in India with four brothers.'

'*What?* How does that—'

'James. It will be one blow. One clean blow.'

'No!'

'Really, James. Don't be a baby. I've done this countless times playing at Ali Baba. You just have to hold still.'

'Please, no!'

They had both failed to hear the sound of the door opening again upstairs, but as Brunswick's cry of 'Please, no!' echoed around the waxwork gallery, a third figure could be heard reaching the bottom of the stairs.

'Aaargh!' screamed Brunswick (again). 'Don't kill us! Miss Vine, please don't!'

'Police!' this third figure cried, bursting in. 'Police with bally truncheons!'

———

Inspector Steine got the call to the incident in Upper North Street. He wasn't in the mood to see two headless corpses and a maniac full of bullet-holes, but it seemed he had no choice. At least these ones weren't innocent visitors to our shores.

'Very well,' Steine said flatly, when he received the news from Sergeant Baines. But Baines was so worried by the traumatised state of the inspector that he decided to accompany him. It was just as well. Most of the way there, Baines was required to hold the inspector's arm and keep him upright, while also holding an umbrella over his head.

When they arrived, the bodies were sheltered beneath a makeshift tent, erected by the pathology team. Steine hesitated before going in. 'So what do we think happened here?' he said weakly, to no one in particular.

A young constable, white in the face, stood to attention but merely bit his lip. It wasn't an easy thing to describe.

Baines took control. 'Come on, son. The inspector asked a question.'

'Well, sir,' said the constable. 'Perhaps you'd better see for yourself?' He lifted a flap in the tent for Steine to enter.

'No,' said Steine. 'That's not what I asked. You tell me. I might not choose … '

'Might not choose what, sir?'

'Look, it's none of your business what the inspector might not choose, Constable,' snapped Baines. 'Just tell him what happened.'

'Right, sir.' The constable took a deep breath. 'Well, first things first, there are no witnesses at all.'

'Oh, come on, lad!' scoffed Baines. He looked around and found the inspector leaning against a low wall, wiping his face with a handkerchief.

'Go on, Constable,' Steine said, realising he ought to speak. 'I'm listening. You said there were no witnesses.'

'I think anyone in the vicinity just ran off when they saw a man with an axe, sir. You can't blame them. But as I see it, judging by the wounds, what happens first is that the axeman assaults the big man, hitting him on the neck. Then the axeman is shot several times by Constable Jenkins at very close range—'

'Jenkins?' said Baines. 'What was Jenkins doing here?'

'Oh, sorry, sir. I don't know. But it seems Jenkins stepped in quite bravely, shooting at the axeman.'

'He shot him?' said Baines. 'With what?'

'He seems to have had a gun with him, sir, but no one can explain why. And it's not at all like a police weapon: it's very small calibre, a gun a woman would use. Anyway, Constable Jenkins shoots at the axeman, who then pauses in his hacking away at the prone big man, and takes a massive swing at Jenkins as well and takes his head clean off.'

'Good God,' said Baines, shocked. He turned again to the inspector. 'Are you hearing all this, sir?'

'Yes, Sergeant Baines. Yes, thank you. Loud and clear. Poor Jenkins is dead,' he said, trying not to sound too happy about it.

'Once the heads are completely severed, the axeman takes the gun from Jenkins and shoots himself in the head, sir. We can't be sure why he does that, but presumably because he has realised the magnitude of what he's done.'

Steine swallowed, and closed his eyes. The wall seemed not to be solid behind him.

'Sorry, sir,' said the constable. 'I suppose it's quite a lot to take in. Would you like me to run through it again?'

'Absolutely not, Constable,' said the inspector. 'That was admirably clear and I think I'll just lean against this wall for a moment because it's so convenient.'

It was while he was leaning weakly against a low garden wall in the rain that Inspector Steine experienced what he took at first to be a supernatural visitation.

'Inspector?' said a disembodied voice beside him. 'I thought it was you, dear. Need a cup of tea?'

His eyes were closed, and he was almost afraid to open them. But finally he looked, and there she was: the real and earthly Mrs Groynes, under a colourful umbrella, with a fresh cup of tea on a tray, and a plate of bourbon biscuits. In all this gloom, and amid all this aftermath of shocking violence, she seemed to shine like an angel.

'You can come indoors with me if you like,' she said, offering him an arm. 'My house is just two doors along. Evidently there was some sort of hoo-hah out here, but I was swabbing the floors when it happened, and I didn't hear a bleeding thing! What am I like, eh? You don't get many of me as a free gift with Robertson's Golden Shred.'

'Mrs Groynes?' he said, bursting into tears. 'With a cup of tea? And *wittering*?' It was all too much for him. 'Oh, my goodness, have I died?'

Twelve

By nine o'clock that evening, it would be fair to say that a sense of anti-climax was pervasive. Extreme levels of excitement tend to have that effect. 'The day after the Lord Mayor's Show' is the way Londoners colourfully describe such a sense of let-down, with all the connotations of traipsing through horse dung and chip-paper.

Take Constable Twitten. On bursting into the wax museum with his 'bally truncheons' line, he had felt very pleased with himself, especially when he realised his arrival had perhaps prevented the sergeant from having his hands lopped off by a theatrical landlady boasting of implausible knife-skills acquired colonially. But an hour or so later, once he was back in the office, the feeling of elation simply wore off, leaving behind only fatigue and a few nagging doubts.

The fact was, Brunswick was safe and sound (and very subdued). So was the inspector. The danger to both of them had been intensely real this morning, but now that it was over, it seemed to belong to a different reality, along with the extremely violent deaths of the psychopathic Geoffrey Chaucer, the treacherous Barrow-Boy Cecil and the venal Constable Jenkins.

'Adelaide Vine and her dastardly female co-conspirators are nowhere to be found, sir,' Twitten reported to Inspector Steine, after answering the phone on Miss Lennon's desk. Normally, he would have trotted to the inspector's door and delivered this news while standing to attention. Normally, he'd also have sounded interested. This afternoon he delivered the news less conventionally, by sitting down and yelling it.

There was no reply from Steine's office.

'Sir?' called Twitten. 'Did you hear me, sir?' He prayed he wouldn't have to get up.

'Yes,' came a faint voice. 'Thank you, Twitten.'

At his own desk, the inspector was staring out of the window. There was nothing in his mind. He saw, but took no interest in, bedraggled seagulls gathering on neighbouring rooftops. He would have preferred to close his eyes, but every time he tried it, he saw a clock plummeting earthwards off a building, or a car careering towards him, or a discarded and bloody executioner's axe with human flesh and hair adhering to its blade.

For his own part, Brunswick was making no attempt to be normal. He sat, unmoving, for over an hour, moaning 'Ow, my head! Ow my head!' until the inspector, shouting from his office, ordered him to stop. At first Brunswick had taken a proper interest in the related events on the zebra crossing, especially ('Blimey!') the unfortunate part played by those flattened French onion-sellers – but since then he had been simply leached of emotion, aware only of little waves of re-sidual terror, which were gradually lessening in intensity. Did he care that Adelaide Vine could not be found? Well, a bit, yes. But was he prepared to do anything about it? Not if it involved rising from this chair.

When Sergeant Baines popped his head around the door mid-afternoon, he burst out laughing.

'You lot should blooming see yourselves!' he chuckled. 'You ought all to go home, if you ask me.'

Mr Lloyd the scurfy postman shuffled in and dropped an envelope on Twitten's desk. 'Lady gave me this,' he said. 'Say thank you, son, or I'll take it away again.'

'Thank you, Mr Lloyd,' Twitten managed to say. Looking at it, he was struck by the similarity of this envelope to one he had seen before. 'Mr Lloyd!' he called out hastily. 'Could you describe the lady?' But whether Mr Lloyd heard him or not, he left without answering. The standing orders of Mr Lloyd's postal union demanded that once a member has engaged in his egress protocol (i.e. has turned to go), he does not deviate, diverge, revolve, or swerve off.

Twitten, with effort, opened the envelope and absorbed its contents. Then he sighed and slipped it into his desk drawer.

A few minutes later, the inspector decided to address his men. He emerged from his office, clutched the door jamb for stability, and then launched himself in the direction of Miss Lennon's outsized desk, where he sank gratefully onto her vacant chair.

'Men,' he said. 'I don't know about you, but I feel peculiar.'

Brunswick put a hand up. 'Permission to say "Ow, my head!", sir?'

'Oh, very well.'

'Thank you, sir. Ow, my—'

'But only once.'

'Oh. Oh, all right. Thank you, sir.'

'Because if you keep saying it, I will have to insist you go to hospital.'

'Yes, sir.'

There was a pause.

'Are you *not* going to say "Ow, my head", Brunswick?'

'I thought I'd save it up, sir. For when I can't help it.'

'I see.' Steine took a deep breath. 'Look, men, we have all been through our own ordeals, and ordinarily—' He stopped. Had he said that correctly? Ord-in-ar-i-ly? *Ordinarily*? He frowned. Was 'ordinarily' even a word?

'Can we go home, please, sir?' said Twitten.

'Yes!' burst out Brunswick.

'That's just what I was going to suggest, Twitten. If you hadn't interrupted. In many ways, this should be a joyous time, and ordinary—' He frowned again, and decided to paraphrase. 'And in the normal way of things, we would rejoice that we all survived this day. Did you just say that Adelaide Vine has been successfully apprehended, Twitten?'

'No, sir. The opposite. She seems to have bally well got away again. As have the others, namely, Miss Sibert and Miss Lennon. Combined, these three females make a formidable group. They are all highly devious, but with strikingly different approaches and vocal styles.'

The inspector huffed. 'Still, many good things have happened. The annoying Constable Jenkins was revealed in his true colours, and paid the price. And I meant to tell you both earlier, I spoke to Mrs Groynes – '

'Gosh, did you, sir?'

' – and she has indicated that she will return to work next week.'

'Oh, that's spiffing news, sir,' said Twitten delightedly looking at Brunswick and seeing him burst into tears. 'Oh, don't cry, Sergeant!'

'I'm not!' snuffled Brunswick, from behind a handkerchief.

'I think the sergeant is a little bit overwhelmed by the news of Mrs Groynes's return, sir. Which I suppose is understandable since they've always had a special bond, what with all the disgusting Battenberg and so on, and given that his maternal abandonment issues run so deep.'

'She didn't say it in so many words,' the inspector continued, raising his voice a little to be heard over the sounds of unmanly emotion emanating from his sergeant, 'but I got the distinct impression that Mrs Groynes had been twiddling her thumbs, and missing us all dreadfully. She said the hours had dragged and that she had never stopped thinking about us for a second! Anyway, I can see you're moved by this, Brunswick, but contain yourself if you can.'

'Yes, sir.' Brunswick took a deep breath and wiped his eyes. 'Better now, sir.'

'Good.'

'I'm just happy, sir.'

'Yes, well. Good man. Now, we will all go home, take a rest, take stock, and reconvene on Monday.'

'May I just ask, sir?' said Twitten, who was finally dredging up some energy. 'Before we go our separate ways. Does anyone else feel that at no point this week did they really have autonomy? I think that's why I'm so depressed. I feel as if I never had a choice about how to act, as if my unconscious—'

'Oh, not now, Twitten!' interrupted Brunswick, with sudden vehemence. 'Ow, my head!'

But this was all a few hours earlier, and now it was nine o'clock and Twitten was retiring to bed, having rested in his room for most of the afternoon and then joined Mrs Thorpe to eat supper and watch television for half an hour, with General Thorpe's fabulous sword hanging (safely) back above the fireplace.

'Sergeant Brunswick is taking me out to dinner,' Mrs Thorpe explained, when only one plate of ham salad was delivered to the supper table by the trusty Mrs Browning. 'It's his way of apologising for last night.' Twitten noticed she was wearing her favourite coral-coloured frock with the very full skirt, and a crystal necklace. He wondered how much of this going-out-to-dinner idea had been Brunswick's. He also wondered why Brunswick owed Mrs Thorpe an apology in any case. After all, he could hardly help missing the dinner last night, could he? He had been *tied up*.

'Good luck,' said Twitten, as he speared some crunchy lettuce with his fork. 'I think you might have to shoulder the burden of conversation. The last time I saw the sergeant he was so exhausted he could barely string two words together.'

After she had gone, he quickly took his bath and climbed into bed. 'Peace,' he said, switching off his lamp, and closing his eyes. 'A bit of bally peace.'

And then, faintly, he heard a key in the lock downstairs.

At about the same hour, Gerald Winslow, lately governor of Broadmoor, boarded an express for London, jumping on at the last minute and finding himself in a small, dimly lit compartment with three women, all apparently travelling separately and all of them peering intently at their books.

As the train drew out of the station, and rain started to pelt the darkened windows, he took stock. The large woman in the furthest corner was evidently absorbed in *Peyton Place*. Opposite her was a younger woman with glorious chestnut hair, reading the latest from Daphne du Maurier. And opposite Winslow was a small, rosy-cheeked woman with plaited hair pinned up over her head, making notes in a book by Jung.

'Carlotta?' he cried.

She looked up, and he gasped. 'Oh, it's you! I can't believe it, Carlotta. It's me, Gerald. I've looked everywhere for you!'

'Herr Governor?' she said. She seemed both surprised and delighted. She clutched her knees and – rather thrillingly, to Winslow's eyes – wiggled her tiny feet. As Twitten had so sagely remarked, the feminine attractions of Miss Sibert appealed to quite specialised tastes. But when they worked, they worked.

'Call me Gerald,' he corrected her. 'You used to call me—'

'*Jah,*' she said thoughtfully, as she remembered. She reached over and patted his hand. Then she signalled to the others, who both cautiously lowered their books.

'This is Gerald! It is nice coincidence!'

'Good evening, ladies,' he said, tipping his hat.

'Hello,' said Miss Lennon flatly.

'Good evening,' said Adelaide Vine, with eyes narrowed. She darted a glance at Miss Sibert. Being reunited with this man seemed to make her very happy.

But then Miss Sibert's mouth turned down. 'You hear of poor Mr Chow-tza, Gerald?'

'Yes. I'm afraid so.'

'*Mein Gott!*' She pulled a comical face, as if tempted to laugh. 'Shoots himself, *beng-beng*?'

'Yes, poor man. But not before chopping off two men's heads, which means I'm on the run, Carlotta. People already blame me for helping you with the escape. Now I'm an accessory to murder! I don't know what to do.'

She crossed the compartment to sit next to him and took his arm.

'Let me talk to my friends, *jah*?' Her eyes twinkled. 'We see what we can do. Like you, we are "on the run", as you say. We have decide to form a *geng*! Don't worry, Herr Gerald. Your Carlotta will see to everything. Perheps you join the geng, too?'

Why not? he thought. 'I long to be with you, Carlotta.'

'I know, Herr Gerald,' she said. '*Und* even better, I *understand*.'

Elsewhere, the events of the day were reverberating. At home in her North Norfolk bedroom, Pandora Holden reached for her diary. Her surroundings pretty fairly represented the split personality of an intellectually precocious but sexually awakened teenager: while a sophisticated jazz LP played on her portable record player and a copy of Ovid's *Metamorphoses* lay on the bed, there was a poster of Tommy Steele pinned to the wall – a free gift from the fourpence-halfpenny girl's romance comic *Mirabelle* ('packed with all-picture love stories'). Opening the diary at the back, she studied the lists of names for the children she intended to have with Peregrine. On the lengthy train ride home, she had rethought Sappho and Caligula three times at least. 'Andromache', she wrote; and then 'Philoctetes'.

Then she shut the diary and looked at the Ovid and the *Mirabelle*. Which did she feel more like reading? The story of the raped and mutilated Philomela being turned into a nightingale? Or the story of the nicely coiffed Nurse Janet finding love with lantern-jawed Dr Lyle? Without hesitation, she picked up the *Mirabelle* and was soon happily lost in the long-running saga entitled 'I'll Follow My Heart'.

Back in Brighton, Sergeant Baines visited Sergeant Masefield (erstwhile police driving instructor) at his clinic for nervous exhaustion, and told him what he'd missed. The bluff Sergeant Baines was generally very good at cheering people up, and he related the noonday events at the zebra crossing with considerable colour and gusto. But Masefield was – understandably – hard to entertain, especially with anecdotes that involved Constable Twitten at the wheel of a moving vehicle.

'He wanted me to *talk him through the pedals*, Alf!' laughed Sergeant Baines.

'Promise me he'll never drive again, John,' whispered Masefield, grabbing Baines's arm with an icy, claw-like hand.

Alone in the record department of the darkened store, with Elvis Presley playing over the loudspeakers, Mister Harold kept rehearsing the day's events and wondering what he could have done differently. He really wanted to say to himself, with a clear conscience, 'You could not have prevented this terrible state of affairs, Harold!' But then he would remember the clock-installers insisting on the need for chains and concrete – and the memory made him squirm.

Was this the end for Gosling's? Had Hannington's won, without even trying? He looked round at the pegboard record booths; he inhaled the wonderful smell of vinyl. Elvis requested to be his teddy bear. A tear trickled down his face.

What frustrated him most was that his usual mental processes were thwarted. Ordinarily, his thoughts ran along the lines of, *How can I turn this latest thing to the store's commercial advantage?* But even that greatest of retailers Harold Gosling was stumped for how to dig a usable sales pitch out of an example of gross negligence resulting in the crushing to death of four French people (not to mention their exotic alliums). Miserably, he tried a few slogans in his head:

Come and Be Flattened by Gosling's!
Gosling's – Where We Murder Prices and Occasionally People!
Isn't It a Crime Not to Shop at Gosling's?
It Isn't Only Our Pricing That's Criminally Negligent!

And with that, miraculously, he stopped feeling miserable. It really helps sometimes to have a shallow personality.

'That could work!' he said to himself excitedly. 'I think it could actually work!'

At English's fish restaurant in East Street, Mrs Thorpe had ordered half a dozen oysters and the fillet of sole *bonne femme* with asparagus; Brunswick had requested *soupe du jour* followed by steak and chips. They were seated in the little bay window, watching the rain bounce off the pavement outside, but their mood was fairly buoyant. After a solid three-hour afternoon nap at his auntie's flat, Brunswick was definitely beginning to revive. It helped that Mrs Thorpe looked stunning in her coral dress and crystals. He was glad he had worn his blue suit. Reflected in the window, they made a handsome couple.

'You never mentioned before that you grew up in India, Mrs Thorpe,' he said, attempting grown-up conversation.

'Yes, James. I was lucky enough to be born in Simla.'

'Oh. Really?' he said. 'Well, well. Simla. That *was* flaming lucky.' She had said the name as if it should mean something to him.

'But of course our position in the Punjab was much affected by the Amritsar Massacre. And rightly so.'

He bit his lip and adjusted his tie. The early-twentieth-century history of the Indian subcontinent was a bit of a blank page as far as he was concerned.

She tried once more. 'But on a brighter note, my grandmother knew Kipling in Lahore in the eighties!'

Again, there was nothing for him to grab onto. He wondered if he should counter with his own favourite claim to fame, 'Edmundo Ros went to my school', but thankfully decided against it. This unshakeable delusion of Brunswick's that the popular bandleader had attended the London Road Academy for Orphans, Waifs and Foundlings in Brighton did not stand up to the slightest scrutiny.

Feeling miserably inadequate, Brunswick took a sip of the martini cocktail Mrs Thorpe had ordered for them both. To taste buds accustomed to Watney's, it was unspeakable.

'Look, Mrs Thorpe,' he said, choking slightly. 'We need to talk about something a bit closer to home than the flaming Punjab, and God knows, I'd rather not.'

Mrs Thorpe adopted a bright expression, to mask her feelings of dismay. Was this it? Was he choosing this moment to finish with her? Why, oh, why, had she plumped for a famous and expensive seafood restaurant without checking with Sergeant Brunswick first?

'Go on,' she said bravely. 'Tell me. I can take it. Is it because of the fish?'

'What? No.' He frowned. 'No, this is about today, Mrs Thorpe. I don't think you realise that you put yourself in terrible danger. You keep making light of it.'

'Is that all?' She was relieved. 'But I really didn't mind, James. I found it very exciting.'

'No!' He banged the table, which startled her. Several other diners craned their necks, and a glaring waiter made a very obvious mental note to keep an eye on Mister ruddy Steak-and-Chips.

'Look,' Brunswick said, with emotion. 'I'm no good at this, Mrs Thorpe. Oysters and what have you. Linen serviettes. Everything in French. This knife is so flaming heavy I can hardly pick it up! But I'm doing my best.'

'Of course you are.' Mrs Thorpe's face was all concern. 'We can leave if you like, James.'

'No, no. There's just something I need to say. At the wax museum, I was very frightened. The danger was real. And I've been thinking about it all afternoon and I just can't flaming get over it.' He lowered his voice and took her hand, which made her gasp. 'I can't get over it,' he repeated quietly, 'that you, a beautiful posh woman who can do much better than me, would put yourself in danger on my account.'

Tears formed in Mrs Thorpe's eyes. 'James,' she said gently. 'That's the nicest thing you've ever said to me.'

The waiter chose this precise moment to arrive with the main courses. 'Go away at once!' she snapped, and he stepped back so violently that a quantity of *bonne femme* sauce slopped up his sleeve.

'I'm very fond of you, James,' she continued, adopting her former cooing tone as if nothing had happened.

'I know that,' he moaned, aware of the waiter hovering and muttering. 'But—'

'I would like it very much if we were a couple.'

'I know that, too. But *why* do you want me? I just don't understand it. And the more you tell me how dotty you are about me, the worse it gets! I'm flattered, very flattered. But the more you go on about it, the more it feels like – well, like you're flogging a flaming dead horse!'

'That's a horrible expression, James.'

'I know. But what you did today, well, what am I supposed to think? You love me so much you saved my ruddy life? How does that help?'

'You're saying I'm too keen?'

'Well, yes. Yes.'

'It puts you off that I express my feelings, even though my words are meant to encourage and reassure you?'

'Yes. I'm sorry.'

She lowered her voice to a whisper. 'You did *kiss* me, James. Not long ago. And it meant so much to me.'

'And that's exactly the sort of thing I'm talking about!'

'I see.'

She sat back and signalled to the waiter to approach, which he did with a very bad grace.

'Ready now?' he said pointedly, as he set down the dishes.

Back at Mrs Thorpe's house, the door to Twitten's bedroom creaked open.

'You there, Constable?' said the expected voice in the dark.

Clive Hoskisson was dithering on Inspector Steine's doorstep with an envelope in his hand when – without warning – the door was yanked open and the inspector appeared, dressed in a royal blue monogrammed dressing-gown, and holding a rinsed-out milk bottle.

'Hoskisson? Good. Thank you for coming. As you can tell from my informal attire, I'd rather given you up.'

Both men went inside, and Steine showed the reporter to the front sitting-room, waving him to a chair.

'I just need to ask you some questions,' said Hoskisson, laying his notebook on a table. 'But don't worry, it's not about what happened at the famous milk bar. It's about what happened outside the department store today.'

Steine looked at him and shrugged.

'Your desk sergeant gave me the address. He said you had something you wanted to tell me.'

'That's right.' Steine closed his eyes and gathered his strength. He hated talking to reporters, but this had to be done. 'Look, Hoskisson, I'll be brief. It was pointed out to me this afternoon that my actions at the zebra crossing might be open to misconstruction. What I mean is that my saving your life while putting my own at risk might be erroneously construed as "heroic". I want to make it very clear to you – and to those intensely curious mythical readers of yours, of course – that it was *not* heroic, I merely acted on instinct, and I'm sorry if that's less interesting as a story but it's the truth.'

Hoskisson pulled a face. 'Why are you being so obtuse, Inspector?'

'Obtuse? I am not being *obtuse*. How dare you? I just explained—'

'But you just said it. You saved my life by putting your-self in danger! That's what heroism is. I admit, I previously thought less well of you. I had learned some very shocking things about your conduct regarding the shooting of Terence Chambers. But I know what you did today, and it was magnificent. I have half-written my piece already: I just need some quotes from you to complete it. Naturally it will suffer alongside the other sensational stories from today, but the headline will be: "MY LIFE SAVED BY MILK-BAR HERO COPPER".'

'Well,' said Steine quietly, 'I wish you'd had the courtesy to consult me before you started writing it.'

'I couldn't get access to you, Inspector!' Hoskisson spoke with passion. It had been quite an exhausting day for him, too, what with the sensational bloodbath on Upper North Street to report, not to mention the wildly dramatic crushing-to-death of four heavily disguised members of the Chambers gang from London. His editor back in Fleet Street was pleased to bits with him, especially for the way he had immediately recognised the Soho hoods in question and could personally testify to the way they had met their gruesome end. Until tomorrow morning's edition of the *Mirror* hit the news-stands, everyone else would still believe the four victims of death-by-enormous-clock were innocent French onion-sellers.

'Look, Hoskisson,' sighed the inspector. 'I'd like you to kill the story about me saving your life.'

'Kill it?'

'On that zebra crossing, I did what needed to be done, and that's all I'll ever say on the matter.'

'But why don't you want people to know?'

'Oh, for goodness' sake!' Steine exploded. 'Because I could not bear to be treated like a hero again!'

Hoskisson was bewildered. 'I don't believe you,' he said.

'Look,' said the inspector, 'I apologise for the outburst. But I mean it. Being a celebrity was not to my taste at all. I mean, it was wonderful to meet Roy Plomley, and I was overwhelmed to receive the Silver Truncheon. But they made me have my photograph taken with scantily clad women described as "Rank starlets", Hoskisson! And I sat at dinner with a slimy fellow whose business card called him a "society osteopath"! A *society osteopath*! What does that even mean?'

He shuddered to remember it all. 'And then the very *Commissioner of the Metropolitan Police* sent this woman Miss Lennon down here to be my secretary, and if it hadn't been for him doing that, none of these zebra-crossing shenanigans would even have come about, and … ah. Hang on. I just need to … '

Steine frowned, his eyes swivelling. It wasn't often that he had an epiphany. In fact, he might never have had one before. Perhaps fatigue had something to do with it. But something annoyingly hinted by Constable Twitten earlier in the day had just started to make sense.

'What is it?' asked the reporter.

'Hush a moment, would you?' said Steine. It had been just a few days ago, but it seemed like a distant memory: him standing with the commissioner in the office at Scotland Yard. What exactly were the words the man had said to him, in that misleadingly genial tone?

'*I hope my Soho chaps haven't been too hard on you over this Chambers business.*'

'For what?' Steine had asked, genuinely puzzled.

'*Well, for halving their income, in some cases! I mean, I shouldn't say it, but between you and me, my own lady wife is furious with you. Furious! Chambers flew us out to Torremolinos last year for a fortnight, and she said it was the best holiday she ever had. And then of course there were the cases of spirits at Christmas.*'

Hoskisson coughed. 'Would you like me to go, sir?'

'No. Wait.'

'I do have a deadline, and if you really don't want me to file this story, I shan't insist—'

'No! Stay there!'

Perhaps if the inspector hadn't been so tired, he might have applied more caution, considering that his interlocutor was a journalist famous for his idealism, his distrust of the police, and his stalwart limpet-like qualities. But the more Steine dwelled on what had happened to him this week, the angrier and more justified he felt. Had the *commissioner* been complicit in this Chambers revenge plot? When he so generously dispatched Miss Lennon to Brighton, did he *know* that she was Terence Chambers's sister, thirsty for revenge? Twitten had been so right about police corruption: as a subject you keep happily forgetting all about it, and then, *crikey*! It does just pop up again.

He felt slightly underdressed for the momentous decision he was about to make, but so be it. The dressing-gown and slippers would have to do.

'Look, Mr Hoskisson,' he began. 'If you want a story, how about this? Forget about what I did. Have you ever heard of a place called Torremolinos? It's where the Commissioner of the Metropolitan Police and his wife sometimes go on holiday ... '

Back in Twitten's bedroom, it was time for the usual debriefing. He regretted the absence of a cup of tea and a slice of fruit cake, which normally helped such sessions along, but on the plus side, the darkness helped him concentrate.

'So I'm guessing it was Barrow-Boy Cecil who was your hidden enemy all along, Mrs G?' said Twitten sympathetically. 'You must have been jolly disappointed when you found out.'

'Disappointed? Bleeding furious, more like. If he wasn't dead already, I'd wring his neck and drown him backwards.'

'He cut off his own little finger to send to you, then?'

'No, dear.'

'Oh? Then whose was it?'

'I reckon he just put his ring on one he happened to come across.'

'Oh, I see, gosh.' Twitten didn't want to think about how anyone 'came across' a spare little finger. 'I always got the impression you trusted him completely.'

'Exactly, dear. I did trust Cecil. I hadn't forgotten that aspect of it, as it happens, but ta very much for rubbing it in.'

He resisted the impulse to switch on the light, but he wanted to look at her. Was Mrs Groynes *truly* as well as she sounded? Hadn't she been through a serious emotional ordeal, involving high levels of anxiety followed by her own near murder?

'Well, I'm glad you're all right, Mrs G. And I honestly don't mind a bit that when you confide in me like this about your criminal activities it just reinforces my helpless position vis-à-vis bringing you to justice.'

Unsurprisingly, it took her a little while to absorb this statement – and she didn't, not fully. 'You couldn't run that past me again, dear?'

'It was just something Miss Vine said to me.'

'Oh, *her*. You don't want to listen to *her*.'

'But perhaps I do, Mrs G. She was urging me to see my true position, you see, as an ambitious young policeman with a stellar career in prospect. It was a bally revelation, actually. She explained, for example, that deep down I had no respect whatever for Inspector Steine, although—' He stopped to consider. 'Although, after what the inspector did today, well,

I *was* genuinely impressed by him, so I don't know if that's entirely true any more.'

'You've lost me, dear. Go back to all that about you and me and vis-à-vis.'

'Ooh, well, what she said about *us* was that since I hadn't yet revealed the existence of the incriminating photograph, I was clearly invested in maintaining the cosy status quo of you being a wicked villain and me doing nothing about it.'

'Well, that *does* sound attractive, dear.'

'But then she said I should resist the pull of this status quo, *however cosy*, because deep down I have great ambitions, and these ambitions are not served by allowing myself to be manipulated by you, even if you tend to manipulate me by means of kindness and fellowship, which are otherwise in short supply. She also said every decent criminal already knew all the stuff in my book, *The Hidden Persuaders*. Apparently it isn't revelatory at all; it's basic. If you want to persuade some-one to do something, you just appeal to their deepest ideas of themselves, or supply their deepest needs. And if you want to upset them, you undermine that deep idea or deprive them of what they want most.'

'It sounds less like a word to the wise, more like an episode of *The Brains Trust*.'

'Well, I suppose so, but it was bally effective, Mrs G, because now I'm confused!'

'Confused by what?'

'By whether to expose you. You see, for once I have the means.'

'I see.' She paused. 'Look,' she said kindly. 'You're obvi-ously on the horns of a dilemma, dear, and it's making you unhappy, so I'll make it easier for you.'

'Really? How? You aren't going to give yourself up?'

She laughed. 'Good gawd, no. I'm just going to say that I know what you're thinking about: it's that photograph your girlfriend brought all the way back from Norfolk and that you hid, in a bit of a panic, in Mrs Thorpe's jelly-mould cupboard in the kitchen downstairs.'

Twitten gasped. 'You know where the photograph is?'

She didn't reply. The stupidity of this question answered itself.

'Ah,' he said, with resignation. 'You found the photograph.'

'Yes, dear. Of course I did.'

'And destroyed it?'

'Bingo. I wouldn't have found it in Norfolk, I grant you. But in a bleeding jelly-mould cupboard … '

'I understand, Mrs G. Oh, well.'

They sat together in the dark. Mrs Groynes lit a cigarette, and took a drag. Twitten hugged himself. She thought she had won! But what Mrs Groynes didn't know was that a further sheaf of incriminating pictures evidently from the same stolen set of duplicate prints had been delivered to him just this afternoon!

'Oh, and I took care of that other batch in your desk drawer, dear,' she added, blowing smoke at him. 'So that's all sorted, too.'

———

Brunswick and Mrs Thorpe finished their meal at English's quite quickly, and mostly in silence. Mrs Thorpe felt more wretched than she could ever remember feeling. Her friends would have been furious with her. They had no sympathy for this infatuation of hers. 'This common police sergeant really isn't good enough for you, Eliza,' they all said, over afternoon teas at Hannington's. 'Stop mooning over him. Your grand-mother knew Kipling. You are related by marriage to Louis Mountbatten. John Gielgud has stayed at your house!'

But such arguments were futile. Whenever she looked at Brunswick, or even heard his name, the arousal was auto-matic, entirely beyond her control. It was as if an ignition was fired in her very loins. His attractive eyes, his manly neck, his strong arms! He had once sat down in the front sitting-room at her house, and when he had gone, her heart stopped every time she caught sight of the barely visible dip that his backside had made in the upholstery. 'Oh, Eliza, that's so adolescent!' her friends said, recoiling in disgust, when she confided in them. 'You're forty-one!'

But she was in the grip of Brunswick fever, and there was nothing she could do. She hated the pain of rejection, and struggled with the need to accept it. And here was the crux of the matter, obviously. Because Brunswick, by contrast, was clearly struggling with the idea of an attractive female person who *wasn't rejecting him.*

So, things might have gone either way on this momentous evening as Brunswick and Mrs Thorpe left the restaurant. He helped her with her umbrella and took her arm. They began to walk to the corner of North Street, with car headlights bouncing in the shop windows, and the sodium street lights leaching the colour from their clothes and faces.

'You didn't enjoy that celebratory meal much, did you, James?'

'I'm still very tired, Mrs Thorpe,' he said apologetically. 'Perhaps we should have done it tomorrow night instead.'

She stopped walking, and he jerked to a standstill, thinking in dismay, *Here we go again; more flaming lovey-dovey.*

But he was wrong. Today had been a big day for Mrs Thorpe, and it was time to make a desperate play. If it worked, wonderful. If it didn't, it was time to say goodbye, accept reality, and move on.

'I'll tell you what I enjoyed today so much, James,' she said pleasantly. 'It was when we were arguing over whether you needed to apologise to me. The thing is, I'm aware of it, too – this *flogging a dead horse*, as you so unpleasantly phrased it. Whenever I'm nice to you, and flatter you, and tell you how passionately I feel about you, instead of it filling you with pleasure, you go completely limp—'

'Limp?' This was rather an offensive word in Brunswick's opinion.

'Yes, *limp*. You go limp and lifeless and hopeless! But when I challenge you, or am critical of you, it's as if your eyes suddenly open to me, and for a moment you actually bloody desire me.'

'I'm glad you didn't say any of that when we were still inside,' he said. 'That waiter hated me enough already.'

She laughed, but then took a breath and became serious again. 'So I'm going to tell you something you might not like, James.'

'What's that?'

'Despite everything I might have said to the contrary over the past few weeks, I think we must both accept it. You are simply not good enough for me.'

'What?'

She felt his grip tighten on her arm.

'You are a common policeman and an ungrateful man, and I wish I hadn't saved your life because you plainly don't deserve it.'

His eyes blazed indignantly. 'How can you say that?'

She looked up at his face. *Oh, my goodness*, she thought. *It's working. If he doesn't kill me, this could be it!*

'You grew up a poor orphan while I've played host several times to some of the greatest Shakespeare speakers of our time!'

'Stop it.'

Still working.

'I grew up in Simla and you don't even know where that is! I could tell you didn't!'

'That's not fair.'

Keep going.

'I won't have you touch me again, James, never! Your touch is disgusting to me!'

'Eliza!' he moaned, taking her by the shoulders. 'Oh, flaming hell, you're so beautiful!'

'I'm sorry I didn't help you much, in the end,' says Twitten, after a while. The news that Mrs G has scuppered all his hopes of exposing her is taking a bit of getting used to.

'Oh, you played your part, dear.'

Time is ticking by calmly in Mrs Thorpe's house. Both Twitten and Mrs Groynes are sweetly unaware that about three minutes from now two sexually enflamed people will burst through the front door and start noisily undressing each other while one of them hurls snobbish insults to maintain the erotic momentum.

'What I don't understand, Mrs G,' says Twitten, 'is why you destroyed all those files on Mr Chaucer at Inspector Steine's house. Luckily the key document relating to Doris Fuller escaped the flames, otherwise I would never have known about the *ein, zwei, drei*. And then I wouldn't have driven at top speed in first gear to the inspector's rescue.'

'You think that file just happened to *escape the flames*, do you?'

'Well, yes. Of course. You had burned most of the others.'

'Oh, give me strength,' she remarks, with feeling. 'Look, dear, when I went through everything in that box, I found a lot that might have sent you in the wrong direction, didn't I? That's what I destroyed. The important thing was that the plotters believed in the *ein, zwei, drei*, and were acting on it, with the black-and-white patterns, and the clock chime and everything. So that was what you needed to know, too.'

'So that's why the Doris Fuller file was left … *for me to find*?'

'Yes, dear. Give that boy a mandarin.'

'There's no need for sarcasm, Mrs G.'

'If you'd had all the other documents, you'd have seen what I saw: that actually what triggered the poor blighter was much simpler. Just a woman in distress, dear.'

'Really?'

'Yes. All the other stuff – well, it was pure coincidence that it was there at the other scenes. There was no *ein, zwei, drei*. All this Chaucer bloke needed to set him off was a woman calling for help, like his poor dear mummy had done.'

'So those Frenchmen at the scene were surplus to requirements? Their deaths were even more pointless than it first appeared?'

'Well, I wouldn't go that far. Look, this is just between you and me, but those blokes were some of Terry's hoods in cunning disguise. So talk about hitting the jackpot.'

'No!'

'They were armed and everything. That Miss Lennon of yours didn't want to leave anything to chance, you see.' She takes another drag on her cigarette. 'Ironic, really.'

Twitten shakes his head thoughtfully. 'So you knew what Chaucer would do if you got Cecil to hit you? You knew he would attack a man who showed violence to a woman?'

'Precisely.'

It is always nice to clear up some loose ends, but Twitten can't help feeling, vaguely, that they are filling time until something bigger occurs.

'I suppose Professor Milhouse was killed just to draw police attention to the shop.'

'Probably.'

'Also, I think Miss Vine didn't like being lectured on a subject she understood better than he did.'

'Probably,' agrees Mrs Groynes again, yawning. She has never been interested in poor Professor Milhouse.

He changes the subject. There is something that's been nagging at him. 'I'm a bit hurt that your so-called weak spots didn't include me, Mrs Groynes. Your enemy had designs on both the sergeant and the inspector, but not me.'

In the dark, she smiles. 'So you never realised your brakes weren't working?'

'What?'

'Oh, yes. Constable Jenkins had fiddled with your bleeding brakes, dear.'

'Oh, flipping flip!'

'Yes, but luckily they didn't know you're such a terrible driver you never have cause to use them.'

Just a minute to go now before the front door crashes open. Still they are blithely unaware.

'The inspector says you're coming back to work.'

'It'll be like I never went away, dear. I took advantage of your absence this afternoon to move all my stash back into the cupboard and everything; Vince and Shorty helped me. That's when I found those extra photos of yours, so I killed two birds with one stone.'

'Of course.' Despite everything he has said about his duty to resist the cosy status quo, it pleases Twitten to think that next Monday the office will be back to normal, with the new kettle switching itself off (with a 'tock') while they all stand around admiring it. The brave new world of 1950s consumerism isn't all bad.

'How did you avoid Sergeant Baines seeing you bring your stash through the front door?'

'By using the bleeding back door, dear. Use your loaf. Blimey, what's that?'

It is, of course, the bigger thing starting to occur downstairs.

'Shhh,' says Twitten. 'I think I can hear Mrs Thorpe coming home.'

They both listen, in the dark. From outside on the top step comes the sound of raised voices, as if in argument, one of them a man's.

'That's Sergeant Brunswick,' whispers Twitten. 'Don't worry, he won't come in. He never does. He knows she wants to manoeuvre him into bed, you see. In a minute she'll come in on her own and then burst into tears and have a very big drink with the record player blaring.'

'This is a bit awkward,' says Mrs Groynes redundantly.

'Yes, it is. But if I may say so, it's not my bally fault that you're here.'

Downstairs the front door bangs open, and there are stumbling, scuffling noises, accompanied by loud kissy sounds.

Twitten gasps in horror.

'What?' whispers Mrs G.

'This is different!' he squeaks. 'I think he came in!'

'He definitely did,' she agrees.

'Eliza!' Brunswick moans distantly.

'Gosh,' whispers Twitten. 'I wonder how she—?'

'Oh, James! James, unhand me, you uncouth brute!' says the far-off Mrs Thorpe, in a passionate voice. 'But wait till I get my coat off.'

'Eliza!' moans Brunswick again. 'I am so confused!'

'You're a mere waif and a foundling, and you deserve to be shot in the leg over and over, and over and over.'

'Don't say that!'

'They're coming upstairs!' squeaks Twitten. 'Can we talk about kettles, Mrs G?'

'What? Kettles? Why?'

'Please! Talk about anything! Anything other than what's happening out there!'

Then the door to Mrs Thorpe's bedroom slams shut and Twitten says aloud, 'Oh, for flip's sake,' and switches on his bedside lamp.

In the unaccustomed yellow light, he looks at Mrs Groynes and she looks at him.

From downstairs can be heard thumps and moans and laughs. From Twitten's point of view, this certainly makes a change from the usual tempest of sobbing and Frank Sinatra belting out 'One for My Baby' at maximum volume, but on the other hand, it is not an improvement.

'You've got a bruise on your face, Mrs G!' he exclaims, belatedly noticing. 'Barrow-Boy Cecil hurt you!'

'Oh, it's nothing,' she says, reaching out to pat his arm. 'You know what? I'd rather go through that whole bleeding malarkey again than listen to those two down there. But as you so rightly point out, it's nobody's fault but my own. I wasn't exactly invited.'

They look at each other steadily, and then she reaches out to switch off the lamp again. They strain to listen. There seems to be no other choice.

'Does this mean you won't be letting yourself in here any more at night, Mrs G?' Twitten says tentatively in the dark, his voice low.

She huffs. 'Are you kidding?' she says, extracting a key from her pocket and placing it on his bedside table. 'You win, dear. It's all yours. Accept it with my bleeding compliments.'

Afterword

In researching and planning these books, the greatest pleasure has been in choosing Twitten's latest intellectual obsession. For *Psycho by the Sea* the publication in 1957 of *The Hidden Persuaders* was a bit of a gift. It suits Twitten so well that he should be excited (and shocked) by the new science of 'motivation research' – and that he would want to apply it to the case before him. Digging a bit deeper, I was slightly startled to find how precisely topical this subject was. On Monday September 16th 1957 (i.e. at the start of the very week covered in this book) *The Times* ran a story from its New York correspondent, 'Split Second Advertising Aiming at the Subconscious', detailing an experiment in subliminal advertising that had recently taken place in a cinema in New Jersey. (The practice was banned soon after, in 1958.)

I do recommend the 1950s sociology Twitten latches on to in this book. It is fascinating in the light of the modern world. The idea of the average person's inner gyroscope giving way to an inner radar, which Twitten says is "such an elegant idea that I can't bally well stop thinking about it" (page 109), comes from David Reisman's classic *The Lonely Crowd*. As it happens, there *was* an American sociologist in Brighton researching crowd behaviour in September 1957: this fact was what got me thinking about the whole subject. You will be pleased to hear that the real man came to no harm, although a trip to the races with a reporter from the *Argus* was evidently extremely unpleasant.

I am indebted to Mrs Gwen Barden who wrote to me about working in a tube room in 1945, when she was 14 years old. A brief mention of a job in a tube room in Virginia Nicholson's brilliant oral history of the 1950s, *Perfect Wives in Ideal Homes*, prompted me to research the Lamson pneumatic system, which I then wrote about in a column in a newspaper. Mrs Barden kindly got in touch with me as a result of that piece. Gosling's I named after a long-ago department store in Richmond, Surrey (for many years now, the site of Dickins & Jones). The lively twins Joan and Dorothy are so named as a tribute to my mum. I would like to point out that I know Broadmoor did not have a 'governor' at this period (or any break-outs). In 1957, in fact, the father of the novelist Patrick McGrath became the tenth and last medical superintendent. The Puffins cigarette brand is a knowing reference to *Murder Must Advertise* by Dorothy L. Sayers. Barrow-Boy Cecil's 'See the bunny run' may remind alert cinephile readers of the excellent 1956 British crime film *The Long Arm*, which I watch at least twice a year. Lastly, the joke about the French baguette being sucked up the tube is an overt homage to the film *Paddington*, in my opinion the best film thus far of the 21st century.

Thanks are due to The Keep, Brighton's local history research facility, where the staff are unfailingly patient with people who are unable even to wrench a roll of microfilm from a spindle without expert help. As ever, I would like to thank everyone at Raven Books in London and Bloomsbury in New York, and also my wonderful agent Anthony Goff, who has provided much-appreciated moral support while I've been writing all four of these Twitten books. Thanks also to the Detection Club for electing me a member. Crime writing is a venerable profession and I feel honoured to have joined it, in however minor or short-lived a way.

A Note on the Author

Lynne Truss is a columnist, writer and broadcaster whose book on punctuation *Eats, Shoots & Leaves* was an international bestseller. She has written extensively for radio, and is the author of seven previous novels, as well as a non-fiction account (*Get Her Off the Pitch!*) of her four years as a novice sportswriter for *The Times*. Her columns have appeared in the *Listener*, *The Times*, the *Sunday Telegraph* and *Saga*. She lives in Sussex with three dogs.

A Note on the Type

The text of this book is set Adobe Garamond. It is one of several versions of Garamond based on the designs of Claude Garamond. It is thought that Garamond based his font on Bembo, cut in 1495 by Francesco Griffo in collaboration with the Italian printer Aldus Manutius. Garamond types were first used in books printed in Paris around 1532. Many of the present-day versions of this type are based on the *Typi Academiae* of Jean Jannon cut in Sedan in 1615.

Claude Garamond was born in Paris in 1480. He learned how to cut type from his father and by the age of fifteen he was able to fashion steel punches the size of a pica with great precision. At the age of sixty he was commissioned by King Francis I to design a Greek alphabet, and for this he was given the honourable title of royal type founder. He died in 1561.

Also available by LYNNE TRUSS

A SHOT IN THE DARK

A CONSTABLE TWITTEN MYSTERY

WINNER OF THE CRIMEFEST LAST LAUGH AWARD

Brighton, 1957. Inspector Steine rather enjoys his life as a policeman by the sea. No criminals, no crime, no stress.

So it's really rather annoying when an ambitious – not to mention irritating – new constable shows up to work and starts investigating a series of burglaries. And it's even more annoying when, after Constable Twitten is despatched to the theatre for the night, he sits next to a vicious theatre critic who is promptly shot dead part way through the opening night of a new play.

It seems Brighton may be in need of a police force after all...

'This is crime fiction turned on its head
– a giddy spell of sheer delight'
Daily Mail

'Funny, clever, charming, imaginative,
nostalgic and gently satirical'
The Times

'A perfect summer read'
Guardian

Order your copy:

By phone: +44 (0) 1256 302 699 • By email: direct@macmillan.co.uk • Delivery is usually 3–5 working days.
Free postage and packaging for orders over £20. • Online: www.bloomsbury.com/bookshop
Prices and availability subject to change without notice. • bloomsbury.com/author/lynne-truss